PRAISE FOR
KNOWING

"True-to-life, funny, and sometimes biting dialogue. . . .
Looks at passion between and beyond the sheets. . . .
Explores a situation that many women can relate to."

—*USA Today*

"An enthralling first novel . . . cuts across ethnic lines."
—*Entertainment Weekly*

"Recommended. . . . Will appeal not only to African-
Americans, but to most women struggling to make
sense of their lives."

—*Library Journal*

"Ultimately it's the story of everyone's struggle to find
that faith, that happiness. Turn the pages fast, though,
or you'll burn your little fingers!"

—**Patrice Gaines, author of**
Laughing in the Dark

"An engaging, vividly rendered story . . . undeniable
momentum."

—*Kirkus Reviews*

"A good-hearted novel. . . . It's about who's most
important, your husband, your kids, or yourself."

—*Washington Post Book World*

more . . .

"McMillan has this kind of novel down to perfection, snappin' on the menfolk, crying on cue, and standing tall for the Sisterhood."

—*BookPage*

"A tale of love, lust, family ties, deception, dreams, relationships, and fulfillment . . . peppered with something for everyone: lustful sex scenes, passionate sermons, [and] bittersweet and powerful moments with families."

—*Grand Rapids Press*

"Warmth and down-to-earth richness . . . humorous. . . . McMillan's strong point is certainly her powers of description and imagery."

—*ACE* magazine

"KNOWING gives frustration a voice."

—*Virginia Pilot*

"Rosalyn McMillan has a knack for capturing the directness and humor of modern black female speech. She manages to bring out the glamour, passion, and fabulous interior design in the lives of everyday, working-class people."

—*United Autoworkers Solidarity* magazine

Knowing

ROSALYN McMILLAN

Knowing

WARNER
VISION
BOOKS

A Time Warner Company

This novel is dedicated to my mother and father,
Madeline Katherine and Edward Lewis McMillan

The poem "Complicated" on page viii is reprinted courtesy of the author, Angelica R. King.

Lyrics on page 85 from "Reaching for the Sky," by Peabo Bryson, ©1978 WARNER-TAMERLANE PUBLISHING CORP.
All Rights Reserved. Used by Permission.
WARNER BROS. PUBLICATIONS INC., Miami, FL, 33014.

WARNER BOOKS EDITION

Copyright © 1996 by Rosalyn McMillan
All rights reserved.

Warner Vision is a registered trademark of Warner Books, Inc.

Cover design by Diane Luger
Cover photograph by Herman Estevez

Warner Books, Inc.
1271 Avenue of the Americas
New York, NY 10020

Visit our Web site at
http://warnerbooks.com

W A Time Warner Company

Printed in the United States of America
Originally published in hardcover by Warner Books.
First Printed in Paperback: April, 1997

10 9 8 7 6 5 4 3 2

Acknowledgments

I would like to thank God for the power and creativity that facilitated me in writing this novel.

I would like to thank my best friend for a lifetime, my lover and husband, John D. Smith. Also my four children, Vester Jr., Shannon, Ashley, and Jasmine, who were and always will be the inspiration, the motivation, and the loves of my life.

Equally important are what my special sister Crystal Joy calls the shopping network: my three sisters, Crystal, Terry, and Vicky McMillan, whom I love and cherish dearly. Let's give new meaning to the phrase "shop 'till we drop," girls! See you soon.

My agent, Denise Stinson, is a miracle; she's also my friend. She worked very hard and lobbied for me and the success of this novel on unlimited occasions. I thank you, Denise, for your hard work and enthusiasm on this project, and I unequivocally appreciate everything you've done.

Research is very essential also, and I've learned to enjoy the process. I would like to thank the Southfield Public Library for the generous help they've given me.

It's very important to have someone in the publishing industry who believes in you and your work. Anne Hamilton was that person. I would personally like to thank Anne, who loved *Knowing* first, and my editor, Rob McQuilkin, who loved it last.

And finally I'd like to give honor to my mother, Madeline Katherine, who could have been a stand-up comedian in her lifetime; but she chose to be a mother. We'd be on the telephone talking and I'd say, "Mama, wait a minute, let me get a pencil so I can write this down." And she'd say, "Child, I can't remember everything I say." Her remarks were always so spontaneous, so on the money. I am still enamored by her words of wisdom and can still hear her laughter today.

My mother left this world two years ago, but I am content in knowing that she is telling jokes to the angels up above, and that she is an inspiration to them as well as to the loved ones she left behind who still cherish her memory.

I feel your power, your sweet spirit, Mama, radiating over me. In the evenings, as I look up toward the heavens, I feel and I know that it's your single star shining bright down on me. I miss you and I love you, Mama.

Twinkle, twinkle, little star, now I know what you are.

Complicated

November light streams through the window
and lays in yellow slices on my bedspread.

And I can't help but stare at you as you lay helpless,
still fully succumbed to the throes of sleep and slumber.
I sit up slowly so as not to disturb your sleeping form.

Curly black hair,
long lashes and sleep-smoothed skin
the same exact color as strong black coffee.
And I love strong black coffee.

Chest covered
in dark and silken softness.
I long so much to reach out and touch you
and feel your heat
beneath my hands, but I do not.
Instead, I sit thinking,
mute and melancholy.

I love you. It really is that simple. I love you more
than I have loved anyone in my whole life.
But I can't tell you. You might laugh
or blow it off, or what's worse,
you may tell me that you don't feel the same way.
That makes this complicated.

And so I sit,
a prisoner of myself,
a prisoner of you,
serving hard time and waiting
for my daily ration of bread and coffee.

—Angelica R. King

1

Sexual Healing

Ginger waited until she heard the familiar faint, even snoring from the man lying next to her in their usual double-spoon sleeping position. She lifted his arms from her waist and slid out from under the comforter of their king-size bed, pausing to trace a light caress as feathery as butterfly wings across his thighs. She knew nothing would wake him for a few hours after a serious session of sex. She never could understand how men were able to go to sleep so suddenly after sex, while their women, listless, would lie staring at the ceiling, counting the spots on the walls, straining to listen for sounds from children's rooms.

In her closet, Ginger slid a pink satin gown over her nude body. She stepped into a pair of matching satin slippers and walked out of their bedroom, glancing back over her shoulder for a last glimpse of her husband sleeping peacefully.

She carefully cracked open the door of her daughters' room, knowing the television would still be on from their unsuccessful attempt to stay awake and watch the Friday night comedians on the cable channel. She went in, lifted Autumn's leg, which was dangling over the edge of the bed, and tucked the cotton coverlet securely under her chin, careful not to disturb Suzy Scribbles, the doll her five-year-old daughter never slept without.

Turning off the set, Ginger leaned over and kissed her daughter Sierra, who was in the fifth grade. If only she could put a timer on the television set to turn it off automatically at 11:30 on Friday and Saturday nights, Ginger thought, she'd save herself a fortune on the electric bill.

Christian, sucking on his bottom lip as usual, had gone to bed first on the weekend. Ginger smiled, shaking her head as she left his room. She'd wager none of his friends approaching their first year of high school hit the sack before his younger siblings. Never had she seen a child who loved to sleep so much. He must have gotten it from his father's side of the family. She hoped the rest of his body would soon catch up with his large, round pie face and pearly white chipmunk-sized teeth.

"Mama, is that you?" Jason called from his room. The faint sound of rap music could be heard in short, choppy waves, emanating from his stereo system. He'd rushed across the street to ABC Warehouse after his fifth paycheck from working as a bagger at the grocery store and laid out his hard-earned cash. Ginger was astonished that he hadn't bought the latest Michael Jordan gym shoes. She came home from work one night to find him and Christian huddled together trying to figure out the instructions for assembling the glass-and-oak cabinet that housed the unit. She noticed Jason's increasing addiction to the harsh lyrics that no one in the house but he seemed to enjoy. Ginger hated rap too, until she saw L. L. Cool J on the TV American Music Awards, his shirt off, moving his pelvis in a titillating, scandalous imitation of sex. . . . It left Ginger perspiring all over. Later, she heard from a friend that other women, heated from his gyrating performance, had also left smiles on the faces of their unsuspecting husbands that night.

"Yes, it's me, Jason."

Modestly covering himself with his top sheet, Jason whispered, "Anything wrong, Ma?"

"No. I can't sleep." The neon digital clock cast a turquoise glow over the posters of various basketball players and rappers papering his walls. He sat up as Ginger pressed the Off button on the stereo. "Don't you have to be at work at six-thirty in the morning?" She closed the door to his closet. The smell was overbearing. She barely heard him mention they'd changed his schedule from 11:00 A.M. to 7:30 P.M. "Drop those stinking gym shoes in the laundry room when you get up. All of 'em," she instructed.

Jason wrapped the crisp, white sheet around his muscular body, like a Roman emperor, gave Ginger a quick kiss on the cheek, and guided her out the door. "Okay, Ma."

He loosened the toga and flopped down on the bed, reaching underneath to retrieve his Sony Walkman. Adjusting the earphones, he crossed his legs at the ankle, laced his fingers behind his head, and began nodding to the beat of the radical refrain. Hearing the faint sound of the blaring music outside his door, Ginger shook her head.

As she descended the circular staircase leading to the first floor, the coolness of her satin robe teased the tips of her breasts. A trace of lemon polish hung in the night air from the carved oak panels that covered the walls of the spacious circular foyer. Raking her fingers through her hair, she leaned her head forward, and massaged her temples with the tips of her fingers.

Through the soles of her delicate slippers, she felt the cool brick ceramic tiles that bordered the shiny oak hardwood floor of the entrance hall. Stopping for a moment to admire her beautiful home, she was surprised by the newly fallen snow outside the windows of the music room. She headed toward the kitchen, where, reaching inside the cabinet, she selected an ornate crystal wine goblet from the impressive array of cut stemware.

Her mother, Katherine Lee, had taught her well. As poor as they were when she was a young child, her mother had refused to purchase anything but the best, even if it had to be second- or third-hand. Ginger followed the same practice, stopping at auctions and garage sales, always looking for that rare, undiscovered treasure and oftentimes finding a gem among junk, under a stack of old books or wedged in the corner of an old curio cabinet.

Turning toward the garden window, she admired the winter wonderland outside. Inside, she fingered a leaf of the carefully tended African violets nurtured by her husband, Jackson. He loved to display his natural ability as a gardener, and as a result, their home was filled with Chinese fan palms, bamboo palms, large, leafy dumbcanes, and dozens of ivy baskets.

A single snowflake stuck firmly to the leaded pane. Of the millions of white speckles falling in large clusters, growing larger each moment, the solitary flake managed to cling on, to survive. If only for a few fleeting moments, it stood out and acknowledged its own existence and resilience briefly, experiencing the splendor of freedom. She pressed an outstretched palm against the frosty window in awe of the snowflake's courage, the courage to break away from the crowd and become a singular entity standing alone, above the rest.

Closing her eyes, Ginger repeated a prayer she'd memorized. "Come, my soul, thy spirits prepare; Jesus loves to answer prayer; he himself has bid thee pray, therefore will not say thee nay."

Cupping her hand over her mouth, she held her breath for several moments as her eyes misted.

She flicked the light switch by the stairway off the kitchen that led to the wine cellar. When she opened the cellar door, she felt a slight chill and hurriedly selected a vintage bottle of Chardonnay.

She walked through the music room sipping the rich wine, tapping the keys on the white baby grand piano that stood proudly in the center of the pale pink wool rug, which was bordered by the plush off-white carpeting that covered the floors throughout most of the home. This was her favorite room downstairs. It was shaped in a circular design, and leaded Pella French doors surrounded three-quarters of it. The rear of the broadfront English Tudor house boasted 140 windows on three levels of its 5,000 square feet.

Placing the wine on a glass table, she slid onto a velvet

chaise, kicked off her satin slippers, and tucked her feet beneath her.

The sting of the cold, wintry air whistled through a break in the velvet-draped windows, even as the wine warmed her from within. Silent tears streamed down her cheeks. Why, suddenly, did she feel so alone? Was this what being in love was supposed to feel like? Was Jackson's and her love for each other real, or just an illusion? Something inside her knew, and didn't want to accept, that illusions can change from time to time.

Again Ginger combed her fingers through her hair, savoring the smooth texture. More in sorrow than in anger, she felt a sinking depression on being forced to deal once again with the impending loss of her hair. Though in her heart she knew it was coming, she prayed that the problem would somehow not return.

The cycle of alopecia areata, which doctors could not explain, lasted approximately two years. She lost her hair and often suffered the added burden of migraine headaches. Her doctor prescribed Valium for the stress, but the medication left her tired. Her lethargy was an effect neither her children nor her husband could understand, since they were accustomed to her workaholic disposition.

She had been only eighteen years old when the first of the bald patches appeared in her scalp. The problem was eventually diagnosed by a local dermatologist. She'd lost her hair a total of eight times over the years. It had always grown back, but each time she noticed that the loss had become progressively worse. The small dime spots on her scalp advanced into complete baldness, and loss of her eyelashes, then all her body hair.

Ginger had the most severe type of alopecia—alopecia totalis—she was told at the University of Michigan Hospital. She'd been praying for years for someone to find a cure.

She felt numb all over. No one could possibly understand the personal anguish and pain she felt. It was like a slow death, happening over and over again.

Lifting her half-filled glass in the direction of their bedroom, she saluted yet another exemplary performance by her husband. Slowly, she lowered her glass as sadness enveloped her like an old friend, and she became acutely aware of her fears. Did he truly love her? Or did he only lust after her body? Was there that much of a difference?

She'd read an article in the newspaper during Black History Month about how Black women should treat their men. We should treat them with the utmost respect, love, kindness, and recognition, which they rarely experience in the world. We should be enthusiastic about their aspirations and triumphs. We should encourage them to seek brighter horizons beyond merely being athletes, to strive to become scientists, attorneys, and congressmen, so that they can help to write the laws that govern them and our country, the article had told her. But what of *our* hopes and dreams? Ginger wondered. Were they insignificant? Who would help the women deal with pain and suffering?

She had four healthy children, a beautiful home, with lots of beautiful things: expensive paintings, precious antique furnishings, and a closet of designer clothes to die for. Why, then, did she feel such emptiness, such shallowness? Something was missing, something she couldn't bring herself to think about.

Despite their best intentions, Ginger and Jackson's eight years of marriage were often an emotional ordeal of cautious speeches and angry silences during the day. But as evening approached they surrendered to the volcanic passion that couldn't be ignored. Their silent obsession. Reality disappeared in the zest of their union. It was the one aspect of their marriage they never argued over.

But at this stage in her life it wasn't enough. She had played this scene before with her first husband, Michael Carter, who also claimed to love her to distraction. She had grown up believing in Cinderella, but after eleven years of her first troubled marriage, she found that her husband wasn't Prince Charming. He was just a man. Still, she wanted desperately to believe in the fairy tale of finding the man of her dreams. So without hesitation she had married Jackson Montgomery.

She knew her intelligence was above average—something her high school transcripts verified—and she was as proud of her intellect as she was of the combined African, European, and Native American features blended in her face. It was a struggle, however, to change Jackson into a man who wasn't just interested in the shape of her body but also the shape of her mind. She respected him for who and what he was, and expected him, in turn, to respect her for who and what she was, and the person she strove to become.

She chastised herself for spoiling him, making him believe that sex was the priority. She had already sold him on the idea that their bedroom turned into "The Best Little Whorehouse in Texas" when the lights went off. She sighed, inhaled, and took another long sip of her drink.

Yes, she'd gone to bed with him on their first date. But how was she supposed to know what to do? She'd never been on a date before, even though she was nearly thirty years old at the time. She'd been married at seventeen. Still in the process of divorcing her husband, she hadn't had sex for nine months and was horny as hell. It was ridiculous the way attorneys expected a woman to stay celibate during divorce proceedings, so she wouldn't be considered a slut during the custody hearings, while a man could go out and screw anyone anytime, and was rarely questioned about his dalliances.

So it was only natural that she wound up in Jackson's bed, feeling like a teenager. Carefree and happy. A few dates later, they decided to drive his brand-new black Bronco to Port Huron, where she lived. They'd just come from the Masonic temple and she had on a sexy antique white lace dress with iridescent sequins sprinkled around the bodice. His olive green silk suit flattered his sleek, muscular frame. He was totally appetizing. Utterly inviting.

Desire overwhelmed them, before they'd even reached her house. She couldn't wait. Neither could he. She ended up straddling him, having sex down the freeway at eighty miles an hour. She'd never forget it. Neither would he. Two weeks later he asked her to marry him. A few years later they had a baby daughter, Autumn. She was his spitting image. Jackson was happier than he ever would have believed. You'd think he'd had her all by himself, the way he carried on about his little girl.

Jackson Montgomery could charm the rattle off a rattlesnake. He was intelligent, articulate, suave, and charismatic without even trying to be. When he walked into the room, you couldn't help but stop and stare at his tall, slender, poised body. Ginger had been mesmerized the first time those seductive hazel eyes gazed into hers and seemed to look straight through to her heart. She was helpless, and who wouldn't be?

Getting up, she went into the kitchen and washed the delicate goblet and placed it back inside the cabinet. She'd finished the entire bottle of wine, but inner tranquillity still eluded her, and the desperate yearning she felt for Jackson had only been heightened. As she walked toward the circular staircase, she felt as light as the feather flakes that blanketed the ground outside. As quickly as it had begun, the snow had ceased.

When she opened the door to their master suite, barely making a sound, a familiar husky voiced called from the bed, "Baby, come back to bed, baby."

She stood in the center of the room, letting her flimsy garment fall to a fluffy puddle around her ankles.

Sliding beneath the cool sheets, Ginger snuggled close to Jackson's heat, two animals, bodies melded.

Gliding his palms against the round of her hips, he whispered in her ear, "I love you, baby."

The pungent aroma of dirty gym shoes greeted Ginger before Jason did. Turning toward the open doorway, her teacup in hand, she grimaced. "Mornin', Jason."

"I'm gonna put these in to soak, Ma. Is anything in the machine?" asked Jason, dropping one of the size-twelve sneakers.

She called over her shoulder as he walked toward the rear staircase, "No. But add a little Pine Sol to that water. Those shoes need some disinfectant."

She turned back to the magazine article she was reading on new businesses with low start-up costs. Ginger knew one day she'd be working in a professional field. As her eyes traveled down the page, she couldn't help but notice the protruding blue-green veins on both her hands, a result of the hard work they'd done.

Years of healed scars covered her hands. Though some were barely visible, she knew the location of each knick and mark. Lumps on either side of her fingers, the size of thumbtacks, were more prominent, calling attention to the fact that she worked in a factory. Ginger knew that, in order to be a professional, she had to look the part. Acrylic nails would do for a start.

The sun raised its sleepy head, streaming light through the room. Jason had been up for nearly two hours, and Ginger sat drinking her fourth cup of tea when Jackson decided to make his grand entrance.

After looking over her shoulder to see what she was reading, Jackson kissed Ginger fondly on the cheek. He tensed, quickly assessing the situation and Ginger's mood. Several issues of *Entrepreneur* and *Women's Entrepreneur* magazines were folded back, signifying that something had piqued her interest. Not this again, he thought to himself. Walking into the kitchen, he opened the cabinet door, reached for the coffee, opened yet another cabinet for a coffee mug, pulled out the silverware drawer, . . . and again, left it sticking out like a red flag.

"Can't you ever close a door?" asked Ginger, walking behind him and slamming the doors and drawer. She knew she should be used to it by now. Jackson never shut a cabinet door or pushed a kitchen drawer to its original position no matter how many he'd opened. Boy, did that get on her nerves. Their kitchen also had a spacious butler's pantry with its own sink, storing trays, and serving counters, with a total of fifty upper and lower cabinets. Fortunately, his meanderings this morning hadn't taken him that far.

Often, she would come home from grocery shopping, tired and angry, only to find almost every cabinet door in the kitchen wide open. Did she think maybe it was the kids trying to help out, making it easier to put up the groceries? Oh, no. The culprit was none other than Mr. Montgomery looking for crackers to snack on, cheese spread, or a plate—he could never seem to remember where they were stacked.

Ginger had asked Jackson on numerous occasions to have the kitchen remodeled, so at least the hinges would swing back on the cabinet doors and the needless arguments would cease. But no, he'd always refused, saying it would mess up the architecture of the house if they installed a modern kitchen.

Their home, built in 1923, was the epitome of old-money extravagance. The third floor held two bedrooms for the maid and butler with a large full bathroom—they didn't employ either. A spacious cedar closet completed the arc of rooms, which were circled around a massive skylight. They rarely used the third floor. They had plenty of other rooms as well as the twin sofa sleepers in the basement to use whenever relatives decided to stay over.

Dressed in a pair of tight, worn jeans, Jackson curled his fingers around the handle of the mug, and braced himself against the counter. The strong aroma of rich, black coffee filled the air. He took a long sip. "Did you enjoy last night?" He looked her in the eye as a slow, devilish smile eased across his face.

"Don't I always?" said Ginger, resting her hands on her hips.

Easing off the counter, swiftly untying her pink chenille bathrobe, he pulled her into his arms, forcing hers to drop at her sides. His large, nut-brown hands cupped her buttocks, pulling her up on her tiptoes to feel the bulge in his crotch. Her gown molded between her thighs as he thrust his knee to spread open her legs. Closing his mouth over hers, he kissed her. Ginger felt the velvety smoothness of his skin that stretched over his muscular shoulders as she struggled to disengage their bodies.

"Come on, baby," he whispered in her ear, licking the lobe. "We can go upstairs for a quickie before the kids wake up."

"I don't feel like screwing, Jackson. I've got a lot on my mind," said Ginger, finally freeing herself from his embrace.

Jackson glanced in the breakfast room, and then looked at her. "We're not going through this again, are we?" His muscles flexed, his breathing quickening.

As he followed her, Ginger nervously stacked the magazines neatly in a pile, and gathered them up against her bosom. Turning to look him in the eye, she said, "I don't care to discuss this with you this morning. We'll talk about it this evening. I'm going to take a shower." She stormed up the stairs. He followed her, swearing under his breath.

"What did you say?" she fired. She turned at the landing before the flight of stairs leading to their bedroom, and looked down into eyes staring up at her from three steps below.

Jackson propped himself against the wood railing. "You got a one-track mind—"

"So do you. It's your way or no wa—"

"That's why it don't do no good to tell you nothin'."

"What!"

" 'Cause you got your mind made up already. That's why I can't help you with nothin'."

"That's not true, Jackson, and you know it."

"I can't give you no suggestions because you got a one-track mind. I try to help, and tell you how I feel about things. Ain't that important?" His eyes begged understanding.

"Not when they differ from mine. Which is all the time. Are my feelings important to you?"

He expelled a few exasperated breaths. He was getting nowhere fast. "Ginger, it's always your way or no way. If you would just take time to listen to me once in a while, you'd save yourself a lot of time. You know I want to help."

As Ginger took a step down, her eyes grew wide in fury. Her right hand made a half-arc above his head. "How dare you! When's the last time you offered to help me at anything?"

"I don't waste a lot of good advice on you because you don't take it." Jackson's knuckles gripped the banister as he pushed himself up a step closer to Ginger.

Her tone became angrier. "Because you're manipulative, Jackson—"

"No. No. You can't recognize good advice. What you're looking for is someone to support your thinking. Your imagination runs away—"

It's too bad you don't have a little imagination outside the bedroom! Ginger thought to herself before shouting, "There isn't a damned thing wrong with my mind." She stepped back, gripping the rail.

"Can't you step outside yourself for a moment, look at the situation and be objective?"

"I can't. Suppose you try stepping inside yourself and being a little objective? I'd like you to tell me your short-comings. You're so quick to pinpoint mine. Lord have mercy, I can't believe how well you know me. We should get along like two peas in a pod."

"Knowing you is one thing, being able to speak the truth to you about you is another thing altogether, Ginger."

"Are you willing to sit down for a few hours and listen to me tell you about yourself, like I'm supposed to be willing to let you tell me about me?"

"I'm not going out trying to open a business, Ginger."

"Oh! So you don't think Oprah had any personal problems when she started out?"

Jackson crisscrossed his wrists on his knee and spat out the words "You ain't Oprah."

Jackson had long since tired of hearing Ginger brag about Oprah's success. Oprah was a goddess in Ginger's eyes. Her mentor. She could do no wrong. If he happened to be in the room when her show came on, Jackson would get up and walk out, saying "I don't want to hear this shit today." That always pissed Ginger off, and he knew it. She liked him to watch the show with her. Every now and then he would. Whenever he thought Ginger was on the brink of coming up with another big idea, he knew where it came from. Oprah was causing problems in his home she wasn't even aware of. There were probably a lot of other husbands out there who felt the same way he did: Leave my woman the way she was, I liked her better that way.

"And you ain't Michael Jordan either, but do you hear me complaining?" She knew that would piss him off, because he knew how she felt about Michael.

He ignored that retort, and continued honing in on his point. "Listen to me for just a minute, baby. You have a good head on your shoulders. We both know that. But sometimes you get too far ahead of yourself—move too fast. If I don't support your first thought then I'm accused of being unsupportive. Sometimes your ideas are so farfetched I can't be-lieve it. And I just go along with you—"

"What!"

Jackson snapped his fingers. "And sometimes I just go on along with you knowing you're wrong. But knowing if I go along it'll make you happy as can be. Just to go along with your wrong idea . . ."

Ginger felt the veins popping out on her forehead. *You bastard!* She thought for a second, regaining her composure. A slow smile eased across her face. Lifting her gown, she turned back to Jackson. She wiggled her hips as she climbed the stairs. "It's been quite a while since you had a good thought worth pondering over. The single revelation you ever had was when you decided to marry me, and I gave you that one!"

Jackson disregarded that remark, electing to make his point quickly. "I got sense enough not to leave over twenty years of seniority. A company that made it possible for you to live like you do." Jackson's gangly arms lifted to praise their beautiful surroundings. "Or have you suddenly forgotten where you live? Don't you feel your seniority at the company deserves more respect than a fast money-induced advertisement for suckers like you?"

Ginger turned and marched silently up the stairs.

2

Ain't Too Proud to Beg

Leaning over to fill the tub, Ginger replied through stiff lips, "No, I haven't forgotten about my seventeen years at the plant." Turning around to face Jackson, she sat on the edge of the tub and crossed her arms. "We've discussed my job at the plant and my endless jobs at home," she huffed, "and you know exactly how I feel about both." The sound of gushing water cut their conversation short.

As he walked toward her, Jackson inhaled deeply, then put an arm around her shoulder. Ginger stiffened, continuing to pour generous capfuls of jasmine bubble bath into the tub. Running his fingers through her hair, he turned her head toward him. His lips brushed against her neck as he spoke "Baby, let's not argue today," while kissing an exposed shoulder.

The warmth of her breath bounced off his face as she uttered softly, "I don't enjoy arguing with you, Jackson. I would just appreciate a little understanding." She stared innocently into his face. "Is that too much to ask?"

Knowing where the conversation was leading, he folded

his hands together in a nonhostile gesture. "What is it this time, Ginger?" he asked in a civil tone. "You promised me the last time you spent thousands of dollars on that . . . that . . ."

Her head lowering, she whispered, "Body Shop." Ginger knew every angle from which he would come at her. They'd had this same argument so many times that she'd memorized his speech. He'd bring up the kids. Her job. Her responsibilities at home. Finally end with "You must be losing your mind."

"Yeah," he continued. "That lotion and perfume business that you were so sure would be a success here in Detroit." He stood and walked toward the window. "Isn't that what you said!"

"Yes, but—"

"But nothing. I can't take this constant juggling in our home life every time you come up with a new business idea. It hasn't been so easy on the kids, either. How many times do we have to go through this? Every year?" He paused. "Are you that selfish? Can't you think about anybody but yourself? Are you losing your—"

"If I don't get out of that plant soon, I *will* lose my mind. It's always going to be the kids. You. Champion Motors. This damned house. What about what's important to me?" Her voice broke. She walked into their sitting room and flopped down on the couch. Every Saturday the set in this room was turned to the Westerns on TNT. Plush, pale pink carpeting stretched the forty-foot expanse of their bedroom suite. White walls complemented the pink-and-green floral café curtains covering the numerous windows. Ginger turned her head to focus on the fairyland the night's snow had made of the park a few yards away.

"Listen, Ginger. You knew what kind of woman I expected you to be when I married you. I can only take so much—"

"And you knew what kind of woman I *was* when I married you." She eased forward on the sofa, flicking the remote, cutting off the noise. Then, silence. "Jackson, why did you lie about helping me with my career? You knew from the beginning of our relationship how much it meant to me. I was upfront about getting into a business."

"I would've said anything to get you, Ginger."

"So you lied?"

He shrugged his shoulders.

"What about my needs?" Ginger asked.

"Nobody knows better than me what you need," he said seductively.

She raised her voice. "I need a career. I can't take working at that factory too much longer. When I look at that place at four forty-five every morning, I cringe. When I walk to the door, I dread opening it. It's getting harder and harder not to turn around and walk back out. If I hear another person tell me 'Ginger, you're so pretty . . . so talented . . . you're so intelligent, I can't understand what you're doing here,' I'll scream." Her fingers trembled as she massaged the veins in her forehead.

"If you didn't go around broadcasting your latest venture to everybody, you wouldn't have to hear it. I've told you time and time again to keep your mouth shut. But no—"

She shot off her seat. "I talk too much. So what. If you don't talk to people and network, you won't learn anything."

"You got it wrong, baby. You have to *listen* to learn." The muscles in his jaw tightened as he snatched a sweatshirt from the bureau.

"Jackson," she pleaded. "Why then haven't you been listening to me these past eight years? I'm almost thirty-seven years old. I want my life to have some significance—some meaning. I want to be able to be something or do something better than anyone else."

"Ginger—"

She waved him off. "I have four children, each of whom I love dearly. I've got a husband whom I love. I want to be a good mother and wife, but I can't do everything for you and the kids and not spend time on seeking my own happiness. It's just not fair, Jackson."

"My mother managed to take care of *nine* children and a husband and never complained once." Slipping his size twelves into a pair of cowboy boots, he stood over her like a giant admonishing his servant. "Every morning Hattie B.

Montgomery woke at four-thirty A.M. to make us fresh homemade biscuits and gravy. She served us plum preserves from the orchard trees in our backyard that she'd canned each year, got hand-churned butter and buttermilk from the farm a half mile down the road. And she made sausage, bacon, rice, and eggs as well. Every morning!"

Damn this man. Not this sermon again, thought Ginger. In Jackson's eyes, his mother epitomized the perfect woman. Whether it was cooking, cleaning, washing, or rearing the kids, Ginger could never quite measure up to his mother's legacy. Hattie B. Montgomery was a living legend.

"Yes, that woman was the first person up in the morning and the last one to go to sleep at night."

"Stop it, Jackson. I'll never measure up to your mother's standards. And quite frankly I'm getting a little tired of trying," said Ginger adamantly.

"I've never tried to compare you to my mother!"

" 'Cause you don't even know that you're doing it. But you *do* do it."

"That's your opinion."

"It's a fact, Jackson. Unconsciously you've done it since we've been married."

"Why should I—"

"So I can work harder. Turn flips to constantly be better, satisfying your every whim, because that's what your mother did for your father."

"You're taking my admiration for my mother totally out of context."

"You know, Jackson, most men secretly want to marry a woman who mirrors their mother. I can respect that. But I'd also like to be respected for doing the best I can. This is the nineties, not the fifties. Times have changed."

"You're right, baby," he said, wrapping a protective arm around her shoulder.

Ginger pulled away. She wasn't buying his concession, because she knew before the month was out they'd be having this same conversation again. "Jackson, I've told you on numerous occasions that I'm not your mother. I will never be your mother. I resent your constant comparisons, always making me fall at least five steps short," said Ginger, staring up at him in defiance.

He made another effort to stifle an argument. Sitting beside her, he caressed her chin. "I didn't mean it that way, honey. Forgive me." He kissed her lovingly on the mouth. "I'm an old-fashioned man who wants his woman at home."

Noticing his apologetic mood, she tried a different strategy.

"Jackson, I'm not going to spend any money. I've found something that I'd be good at and enjoy doing without spending a dime." Her eyes pleaded with him. "Selling real estate. You know how much I know about and love homes. I've been to every model home in the tricounty area. There's nothing I don't know—"

"Ginger!" His voice deepened to a deadly tone. "I said, I want you at home."

She turned her head shamefully. "It sounds like you want to own me—like a piece of furniture."

"It sounds like commitment to me."

"I can't for the life of me believe you would want your wife to work like a dog in that factory for thirteen more years. I can't believe that you won't encourage me to get out of that prison."

"Grow up, the pension you would get in thirteen years is worth it!" he said.

The thought of thirteen more years confined in that gray cement barrack sickened her. How could he be so insensitive? "I want something better for the rest of my life, Jackson."

He looked around in their huge bedroom suite, sweeping his arms wide. "You've got one of the most beautiful homes in the subdivision."

She stood erect, as her eyes held his. "I want a career. I want to get into real estate."

"No. I told you, I want you at home. Not off running around all over town with every Tom, Dick, or Harry. My wife belongs at home with her family in the evenings. Not off showing houses. You know how I feel! Give up this idea, Ginger."

"What? Is this an ultimatum? I can't believe it."

"Believe it!" He walked out the door and slammed it behind him.

Returning to the bathroom, Ginger sat on the edge of the tub, feeling the cold porcelain against her buttocks, then leaned over to refill the cool tub with steaming hot water. Dozens of jasmine-scented bubbled lined the edge of the water.

Was he testing her love for him? Why did he feel he needed to have so much control? How much could she give without exhausting herself? Wasn't she allowed to have a dream or two of her own? Or was she, as a woman, obliged to give, give, give, and that was to be her reward? Was it wrong for her to aspire to be that other person she saw at the end of her rainbow?

Was it too much to ask to feel that she was someone beyond her family?

Sipping on a frosted glass of Colt 45, Katherine Lee surveyed her work. She'd just completed the task of polishing the brass ornaments in her living room. Nancy Wilson's melodic voice filled the room like warm caramel, lazy and sweet, skipping over verbs every now and then because they were too much trouble to bother with.

Aggravated by the unwelcome ring of the phone interrupting her reverie, she snapped, "Hello." She drained the beer, and wiped away a foamy mustache with her sleeve.

"Mama. I need to talk to you. Are you busy?"

From the tone of her daughter's voice Katherine knew that Ginger had just finished another argument with Jackson. "No. What's the problem, sweetheart?" One of these days her daughter was going to learn how to handle that man. Katherine had learned early on how to handle hers. She couldn't have been more than twenty-two before she'd learned all the ropes. But here Ginger was approaching forty and still hadn't learned. Well, she thought. Another lesson. Another day. Maybe Kim could talk some sense into her. Sometimes her niece acted more like her than her own daughter did.

"Not what is the problem. But who is the problem? I think you already know the answer to that, and that bastard has really pissed me off this time!" Ginger said scornfully. "I've finally figured out how to get out of that plant, and I thought Jackson was going to be so happy about my decision. But was he? Oh no. Not my loving husband."

"Ginger, you know how Jackson is. He tells you he wants you to quit, but he doesn't really mean it. That man wants you in that plant every day so he can keep an eye on you. You couldn't pay me to work around my man every day. Yeah, yeah. I know what you're gonna say. He's in the office. You don't see him all day long. But the point is, you see too much of each other. Two hours on the road every day and eight hours in the plant. It's too close."

"I know, Mama. The whole situation is becoming almost unbearable." Ginger thought for a moment. "Mama. You remember the last time Gwen was here, and she told me that she thought that I'd make a good real estate agent. And that if I ever took the time and thought about it seriously, I'd come to the same conclusion?"

"Yeah, I remember. That was a few years ago."

"I never forgot what she said. As a matter of fact I went to talk to a broker. I had an interview last week. I didn't tell Jackson. I just went."

"Cut the bullshit. What happened?" Katherine poured herself another tall glass of beer and sat back in her chair, relaxing, smiling to herself.

Ginger sighed. "They were very interested in adding a female to the staff. Especially a Black one. But he didn't say that, and he didn't have to. One glance around the office, and I knew what I would be. A token. But so what? I don't have a problem with that. The point is, I signed up for the classes, and they start next week. But . . ."

"So, what's the problem?"

"Jackson. I didn't even get to tell him about the classes. He told me it was out of the question, and to forget it. His wife wasn't going to be running all over the city of Detroit."

"And you're surprised?"

"Yes and no. I thought he would be more worried about me spending money, but he didn't mention it. Anyway, the training and license fees are under a hundred bucks. Forty hours of training is required before taking your test. I'll have that completed in less than three weeks, and I can start working immediately after that. I've discussed it with Kim, and she thinks it's a good choice too. And you know how independent she is."

Slow down, Ginger. You're going too fast, thought Katherine. Out loud, she said, "I love this idea, I think it's the best one you've had yet. But the point is, what are you planning on doing about Jackson? You knew he was selfish before you married him. I doubt seriously if he's planning on changing anytime soon. So what's it gonna be? It's getting a little late in the season for you to keep changing careers. I'm concerned more about my grandchildren. Have you thought about the time you'd be spending away from them?"

"Yes, Mama. I've thought about a lot of things. Namely me. I've made the kids, Jackson, and the plant my whole life. I think it's about time I started thinking about what's really going to make me happy, before I get too old, and too tired to do anything about it. I made a mistake ever going to that plant, and if it takes the last breath I have, I'm gonna get out of there. I'm giving myself two years, and if selling real estate doesn't work out, I'll stick it out at the plant 'til retirement. But if everything works out like I think it will, the kids and Jackson will benefit in the long run, with me being able to be there in the mornings before they leave for school. I hate calling them every morning doling out instructions that they half-listen to, and coming home to see Sierra's changed her clothes from what I had laid out for her. Lord knows what her teacher thinks about me, allowing my daughter to dress like that. And—"

"Don't worry about Sierra's teacher. I'm sure they know you work. More importantly, what are you going to do about Jackson? I'm gonna tell you something about a man and a woman, and I want you to listen. You pay attention to what I'm trying to tell you, because I'm not going to repeat it again. It's time you grew up and faced some facts about marriage."

"I'm listening, Mama."

"You know what this universe is all about?" After hearing a hesitant yes, she continued. "It's about love and sharing. Selfishness, holding on to something . . . that's just a waste of time. It's about taking care of your man and him taking care of you—in a good relationship, the kind that lasts and stands the test of time. But . . . never, and I mean never, tell a man exactly what's on your mind. Then he knows how to play you. The name of the game is how good you can play."

"But I don't want to play any games."

Katherine let out an exasperated sigh and rolled her eyes toward the ceiling. "Just listen to what I'm telling you. Games between a man and woman have been played and won since the beginning of time. And any woman with any kind of sense has found that out already. That's why those women take separate vacations and go out and have a fling to make them feel good about themselves. Not just to have sex with another man. Occasionally they do, but the main purpose is to build up their self-esteem and self-worth so that they can deal with that bastard they're married to when they get back.

"You've got to learn to cope with Jackson, and still make yourself happy. Everybody who loves you knows how intelligent you are. How talented you are. You don't have to prove anything to anyone. Don't seek Jackson's approval in everything that you do, because you're not gonna get it. And quite frankly, you don't need it. If you plan on quitting work, and changing your lifestyle, I'm all for it. You know how I hate you working in that factory. But try to be more consistent for the kids' sake, and stick to it this time. You won't get too many more chances.

"You can do this. I know you can. But, don't just do it. Be the best you can be. You have to want it more than anything else, because when panic steps in—and you know it will—you'll need to be focused. If you can believe in yourself, no one can take that from you. It's something you have to know about yourself, and not have to be told. You wear it like armor.

"Something has to keep you going, something deep within you, and it'll carry you further than talent ever will. Talent gets you to the top, but character keeps you there. You have to have guts. That's what'll keep you going."

"I've got guts, Mama."

"You're gonna need 'em. Sounds to me like you've made some decisions."

"I have," said Ginger matter-of-factly.

"Which are?" Please let this child have the good sense to know she doesn't need Jackson's approval. He'd end up giving in eventually to anything she asks for. He always has, and probably always will, just like most other men who truly love their women, Katherine prayed silently.

"Century Twenty-one will see me promptly next Wednesday, come hell or high water."

Yes, God did answer prayers. Katherine Lee beamed.

Katherine didn't want to hurt Ginger's feelings by saying that if that bastard was working his ass off sitting at a sewing machine eight to ten hours a day like she did, instead of relaxing in an air-conditioned office, he'd be a little more understanding. Katherine couldn't stand the fact that a child of hers was working in a factory. She didn't raise Ginger to be anyone's slave, not even Jackson's.

Katherine had cried when Ginger told her that she was quitting her keypunching job at Michigan Bell Telephone to go to work for Champion Motors. They were hiring three hundred sewing machine operators, and she planned on being one of them. Katherine had taught all four of her daughters to sew. Ginger had even designed her own clothes, and tailored men's suits. Ginger told her mother that she knew she wouldn't have any trouble passing the sewing test.

After working several years in the plant, Ginger finally understood why her mother had cried. Katherine had known that Ginger would get so comfortable with the money that she would never leave to venture out on her own.

Katherine knew, as Ginger would come to know, that many factory workers have bachelor's and master's degrees, and some even boast Ph.D.s. The fast money, large checks—these were the trump cards that kept most people there, eventually destroying their desires for a job more suited to their qualifications.

Katherine had insisted that she'd suffered too hard and too long for a child of hers to give in to a slavish form of employment. She'd taught all five of her children that education was the key to success. She had demanded excellence, knowing what each of them was capable of, and wouldn't accept anything less.

Katherine had been taught by her own mother the importance of education for women. The school system had it backwards. They felt that male children deserved the right to an education before their female counterparts, that one day, those young men would become senators, governors, or presidents, the leaders of our nation. Now women aspired to those same goals.

Katherine had often explained to her daughters, "If you teach a man, you teach one man, if you teach a woman, you teach a nation."

Katherine had instilled confidence in them as well as the fear of not performing; letting them know that though they'd be punished if they didn't live up to her standards, she believed in their abilities. Hailed as the Jackson Five of Port Huron, they had danced to the tune of academic excellence for their exacting mother.

Katherine had known that Ginger was gifted, and wouldn't be satisfied with her immature decision to work in a factory. She couldn't understand why Ginger hadn't realized this earlier.

Even though Ginger's salary was double what she had made keypunching at Bell, she'd admitted to Katherine that her primary motivation was to build a new home with the exorbitant overtime pay she made. Eighty to a hundred hours a week—Lord have mercy, she'd build a castle.

Years later, after living in and loving her new home, Ginger realized that she'd made a mistake. The twelve-hundred-dollar checks didn't seem to silence that inner voice crying out for release: *Listen . . . Listen to your dreams! You can be anything you want to be in life.*

Katherine's other four children had taken the time to attend college, doing without the amenities that had so enslaved Ginger.

Ginger had thought that she was ahead of the game by acquiring all the trappings of the middle class—until she figured out that she *was* indeed trapped. The new home (yes, she'd finally managed to build her dream home in 1979), the cars, elegant furnishings, money in the bank.

How sad. To allow herself to think that possessions would fill the void in her life. Personal satisfaction. Self-expression. Doing what you loved to do for a living, instead of what you *have* to do. Allowing yourself to grow personally. That was what was important, she'd humbly admitted to her mother. But though she talked about it more and more, she had not yet succeeded in breaking away.

When Katherine hung up the phone, she felt encouraged. Ginger is getting some sense, she thought. She's finally managed to keep something from Jackson. Yes, that child is getting more and more like me every day.

3

For Once in My Life

Thinking over her mother's words, Ginger headed for the bathroom. She knew that the only thing that would take her mind off Jackson was a trip to the mall. She placed her cosmetic tray next to the sink and began applying her makeup. As she reached for the translucent powder, she studied the large veins in her right hand for the second time that day.

She turned her attention back to the mirror and used a thick sable brush to stroke her face with a thin layer of golden flecked powder. Ginger looked younger than she was, but after seventeen years in a factory, her body didn't feel youthful.

Jackson's reaction earlier bothered her more than she cared to admit. She wanted his approval. She needed his approval, and his unconditional love. If she accepted less from life, how could she expect her kids to make that giant step and struggle for independence? She had drilled it into their heads for years: "After college, work at a place of business for a couple of years, then strike out, after you've learned the tools of the trade, and work for yourself."

Ginger wanted to set an example for her children. To teach them the importance of education. Especially for her two sons, who thought athletes were it. Though she loved sports, and had nothing but praise for superstars like Magic Johnson, Isiah Thomas, Shaquille O'Neal, and Clyde Drexler, she wanted them to understand that sports couldn't always secure a future. She'd told Jason and Christian that though she took pride in watching the Black male superstars excel in their chosen fields, she wanted her sons to be able to fly not just in a game, like Michael Jordan, but to fly in life.

Most children desire to do things for themselves. Ginger knew that it was up to her to instill in her children a strong sense of self-knowledge and an understanding of the power of God. So much to teach them in so short a time. Would they listen? God willing . . . Would they trust in her learned knowledge about life? God willing . . . Would they respect her decisions as a parent, as their mother? God willing.

Children . . . her children, the living art of God and man, a product of nature. Like a web of God, spinning out of itself—a pattern, a design, a geometry, a journey back to God himself. Oftentimes we see ourselves better through our children. We connect with our feelings. These feelings become *knowing*. Ginger knew her life was not the example God wanted her to set for her children. How could she expect so much of them if she didn't fulfill her own destiny?

She knew that she had to trust in the power of God that was within her. Ginger crossed her palms over her chest. Her spirit and part of her blood were running through each of her children's bodies. She felt the deep beat of her heart. Time . . . life . . . love . . . children.

Jason stood outside her bedroom door and tapped twice before he entered the room. Peeping around to see what his mother had been doing in there so long, he stared wide-eyed into her sad face. "Mama, Kim's on the phone," said Jason. "You want me to tell her to call back later?"

"No, that's all right, Jason." She forced a smile. She hated for her son to see her so depressed; she always wanted to project a positive attitude. "Tell her just a minute." Placing the unused Q-tips and sponge wedges back in their containers, she wiped away the traces of powder staining the white porcelain of the sink. "Jason," she called out, after he'd left the room. He poked his head back around the door. "Are the kids okay?"

"Fine, Ma. I fed them some pizza downstairs. They're watching cartoons."

"Pizza for breakfast, Jason?" She picked up the receiver.

"Yo, Mama. Chill. It won't hurt 'em." He bounded from the room, before he accidentally mentioned he'd served it to them cold. The way they liked it. Cold cereal, cold pizza for breakfast. What was the difference?

"Hi, Kim." Extending her right arm, Ginger stretched out her hand. Making herself a promise, a promise that she knew she would keep: If she wanted to be a professional, she had to start looking like one.

4

Ain't No Woman Like the One I've Got

In the center block of Market Street near Fenkell, formerly Christ Temple Baptist Church, the newly acquired building was being renovated as the current headquarters of the Production 10 Motorcycle Club. This building was their second acquisition. Little Bubba and Jackson, along with twenty other lifelong members, had formed the club in 1970, and each owned a share of the structure. Monies made from cabarets and party rentals were used for utilities and the upkeep of the building. Occasionally they went on field trips; their intention was not profit but pleasure.

"Damn it's cold in here, man!" said Little Bubba, blowing into his cupped hands, then vigorously rubbing them together. He walked over to the thermostat and turned it up. "Man, I'm surprised to see you down here this early in the morning." He eased onto the bar stool next to Jackson. The ten-foot-long mirror stretched across the wall behind the bar, reflected the image of two old friends. Looking at the heap of plumbing apparatus covering the dance floor, Little Bubba said, "I thought we set the meet-up time at noon"

Jackson fumbled with the wrench on the counter. He hadn't expected anyone to show up here at the club before 12:00 P.M. He wanted a few hours by himself to think. "Been talking about bringing down that extra toilet and sink of mine for the last few months. Thought I'd do it today. Might as well get both of the bathrooms installed at the same time."

Little Bubba looked puzzled for a moment. Lifting his hat, he scratched his gray-speckled crew cut. Jackson never missed his Saturday morning Westerns on the cable channel at home. There was a television set at the club, but they didn't have cable. "Your satellite dish still working all right?"

"Yeah," Jackson said. "Same old reruns."

Walking around the bar, Jackson opened the refrigerator door and peered in. He put two cold beers on the counter and then leaned his back against the cool surface. The smell of cold beer filled the air. "Watching the game tonight?" asked Jackson.

"Wouldn't miss it. The Pistons are playing Cleveland tonight. . . right?"

"Yeah, at the Coliseum." Jackson turned on the television set, and sat down beside his friend to watch the morning news. "Gonna be a good game. Pistons need to win this one tonight."

"Got twenty dollars bet on 'em suckers, they better win." Little Bubba, feeling the warmth of the furnace, shed his wool jacket. Shuffling through his deep pockets, he extended a small yellow bag to Jackson and opened his own.

"Hey man . . . thanks." Just like old times, thought Jackson. "Man, this bag must've come all the way from Mississippi, they're tough as hell." Biting down on a curled pork crackling, he cursed from the side of his mouth through clenched teeth.

"Them big teeth you got shouldn't have no trouble biting nothing." Little Bubba smiled. He and Jackson had grown up together down South. Little Bubba stood barely five feet five inches tall. Because his baby brother hadn't learned how to say *brother* correctly he'd always called him Bubba, and the name stuck. After Jackson and Bubba entered high school, though, Bubba's younger brother grew like a weed and shot

up four inches taller than Bubba, so he changed the nick-
name to Little Bubba. "How's the kids and Ginger doing?"

"They're doing fine. Just fine." Jackson pondered for a bit,
then added, "Her oldest son Jason got a job bagging groceries at Krogers. It's working out pretty well. Plans on buying a car before the summer's gone. . . . Henry ain't in no
more trouble is he? He found a job yet?"

"My boy still ain't found no job. Don't think he want
one." Little Bubba shook his head shamefully. "Giving up
them drugs ain't easy. I promised Lillian 'fore she died, I'd
do everything I could to put him in a drug rehab, and see that
he got back right." He jockeyed himself toward the pool
table. "Three years, and each year been worse than the last
one. Last night . . . no, this morning, he came in around five
o'clock looking like he been rolling around in a gutter. I pray
to God Lillian can't see him, otherwise she'd be turning over
in her grave. I had to get outta there this morning before I
killed him."

Little Bubba fetched another cold one for each of them.
They talked and joked about the easy days of growing up
back home, reminiscing with the same old stories they'd told
each over the past twenty years, knowing they'd still provide
a laugh or two.

Z.Z. Hill's down-home blues bounced off the freshly
painted black cement walls of the renovated church building.
Five black and white and red hands of cards—aces, kings,
queens, jacks, and tens, of hearts, spades, clubs, and diamonds—were stenciled in three-foot sections at various intervals around the room. Jackson shuffled his feet to a slow
dance, using the pool stick as his mate. Turning up the volume, he watched Little Bubba smiling to himself, nodding
his head to the melancholy beat.

The digital clock above the bar registered 11:47 A.M.
"Man, it's almost noon," Jackson said, clearing the empty
beer cans lined up along the bar. After consuming a twelve-
pack, playing fifteen games of pool, and making several trips
to the newly installed men's toilet, they were both beat.

Little Bubba flushed the toilet with a bucket of water, and
took a seat at the bar. "Jackson, we gotta get that toilet finished. I can't haul too many more buckets of water. I'm too

old for this. I think I'd be better off waiting 'til I get home to use the bathroom."

Rinsing out the last beer can, Jackson placed it back inside the carton, which he stored next to several boxes of empties by the door. Joining Little Bubba back at the bar, he picked up a discarded wrench and began tapping it against the counter.

"Okay, pal." Little Bubba turned to look Jackson square in the face and exhaled. "We've been friends for a long time. What's botherin' you?" Jackson waved him off. "Don't tell me it ain't nothin'. I been knowing you too long. Something must've pissed you off to get you away from John Wayne and Matt Dillon."

Jackson couldn't help but smile. The beer had relaxed him somewhat, and he'd begun to feel like talking. "It's Ginger. We argued this mornin' before the kids were up."

"Man, don't you go getting that pretty little wife of yours upset. You got a fine woman. A hardworking woman. If I had—"

"What makes you so sure I did something wrong?" Jackson started to get defensive. "She is the stubbornest woman I ever met in my life. I didn't have no trouble like this with my first wife."

"I don't mean no offense, Jackson, but you know these women up here ain't like our women back home—they a mite feisty, but they still good women. Now you know I was sorry, too, when your wife passed ten years ago. But—in the time you and Ginger been married, you seem happier to me. I knew she was good for you when you stopped hanging down here at the club until all hours of the night like you used to. Ain't no married man got no business hanging around all these single men night after night. 'Cause you know they ain't up to no good."

"Yeah. I'm getting too old for that kind of life. I'll be forty-four in a couple of weeks. Got twenty-four years in at the plant, and six more to go 'til I retire. I'm gonna work two more years after that, and that's it. Ginger doesn't know it, but I'm looking at buying some property this summer when we go home for our family reunion."

"You planning on moving back?"

"Yeah. In eight years her daughter Sierra'll be graduating from high school. She doesn't like going down South, anyway. None of Ginger's kids like it, just Autumn. She's a Montgomery through and through. We stopped making the boys go last year, and let them stay with their father until we get back. I wouldn't dream of taking Sierra away from her father—she's crazy about her daddy. I can't stand the son of a bitch. I hate to see him coming every two weeks. He's got her spoiled rotten."

Little Bubba eyed Jackson, lifting an eyebrow. "About as spoiled as your Autumn?"

Jackson's face lit up like a Christmas tree. "Hey, that's the only baby I've got. She'll always be my baby."

"You talked it over with Ginger? How does she feel about moving to Mississippi?" Little Bubba asked.

"She doesn't know."

"So it's like that."

"Yeah, it's like that." Jackson reached behind the bar and pulled out two foam cups, and turned down the volume on the radio. He could only stand so much music. He liked listening to the news station. "I need a drink. You want a shot?" Little Bubba nodded. Jackson poured them each a hefty splash of Christian Brothers, topping it off with a bit of Coke.

The clock ticked noisily in the background as they sat sipping their drinks. Jackson described the scene with Ginger that morning while they had their third drink.

There was a long pause before Little Bubba spoke. "I hate to tell you this, man, but you're wrong."

Jackson's hazel eyes held a lethal calmness. Setting down his drink, he leaned his elbows back on the bar. He respected his friend, but he wasn't going to listen to someone trying to tell him how he should run his home or his wife. He said coolly, "How do you mean?"

"I've talked to Ginger occasionally at the club's family picnics. She's very intelligent, and I won't even mention how everybody in the club raved about the leather chaps and vest she made you. It's obvious she's talented too. Man, you can't hold a woman like that back. I wish Lillian had pursued her gift of painting with the same passion. After working all them years in a factory, I can't blame Ginger for wanting to get out. Personally, I wouldn't want my wife working like a dog in that car plant."

Jackson bristled at his comments. What did Little Bubba know? Or more, what right did he have telling Jackson anything? "Last time I checked, you didn't have a wife." Jackson knew that was below the belt, but he felt his friend had crossed the line, so why shouldn't he?

Little Bubba knew deep down his old friend didn't mean any harm. If any other man this side of heaven had made that remark about his dead wife, he would have pushed his size eight and a halfs down the crack of his ass. He drained the bottom of his drink and grabbed his coat. "If I had a wife like yours . . . I'm telling you man, these nineties women ain't taking that male chauvinist shit no more. They're walking out, and ain't looking back. I just hope that you wake up before it happens to you."

"Sierra, you and Autumn get down here," Ginger hollered. Two pairs of feet pounded down the stairs as Ginger cleared the half-full cereal bowls from the breakfast table and set them on the sink. "Didn't I tell you not to pour more cereal in the bowl than you were going to eat?" Their heads nodded in agreement. "Then why are they half-eaten?" Ginger raised her voice and the bowls simultaneously.

"Mama—" Sierra kicked Autumn in the leg—"we were planning on coming back downstairs to finish just before you called us." She handed Autumn her bowl and spoon. "See . . . we were gonna finish." Autumn, following Sierra's lead, lifted the bowl to her mouth and drank the remaining milk. They were still stuffed from the leftover pizza Jason had fed them earlier.

"Where's Christian? I want this house clean in the next two hours. I've got a lot to do today. Let's get with it," Ginger called, already climbing the stairs.

When Ginger wasn't looking, Sierra kicked at her sister— then snarled, "I told you to let me fix it. My stomach feels like it gonna bust open."

*   *   *

"I know, Ma. I'm getting my room cleaned up, Ma," said Christian, rolling his eyes toward the ceiling. "Yes, I saw the list you left on my dresser." Every Saturday, the same routine.

Ginger left a similar list on Jason's dresser. When he came in from work, she'd let him rest for a couple of hours, and then he'd have to pitch in and do his part like everyone else did. He grumbled and mumbled, as they all did. Well, she was just as sick of cleaning every weekend as they were. Maybe she'd find out how much it would cost for someone to come in and do the heavy cleaning every two weeks.

Jackson waved to Autumn, Sierra, and Christian building snowmen in the yard as he pulled into the driveway. The leather seats squeaked at the release of his 220-pound frame. He was surprised to see Ginger's minivan missing from her section of their three-car garage.

The smell of Pine Sol greeted him at the back door, and he knew without looking that the house was spick-and-span. Although as he walked down the upper hall, the familiar odor of teenage funk funneled from Jason's room. Kicking off his cowboy boots, he discarded them along with his jeans and shirt in a cluttered pile near the bed and stretched out on the mattress.

Later that evening Ginger returned home, carrying a large box. "Where have you been all day?" asked Jackson, looking up from the television set.

"I've been over at Kim's. I called home to speak to you, but Jason said you were still sleeping." She placed the black box on the chaise next to her purse. Walking into her closet, she slid off her gym shoes, scooting them into their cubbyhole. She folded her jogging suit, and placed it in her bottom drawer. Up above her were rows of large white, square hat boxes stacked on top of each other. Several round black glossy boxes were imprinted with the name of Henry and Hatter in gold letters—a men's hat store. Ginger loved the way she looked in men's hats. After changing into her nightgown, she retrieved the box from the sitting room and rearranged the shelf to accommodate her latest purchase.

"You bought a new hat?" Jackson asked over the loud

cheers coming from the set. He wanted to talk about anything other than the problem at hand. He hoped she had forgotten the real estate idea, but after talking to Kim all afternoon . . .

"Yeah. Kim and I went shopping. She bought one too." Ginger wondered if he was going to broach the subject again. Well, she'd tell him about her decision when the time was right. "I'm going to check on the kids' clothes for church tomorrow. You going?"

"Yeah, set my suit out, will you?"

Ginger felt her anger rising, but said nothing. She didn't want to start fighting yet.

Later, as Ginger slid into bed, she tried to neutralize the anxiety now stirring inside her, and she prayed for the spiritual peace that fellowshipping in church the next day would surely bring.

Jackson cussed and shouted as the Pistons' lead over the Cleveland Cavaliers narrowed. Cleveland had two chances to tie the score after Steve Kerr cut Detroit's lead to 92 to 90, but it wasn't to be. Isiah Thomas hit a three-point with 2:34 left to make it 101 to 96, and finished with nineteen points. The Pistons were victorious, 105 to 100.

Pushing the remote, Jackson turned off the set and climbed in beside Ginger. He pulled her close, smelling the scent of the China Rain cologne and Shower to Shower body powder that was forever present on her pillow. He lifted a tendril of hair and kissed her neck. Shrugging him off, she moved to the outer edge of their king-size bed. He got the hint. He turned his back, and replayed the Pistons game, over and over in his mind until finally, he drifted off to sleep.

"Shhhh, Autumn. You're going to have to be quiet while the pastor is speaking, otherwise you'll have to go with the children to the children's section next time." *Where you should have gone today if your daddy hadn't been so insistent that you had a little sniffle and needed to stay with us,* Ginger added to herself. Autumn's small hand continued to tap her mother's leg as she tried to prompt her mother to let her speak. "Okay, Autumn, what is it?" asked Ginger, wondering why Jackson never seemed to notice how much trouble the child was when she stayed in the service with them. Autumn pointed to the elegantly dressed woman, clad head to toe in black, sitting next to Jackson, and whispered that she hadn't put any money in the collection plate when the usher passed it down the row. Ginger patiently whispered to her observant baby daughter that not everyone who looked like they had money always had it.

"The good Lord wants his children to come to church whatever their circumstances," she explained in a whisper. Autumn seemed satisfied and sat back quietly.

The pastor wiped his sweaty forehead, hesitating for effect as he continued his sermon. "These young people around here talking about 'fresh.' They don't know God's got his own interpretation of fresh." The preacher patted the perspiration raining down his forehead and continued his fiery message. "F-R-E-S-H. The Lord wants his saints to be fresh. You want to know how the Lord wants you to be fresh?" The congregation chorused a resounding yes.

"To be reverent, respectful, positive. 'F' meaning being focused—'R,' having responsibility—'E' for developing a level of efficiency, something to distinguish you from everyone else—'S,' meaning self-sufficient, having self-esteem—and finally 'H,' being holy, having hope." Sister Staten stood up, clapping and uttering a loud "Amen."

"A man worries about dying while he's living, but he should be worrying about what dies in him while he lives."

When the choir marched down the aisle robed in flowing gowns, singing the postlude, led by Jackson's cousin's wife, Mae Thelma, a nodding Jackson suddenly became wide awake. Ginger felt a tinge of jealousy, wishing with all her heart that she were blessed with such an amazing voice.

Mae Thelma's soprano voice, melodic, and spiritual, left the entire congregation misty-eyed, filling their hearts with supreme pleasure.

5

The Love I Saw in You
Was Just a Mirage

As Mae Thelma gathered her boys from the children's church, several of the sisters stopped to compliment her on her wonderful solo. With a thick, southern drawl she answered softly, saying, "Why thank you, Sister Washington, Sister Armory, and may God bless the both o' ya." Mae Thelma shook their hands, smiling from ear to ear, gold crowns glittering on her two front teeth.

"Robert Earl Jr., David Earl, you chillins come on heah now. We gotta hurry afore we miss the church van."

"Mama," her eldest son, Robert Earl Jr., said, "when you gonna learn how to drive Daddy's car? I'm tired of riding that bus. We can't even stop and get some goodies afore we go home. You promised us three months ago you was gonna take driving lessons. Why can't Uncle Jackson teach you how to drive?"

"Hush boy, here they come now." Mae Thelma had already secretly appealed to Jackson for help. She had some knowledge, but was scared to drive in the unpredictable Michigan weather. Back home in Guntown, Mississippi, where she and Jackson grew up, she'd never even seen a flake of snow. But she didn't know how long her husband, Robert Earl, would be in jail. She was all alone now with two young boys who needed a man to set an example of how to grow up Black in this White man's society.

Mae Thelma stood five feet eight inches tall, with hair that tumbled to her petite waistline. Beautiful black wavy hair that she always wore in a french braid coiled atop her head like a halo when she was in church, which was five out of seven days a week. Her skin tone was the color of a ripe Georgia peach, as smooth as the finest leather, and thick black eyelashes bordered her slanting, exotic eyes.

She moved quickly toward Jackson, smiling provocatively. The heavenly essence of honeysuckle floated around her. "We've been looking for you," said Jackson, hugging Mae Thelma and patting her boys casually atop their heads.

They were always happy to see their Uncle Jackson, as they called him, even though their father and he were only first cousins. He drove a motorcycle. How could anybody who drove a motorcycle as fast as he did be anything but cool?

Jackson looked immaculate in his charcoal gray double-breasted pinstriped suit. His eager smile as he admired his cousin's saintly wife looked somewhat devilish, like that of a young man with silent temptations. "Ginger and I would like to invite you and the boys over for dinner next Sunday after church," he offered. The shouts of glee from her boys elicited a smile from Jackson. But the children beside Ginger stiffened and whispered among themselves.

Ginger prodded Jackson to answer her questioning eyes as to when all this inviting had been decided. Besides, she'd already made other plans.

"Sweetheart," said Ginger, getting in the car and buckling her seat belt, "I already invited Kim, Bill, Aunt Jewel, and Mama over for dinner next Sunday. You could've asked me first before you extended invitations. After all, we both know who is going to be doing the cooking, and it certainly ain't you."

Jackson wove the Bronco through the maze of cars lined up behind the church. He stopped at the light and turned toward Ginger. "You could've also mentioned to me that you'd invited your cousin and her fiancé over. Katherine, Kim, and her mother I can deal with, but Bill—You know perfectly well I can't put up with Bill and his militant speeches for more than ten minutes."

"Well, bucko, an afternoon with the sanctimonious Mae Thelma talking about God every two minutes is a little more than I can tolerate myself. And those bad-ass little heathens she's got. She needs to stop spending so much time praising the Lord and whip their little asses. I swear I'm gonna slap that little David Earl one of these days."

She paused for a moment. "Have you forgotten the last time they were over he knocked that ivy hanging plant on my white carpet?" The sound of leather crunching as Jackson shifted uncomfortably sliced the mounting tension in the air. He loved his precious plants; if anything got his attention, that would. "And you know I've tried everything, and that stain still won't come up."

"Baby, the boy's only three years old. Give him a break, will you? I've heard this story every time I've mentioned Mae Thelma's name. How many times are you going to repeat it? I get the point, okay?"

"I'm only telling you because they're eating dinner with the kids downstairs. After dinner they can play in the basement, not in the kids' bedrooms, and when they finally come up for air, it'll be to go home sweet home."

Christian spoke up to complain that Robert Earl had gone in his room and taken some of his experiments out of his chemistry set. "If he goes in my room again, I'll kick his butt," Christian added. Jason joined in, saying one of them stole one of his tapes. Sierra and Robert Earl, who were the same age, were secretly in love with each other and always got along well. So she said nothing.

"And David Earl stole the batteries out of Suzy Scribbles," Autumn chimed in. Everyone turned to look at her, knowing she was fibbing, except Jackson, whose eyes were focused on the sluggish traffic.

"Where was I when all this thievery was going on?" Jackson asked. "I don't want to hear any more complaints." He gave Ginger a quick look. He meant her, too. "You all are going to have to get along. I promised my cousin I'd keep an eye on his wife and kids while he was in jail. So everyone might as well tuck in their lips and get used to them being around." An angry silence descended over the vehicle as they drove home over Palmer Park and through the woods.

"Sierra, are you almost finished?" Ginger called from the family room.

"I can't get these creases straight." Sierra's long, delicate fingers were frantically straightening and restraightening the fabric of her baggy Used jeans.

As Ginger closed her book and gathered up the pile of wrinkled clothes lying next to her, she felt a sharp pain stab at her temple. She walked toward the laundry room, trying to shake it off, massaging her forehead with her free hand.

Jason caught a glimpse of the grimace on her face as she walked past the exercise room. "Ma, you all right, Ma?" He set down the hand weight and put his arm around her shoulder. A shock of black hair and funk hit her at nose level. She patted him off. "I'm okay." Pushing him back into the room, she returned, "You got fifteen more minutes to work out and I want to see and smell you showered and fresh for school tomorrow."

After showing Sierra for the fiftieth time how to match all four seams together and steam in a hard, razor-sharp crease, Ginger ironed her own clothes along with Autumn's. Next year, she thought to herself, when Autumn turned six, she'd be joining Sierra down in the basement to iron her school clothes, too. Jackson had babied Autumn long enough. It was about time to let her do some of the chores along with the other kids.

Ginger spied Jackson in his familiar napping position as she gathered her nightclothes. Running a few minutes behind schedule, she elected to take a quick shower before the hot water ran out, instead of the relaxing bath she desperately craved.

By 9:01 P.M. Ginger kissed a loving good night to each of her children, who were bathed and dressed in their PJs, and issued last-minute orders that they knew by heart: lights out, TV off by 9:30.

Closing her bedroom door, she rested her head against its smooth oak surface. Her headache had subsided after she took two extra-strength Tylenols and a cup of strong Lipton tea.

After cleansing and moisturizing her skin, she brushed her teeth and finished preparing for work the next morning. Then, sitting across from Jackson's slumbering figure, she prodded him with her feet.

After several kicks, he sat up straight and scooted to the front of his seat. "What time is it?" He checked his watch and jumped up, quickly peeling off his clothes. "Honey, I asked you not to let me sleep so long. You know I won't be able to sleep tonight."

She coiled a long auburn lock of hair around a pink plastic roller, clasping the cover between her lips. Through clenched teeth she answered, "I was busy with the kids, I forgot to wake you." She watched him peeling off his clothes, leaving a trail behind him.

Within minutes he'd showered and slid next to Ginger between the freshly powdered sheets, his cologne mingling with the fresh scent of the talc. He pulled her close and planted kisses along her shoulder. "It's okay with me, baby, about the real estate thing." She turned to face him, surprised. "I don't want to feel any guilt about holding you back. If that's what you want, and you're sure about it, I won't give you any more arguments." She kissed him on the mouth, silencing his next comment.

"But," he said, after coming up for air, "I want you to promise me. And mean it this time. Because this is the last time I'm going through this—promise me that this is it. That this is the last time you ask me to go along with any more of your ideas, okay?"

"I promise. I promise," said Ginger, hugging him.

"You've got a year. That's it. A year . . . to get this out of your system and see if it's for you or not."

"That's all I need, honey. You'll be proud of me, you'll see. You and the kids will be proud of me. I know I can do it. All I need is a chance. Just a chance." She whispered the words more to herself than to her husband.

She felt him pushing down his underpants hurriedly and

kicking them off, and turned to pull her gown over her head full of curlers. Plastic curler clamps landed on the floor alongside the discarded gown, but were unnoticed. Kissing her passionately on the mouth, he guided her hand to his growing sex. She stroked him gently at first, massaging the tip artfully, as he sucked the tips of her breasts until they peaked with desire.

He felt a tiny drop of clear liquid ooze from the source of his heat. His excitement mounting, he teased the mounds of her breasts with his tongue, while his hands toured the satiny landscape of her buttocks.

Her breasts rose and fell with the erratic beat of her heart. She inhaled the scent of his cologne, her breath becoming shallow, as he continued to explore the softness between her thighs.

She knew that neither could wait another minute. After years of lovemaking, their bodies were perfectly in tune. Each time they made love, their desire increased, taking them to a higher level than they thought possible—each time was better than the last. Jackson shifted his weight, positioning his long body above her.

She whispered "Let me" and kissed the nipples of his breasts. Guiding him to lie back against the feathery pillows, she stroked his sex until she felt his veins straining for release. Easing her leg over his lap, she straddled him, and bending her head to kiss his full, sensuous lips, caressed his luscious mouth with her tongue. She guided him inside her. Slowly, she felt his pelvis move with a quick assuredness that rendered her more helpless with each stroke.

Her heart pounded as if it were a talking drum of Africa. She met each stroke with a rhythmic thrust of her hips. Her eyes were closed, her mouth half-open, whispering his name. Her breasts swayed as strands of sweat ran down them and clung to the nipples, cold mingling with the heat of her passion. The warmth of Jackson's mouth closed around her taut areola, sucking, licking, loving. Her entire body felt so relaxed, yet desperate for total sexual fulfillment.

She uttered a soft scream that told him she was near to release, and he lifted his lean hips to drive deeply against her, giving her the pleasure she needed. Holding back his own release, he felt the hot juices of her love crown the head of his manhood.

Her blood was making explosions through her body. She cried out in release, feeling as if a strange spiritual intoxication had taken control of her. . . . Her eyelids closed tightly as a kaleidoscope, swirling, eddying, appeared to dance before her eyes.

Jackson cupped the velvety halves of her bottom, guiding her to the final moment of rapture. He felt it his job as a man, to satisfy his woman first before he indulged in his own gratification. He'd finally met a woman whose sexual desires matched his own.

Knowing that his climax was imminent, she whispered "Faster." She felt his body arch beneath her, gyrating his pelvis, lifting her higher with the ease of a thoroughbred stallion. His breathing ragged . . . hers in soft pants . . . their bodies in exquisite harmony . . . his raw sensuality carrying them to greater heights.

"That's it baby . . . deeper . . ." cried Ginger as she felt the power of his throbbing penis. She worked the muscles of her vagina, relaxing then contracting, suckling him, grabbing hold of his shaft.

Timing their orgasm to catapult them to another place in time, they rode the waves of carnal passion together. They shuddered simultaneously.

As Ginger lowered her head, her eyelashes grazed his face while he massaged the center of her back, kissing her lightly on the tip of her freckled nose.

"Baby, it don't get—"

"—no better than that. I know, sweetheart," said Ginger, lying exhausted beside him. His strong arm tightened around her, pulling her close.

Polishing the white Formica counters and chrome fixtures until they gleamed, Mae Thelma harmonized "Tomorrow" along with her favorite tape by the Winans. Satisfied that the kitchen was sufficiently clean, she gathered her sponges, polishing cloths, and mop bucket and lined them in precise order in her immaculate utility closet. As she paused for a final inspection, the phone rang.

"Yes, hello."

"It's me, Mae," said Robert Earl. Her husband's deep voice was instantly recognizable. "I'm calling to make sure you're coming down to see me in the morning."

Annoyed at the pleading tone in his voice, she wiped the sweat from her forehead. She untied the diaper-style scarf from her head, allowing her hair to cascade down to her waist. She ejected the Winans' tape and dropped it into her apron pocket. Her southern accent offered a sweeter tone. "Why Robert Earl Collins, I do declare. Don't I visit my husband dutifully every Monday morning?"

He didn't bother to answer; instead he asked, "Did you and the boys go to church this evening?"

"Yes, Robert Earl, we went to church tonight, and after dinner I read the boys a Bible story before I put them to bed. I wish you'd call early enough to speak to them—they can't come and visit you like I can." Tears welled in her eyes, and she tried to hide her emotions with her voice. "You know how much they miss you, honey."

"I hate talking to them while I'm in here. It just ain't right. Mae, you gotta talk to my lawyer about getting me outta heah. I can't stand being cooped up like this too much longer. Baby, please, please call the lawyer in the morning and talk to him before you come down." There was a pause, then, "Will you promise me you'll do that?"

He sounded so pitiful it almost broke her heart. She hated it when he begged like that. For months the judge had been pushing back his trial, always on some kind of technicality, always needing another piece of evidence.

Robert Earl sat looking out of the barred windows of his cell as he contemplated his situation. One of his cellmates had been arrested for the same crime and was looking at five years in Jackson prison. This wasn't the first time the other man had been arrested for selling drugs, and he told Robert Earl he'd do his rap, and his woman would work his business until he got out. Start the whole cycle over again. No White man was gonna tell him what to do with his life. What else did they expect him to do for a living? There weren't any decent jobs for a Black man in this city.

Robert Earl's guilt had grown in the months he'd spent
locked up. He began rethinking his situation. What he'd do
when he got out. How he'd make it up to Mae Thelma and
the boys. He wasn't a hardened criminal like the rest of
them, and he did have a choice. He really hadn't tried hard
enough to find another job. He'd taken the easy way out.
Hell, he should've moved back home to Mississippi and
worked in the blue jean factory where his sister was the supervisor. She'd promised him when he left that if he ever
wanted to come back home, she'd always have a job waiting
for him.

No thank you, he had told her. The factory life wasn't for
him. His dream was to pursue a career in computers. Leaving
his southern home wasn't easy, but the high-profile jobs just
weren't there.

After graduating third in his class, he'd moved his family
to Michigan. With the excellent recommendations from his
professors, he'd found a job programming computers in two
weeks. After weeks of scouring the city, he'd found a home
in a nice neighborhood close to an elementary school for his
two boys. But when the car business had slowed down, it had
a domino effect on every field. They'd lived well for the past
seven years on a salary of almost thirty-five thousand dollars
a year. How could they possibly survive on unemployment,
and when that ran out, welfare? It was incomprehensible. Instead, he chose to invest the last of their savings to start up
his drug business.

He'd kept it a secret from Mae Thelma until one of his
customers made the mistake of calling his home for a quick
buy. She overheard his conversation, and prayed to God to
touch his soul so he could see the error of his ways. But she
didn't yell—maybe her silent disappointment was worse than
anger.

Looking back on that awful night of the bust, Robert Earl
still felt embarrassed. He'd begged Mae Thelma to keep the
boys in their room while the police cuffed him and searched
their home for drugs. It was humiliating, their neighbors
looking on as their home was turned upside down. It seemed
to take forever for the Narcotics agents to find three small,
plastic bundles of white powder and a canister of marijuana.

If only the lawyer could get him out of here, he'd never play the fool again.

"This is Ms. Bell, his secretary, Mrs. Collins."

"Ma'am, I'd 'preciate it kindly if he'd call me regarding my husband's case. He's getting a mite anxious being locked up so long—what with all these postponements. Can you ask Mr. Bowman if he'd go up and see Robert Earl in jail and let him know what's going on, please ma'am?"

Ms. Bell cleared her throat several times before answering, "Mr. Bowman has asked me to send out a letter informing your husband than unless you are able to pay him an additional retainer of two thousand dollars, you will have to seek assistance of another attorney, or have free counsel provided for him. You should receive verification and an itemized list of Mr. Bowman's services and time expenditures while representing your husband in two to three days."

Mae Thelma was silent. They'd already withdrawn the last of their money from their savings account. Where would she get two thousand dollars? She took a deep breath. "Thank you," she said as cheerfully as she could before hanging up. Tomorrow's visit would not be a pleasant one. She couldn't bear to see the disappointment in her husband's eyes, yet again.

That next morning she had to run to catch the bus, she was so nervous, having taken extra care to look her absolute best. Mae Thelma dropped her precious coins into the glass receptacle as the bus traveled south toward the heart of the city. Rocking, rolling along, she sang in a low monotone, "Since Jesus Came into My Heart": "I'm possessed of a hope that is steadfast and secure, since Jesus came into my heart. There's a light in the valley of death now for me, since Jesus came into my heart! And the gates of the city beyond I can see, since Jesus came into my heart! And I'm so happy, so happy as onward I go, since Jesus . . ." Her voice suddenly cracked and, like a wide-mouthed ceramic wine crock, became deep and absolutely unusable—it would hold nothing of what was poured into it. She was silent.

6

Two Lovers

Awakened by the blaring of the alarm, Ginger moved away from Jackson's arm and carefully slid out from beneath the cool powdered sheets. He didn't like satin sheets. Instead he preferred the smooth, clean feeling of the talc against his body. Jackson insisted on sprinkling their bed nightly with baby powder. He'd told her when they first met that he didn't like to sweat. The crease behind the back of his calf was the only place where he allowed any perspiration. In the darkness his dusted body seemed to be coated with silver velvet, as smooth and as hard as marble. Throughout the night she would reach over and glide her hands over his lithe, sculptured body—perfection. His luscious sweet lips and the cottony cushion on the bottoms of his feet were the only soft parts of his sleek frame.

Splashing her face with cold water, she banished any thought of returning to bed for a few more moments of sleep. She began the ritual she practiced every day, morning and evening, of cleansing her skin with clear glycerin soap and using Vaseline as her moisturizer. She loved her Crabtree and Evelyn and her other toiletries, but she left her face in the care of Johnson & Johnson.

When she was a child, Ginger had noticed that her grandmother's skin was taut, tight—ageless. At sixty-five years old, the woman still hadn't had a wrinkle visit her face. She'd told Ginger then that petroleum jelly was all she needed. Now Ginger agreed. It lasted longer than lotion, was cheaper, and was better than the best moisturizers on the market.

Drying her hands, Ginger turned to see a small figure standing in the darkness outside her bathroom.

"Mommy, I'm wet," said Autumn, dragging Suzy Scribbles by the hair. Ginger couldn't understand why her baby couldn't stop wetting her bed. She'd tried everything. Taken her to doctor after doctor, who'd all told her that Autumn would have to grow out of it. But Autumn slept deeply and was unable to wake herself when the alarm in her brain signaled for her to go to the bathroom. Sometimes she would be able to hold off until morning, but more often not.

Not only did Autumn look like her father—she even had the same birthmark on her thigh—but she'd inherited his ability to sleep. Sometimes Ginger felt as if she needed an atomic bomb to get the man out of bed in the morning before he went to work. After she woke him, he had to sit on the side of the bed for at least ten minutes before he could place one foot in front of the other.

Knowing that Autumn had to be awfully wet to wake by herself, Ginger grabbed a fluffy towel from the rack. "Come here, sweetheart. Mommy'll change you."

She called out into the darkness, to the still form, "It's time to get up, Jackson." She quickly washed and changed Autumn.

His large hands between his inner thighs, his head lowered, he sat recalling their previous night. Lord have mercy, that woman was something else. Reaching down to rub the bulge in his briefs, he knew he needed to take a piss. But that could wait for a few more minutes.

Jackson enjoyed the role of the aggressor, the conductor who orchestrated the tempo of their lovemaking, the momentum, the facets, the emotion, when it began and how soon it would end. But Ginger had taught him that she too was a conductor. He'd slept with many a woman in the forty-odd years of his life, but never, never, had he felt such oneness. No one had touched off the warmth of his love as she had. He had to have her, forever.

"Whew!" said Kim, turning up her nose as the smell of Lysol welcomed her and her mother, Jewel, to the second floor of the nursing home. Her father, Ollie Lee, had been a resident of the home since having a stroke almost a year earlier.

Kim moved at a slow pace to accommodate her mother, who at sixty-nine years old was constantly being mistaken for her grandmother. Kim was tired of explaining to people that she was a change-of-life baby. She resented not having any family. She'd had no sisters or brothers to share secrets with as she grew up, and had had to learn everything on her own.

When she finally came along, her parents, having almost given up on the idea that they would ever have a child, tried to be perfect. God had created a miracle in their lives—a healthy, beautiful baby girl.

Jewel was afraid to let Kim outside to play with the other children, worrying that she might hurt herself. Jewel explained to her crying child that the other children were too rough, and hadn't been properly raised. It was always something, some excuse to keep her inside. Consequently, Kim found it difficult to make friends and was often sad and lonely as a child. Those feelings turned into rebelliousness later in her life.

Her father, Ollie, not wanting to rock the boat, never overrode any of his wife's rules and regulations.

"Mrs. Lee," the nurse called out from the front desk. The nurse approached the two women exiting the elevator. "Your husband's had another visitor this morning." She smoothed the invisible wrinkles from her uniform. "He's been asking for his sister-in-law. Her name is on the visitors' list, so we called her yesterday afternoon. When I came on duty this morning, she had already finished feeding him his breakfast.

He hasn't been too well lately." Then as an afterthought, she added cheerily, "She brought him a real nice bouquet."

"Hard to believe Katherine came all the way here in this kind of weather," said Jewel, looking at Kim. "It's been snowing and raining for the last couple of days. She don't go outside when it's raining. You know how bad her asthma is getting. Can't rightly figure it."

The nurse left them outside the room, explaining that she would discuss the new treatments the doctor had recommended for Mr. Lee after their visit.

As Jewel entered the room, she paused to admire Katherine's lovely flowers perched on the tray next to the hospital bed. Her husband lay sleeping on his side, his back turned toward the window. Kim took her mother by the arm, guiding her slowly toward the bed. Ollie moved slightly at the sound of the old familiar footsteps.

"Jewel," he uttered, as he inhaled the sweet fragrance of her rose perfume. Every day of their past fifty-one years of marriage, she'd worn the essence he'd given to her on her eighteenth birthday.

"I'm here, honey," said Jewel in a hushed voice. Reaching out to touch his face, she felt the warmth of his skin. She kissed his forehead. "Sweetie. I miss you, sweetie."

Kim rubbed the top of her father's shiny bald head, kissing it tenderly. "Hi, Daddy. You feeling all right today?" He nodded. The faraway look in is eyes belied the assertion. She loved her father dearly and couldn't bear to see him like this. His sense of humor had helped her through many a night of crying after an angry breakup with a boyfriend. In her teens, she sought out his opinion, allowing his wisdom to guide her through difficult growing pains. She told him her secrets. He never judged, just listened and gave his advice as well as he could.

"Mama, I'm going outside for a cigarette. I'll let you two be alone for a while. Be back in a few minutes." Kim realized the two lovebirds needed time alone before she asked her usual questions. Besides, she couldn't wait to make a quick exit; the overpowering scent of the carnations and her mother's excessive rose perfume reminded her of a funeral parlor.

Jewel patted the back of her husband's hand. She hated this room. The walls were painted a dull army green. Not a picture or a plaque on them. Just an ancient black and white clock, ticking angrily. Beige, water-stained drapes drooped and sagged, missing several hooks. Outside the metal-encased window, the drizzling rain tapped incessantly against a backdrop of a dull gray Monday-morning sky.

Jewel took a deep breath and continued quietly. "Honey, we got to get you outta here. You got to do what the doctor says, so you can come home." His head sank farther back into the pillow. Moving his lips, he tried to speak, but the words wouldn't surface. He turned his head, looking toward the window at the silvery sprinkles.

Driving home, Jewel confided to Kim that she thought Ollie wasn't getting any better. He'd barely spoken five words during the time she was there. For a moment when he stared at her, she was sure he didn't recognize her. Wiping her eyes with her lace handkerchief, she admitted to Kim that she didn't know what she'd do if something happened to Ollie.

"Mama, Daddy's gonna be just fine," Kim said softly as she pulled fresh tissues from the box, offering them to her mother. Jewel's favorite handkerchief was soaked clear through. Rain clouds darkened the sky. Silvery threads of lightning veined the atmosphere. "The doctors said—"

"What do they know!" Jewel fired. "They've been saying the same thing for months. 'Mr. Lee's prognosis for a full recovery is good, Mrs. Lee. Just a few more weeks of physical therapy and his mobility should be back to normal.'" Jewel turned her face away. A watershed of fresh tears trailed down her softly lined cheeks.

Kim slowed her gold Mazda and waited for the red light. Rain streaked the windshield like welts. She had no idea how to reach her mother. Their conversations never lasted more than a few sentences. Whenever problems arose, her father was always there with the right words, the needed hugs to bring Kim out of her angered state. Jewel was seldom irritated or impatient. But she believed in taking her problems to the Lord. Prayer was her answer for everything.

Clasping her hands tightly upon her lap, Jewel rocked

steadily. "I should have never taken him to that place." Her rocking slowed as she turned her head slightly toward Kim. Her eyes looked up at the bleak sky.

"Daddy had a stroke, Mama," said Kim as she changed lanes. She felt a headache coming. "He needed hospitalization. You couldn't possibly—"

"You trying to tell me them doctors can heal better than the Lord can?"

"I didn't say that." Kim pushed her foot a little harder on the gas pedal. The speedometer edged up to fifty-five. "It's just that sometimes the Lord uses the doctors to heal too. God don't have time for everybody, Mama, He's busy."

Jewel whipped her head to her left, pressing her right elbow on her cocked, right knee. "Seems to me you the one too busy 'round here. You need to take some time away from that job and get down on your knees and pray." Jewel hmmphed. "Lord knows most of them folks working there ain't going nowhere but to hell. Can't you stop worshiping the devil's money long enough to spend more time with your own father? Care more about money than you do your soul."

Kim's fingers gripped the steering wheel. "Mama, can't you understand how hard I worked to get this position? It's not the money—"

"I'll take a taxi to visit your father tomorrow," said Jewel, cutting her off abruptly. "You don't have to worry about rushing home." Jewel sat back stiffly. "I want some definite dates in determining his progress. Otherwise, he's coming back home where he belongs."

"Please think about Daddy, Mama. He needs nurses monitoring him twenty-four hours a day. You're not able to—"

"Young lady, don't you begin to tell me what I'm capable of doing. If you were any kind of daughter, you'd offer to take a little time off that job and help me."

"How can I help you? I know about numbers, not medicine, Mama." Kim felt a rush of blood up the back of her neck. "I wish you could try and understand that the best thing we can do for Daddy is—"

"You're just selfish. Don't think about no one but yourself. One of these days you're gonna need me and your daddy, and you know what? We won't be there."

"Please don't say that, Mama. I love you and Daddy.
You're all I have."

"You don't need us—just that job. Don't even want any
kids, that's how selfish you are. Got no time for nobody but
Kim. I don't know how Bill puts up with you. He must have
the patience of Job."

Bill. Kim needed a night alone with Mr. Bill. A good
screwing—now that would take her mind off the problems of
her parents. Biting her tongue so as not to lash back at her
mother, she prayed silently for mercy to follow her, not just
all the days of her life, but Lord, just grant her the calmness
to make it through today.

"How'd your lecture go at Wayne this afternoon?" asked
Kim as she watched Bill devouring his steak.

"Okay. Dr. Ingram's speech was far more interesting,"
Bill answered between bites. He took short, quick, glances at
her over his black-framed glasses.

Dr. Ingram had been Bill's professor when he attended
Wayne State University, and they had remained friends over
the years. Kim loved to listen to Bill speak. He sounded so
much like her father. He had most of his qualities: maturity,
level-headedness, wisdom. But best of all, he took the time
to listen to her whenever she came to him with a problem.
The only trait Bill lacked was her father's sense of humor.

The smell of sautéed onions and buttered mushrooms
hung in the air over the tiny table in Bill's small apartment.
As Bill continued sharing the day's events, Kim cleared the
table and placed a mouthwatering strawberry cream puff before him. His wide boyish smile signaled that he was
pleased. He thanked Kim for surprising him with a home-
cooked meal. They rarely had time for such luxuries these
days, both of their schedules were so hectic. Kim kissed him
on his forehead. She knew his weakness for sweets, and had
picked up one of his favorites at the bakery when she
shopped for their evening meal.

"A few students even volunteered to help with the refresh-
ments, and clean up during the open house of the clinic and
workshop."

His own clinic was to open in May, less than three months

away, and he was taking great pains to assure that it would be a success. By mailing out flyers to other professional organizations and making personal appeals to neighborhood YMCAs, he'd reached out to the community and explained the long-term effect his clinic would have on the numerous gifted young children who needed a little extra help and guidance. He believed their knowing they had somewhere to go, someone they could talk to, someone who genuinely cared about them, would help the youths who had gone astray, and he wanted to make some changes in their lives.

Bill admitted that he had gotten somewhat emotional when he had explained to Dr. Ingram's students the vow he made to a dying youth, killed senselessly by a stray bullet in his apartment building.

Kim was familiar with Bill's story of how, while holding a dying nine-year-old in his arms, he'd vowed to dedicate his life to saving Black children. But she never ceased to be moved when he finished.

Both sat in silence for several moments. Then Kim, who knew she needed love and tenderness tonight from the man she adored, especially after the horrendous afternoon at the nursing home, decided it was time to change the tempo of the evening. Time to talk about the two of them, their love, their need for each other.

Picking up their after-dinner cocktails, she led Bill to the sofa. Then she casually removed his glasses, his stiffly starched white shirt, and loosened the buckle of his trousers. Kim massaged Bill's tense shoulders until he relaxed a little. Kissing his shoulder, she whispered that she'd be back in a moment, and went to get her purse. She took out a small vial of aromatic oil that she'd had the foresight to bring with her.

In the kitchen, as the oil warmed in a small pot on the stove, she stripped down to her underwear. Next, she slipped a classic George Benson cassette tape in the stereo and dimmed the lights.

Moments later, the evening began to happen just as she'd planned it. She loved taking the lead, rendering her man helpless with her ardent seduction. Yes . . .

7

I Can't Get Next to You

After completing her daily production allotment, Ginger cleaned her sewing table and stacked the leather cushions neatly for the next day's workload. Waving *adiós* to her sewing partner, Veto, she left her work area and headed toward Jackson's office.

She walked down the center aisle past sewing units similar to hers. Each unit was equipped with seventy or more power sewing machines by Singer, Juki, and Adler. The machines were attached to the top of green Formica tables roughly eight feet long, with half-moon cutouts for the sewing operators.

To her right were several multineedle machines used for stitching continuous lines on single-cushion pleats. Beyond that was a small embroidery unit that created intricate designs on leather and cloth with computerized needlework for the luxury model cars.

Looking around, Ginger thought, as she did almost every day, How in the world did I end up here?

As she entered Jackson's office, he glanced up from the

phone, signaling her with a lifted finger to wait a minute. His thick black mustache parted like two birds above his lips as he spoke into the receiver, his lips expanding to a flat, thin line. Leaning forward, Ginger eyeballed him, trying to decipher his conversation. She decided he must be talking to his mother, and rose to leave. She knew he'd be a while.

"Wait a minute, baby. I need to talk to you." The day's news wailed from the small radio on top of the file cabinets as she stood waiting. Jackson said a few more words and hung up the phone. "My mother's sick," he said, lowering his head. "She's scheduled for an operation Wednesday. I need to catch a flight out in the morning. I called for reservations for a layover in Chicago, so I could pick up my sister Annie."

"Oh . . . I see. You've already made reservations."

"Yeah, for me, you, and Autumn."

"So I'm supposed to leave Jason, Christian, and Sierra home alone, is that it?" She leaned over the desk, her head thrust forward.

"Sweetie, let's not argue. Jason is old enough to watch the kids. Or we could ask Mrs. Johnson to come over for a few days." As he picked up the phone, Ginger clamped her hand on top of his, silencing the dial tone.

"Perhaps, but my boss will be mad at me if I tell her at the last minute. She has to have time to get someone to cover my job, and I don't feel like being hassled right now." She looked around his office, staring at the numerous photographs of Autumn covering the beige canvas walls. Potted aloe vera and ivy plants covered the tops of bookshelves and file cabinets. She should be working in an office, she thought, not at a noisy machine that was ruining her hearing.

Taking a deep breath, she walked toward the open door. "No, you go. You and your sister." Shaking her head, she said, "Besides, I really don't want to take Autumn out of school—she's doing so well." A proud smile spread across her face. "Every day she comes home with something new that she's learned. She loves doing her homework every day like the rest of the kids. Carrying her little notebook around with her." Looking away, Ginger tried to mask the disappointment in her face. This would be the first time in their eight years of marriage they'd be away from each other overnight.

Jackson walked around his desk, lifted up her chin, and kissed her. "Okay. Anyway, I kinda figured you wouldn't want to go. And we both know the kids hate Mississippi. Just getting them down there every summer for the reunion is punishment enough. You know I didn't mean any harm."

He sat on the edge of his desk, pulling her toward him. "I probably wouldn't be very good company. I'm really worried about my mother getting through this operation. She's going to be seventy in a few months, and the odds of her healing correctly or at all aren't great."

Ginger felt the familiar jealousy about Jackson's mother spreading throughout her body. The anger she felt as she constantly tried to compete with the perfection of his mother's legacy surfaced again now. She tried to be the woman he wanted, a woman close to his mother's image. But it seemed an impossible task.

After dinner she would talk to Jackson. He would know how to handle the kids, and when to tell them. One of the many things Ginger loved about Jackson was that he had an easygoing way of handling serious situations. Her hair was so thin on top, she knew he was aware of what was happening.

Ginger dreaded the thought of explaining to the kids that yes, Mama was fine. Yes, she would get through this just like all the other times. She knew Autumn would ask so many questions. "Why, Mommy? Can't the doctor fix it, Mommy?" Tears formed in her eyes at the thought of the hurtful look. . . .

Jackson gave Ginger a firm pat on the buttocks as he kissed her on the neck. "Dinner almost ready, baby?"

Pulling away from the steaming pot of spaghetti, she felt the fine texture of her hair with her fingertips, and said, "Jackson, I need to talk to you. Can we talk after dinner?" She began adding oregano to the bubbling tomato sauce.

Slicing a chunk of sharp cheese, then grabbing a roll of Krispy crackers, along with a hunk of garlic ring bologna, Jackson pinched Ginger on the behind and said he'd see her upstairs later.

"Daddy, telephone. It's Mae Thelma," said Autumn, taking a bite of his cheese.

"I'll get it upstairs, thanks baby." He kissed her cheek before he dashed up the stairs by twos.

Ginger concentrated on dinner, not on what might happen tomorrow. Feeding the kids their favorite meal always made the conversation lively at dinnertime. At times Jason could put away three plates of steaming Italian spaghetti smothered with parmesan cheese.

Her son's physique was that of a bodybuilder. With broad chest, muscular shoulders and thighs, and a perfectly flat stomach that would make a quarter bounce and spin around, he caught the eye of many an amorous teenage girl. Ginger thought his buttocks a tad too big for a young, mature male—a burden he'd inherited from his mother, and his gyrating grandmother, Katherine—but Jason insisted the girls loved it. That the girls couldn't wait until summertime so they could watch him play basketball in a pair of Lycra biker shorts. Still, Ginger hoped he would stop eating so much.

Later, while the girls stacked the dishwasher, Sierra told her mother that she was worried about a math test she was taking the next day. "Mama, could you ask Christian to help me?" said Sierra apprehensively. "I asked him already, and he said no."

Christian had been hiding on the back stairs, listening. He knew Sierra was going to tell on him. Sucking on his bottom lip, he made a casual entrance to tell his side of the story. "That's not quite all the truth, Ma." He glared at Sierra.

Sierra's petite little body seemed to droop. She looked from Christian to her mother helplessly. Her gray-blue eyes filled with tears because she knew that Christian would be calling her stupid as soon as they were out of their mother's sight. Sierra wrapped her arms around her mother's waist, and began crying. "I can't help it if I'm not as smart as they are, Mama."

"She daydreams, Ma."

"I don't!"

"You do too!"

Sierra buried her head in her mother's bosom. "I just don't understand him, Mama. He goes too fast."

" 'Cause you don't pay attention," said Christian, sounding like a little professor.

"He calls me stupid if I forget something, Mama."

"I don't," yelled Christian.

"You do." Sierra's bottom lip quivered. Tears tumbled down her golden cheeks. "I'm stupid! Stupid! Stupid! Stupid!"

"Baby," said Ginger, swaying Sierra in her arms. "It's just going to take a little longer for you to understand things, that's all. You're not stupid." Ginger bent down and tugged at her chin, smiling. "Ain't none of my babies stupid."

Sierra forced a weak smile. She hugged her mother's neck.

Ginger glared at Christian. A silent "See what you've done" was written all over her face.

"It's okay, sweetheart. Christian's going to help you with your science and math homework every weeknight for the rest of this marking period. Aren't you, Christian?"

Christian pushed both fists into his jeans pockets. "Yeah." He turned to leave before adding, "No radio, Sierra, while we're studying. That's why she can't remember nothin', she's too busy straining to listen to EnVogue."

Ginger smoothed Sierra's sandy brown hair, saying, "Are you gonna pay attention, and listen to everything Christian's trying to teach you, Sierra?"

Sierra eagerly nodded her head yes as she wiped away remnants of tears.

Ginger swatted her on the butt. "Now you to go on upstairs and see what Autumn is doing." Ginger shook her head, smiling to herself as she filled the teapot with fresh water.

After wiping off the kitchen counters, she prepared a cup of lemon tea, then tiptoed up the back stairs to look in on Jackson, who was watching *Hondo*. She hated *Hondo*. Couldn't stand that dog. Where on earth did they find such an ugly dog? Strolling in to give her husband a quick peck on the cheek, she told him she'd be out after her shower for their talk. Glancing at the set, she noticed it was the scene where Hondo's dog had gotten in a fight with a wolf, and they thought he had rabies and were going to shoot him. She sighed, thinking, I've seen this at least five times. Lord knows how many times Jackson has seen it.

Pausing by the girls' door, she checked to see if Christian was tutoring Sierra. He was. The girl's reddish brown ponytails swayed as she nodded to his questions. Autumn sat on the floor, reciting verbatim the same lessons to Suzy Scribbles.

Slipping a shower cap on, Ginger stepped into the steaming hot shower stall and lathered her body with a lavish amount of bath gel. As she reached for a fluffy lavender towel, she glanced in the steamed mirror, and gazed momentarily at the silhouette of herself—she did not admire the misty reflection that stared back.

Cupping her hands, she splashed cold water on her face. She was determined not to feel sorry for herself about a problem over which she had no control. But she needed Jackson's support—needed him to tell her yet again that it didn't matter about her hair. Maybe this time she would finally believe him.

When she walked into the sitting area of their bedroom, Ginger was mildly disappointed to find Jackson asleep, his bottom lip gaping open slightly. She touched his arm to wake him. Jackson was still clutching the remote control, and it took him a few seconds to get his bearings. She snatched the remote from his hand and kneeled down in front of him. "Can we talk now, sweetheart? What did Mae Thelma want?"

"Nothing. Nothing important. Baby, let's go to bed. We can talk in the morning. Besides, I saved you the trouble and I already gave myself a lecture about how to conduct myself in Mississippi while I'm not at the hospital." He gave her a devilish smile. "I'll be too busy to see any of my old friends, I'm planning on paint—"

"Jackson. I'm not worried about you and your old friends down South. I wanted to talk about . . . something more personal." Placing her hands on his thighs, she rested her head on his chest. His arms encircled her waist. He stroked her hair, and kissed her neck, his lips brushing past her as he spoke, "I know you're gonna miss me, baby. I miss you already."

"Jackson, wait—"

"Come on, baby. I know just what you need." She held her tears in check as he gathered her into his arms and moved her onto the bed, kissing her passionately. He peeled off his clothes quickly, and lifted the hem of her gown above her waist, massaging her buttocks, which felt as soft and sweet as cotton candy to him.

Acquiescing to his charms, she knew the moment had passed for a serious discussion. She needed him now, but would have to wait for any words of reassurance.

"Hey, girlfriend. What's up?" said Kim, hanging her coat in the front hall closet. "Damn, it's cold out there."

Ginger looked at her cousin. "If that suit had a few more yards of fabric on it, I doubt if you'd feel a chill." Decked out in an Aztec gold three-quarter-length wool-crepe collarless tapered jacket and matching miniskirt, Kim looked all the part of a young executive. "I got to give it to you, girl. The suit is bad. I wish Jackson would let me wear miniskirts. He says my knees are too big."

As they walked toward the blaring music in the family room, Kim moved slowly, her hips swaying to the beat. She played with the strands of gold chains above her breasts. "You give that man too much power. No man is ever gonna tell me what I can and can't wear. Just like the guns of Will Sonnett, 'no brag, just fact.' "

As soon as the girls saw Kim they steered her downstairs to watch the new dance routine they'd worked out. Kim watched patiently and then gave them a few new pointers she'd learned from Detroit's daily televised *New Dance Show*, which she sometimes frequented.

Ginger envied Kim's natural talent for dancing, and treasured her cousin's patience with her overzealous daughters. Ginger hadn't danced in years, though in her teens she'd won plenty of dance contests—something her girls never quite believed.

Kim and Ginger finally managed to break from the girls for a steaming cup of orange spice tea. "Those outfits the girls have on are tough, girlfriend," Kim said, blowing into her cup. "I just don't know how you find the time to sew at home, and sew at work. Don't you ever get sick of sitting in front of a machine?"

Ginger smiled as she spoke. "That's the reason I asked you to come over. I'm hoping to change that soon." She leaned back and pulled a briefcase from beside the buffet. "Look," she said, opening the brown leather case. "I'm going to start selling real estate."

Setting down her cup, Kim gave her a feline smile. "I'm impressed, Ginger. I think it's a wise decision. An excellent choice, considering how much you love houses." She looked around the tastefully decorated breakfast room, done in lavender and peach. "Anyone seeing this house for the first time would think you'd hired an interior decorator."

"Thanks, Kim." Ginger leaned across the table and patted her on the shoulder. "You're more than a cousin. You're the best friend I've got. I don't know what I'd do without you."

"You're right, what would you do without me?" They saluted each other with their teacups, exchanging mischievous grins.

Kim gave Ginger a lecture on how to become a successful businesswoman, pointing out the ways she could develop her particular strengths. She encouraged Ginger to learn not only the administrative duties the job entailed, but to learn the logistical and technical aspects of marketing, too. She advised Ginger to read the marketing textbooks from Jackson's college days she'd seen on their library bookshelves.

She advised Ginger to make a long-range plan of where she wanted to be and when, to remain focused on the job at hand, but to be aware of the next job on the ladder—managing the agency. "Create a goal in your mind and stay on that course, and you'll find the wind behind the sails of your career," she told her.

"Remember," she concluded, "as some famous person once said, 'Boldness . . . is the first, second, and third thing.' " Kim tapped a sculptured fingernail on her arm. "Don't forget it."

"I have so much respect for you, Kim. You know so much for someone so young," said Ginger, clearing the table.

"I had a good teacher." She leaned against the counter as Ginger washed and dried their cups and saucers. "Remember that guy that helped me get my job at the agency? Randall. Randall Pierce." Ginger shook her head no as she folded the dish towel and looped it through the oven handle. "Anyway, we went to school together at Michigan State. After the first semester, we seemed destined to meet. We had the same classes. Sometimes with different professors. But over the four years we became fast friends, doing our homework together, sharing stories about our childhood and domineering parents."

"And you say the guy helped you get your job at Pierce-Walker?"

"Yeah. He pulled a few strings because his aunt owns the investment company." She threw her hands in the air. "Otherwise, I would have had to have at least two to three years' experience after college before I landed a job like this."

"Lucky you," said Ginger, feeling envious. Her cousin had done all the things Ginger had wanted to do when she was younger. She had lived on campus at an impressive university, dated men from different social backgrounds, and shopped whenever she felt like it, thanks to a generous allowance from her parents. And, most importantly, had chosen a good career early on in life.

"No, Ginger. You make your own luck. Contacts. Networking is important to succeed in business. I've negotiated a lot of deals for that company. They gave me a job, but I've paid them back tenfold with my impressive lists of satisfied clients. I'm good. Damn good." She glanced at her watch. It was getting late. "No brag . . ."

"Just fact," said Ginger, completing the phrase. She turned toward Kim and asked, "Wouldn't you like to open a business with Bill as your partner?" She handed Kim her purple leather coat from the hall closet.

"No." Kim stood motionless in the middle of the foyer. "Bill is good at his job, and I'm good at mine. I enjoy knowing that I'm superior to him at something." She thought about it for a moment. "You know how intellectual he is. I admire him for it. I respect his dedication and genuine concern about the importance of his work with troubled Black children"—she paused—"but I expect the same respect. I'm educating affluent Black clients on how to invest their money. Money is power. Without power, we're defeated before we begin.

"Sure, I have White clients. Satisfied White clients. Every now and then they lose a few grand, but they can afford it." She thought for a moment before adding, "Scratch that. The only dissatisfied Caucasian around me is my boss, Cameron. Randall's uncle." She eased into her coat.

"He resents my friendship with his nephew. Says I'm using him to climb the corporate ladder. Of course Mr. Cameron didn't start complaining until I stopped fucking him." She waited for the shock to register on Ginger's face.

Ginger's mouth formed a large O. "You what?"

"Grow up, Ginger. I fucked him. He was the boss. I thought he was the key to a managerial position. Boy, was I wrong. His wife holds the strings. He's only a puppet." Kim sucked in her breath. "Listen, Ginger, this was before I met Doctor Bill. Before he used his charms on me, and I developed a conscience."

Kim put her hands over her heart defensively. "Look, I'm human. I've made a few mistakes. Will probably make several more. Bill's taught me to look forward in life. To create a positive future without looking back. I can't change the past, and the immature decisions I've made." She looked deeply into her cousin's eyes. "I'm sorry if I've lowered your opinion of me—but life's full of surprises."

"Let's not get so dramatic," said Ginger, trying to lighten the mood. "Hey, Jackson's going to be gone until Sunday or Monday, why don't we meet for lunch Friday afternoon?"

"Aren't you going . . . I forgot, you have your real estate classes on Thursday and Friday, right?" She admired her cousin's tenacity. Changing her life with a husband as jealous as Jackson wasn't going to be easy. Even though Ginger would never admit it, Kim had seen from the moment they first met how he overpowered her, dominated her. Maybe with him away, she could coax Ginger into a heart-to-heart before her cousin sabotaged what would probably be her last effort to leave the factory life behind.

"I forgot. I've got to call Mama before I go home. She wanted me to stop by the store for something, I can't remember what. . . ." Kim patted the girls on the head as they sped past her in the kitchen. "Mama's not feeling too well herself, I'm afraid."

As they made their way to the foyer, Ginger asked Kim if she and her mother were getting along any better. "Oooohh, that woman gets on my nerves! Complain. Complain. Complain. She never compliments me on anything. In her eyes, I'm just a selfish spoiled child looking for somebody to take care of me after I leave home." She took her car keys from her purse and walked toward the front door. "She seems to have forgotten I haven't asked her or my father for a dime in the last year and a half."

"Why would you? You've told me time and time again how much your commissions brought you. You should be loaded living at home with your parents. I know for a fact that Aunt Jewel isn't charging you any rent."

"If we weren't cousins, I'd tell you to mind your own business. But, I'll let you in on one of my goals. I've invested half my take-home pay since joining the firm in high-risk investments. Randall helped me set up my portfolio." She gave Ginger an innocent smile. "Bill doesn't even know about it. I let him think I spend all my money on clothes— he'll never know how many store managers I've got calling me when the suit I've been waiting for gets the final markdown. I shop on my lunch hour at least three times a week searching for a bargain. And believe me, you can always find one. Guess how much I paid for this suit?"

Ginger was impressed. She turned her head from side to side. Kim knew she'd been sewing for years and knew the quality and price of a tailored suit. "Maybe two-fifty, or three hundred dollars."

"Try sixty-five dollars. Give the lady a star—it retailed for two ninety-nine." She held Ginger's eye for a moment before adding, "You know what I tell Dr. Bill?" Ginger's eyes rolled upwards. "I tell him I need a beeper. I need a car phone, and next month I need it turned on. I need some tires for my car, and I need my windows tinted."

Ginger laughed playfully. "Go on, girl."

"Look. I got what he wants. We both know it. He's got enough sense to say no if the price is too high, don't you think?"

"Amen," said Ginger, giggling.

"And I'm going to reward him generously." She gave Ginger a provocative stare. "And don't let him get me a CD player. Have mercy. He'll really get it good then."

Ginger couldn't contain her laughter. "You're scandalous, girl."

"Just call me an enterprising woman." She went to the front door. "It'll probably take Bill 'til Christmas time next year to buy me everything I want. He's so tight. He watches every dime. He's almost worse than I am. But," she said, lifting a single finger, "he's got several investors backing his clinic so he won't have to spend any of his savings." She kissed Ginger on the cheek. Then suddenly a coldness passed over her face for a fleeting moment before she turned the handle on the front door.

"You worried about Jackson?" asked Kim, cracking the door.

Ginger hoped Kim would understand her feelings without being too judgmental. "A little. I've always tried to include him in all my business ideas, hoping we could run a business together one day. . . . He doesn't seem to share my same enthusiasm. He's so intelligent, he could go so far if . . ."

Pushing the door closed, Kim shut out the cold air before turning back to her sulking cousin. She cocked her head sideways and said, "Why do women insist on loving men for what they want them to be, instead of what they are?"

A surprised look came over Ginger's face. Kim hugged her, tied the belt on her leather coat, and left. She wanted to say more but felt it was better to let Ginger do a bit of soul searching on her own before she bombarded her with all her theories about men and marriage.

Kim had heard on numerous occasions from Ginger about how intelligent Jackson was. How articulate and what potential he had. But Kim knew that what Ginger had failed to take into consideration was the fact that the potential you see in other people, especially your mate, doesn't mean anything if they have no desire to climb any farther than the level at which they are comfortable. Knowing Jackson, Kim thought, with his quiet ways, his love of television and the easygoing life, he was quite comfortable, indeed.

8

I Can't Help Myself

Kim shivered slightly; small goose bumps made a trail along her arms as the cool night air touched her bare skin. As he drew her near, his gaze dropped from her eyes to her shoulders, to her full breasts. His look was as soft as a caress. His fingers traced small circles of sensation around the globes of her breasts. Kneading, massaging until her dark nipples peaked and stood erect. The warmth of his mouth closed around her rosy brown mound of softness, kissing, sucking her smooth roundness. He cupped them with his hands, his thumbs briskly feathering their tautness. Her kiss told him of her arousal.

His breath was just faintly perfumed with wintergreen as his lips met hers. Their tongues touched, circling each other in an erotic ballet of moist sensation. Her breath caught in her throat as she felt his fingers teasing her tufted mound. His two thumbs gently pulled the folds apart, and he dipped the tips of his fingers into her sweet flesh. He caressed her tiny jewel, urging her to whisper his name—"Bill, ahhhhh

Bill." Knowing she was ready, his mouth covered hers hungrily.

Bill raised his mouth from hers and gazed into her eyes. "I love you, Kim." She watched as his head bent forward, his woolly brush cut grazing her skin, pushing between her open thighs. He took her tiny pearl between his lips and tongue and sucked on it, at first gently, then harder. She closed her eyes, her head rolling from side to side. She clutched his head, encouraging him not to stop. She made a soft sound and arched her body to meet his plunging tongue.

She could feel her clitoris growing, expanding, getting hotter with each thrust of his tongue. She was sweating, though she couldn't remember it being hot in the small room. She shivered, and then quite suddenly relaxed. She made a soft moan aloud. Then it began. Her legs began to tremble, her pelvis lifted itself off the mattress as if it were out of control.

She felt her orgasm. Her tiny jewel made one last jab forward, the lips of her vagina opened to grab whatever was available as her insides clamped together like a vise. She groaned aloud. She was coming, and he kept sucking the juices of her honeyed cream. Her legs closed around his head, and he didn't seem to mind, as he continued his love affair, sucking and eating on her like a hungry animal starved for food. Again she came. And again. She sighed and her eyes closed of their own volition, her body buoyant and languid.

"More . . . I want more, Bill," she said shamelessly. "Fuck me. Fuck me now." She shuddered, as his head lifted from her quivering thighs. His body was hot and wet. She could feel the sweat on his back as she ran her fingers along the crevice of his spine. She grasped his shaft between her two hands and guided him into her. Her vagina was still hot and tight from her orgasm. She clamped her muscles around his shaft, as if to lock them together for eternity. He buried his head in her breasts, but she searched his mouth to kiss him, to kiss herself. It made her shiver. The air was heavy with the scent of lust and her exotic Satin perfume.

She grabbed his butt so that his pelvis ground hard against hers, forcing him to plunge deeper and deeper into her. And then he came, moaning her name with a cry of ecstasy as he finally released his passion.

Soft jazz flowed through Bill's small apartment as they lay silent, enjoying a short moment of reprieve.

"The drywall was delivered this morning," Bill began as he wrapped the sheet around Kim's half-nude body.

She turned over onto her back, staring at the ceiling. "So you think the clinic should be finished on time for the grand opening in May?"

"Should be." He slipped on his boxer shorts and handed Kim a manila envelope from his dresser drawer. Several volumes of leather-bound physicians' texts lined the bookshelf above his bureau. "These are all the signed contracts from the investors." Sitting beside her as she inspected the contents, he smiled happily to himself. She was everything he ever needed in a woman. When everything was under way he planned to ask her to marry him.

"I'm proud of you, Bill." She traced the line around his lips with her index finger and kissed him lovingly on the mouth. "I knew everything was going to work out all right. I don't know why you worry so much."

He rested the back of his head against the headboard and crossed his ankles. "I'm not worried. Just careful. I've got a lot at risk, and it's important to me to be successful. I've got other plans that revolve around the progress of this practice." He looked around his cramped apartment. "I can't wait to move into a larger place." He glanced at Kim quickly, hoping she understood his meaning.

Taking her hands in his, he brought them to his lips, kissing them tenderly. "I want you to understand that we'll have less time together soon. I'll be working more hours at the clinic, trying to get it established—regular hours will be a thing of the past. But in the long run it'll all pay off. The outlook through the year two thousand is excellent for child psychiatrists. Health and welfare agencies need expertise like mine.

"I've already been approached by government agencies who have patients in need of the treatments our clinic is offering. We're also working with teachers, principals, and administrators to provide a network for Black educators to exchange ideas, and strategies for the troubled youths we'll be seeing at the clinic.

"We're going to be hosting monthly professional development seminars, reports on effective strategies for teaching Black children, encouraging the Detroit school system to teach history that is relevant to our Black children. The school system is, after all, eighty-five percent Black.

"We want parents to become more actively involved in helping their kids eliminate the gap between potential and achievement."

Kim looked into the eyes of a man who was dedicated to his chosen field. He stood to make a good living, but he clearly loved helping Black children. Her heart was full of love for her lover, and she longed to utter the words to tell him so. But somehow they remained frozen behind her lips.

Wiping the sleep form her eyes, Ginger fumbled for the telephone. "Hello," she said huskily.

"It's me, baby—"

"Jackson?"

"Hi, baby. I'm sorry to call you so late." Ginger focused her tired eyes on the clock, which spelled out 10:50 P.M. "There was so much to do down here, I lost track of time."

"Oh, I forgot about the time difference." Folding back the comforter, she got out of bed and sat on the edge of the window seat. Pulling back the floral drapes, she peered out the window. "How's the weather?"

"It's about sixty degrees."

Outside the sky was clear. High above the tops of the pine trees hung the crescent of a new moon like a pale eyelash. "It's barely twenty degrees here," she said, sliding back beneath the warmth. "How's your mother doing?"

"You know Mama. She won't admit she's in any pain, but I can see it in her face just as plain as day. She don't like us fussing over her."

"Is everybody there?"

"Everybody except Jab. He's on the road. I think he's in Florida. Elmyra called this afternoon and said he'd try to make it by six tomorrow evening."

"What time is her surgery scheduled for?" Ginger propped her head on her elbow, listening for a hint of worry in his voice.

He cleared his throat and paused for a moment. "It's set for eight in the morning."

"Is she in the hospital now?"

"Yeah. We stayed with her until she fell asleep. That's why I got back so late. She hasn't seen us all together in almost a year. All of us gave her a play-by-play on how her grandchildren were doing. She asked about Lady Bug and the boys."

Her mother-in-law never failed to ask about her kids. Ginger secretly wondered if Hattie B. minded her son marrying a woman with three children from a previous marriage. But in the eight years Ginger and Jackson had been married, she'd never asked about the kids' father, or why she'd divorced him. Ginger had to respect her for that. Most mothers-in-law were so nosy they couldn't wait to pry and find out all the dirt on their nondeserving daughters-in-law, who they usually felt wasn't good enough for their saintly sons. But not Hattie B.

"That was nice. Tell her I said hi when you go back to the hospital tomorrow."

"She told me to give you a message."

"What?" said Ginger, feeling immediately nervous.

"She told me to tell you she's keeping an eye on me. You don't have to worry about your old man running the streets with no strange women."

"Jackson . . . did you tell her I was jealous?" she asked incredulously.

"I didn't have to. Remember last summer when you got pissed off at my class reunion and left me at the party?"

"Yeah. I remember. But how was I supposed to know that was your cousin kissing you?"

"If you had asked, instead of jumping to conclusions, I would have told you exactly who she was."

"I ain't never seen a family with so many cousins in my entire life. Is everybody in Mississippi related?" Jackson laughed, and Ginger added, "Our family is one of the largest in Port Huron, but it doesn't come close to yours."

"I told you I had a big family when you married me, remember?"

"Yeah, I remember. But who doesn't exaggerate a little these days? And when we come down there this summer I'm going to suggest to your sister that we wear name tags. I can't remember all those people's names." She could feel him smiling through the phone.

"Mama gave me six quarts of her homemade plum preserves to bring home to you since she knows you're so crazy about it."

Ginger felt a pang of guilt. Her mother-in-law was so nice to her. Ginger remembered her preserves. She'd never tasted plum preserves in her life and couldn't get enough of it while they were there last summer. Last year the plum trees hadn't borne much fruit and his mother had been able to put up only a few jars. Ginger had emptied the last one before they left to go home in July. And now Hattie was sending her more.

Deep down she loved her mother-in-law dearly. But Jackson's overwhelming love for his mother always made Ginger feel jealous and insecure in her presence. How long would these feelings persist? Why couldn't she understand his respect and love for his mother? Would she ever feel the same kind of undemanding love from Jackson that he demonstrated toward his mother?

A lump formed in her throat before she spoke. "Give your mother a kiss for me, and tell her I love her."

"Thank you, baby. I love you so much. I'll call you tomorrow, after you get home from work, to tell you how she's doing, all right?"

"Okay, sweetheart." Looking at his empty space in the bed, she felt the sting of loneliness mist her eyes. "I love you," she said. "You take good care of your mother, you hear?"

She hung up quickly before her voice broke. Knowing she needed the comfort of his body next to hers. Knowing she needed to feel his arms pulling her close. Knowing she never wanted to be without him again.

*   *   *

Kim opened the door and carefully tiptoed down the hall to keep from alerting her mother to her late return. She hung her leather coat in the front closet and slipped into her bedroom. Feeling safe, she rested her head against the back of the door and let out a long sigh of relief.

She'd taken a shower before leaving Bill's apartment, ignoring his pleas for her to stay. Kim had only hinted about her mother's old-fashioned beliefs regarding sex before marriage. Her way of thinking was outdated, and no matter how much Kim tried to bring her mother up to date on twentieth-century mores, she wouldn't budge an inch on what she considered the proper morals and values for a respectable single woman.

After brushing her teeth with mouthwash so as not to wake her mother with the squeaky faucet, Kim placed her toothbrush back inside the cabinet. She closed her door quietly once again and slid into bed. As she turned on her side, she smiled to herself. Even beneath the cool sheets, her body still felt the warmth of Bill's lovemaking between her thighs. She curled into a fetal position and pushed her hands between her tightened thighs.

"Girl. Don't you have a ounce of respect for yourself?" came a raspy voice through the cracked door.

"Mother . . ." Kim turned to see the small woman standing in the doorway. She felt a flash of resentment that passed even as it came, though she was sure she was about to hear the lecture of a lifetime. She tried so hard to respect her mother's home. Not often, but sometimes, she had to break one of her numerous rules.

"It's after midnight. I won't have you disrespecting my home like this, Kim. I just won't have it."

"Oh," Kim said. "I thought this was my home too?"

"It won't be for long, if you continue to sneak into this house like a common whore," her mother snapped.

"Mama, we shouldn't be arguing about something so trivial as me spending some time with my boyfriend. I'm twenty-four years old, Mama. I'm not a child anymore. You can't expect me to behave like a sixteen-year-old adolescent—I'm a woman, Mama. Can't you see that?" she pleaded.

She studied her mother in the shadow of the hall light. Her skin was smooth, almost slippery, as if the years had worn away all the roughness the way the wind wears away the surface of stone. She still was an attractive woman, even as she approached the age of three score and ten. Didn't she remember being in love? Couldn't she remember the feelings she'd shared with her husband when they were young?

"You'll always be a child in my eyes, Kim." Jewel sat beside her daughter on the bed and looked into her face.

Jewel's eyes had a dreamy, far-away look. "I remember when your father and I were dating. He brought me home at a respectable hour. He walked me to the door, and shook my father's hand good night. Never even kissed me until he placed an engagement ring on my finger and asked me to marry him. Your father was and will always be a gentleman." She took a deep breath, and gazed at her daughter before continuing.

"He'd want your beau to give you the same respect he'd shown me." She patted Kim's hand. "I know he would." She started to rise, until Kim whispered her name.

"Mother. Do you hate me that much to use Daddy against me?"

Kim saw tears form in her mother's eyes. "Child, you'll never know how much I love you. You've never had a child so you couldn't possibly understand how it feels to bring the gift of life into the world. A gift that I will always treasure. Your father and I had given up the idea that we would be blessed with a child when I started going through the change—but there is a God up above. A God that can create miracles." She wiped her eyes with the sleeve of her gown. "You were a vision of love that we had prayed so faithfully for. And I'm so thankful that I received the answer that heaven sent down to me." She paused, catching her breath. "I worry so about you, Kim. If your father doesn't make it . . . you're the only token I have of our love. I can't . . . I can't . . ." her voice broke.

Kim hugged her mother and kissed her on her smooth, wet cheeks. "I'm sorry for hurting you, Mother. I won't come home late again." They rocked together, sharing their fear of losing a loved one.

*   *   *

"Randall, I'm telling you the truth." Kim twisted her college ring around her finger, looping it over the tip of her blood red, manicured nail. She rocked back in her chair. "I was all set to tell her off and tell her I was moving out."

"So what stopped you?"

"Guilt. It would kill my father if I left my mother alone, at her age." She put the ring back on her finger and steepled her hands together. "I can't make her understand that I'm a grown woman, and every now and then I need a few hours of exotic, raw sex. Can you see anything wrong with that?"

Randall walked around her desk, his long jet black ponytail swaying as he bent down to kiss her on the cheek. His turquoise eyes studied her face. "You're a beautiful woman, Kim. After four years of sitting next to you in accounting and economics classes, I know you didn't keep that three-point-eight-seven average by copying off someone else's paper." His tanned hands pulled her to her feet. "Nevertheless, you don't use the brains you were born with."

"Meaning . . ."

"Meaning you should have Bill come over for dinner and have a heart-to-heart with your mother, since your father is unavailable. Have him give her a spiel about how much he loves you and respects her. You know—make his intentions known."

"But I'm not sure what his intentions are." She rested her buttocks against her desk and faced him. "He loves me. I know he does, but I'm not sure that translates into marriage at this stage in his life. I've told you about his plans for opening the clinic." She folded her right arm under her breast, balancing her chin with her left palm. "I don't think the timing is right, either, with Daddy being so sick in the nursing home. I couldn't dream of planning a wedding without him being there." She looked downcast at the floor.

Randall lifted her chin and gave her a brotherly hug. "You don't have to worry about—"

George Cameron stood in the doorway, watching with obvious condemnation. He puffed his El Producto impatiently.

"Don't tell me that you've forgotten that this is a place of business, and not a hotel room."

Kim straightened her suit, and her face, before replying. "I'm sorry, Mr. Cameron, we were just talking."

"I won't tolerate displays of sexual behavior in my agency. Is that clear?" They nodded. "Randall, don't you have an office with a pile of work?"

Smoothing the sleeves of his steel gray Armani suit, Randall straightened his tie, turned up his nose at his boss's wrinkled attire, and walked out of the office, giving Kim a conspiratorial wink before closing the door. "I've got a few questions to ask you while you're here about the King account." She sat at her computer and retrieved the file. "There's a discrepancy on their statement they received last month. Mrs. King seems to think . . ."

George Cameron closed and locked the door and closed the blinds while she studied the figures on the screen. He kissed the back of her neck—she stiffened. He reeked of cigar smoke. His fat white hands reached around to fondle her breasts.

"Don't! I told you not to try that again," Kim said, pushing his hand away.

"There was a time, not long ago, when you begged me to kiss 'em." He spun her around in her chair, pulling her face close to his. She closed her eyes, bracing her hands on the padded arms. He kissed her on the mouth, bruising her breasts as he knelt in front of her.

"Stop. I asked you to stop," she said, pushing him away again.

"I'm not gonna wait much longer for you, girlie. I enjoyed that black pussy anytime I felt like it—now you're trying to tell me it's off limits?" He pinched the tips of her breasts. "I don't think so."

"Please, Mr. Cameron. I told you I'm not like that anymore," she begged. Tears formed in her eyes when she thought of those ugly scenes in his office after everyone had left for the evening. They had had sex at least twice a week on the leather sofa in his office. It didn't take him long to discover her weakness, and he had given her oral sex at their first entanglement. Now he dropped the cigar in the glass ashtray on the desk, freeing both his hands to grab her.

His thumbs flicked around her breasts. She wiggled to free herself from his grasp, though she knew she was only fueling his desire with her fruitless efforts. He ripped open her panty hose with a quick yank, prodding his fingers into the center of her womanhood.

"Please, Mr. Cameron . . . I'm begging you. Please stop."

Feeling the warm juices coat his fingers, he knew it was only a matter of seconds before she submitted. "Ain't never had a woman get so wet like you, honey. Good Lord, I can't wait to taste that sweet cream between your legs." He knew her body's responses to his expert touch. Her head fell back slowly as she echoed a helpless whimper. He slid her forward to the edge of the chair and lifted her skirt above her hips.

He repeated vulgar French words in her ear, tore off her panty hose, and cast aside her flimsy panties. He pulled her forward to greet his elongated tongue, eager to taste and explore. Her hands clutched his head, pressing him closer. Within seconds he unzipped his pants and held his pulsating penis in his hand. His breathing came in rasping shudders as he felt her dark lips contract.

Positioning himself above her, he thrust his penis between her legs and emptied his seed. Minutes later he threw her panties on the desk, and he wiped his mouth and dripping organ with a white handkerchief from his breast pocket. "Don't you think for a minute that you can ever stop me from tasting that sweet pussy." Placing the cigar butt in his mouth, he left the room with a smug smile on his face.

As Kim adjusted her clothing, tears stained her beautiful red silk suit. She closed the door to her office behind him and relocked it. Who did she think she was kidding? He had her number and he knew it. He gave the best head she'd ever had. He had threatened to fire her on several occasions when she'd refused him. She acquiesced, not just out of fear of losing her high-paying job, but because he had also sworn to tell any future employer about her, so they in turn would expect the same thing.

She bowed her head over her desk and cried. Cried for not

being strong enough to challenge him and quit. Cried because his filthy talk had turned her on. How long was she going to let him use her? If her mother ever found out her little girl was indeed a whore, it would kill her. She had to find a way finally to end it, once and for all.

Driving to work, she had experienced another exciting mild ... to News Radio 88 to find out what a working person should listen to every morning. She didn't want to go to work when a ... was somewhere she didn't want to go used to. Since they'd been married, Jackson always drove them to and from work, and they all carpool that it was. She enjoyed his company... and his easy knowledge of the...ry. As the reporter covered the latest news in Germany or Russia, Jackson always had a piece of information to add. Jackson hoped her to see whatever that entailed. His throat sometimes being strong enough to challenge him and quiet. Cried because his filthy hair had turned her on. How long was she going to let him use her? If her brother ever found out that little girl was indeed a whore, it would kill her. She had to find a way finally to end it once and for all.

9

Ask the Lonely

Ginger held the two pieces of leather rear cushions together and placed them evenly under the foot of the machine. She inserted a plastic J-strap at the appropriate notch, lock-stitched both ends, then stacked them in the half-filled cart near her sewing machine.

Unable to sleep after Jackson had phoned, she'd watched the numbers changing on the clock, knowing that time was running out to get a decent amount of sleep before work in the morning. She missed the warmth of Jackson's body.

Driving to work, she had even turned from her favorite soul station to News Radio 95—Jackson's idea of what a working person should listen to every morning. The thirty-one-mile trek to work alone was something she didn't want to get used to. Since they'd been married, Jackson always drove them to and from work, and they discussed the news. She enjoyed his comments, and his easy knowledge of history. As the reporter covered the latest news in Germany or Russia, Jackson always had a piece of information to add, to help Ginger better understand the total picture. She confessed to Jackson that the moment she had left high school (with a B+ average in history), she'd forgotten everything she'd been taught, figuring she'd never visit any of those places, so why crowd her brain with useless information. She also thought remembering north from east or south from west was useless and let that slide from her mind after completing her geography requirements in the eighth grade.

Jackson had been all over the United States. Visited Africa twice, Spain, England, Mexico, and stopped briefly in Brazil. He'd told her of his traveling exploits numerous times, yet she never tired of hearing them. He promised they'd travel the world someday—she was still waiting.

"Ginger! Yo Ginger!" called Veto, breaking her thoughts. The roaring of seventy power sewing machines blared loudly around them.

Standing on tiptoe, she looked over to see an exaggerated grimace on his face. "What is it, Veto?"

"Come up here for a minute."

Before she closed the thirty feet that separated their machines, she could see her mistake. "This whole pile is like that." He pointed to the stack of cushions piled behind him. "Let's check the work on your cart, and see if the rest of 'em are like these."

"Damn, I can't believe I did this," said Ginger, tearing down the cushions. Veto helped her rip apart forty-eight black leather rear cushion seats, which she'd absentmindedly sewn together with the wrong color carpeting.

After trimming the needle holes, she resewed the cushions, using the appropriate facings. She checked her watch. It was ten past twelve. She'd lost ninety minutes fixing her stupid mistake. After stacking another twenty jade cloth cushions on her table, she reached into one of the buckets under the next row of machines and picked up the small bundles of jade carpeting.

A sharp pain whipped around her head. Her veins throbbed along her temples. Standing erect, she pressed the tips of her fingers along her hairline. She felt as if her head were going to explode, the pain was so intense. Dropping the carpet pieces, she headed for her chair, when another spasm sliced across the nape of her neck.

Another worker, sitting across the aisle, called their supervisor when she noticed Ginger's agony. Ginger tried to call Veto's name but, suddenly feeling weak, she could only manage a whisper. Black dots shot into her vision, dots that turned red, purple, and then black again. Her fingertips tingled and dizziness overcame her. Her weakened body crumpled to the floor like a marionette.

She woke minutes later with a cold compress pressed to her forehead. Looking up into inquiring eyes, she felt humiliated and embarrassed. "Everybody get back to work, she's okay," said her boss, waving them off.

Lying on a gurney in the medical department, Ginger welcomed the nurse's various tests. The nurse eased the thermometer out of Ginger's mouth, waving it back and forth before charting her findings. She told Ginger to call someone to pick her up—they were sending her home to see her doctor.

"I can't understand what happened, Mama," Ginger told Katherine, who was steering Ginger's minivan onto the freeway. "I've never fainted in my life." Her mother had packed a satchel of clothes and hitched a ride from a friend in Port Huron. Forty-four miles, barely fifty-five minutes later, Katherine Lee entered the medical department of Champion Motors in Troy, Michigan.

"There's always a first time for everything." Katherine glanced back and forth from Ginger to the freeway. "You don't look like yourself. Is something wrong with you that you're not telling me about?"

Ginger tilted her head, and smoothed her hair. She pulled down the sun visor and looked into the mirror. She turned her head, cupping her face with her right hand, and stared into her mother's pained eyes. Katherine knew without being told what was wrong with her daughter. Ginger was losing her hair . . . again.

"Uh-huh, she's upstairs laying down. I called her doctor. He's squeezing her in tomorrow," said Katherine, sipping on a tall glass of Miller, the last one of the six-pack of beer left by Jackson. Her taste buds felt the bitter difference between her regular Colt 45 and this.

"So you'll be here until Sunday or Monday, you think?" Jewel asked her sister-in-law. She hoped she'd have time to visit with her for a few days. It was lonely being without Ollie to keep her company. Kim was always busy, going to the spa after work, or eating out with Bill.

"Probably. I brought enough clothes with me for a week." Katherine looked in the refrigerator for something to snack on. "Damn, I'm hungry. This girl ain't got no pickled pigs' feet"—she poked through the drawers—"no hog-head cheese. Nothing." She slammed the door and went back to her beer, switching the phone to her other hand.

"You been feeling okay, Katherine? The nurse said you'd been to see Ollie. It was raining on Sunday, is your asthma acting up again?"

"Feeling fine, Jewel." Holding the phone and the beer, she swayed her large buttocks back and forth as she leaned over the orchid countertops. "As a matter of fact, I'm working on finding me a husband." She waited to hear the shocked tone in Jewel's response.

"Don't surprise me none, Katherine. Can't say I blame you much. You've been alone for eleven years. 'Bout time you settled down and got remarried. Who's the lucky man you done set your sight on? Is it somebody I know? I bet it's that old widowman Wheeler. He's been after you for years now, even 'fore Lewis died."

"No. It ain't him. It was about to be Eugene Moore, until . . ." Katherine finally succeeded in getting a shocked gasp out of Jewel.

"Katherine, ain't that Janetta's husband?"

"Yeah, and she can have his ass, too. The motherfucker can't fuck worth shit." Hearing Jewel gasp, yet again, she smiled to herself. "Close your mouth, Jewel, before a fly flies in it."

"No flies in February—if there was, I would've choked by now."

"Anyway, as I was saying, I thought that ornery old bastard still had a few good fucks left in him. I should've known better. He been bragging and whispering in my ear for the past few Sundays at church—that is, while his wife wasn't looking—what he'd do to me if he ever got me alone."

"How could you do that to Janetta, Katherine? You know she's one of God's children. You oughtna mess with a born-again Christian. God don't like ugly, Katherine."

Katherine sucked an invisible speck from a gap in her tooth. "If a woman can't keep her man at home, it ain't my problem. And that sanctimonious bitch ain't been saved all her life. I've decided it was time to pay back a few of them whores who tripped the light fantastic with my husband till the wee hours of the morning."

"Janetta and Lewis? You knew about it?"

"Truth is, Jewel, if Lewis hadn't died unexpectedly, we probably would've been divorced by now. I'd gotten tired of his philandering. It wasn't totally his fault, though. He was damn good-looking, the women just threw themselves at him."

"God rest his soul."

"Anyway, back to my story. After we got to the room . . ."

Jewel and Katherine laughed hysterically as she gave her sister-in-law the play-by-play of her uneventful evening with Eugene. "Well, that motherfucker couldn't do nothing. He ain't have but two moves. Up and back. Up and back. And he wanted me to teach him something. I said I ain't got time to teach an old-ass motherfucker how to fuck. I told him, 'I know the difference between fucking and fucking around, and if you ain't gonna fuck me, get the hell up, 'cause I know where to go to get my ass turned on.' "

Jewel couldn't help but laugh at her promiscuous sister-in-law. It made her feel younger than her seventy years. "So why didn't you teach him a few tricks, Kate?"

She poured the last drop of beer into her glass, gulped it down, then rinsed out the can and put it under the cabinet. "I told that stupid motherfucker school's out. Why should I show him some new moves, so he can go home and use 'em on Janetta. She used to his sorry fucking—ain't no use surprising her. Poor woman might have a heart attack."

Katherine cocked her legs open and started shaking her right knee as though she were rocking a baby to sleep. She continued making a sucking sound with her tongue. "I'm

looking for me a young man. I'm tired of these old-ass men
that don't last long enough for me to get a good nut, before
he's laying over there snoring and farting like forty mules."

They both laughed together like two teenagers.

A youthful fifty-eight, Katherine's ass was as hot as her
daughter's. She needed more than a date once or twice a
month to cool it off. Dating at her age wasn't as easy as
she'd thought. Older men wanted younger women these
days. And finding a younger man of worth was difficult.

Katherine wanted someone to love, someone to call her
name softly at night. She hadn't felt like a whole woman in
years. She was alone—she had no one—and she needed a
man. Needed a man more than she cared to admit even to
herself.

"Katherine? You still there?" asked Jewel.

"Yeah, I'm here," said Katherine, swallowing the tears of
loneliness that stuck in her throat. She shook her head back.
She refused to give in to self-pity, yet. "As I said earlier,
Jewel, I'm looking for a husband. A young one. A friend of
mine hooked me up with someone for next weekend."

"How old is he?" asked Jewel, almost too scared to ask.

Katherine rose from her seat, to turn on the radio. Peabo
Bryson's "Feel the Fire" floated melodiously around the sun-
lit room. "Probably around fortyish."

"You joshing me, Katherine."

"You think I'm worried about these young women out
here? Hell, I'm just getting started, Jewel. My pussy's got
more snap, crackle, and pop than a bowl of Kellogg's Rice
Krispies. These drug-popping, free-fucking young whores
ain't got nothing on me. Shhhhit!"

"Katherine, these young men are only interested in old
women for their money. I know you know that."

"Yeah, I know that. I don't have any money. I'm on Social
Security. I don't have anything valuable around my house
that a young man would want. So I'm taking my chances.
What could he possibly take from me?"

"I think you know the answer to that already, Katherine."

10

Never Can Say Good-bye

I love it!" said Ginger. Her eyes glittered like emeralds. Folding her napkin across her lap, she paused, taking in the beauty of their surroundings. "The Summit Restaurant on top of the Renaissance. Isn't this nice. The Whitney—what a pretty name."

Kim signaled the waiter to take their wine order. "It's all right if you have a glass of white wine, isn't it?"

Ginger nodded. "The doctor said I'm fine. It was the new medication he had prescribed that made me faint. Apparently, I didn't follow his instructions carefully." She handed the waiter the wine list, admiring the plum pink walls. "I'll have a glass of white zinfandel, please." She paused for the waiter to leave before continuing. "How'd you find this place? I've never heard of it."

The scent of fresh-cut flowers honeycombed the place. Sprays of purple, pink, and white dendrobiums in a clear glass bowl decorated their white linen tablecloth, and an underskirt of deep burgundy caressed their ankles. "Working downtown, you find out all the in spots. This is one of the nicest. Randall brought me here four years ago when they first opened, and I've been coming ever since. Remember I told you about my friend Randall—"

"That you went to college with?"

"Yes. Well, we're pretty good friends. One of these days, I'll take you by his apartment. It's beautiful. He's got one of those new loft apartments near Belle Isle." Kim smiled, remembering how she'd helped him pick out all the kitchen utensils. He hadn't needed any help with anything else; his taste was excellent. "You should see the paintings he has. Beautiful. He paints, too. I'll show you . . ."

Ginger sipped her water, swirling the cubes, staring into the center of her glass, avoiding Kim's eyes. "You sure you and Randall aren't more than friends?" She sensed her cousin's nervousness and chastised herself for being so nosy. "I didn't mean that, Kim." She touched her hand, offering an apology. "Let's order lunch. I'm starved!"

While she studied the menu, Ginger breathed in the rich aromas of espresso coffee, sautéed onions, and the sweet bouquet of fresh strawberries.

"This mansion was custom built in eighteen ninety-four for a rich lumber baron—whose name happens to be David Whitney." Leaning forward in her chair, Kim nodded to the large Tiffany clock built into the wall in the hallway. "See that clock? His initials are engraved in it." Ginger swiveled around slowly, admiring the exquisite timepiece. "The mosaic tiles were laid down individually. See how tiny they are, but it's beautiful, isn't it?" Ginger could only stare in amazement.

"It cost over four hundred thousand dollars to build back then, and it's estimated to be worth at least forty million or more today." Ginger's jaw dropped.

"There are a total of forty-two rooms in the house, and twenty-two fireplaces." Ginger nodded. There were three fireplaces in her own home, which they very seldom lit. Yet she had a passion for them. They were so romantic.

"There's a hand-painted ceiling with cherubs playing musical instruments in the music room. You've got to see it before we leave."

Prisms of sunlight danced through the iridescent Tiffany

glass of the windows. The pianist began playing a classical rendition of "All My Tomorrows," and guests acknowledged his appearance with light applause.

Ginger and Kim ate their appetizers of chilled shrimp cocktail, and had a second glass of wine each. Kim ordered a savory chicken strudel. Ginger selected pheasant glazed with a raspberry sauce. She offered Kim a sample of her entrée, saying it was so tender she could have cut it with her breath.

Satisfied after splitting a slice of white chocolate and macadamia cheesecake, they paid the bill, left a generous tip, and headed upstairs to the bathroom.

Walking up the stairs, Ginger paused to admire the splendor. An enormous tapestry re-creating Bottocelli's *Birth of Venus* hung on the landing. Priceless crystal sconces lighted the walls where several antique clocks and smaller but equally breathtaking paintings hung in gilded frames.

Twin fountains of flowers exploding from huge oriental vases languished on pedestals on each side of the archway. Antique mahogany furniture was tastefully arranged throughout the second floor of the Whitney Mansion.

Peeking into every room and admiring the treasures within, Kim and Ginger explored. The third floor was a massive bar that spanned the width of the room. As in the rest of the home, antique treasures filled every corner.

After visiting the elegant powder room, they headed back downstairs. The female maître d' whisked out their coats, draping them over her arms, like matadors before a bull fight. "Ohhh, shit!" said Ginger. "I forgot to get some matches. I always save at least two packs from every restaurant I go to."

Kim touched Ginger's shoulder as she eased into her coat. "I'll get them," she said.

Kim walked back to their table, but her pace slowed as she saw the back of a familiar head. She looked around the room for an empty table with the matches on it and, grabbing a handful from the glass bowl, turned to exit the room quickly.

"Kim. Just a moment!" a raspy voice called after her.

She turned in a semicircle, stiff as a German soldier, clenching her fists. "Yes, Mr. Cameron?"

She smelled the familiar aroma of stale cigars as she faced

him with a challenging glare. She acknowledged his guest with a polite nod of her head. His robust little body reared back in his seat. "Won't you sit down and join us?" He made a gesture toward the vacant seat on his right.

"No, thank you. I was just about to—"

"Oh, but I insist." George Cameron gave her a knowing look as he pulled out a chair.

"My cousin is waiting for me. I can't stay."

"This won't take long." He turned his attention to his lunch date. "This is Brenda, my new assistant. She'll be taking over Sherry's job." Kim eyed the young Black woman, who couldn't have been more than twenty. The long, blond weaved hair and overdone makeup hadn't managed to disguise her youth.

"Nice to meet you, Brenda. I'm Kim Lee." She extended her hand. "Welcome to Pierce-Walker. Sorry to cut this short, but as I said, I have someone waiting." Kim started to leave.

George Cameron cleared his throat before he spoke in a stern tone. "Kim, I'd like to see you in my office after lunch. We have a few things to discuss. Namely, training Brenda."

"Mr. Cameron, I'm not—Why can't Sherry—"

"Sherry is gone."

"I see." So it's out with the old, and in with the new. She'd heard the other analyst whispering about something in the office this morning, but she hadn't paid any attention. She was praying desperately that the gossip wasn't about her. Kim had rid herself of associating with the other female brokers a long time ago. They were just a bunch of toxic-ass bitches. If they weren't bringing a problem, they were causing a problem. Had anyone seen them yesterday? she wondered. He'd been in her office all of eight minutes. That was all it took for him to . . .

"Kim? I asked you if three-thirty was a good time."

"What? Yes. Fine." She turned to see the questioning look on Ginger's face as she stood in the doorway to the parlor. Clutching her purse under her arm, Kim excused herself with a curt nod of her head.

"Who was that?" Ginger asked when she saw the angry look on Kim's face.

Through gritted teeth, she spat out, "My boss. Let's go."

"Something wrong, Kim?"

"What could possibly be wrong? I'm the hardest-working employee he's got. He's crazy about me."

The tone of Kim's voice warned Ginger that something was terribly wrong. But she couldn't imagine what it could be. Kim never missed a day of work. Three months ago when Kim received a bonus commission for securing the hefty portfolio of an affluent client, they had celebrated. Each time they talked, there was always a note of pride in Kim's voice about an interesting client she'd just taken on. Her colorful stories about other professional women working downtown had motivated Ginger's decision to become one herself. If there was a problem Kim would tell her, she thought. After all, they weren't just cousins, they were best friends. And best friends told each other everything, didn't they?

"He did? Did he say what time he'd call back?" Ginger kicked off her black leather pumps and slid back on the chaise in the living room.

Katherine followed suit, propping her socked feet on the pink velvet sofa. "Didn't say. Just said he'd call back."

Ginger rested her head on the back of the chaise, her eyes fixed on the ceiling. "Jason's not home from school yet?"

"You don't remember him telling you last night that they changed his schedule?" Katherine knew it wasn't like Ginger to forget Jason's schedule.

"I forgot, Mama. I'm glad you're here. Did I tell you that already?" Trying to shake off her temporary loss of memory, she closed her eyes, taking a deep breath.

Sinking her Fred Flintstone size nines into the thick white carpeting, Katherine sat up abruptly. "You haven't mentioned what the doctor said was wrong with you."

"Ohhh." Folding her hands under her breasts, Ginger cocked her head to the side, trying to break the tension in the stiffened artery that sent blood to her brain. "It was the minoxidil that made me faint. I forgot"—she looked guiltily at her mother—"I forgot that he mentioned that this particular medication would lower my blood pressure."

"What kind of shit is this? He gives you medication that will lower your blood pressure, when your blood is already low now?"

"Mama. All the tests showed when they gave their patients with high blood pressure this particular medication it made their hair grow. But he warned me that there were side effects. Anyway, don't worry. I can't take the medicine anymore." Her voice dropped to almost a whisper.

Katherine studied her for several beats of silence, seeing the defeated look on her daughter's face. "So that's it—that's all those educated motherfuckers could do is send you home without . . ." Her voice trailed off.

Ginger rushed to fill the silence.

"Mama, I'm gonna light that damned fireplace if it kills me. Will you see if there's any white zinfandel in the wine cellar for me, please?" Not wanting her mother to see her crying again, she made an effort to appear her usual self.

One day ten years ago, when Ginger was married to Michael Carter, Ginger went to sit in the living room and stared at the blank television screen. Then, feeling the onset of a headache, she went to the mirrored cabinet in her cheery yellow bathroom for her medication. The reflection that looked back at her was that same anxious face she recognized from two years earlier. Turning her back, she tried to shake the self-pity that was speedily targeting her heart strings. She went back to her recliner and waited for the medication to stop the pounding in her head.

She could smell the strong scent of Glover's Mane that she'd applied to her scalp when she returned home after working the afternoon shift. Her mother told her that rubbing this medication on every day would stimulate her scalp and help reverse the process of her hair loss. What did she have to lose? She was ready to try anything. The doctors couldn't help her. Maybe one of the old folks' remedies would.

In her bathroom there were numerous other so-called remedies, including some from her mother's old hairdressers. Ginger had spent thousands of dollars over the years running to every reputable dermatologist she could find who said they could help her.

She had even spent a week at Saint Joseph's Hospital in Canada, taking every test imaginable. And she'd left disappointed.

She'd been given cortisone injections in her head that started her hair growing. But it would only work for a period of two or three months, then the hair would fall out again if her body hadn't completed what they described as its cycle of "hormonal imbalance."

Finally, one day after leaving the doctor's office in considerable pain, bleeding from roughly forty to fifty injections into her bald scalp, she had decided the brief improvements from that treatment were no longer worth it.

Later, a friend suggested a new method offered at a health-food store. They had a powerful machine that looked into your eyes and was supposedly able to ascertain every impurity in your body. So Ginger walked into the Honeybee Health Food Store and deposited her ninety dollars on the counter.

She left the store in total bewilderment, however. The therapist had recommended that she immediately stop eating flour. *Flour.* She was told that it coated her small intestines and kept the normal functions of her bowels from performing routinely, causing impurities throughout her system which led to hair loss. He also recommended that she follow a diet low in fats, sweets, and starches. He made a list of several vitamins for her to take daily. Her bill totaled one hundred and fifty-three dollars—a small price to pay if it worked. Six months later she was still as bald as a newborn bald eagle.

When her alopecia finally completed its eighteen-month cycle, and she was once again enjoying a full head of hair, the joy was short lived. Fifteen months later it was back. She had been trying to watch *All My Children.* After all, weren't their problems worse than hers? And without thinking, she had started pulling on one of her braids—then another. They resembled dying trees being uprooted from the dark earth, surrounded by patches of barren soil.

The eerie sound of hair coming loose from its foundation startled her. Ginger sprang to her feet and ran into the bathroom to look in the mirror. She wept aloud, horrified to see two braids clutched in her hand. Angry and shocked, she pulled out the remaining braids, one by one. It was almost like tearing a piece of paper; the long, thin, braids of hair felt like there was no life left in them. Brittle and dead.

She remembered how, hours later, her three small children had found her still sitting in a zombielike state in the living room, staring at the television screen, in total disbelief.

After placing a fluted glass of zinfandel on the glass end table next to her daughter's resting form, Katherine closed the drapes, darkened the room, and added three logs to the fire. The smell of wood smoke filtered lazily from the ceramic-and-mahogany fireplace. The silvery pieces of wood hissed, as various chunks snapped, smoldering into fragments of powdery cinders.

Katherine covered her daughter with a handmade afghan from the front hall closet. She remembered when Ginger had learned to crochet, having been taught by her friends at work. They wanted to make use of their spare time when they'd completed their production for the day. She'd called her from work, so excited to tell her about it. Two months later, Ginger had handed Katherine a beautifully crafted hooded poncho, crocheted in a rich wool yarn in blends of smoke gray, tropic sand, and beige.

Ginger's head swung lazily to the side as Katherine tucked the woolen blanket under her chin. She studied her daughter's face. Her mouth was gaping open as though her dreams had surprised her. Katherine stifled the urge to call her name. Unable to understand or fathom the reasons of her daughter's illness, she felt suddenly depressed.

A mother was a child's first teacher. She was there to ease out that first burp, to teach the child to walk and talk . . . to teach the basics of life. Now she was powerless to help her child. She had to put her faith and trust in the hands of God. A silent prayer was on her lips:

> Seek you first the kingdom of God and all his righteousness
> and all things needed for this life will be added on to you.

He says lean not on your own resources or under-
    standings
If you will lean on him in prayer and meditation—

Katherine knew Ginger was mentally exhausted. The anguish that plagued her daughter every two years was overwhelming. She thought of the quickest way to relieve some
of the pressure from Ginger: organizing and using a few
scare tactics on her half-disciplined, lovable grandchildren.

"What kind of game are we going to play, Granny?" asked
Autumn, tilting her pixy head. Sierra wondered about her
grandmother's strange change in attitude. Earlier she had
cussed them out, telling them how junky and funky they
were. She lined all four of them along the couch in the basement and read them up and down. She told Sierra she
smelled like a rank pussycat. Told Jason his room was so
funky a skunk wouldn't have felt at home. She started in on
Christian, saying after putting a load of white clothes in to
soak that she'd spotted several of his drawers that looked
like they'd been dragged through mud.

Autumn had laughed, and pointed at each of them, thinking she'd escape the wrath of their grandmother. ". . . and
Autumn, your teeth looks like Green Giant corn." Then Autumn started to cry.

Katherine had paced the floor, back and forth, yelling at
all four of her grandchildren. Telling them they were taking
advantage of their mother's working. They knew Ginger
went to bed early. Usually they shammed on doing the work
their mother expected from them.

Katherine wasn't fooled by their innocent faces. They
were young devils masquerading in sheep's clothing. She put
the fear in them that Ginger didn't have the energy to.

Then Katherine guided her two granddaughters upstairs to
their bedroom. She placed her index finger over her closed
mouth, studying their wide-eyed stare. "We're going to pretend that Mama is Sleeping Beauty, and we're waiting on the
prince to wake her up. We can't make any noise until Prince
Charming comes to kiss the princess, otherwise the spell will
be broken and Mama will stay asleep forever."

Autumn looked to her sister for guidance. She couldn't decide whether this was going to be a fun game or not. "We have to be real quiet, and make the kingdom clean and beautiful so Sleeping Beauty will want to live here for the rest of her days."

Sierra shifted her weight onto one leg, put her hands on her hips, and said, "You mean we gotta clean our room, and be real quiet about it, Granny?" Katherine nodded. And Ginger said this girl was slow.

When Ginger woke hours later from a deep sleep the house was quieter than usual. The realization that Katherine was there enabled her to relish the silence. If anyone could control her overactive children, her mother could.

The phone rang.

"Hello."

"It's me baby."

She relaxed at the melodic sound of his voice. "Jackson."

"I called you earlier, but Katherine said you were having lunch with Kim. I thought your classes started this afternoon."

"No. They start tomorrow."

"Katherine come down for the weekend?"

"Uh-huh. She figured I'd need some company with you gone. I picked her up after work today," she lied. Ginger kept silent about her fainting at work the day before. Her physician had given her a note to give to her supervisor stating that she take the remainder of the week off, returning to work Monday. "I guess we're both kinda lonely."

"Your voice don't sound right, baby. You all right? 'Cause if something is wrong, I'll take a flight out in the morning."

"No, sweetheart. You take care of your mother. I'm fine. Is she home yet?"

"Saturday. We're bringing her home Saturday morning."

"Did Jab make it down?"

"Yeah, we're all here talking about old times."

Ginger smiled to herself thinking of all the stories Jackson had told her about the nine of them growing up with hardly any money, and never really noticing they were poor. All their neighbors and relatives around them in Lee County never had any more than they did. Nobody had had a car—or other expensive items.

They had never been introduced to the luxuries of life. They were poor financially, but rich spiritually, physically, and mentally. Their life was so filled with good memories of cherished moments that Ginger couldn't help but feel envious of their love.

11

You've Really Got a Hold on Me

At two o'clock in the afternoon, thick cumulus clouds clustered in the sky. The cold air tickled Ginger's lungs as her breath hung in the atmosphere. Wiping the layer of fresh snow from her windshield, she headed for the freeway.

As she stopped at the light on Jefferson, she noticed the newly remodeled bridge. The serenity of the view beckoned her. She decided to seize a few moments to enjoy the picturesque waterscape. Crossing the Douglas MacArthur Bridge, she entered the thousand-acre park of Belle Isle. The island featured an aquarium, zoo, and Dossin Great Lakes Museum. It had been the city's playground for more than a century.

The place was an oasis where picnicking families flocked in the warm months, filling the air with the aroma of spicy barbecue, fresh sweet corn, and savory collard greens smothered in smoked ham hocks steaming over smoking barbecue pits.

After parking her minivan, Ginger relaxed, opened the windows to inhale the cool breeze whipping across the frozen river, and turned the radio to Light 93.1 She let the soothing music flow through her body. Ginger's eyes feasted on the forest of trees still draped with winter ice. The blanket of snow and frozen glaze across the Detroit River extended to the neighboring Canadian border.

She didn't want to read any more textbooks, talk, or even think. For just a while, she just wanted to *be*. It felt so wonderful to be calm, and just to observe, to merge with nature, instead of enduring the pressures of work and home.

"Where's your overnight bag, Sierra?" Ginger demanded. She closed the second door in Sierra and Autumn's walk-in closet.

Lord knows I don't want to start another argument with this child today, thought Ginger. Nearly every time the kids left to visit their father, Sierra seemed to forget where she put her packed overnight bag. Ginger had bought Sierra at least twelve bags over the nine years since the divorce.

"I just had it, Mama." As she sat on the bed trembling, Sierra's small body was rigid. She hated these scenes of her mother's.

Bulky sweaters, jogging suits, and caps of various sizes were strewn on the closet floor. Moments before they had been stacked neatly on the shelves above Ginger's head. "Then where is it?" Ginger felt her forehead. Pain sliced through her temple. Placing her index finger and thumb over her closed eyelids, she leaned back against the wall.

Katherine stomped into the room, holding the bulging bag as evidence of their futile effort. "If you hadda stopped for a minute in the kitchen instead of running upstairs like a raging bull, I could have saved you the trouble of packing their bags."

Ginger breathed a sigh of relief. Looking at her daughter's eyes brimming with tears, Ginger was sorry she'd jumped to the conclusion that Sierra had left the bag in Port Huron.

For the past year, she and Sierra had been fighting like cats and dogs. Ginger didn't know how to reach her anymore. Sierra possessed an angelic face and an itty-bitty body that made her look seven instead of ten. It surprised even Ginger how such an innocent-looking child could turn into a

pint-sized she-devil when told to do something that she
didn't like.

The women at work had warned her that when their
daughters reached the fifth grade, they entered a crisis stage
that usually lasted until age twelve. The girls were going
through a change of life, and it wasn't easy on anyone.

She pressed Sierra's sandy brown head to her bosom,
rocking her back and forth, and told her she was sorry for
hollering at her. Sierra's large brown eyes widened with relief as she stared up into her mother's face.

"Okay, let's get the show on the road," Katherine commanded. Steering her granddaughter from the room, she
handed Sierra her blue overnight bag. "Granny starched and
ironed all your clothes this morning. The only thing you have
to do is pack your toothbrush. I didn't know whose was
which, so I left it out." She smiled fondly at her grandchild
and patted her on the butt.

Katherine sat on the edge of Autumn's twin brass bed.
Rolling her eyes at Ginger, she chastised her for constantly
harping on Sierra. "I don't know why you can't see it. Everyone else can. You nag her for every little thing she does.
Can't you see how sensitive she is?"

Sitting herself on Sierra's white eyelet comforter, Ginger
crossed her arms and feet, and waited for the sermon she
knew was coming. What her mother didn't admit was that
she'd done the same thing to her and Gwen when they were
little. It wasn't until a few years ago that Ginger and her
mother had become good friends. Now, unwittingly, Ginger
was following her pattern.

"I know I holler too much. I'm guilty, Mama." She threw
her hands in the air. "I just don't have any patience with her.
She tries my nerves."

"You got a lot on your mind, Ginger. We'll talk about it
another time." Katherine pounded from the room, all of her
180 pounds imprinting footsteps in the white carpeting.

Ginger knew that Sierra was struggling to find her place
between Christian and Autumn. But she didn't know how to
help her. It didn't help that both Christian and Autumn ex-
celled in school while Sierra found every class a challenge.
Thankfully Sierra and Autumn got along. In fact, they were

crazy about each other. They rarely fought. Even wore each other's clothes—Autumn being extremely tall for her age and Sierra tiny, and small boned. Sierra suggested they share a room together, which pleased Jackson more than Ginger. Jackson didn't want his baby girl sleeping alone.

Ginger turned to admire her girls' room; she'd redecorated it for them last year. Sierra and Autumn had been so excited about all the changes they could barely sleep for a week.

Thirty clerestory windows encircling the pie-shaped room made the glacier white paint gleam. Stenciled lavender irises bordered the ceiling. Each girl had an antique brass poster bed. Intricate patterns of lovebirds, elm leaves, and berries were woven into the foot- and headboards and romantic coverings of feathery white cutwork canopied the beds.

Two gold-filigreed pink-and-lavender Tiffany lamps adorned the mahogany nightstands. Handmade crocheted doilies danced in twelve sugar-stiffened layers around the center of the bureaus. Silk blossoms of white gardenias and lavender baby's breath sat in hand-painted ceramic vases on the doilies.

It was a place of sweet repose, of sunshine-gilded daydreams tinged with a hint of mystery. A room fit for a princess. Why, then, didn't her children act like the perfect little angels in the fairy tales?

Two porterhouse steaks sizzled in the iron skillet, smothered with sliced mushrooms and circles of Spanish onions. Steam billowed upward as Katherine checked the potatoes and onions simmering on the stove's back eye.

Ginger and Autumn sat at the butcher block slicing fresh vegetables for the salad. Autumn dreaded the bimonthly visits her sister and brothers made to Port Huron with their father. Sierra had tried to explain to her that their mother had been married to Michael Carter before she married Jackson. But Autumn never quite understood about divorce. She only knew how sad she felt when they were gone. Sometimes she cried. That was when she'd go upstairs and talk to her doll, Suzy.

"Mama, when is Sierra coming home?" she asked her

mother. She'd ask this question continuously until Sierra came home.

"Sunday. They'll be home Sunday night, sweetheart." Ginger took heed of her mother shaking her head as she bent over to check the steaks.

Katherine felt that Autumn should be allowed to go with the other children, but Jackson wouldn't have it. Ginger wasn't sure how she felt about it. Katherine hinted at Jackson a few times that Michael Carter had offered to take Autumn along for the weekends. Jackson was vehemently opposed to the idea. After a while, Katherine dropped the subject.

After dinner, Ginger and Katherine cleaned the kitchen together, while Autumn was mesmerized in front of the television with a Ninja Turtle video Ginger had rented. Making a quick stop at Blockbuster Video on her way home from the park, Ginger had picked out the latest videocassettes available for children. She had also grabbed boxes of Raisinets, Milk Duds, and microwave popcorn to keep Autumn busy after the kids had gone.

She always planned something special to do on those Saturdays with Autumn while the others were away. Just the two of them. Sometimes Jackson would come along, but rarely could she convince him to take a few hours away from his marathon of Westerns.

"Just tell me what you plan on doing about keeping this house clean. You're not going to have time to clean this house working in the plant and working at the office part time." Katherine thought for a moment. "How many times a week did you say you had to be in the real estate office?"

"At least four times a week—put in two or three hours. After I'm established I won't have to go in so much. I can do more from home. They want to see that I'm serious about working there. They've trained so many people who have quit after they hadn't made a sale in a month or two." Ginger sighed. "I know it's not going to be easy. But I can do it, Mama. I know I can."

"You listen to me, and you listen to me good." Katherine closed the dishwasher and took a seat at the breakfast room table. Ginger joined her after putting away the scoured skillets in the pantry. "You got good sense, but you don't use it. You need someone to come in every two weeks and clean this big-ass house. I hope you don't think these kids are going to clean it right without you supervising them?"

Ginger folded her hands on the table. "I already asked Jackson about getting someone—"

"Asked?" her mother shouted. "You don't ask, you tell. Are you out of your friggin' mind?" Katherine walked to the refrigerator and came back with a tall glass of beer. After a long cold swallow she added, "That may be a slow-walking back-hill Mississippi son of a bitch, but you better believe his mind clicks as quick as a Bic." She took another sip. "Don't tell me. He said no." Ginger nodded, her eyes focusing on Autumn's gym shoes near the credenza.

Katherine got up from her chair, nursing her beer, and strode to look out the window. She shifted her weight to her right hip, and continued speaking with her back turned. "He wants to tie you down at home, so you won't have the energy or wherewithal to succeed at anything, so you'll just accept what he expects you to be: a factory worker, mother, and wife."

"He wants me to quit the plant," Ginger challenged, half believing it herself. "He just doesn't want some strange person in here cleaning our home."

"Bullshit. They have bonded maid services. You don't have to worry about anybody stealing anything." Two of her other daughters who lived out of state and worked full time had gotten cleaning women years ago. Not wanting to hurt Ginger's feelings, Katherine had never mentioned it; neither had her daughters.

The sound of the phone ringing cut off Ginger's reply. "Mama, will you hang up the phone when I get upstairs, please?" Katherine glared at her, knowing who was on the other line.

Ginger took several deep breaths before leaping into a cheerful conversation with her husband. Why did her mother always try to make her feel so guilty about loving her husband? Was she weak to give in to some of his demands? Or was her mother jealous because she didn't have a man to go home to?

"Hi, sweetheart," she whispered.

*   *   *

Shaking the snow from her purple leather coat, Kim stood at the front door. Katherine grabbed her arm and led her into the living room. She pressed a finger to her lips, begging silence, then turned on the stereo and sat down to chat with her niece.

"Every time I come over, she's either ironing his shirts, matching up his clothes for work, fixing his plate, taking his shoes to the shop to get them polished, and anything else she can think of that he needs. She does too much for that man. The only thing he does for himself is to take a piss." Kim leaned over toward Katherine, glancing at the doorway. "And sometimes she even holds that for him, after they'd had sex, because he's soooooooo tired."

Katherine shook her head and, following Kim's lead, checked for a spying figure lurking in the doorway. "I'm always telling her she do too much for Jackson. But she gets mad. I think she thinks I'm jealous. So lately I haven't been saying anything. When she starts selling real estate next month, she won't have no time to baby-sit him. All hell's gonna break loose in this house. She loves that man so much, I bet every time she looks in the mirror, she sees his face."

Walking down the circular staircase, Ginger thought about the conversation she'd just had with Jackson. After listening to her pleas and arguments about their needing a cleaning woman, he'd still held fast to his original decision: "No way."

She had hoped that under the circumstances, with him missing her and their being apart, he'd be more reasonable.

Ginger respected his judgment, and his knowledge of the world, the world Ginger had been sheltered from by her first husband. Jackson possessed something . . . something she couldn't put her finger on. Something that was missing inside her. Was it patience? Yes. But that wasn't it. Was it his ability to size up any situation and make the correct decision? Yes. But that wasn't it either. He possessed a certain something that she admired and strove to call her own, but yet she couldn't quite put it into words. It was . . . it was . . . maturity.

Overhearing fragments of Kim and Katherine's conversation caused Ginger to hesitate, cringing, before entering the living room.

"These young women today are frantic for a man's company. Marry the first man that asks 'em. Claim it's not just sexual; they need a man to talk to. Child, you can call directory assistance and talk to a man. Just 'cause you got a huuu-uuuuusband don't mean diddly shit. That's your man today—"

". . . and some other bitch's tomorrow," said Ginger, casually walking into the room. "That's the correct phrase, isn't it, Mother?" She saw the frown on her mother's face, smiled, and sat next to Kim. "I thought I heard the doorbell while I was on the phone. How long you been here?"

Kim looked guiltily at Ginger, then at Katherine. Ginger didn't miss the connection. They'd been discussing her. It wasn't as if they didn't have their own problems to talk about. As a matter of fact, Aunt Jewel had called her the other day while Katherine was at the store stocking up on beer. Evidently, her mother had told Aunt Jewel that she was in the market for a man.

"Just got here a few minutes ago. I'm on my way downtown. Would you care to join me?"

"Can I go where?" Ginger asked in a nonchalant tone.

Kim crossed her legs, baring yards of skin beneath her royal blue suede miniskirt. "I'd like you to come with me to a club in Greek Town, now. Can you go?" It was as much of a challenge as it was a question, Ginger felt.

She swallowed hard. Jackson would shit bricks if he knew she'd gone out with Kim, whom he called "hotter than a bitch in heat." "Sure. I have to change."

Knowing Ginger would be a while, Katherine continued her conversation. She was feeling kind of mellow. "Sometimes the only thing worse than not getting your wish is getting it. Ginger wanted that man, and now she got him." She sat on the pink chaise across from Kim, scooted back, rocking a large thigh back and forth.

Kim crossed her bare legs and puffed on a Kool Light, letting the billowing smoke curdle through her nose, inhaling, then softly blowing it out. She wondered if possibly she and Aunt Katherine weren't just a tad bit jealous. After all, she and Bill were a long way off from making a commitment. And if he ever found out about her boss . . .

"Did I ever tell you about a man I was having an affair with while I was married to your Uncle Lewis?" Kim's eyes bucked. Shaking her head, she urged her aunt to continue.

"I almost left Lewis for this boss-sex motherfucker, Curtis Carlton. When I first met Jackson, I thought about Curtis, he reminded me so much of him. Problem was, he was married too." She smiled to herself, thinking of Curtis, and what might have been. "I talked my problems over with my wise old friend Addie; she was in her late sixties. I always had an older woman to confide in. They keep their mouths shut." She wagged a thick finger back and forth. "Don't ever tell girlfriends your own age about your personal problems. First of all, they tell their men everything, next thing you know, your business is all over the streets 'cause men gossip worse than women do."

Kim had thought about discussing the problem of her boss with Ginger. She assumed her cousin would keep her mouth shut. Aunt Katherine did have a point, though. Ginger would probably tell Jackson, and then where would she be? But she needed to talk to someone about it. Maybe she could confide in Aunt Katherine. She'd understand, wouldn't she?

"Anyway, Addie told me not to leave my husband for no high-frequency-sex motherfucker. 'Cause you ain't gonna have him but a minute. She said women been leaving their husbands since she was a little girl. But a woman with *good* sense don't leave their man because he's having an affair. Sooner or later, they always come back home. Ain't nothing changed but the weather.

"Lewis was so damn good-looking, I should have known he'd be a womanizer. Should have married me a ugly man. Men don't want nothing that look better than them, you know. They want scraggly-looking women that treat them like kings." Katherine patted her thick, peppery red hair. "Don't know if you remember, Kim. But your aunt was a fine woman in her day."

"Mama's got pictures of you and Daddy and his brother in her chest. You were gorgeous, Aunt Katherine. And my daddy wasn't doing too bad either." She thought of her father withering away in that nursing home, becoming somebody she almost didn't recognize as her father. He still was a handsome man at seventy-three. But his spirit had left him. He'd given up, lost the zest that had kept him looking youthful even as he aged.

"Anyway, it lasted for almost a year, before Addie's words started sinking in. He kept lying about leaving his wife. Next thing I know, I heard he was going out with one of my so-called girlfriends who happened to be married, too, and having marital problems. Anyway, I didn't have the strength yet to tell him to kiss my ass, because I still wanted to go to bed with him. I'd gotten addicted, and didn't know how to resist him.

"One day, he came over, Lewis had gotten sick again, and was in the TB sanitarium in Saginaw, Michigan. I'd just fried some catfish, had a pot of collard greens on the stove, and was chopping the cabbage and carrots for some slaw. He said, 'That sure looks good, Kate. Them collard greens smell like heaven. Fix me a plate, baby.' I looked at that motherfucker real hard for a minute. Then I told him he wasn't bringing me no money, and had the nerve to want something to eat? I told that potato swinging dick motherfucker that he'll never eat my food and go shit it out in some other woman's toilet.

"Next thing I know, he stopped coming 'round so much. So I said fuck it, Lewis was getting out the hospital soon, and I was gonna try to make it with my man. Hell, ain't nobody perfect. If I hadda let that man blow my mind, my five kids would've been picking maggots out of the dog in the backyard, thinking it was SpaghettiOs."

Kim couldn't help but laugh at the picture of her Aunt Katherine painted so vividly. But then her smile faded. If her aunt could find the strength, she could too. She had to if she was going to have any kind of future with Bill, and she desperately wanted one.

"As I was saying, a man has so many fucks in them, and they pass it around to so many women and let them enjoy it.

About time they get around to the right woman, they don't have shit left.

"Don't let a man get to the bottom of your ass and wear you out, so just in case you don't end up with this man you want to have something left to give and enjoy with someone else. About time he's trying to push down to the bottom of my pussy, I'm steady rearing back so I can save some of it for me."

"Aunt Katherine," said Kim, laughing, "you're too tough for words!"

Katherine stood up, stretching her stocky body. She gyrated her large buttocks, saying, "Screwing is gone out of style anyway. I can't stand a man sweating all over me. He can kiss my toes and paint each one of my nails a different color and get the fuck out of my face. I like smelling my own funk." She started humming Nancy Wilson as she waddled to the doorway. "I got to check on my grandbaby. That tape should be . . ."

"Granny, where's my mommy?" said Autumn standing in the darkened foyer.

"She's upstairs getting ready to go out. Come with me, Granny's gonna fix me and you some ice cream. We're going upstairs in Jason's room so we can get real comfortable, okay?" Autumn nodded. "Say good-bye to Kim. Kim, go upstairs and see what's taking Ginger so long? She should've been ready by now."

Before the words had left her mouth, Katherine felt she'd forgotten something. Her daughter had a closet full of clothes—that couldn't be keeping her. Maybe Ginger was having a hard time fixing her hair. For a fleeting moment it had slipped her mind. Had she told Kim?

Kim turned the knob, then hesitated, knocking first. "Mama?" asked Ginger. "No, it's Kim. Can I come in?" Ginger had just pinned a gold hair ornament alongside her french roll, camouflaging a thinned section of her hair. Good, that looks okay, no one will ever know, she thought to herself. "Come on in, Kim." Kim entered the outer hall of their bedroom, and peered into her bathroom. "You almost ready?" asked Kim.

Ginger, clad in a black lace strapless bra and half slip,

stood staring into the mirror. "I'm just about to put on my makeup. It won't take but a minute. My dress is over there." She pointed to the gold-crepe-backed satin dress hanging on the door of her closet. "Kim, look in my jewelry box on my dresser and get me those gold hooped earrings, will you?"

As Ginger skillfully applied her makeup, Kim sat on the tub watching her. "Ginger, you ought to think about what Aunt Katherine said, about getting someone to come in here and clean." She looked around the huge bathroom, which was bigger than her whole bedroom. "This house is beautiful. Big and beautiful. I don't know how you manage to keep it so clean with all the hours you work at the plant."

"It isn't easy. Mama does have a point. I'm gonna talk to Jackson again when he gets home. It would be a lot of worry lifted off me, knowing these kids weren't suffering from me trying to do something for myself." She bent closer to the mirror, glancing periodically at Kim, wondering why she had such a worried expression on her face. "Everything all right with you and Bill?"

"Sure. Fine. He might meet us there tonight, if he finishes his meeting. He's interviewing another doctor for the clinic. I just don't understand why it had to be so late."

Suddenly, Ginger's eyebrow lifted as she lined her eye with black kohl pencil. "You never worry about Bill. I thought you said you had his number?"

Kim stretched and crossed her legs, smoothing the nap of her suede pump with her heels. "We're doing okay. He just spends so much time on that damn building I hardly get to see him. He keeps telling me to be patient. That it'll only be until he gets things organized." She looked into Ginger's eyes, which showed concern but not intrusiveness. "I just have the feeling that when it's opened in a few months, we'll never see each other." Her voice lowered. "I'd just appreciate a little quality time with him. Lately, it's been hurried sex. Good, but not like when we'd sit and talk for hours afterwards. You know, that afterglow that you feel after you're both satisfied, and you feel you still somehow need to connect. You don't want that closeness to end. So you talk, you touch, you revel in a luxurious time, when you feel as one—knowing that the love you just shared with each other was special, that no one else can make you feel that . . ." She whispered the word *special*. Tears glistened in her eyes.

Ginger knew something was on Kim's mind, but she hadn't thought it was serious until now. Something must be terribly wrong between Kim and Bill. Usually when she spoke about her and Bill making love, she'd always mentioned how much she was in control, how Bill was putty in her hands in the bedroom. She'd hinted that through the years she'd learned sexual tricks from older, experienced men, and that she'd become quite skilled in the boudoir.

Kim did consider herself a triple threat to a man. He had to compete with her intellectually, financially, and finally try to satisfy her in the bedroom. Luckily, Bill succeeded in all of the above. His intelligence and financial status were obvious from the beginning of their courtship, but what had taken her totally by surprise was his fantastic lovemaking. He'd waited three months before making love to her.

Kim had been almost ready to dump him and go on to greener pastures. Until he told her he'd made reservations at a posh hotel for them for the weekend. His psychology had worked its magic on her, and she hadn't even realized it. Figuring that the anticipation was more thrilling than the act, he had been patiently seducing her inner being. Teaching her the subtle yet priceless joy that spiritual contact with another human soul offered. A touch of heaven. When he finally bedded her, the mere touch of his hand on her bare skin sent her to heights unknown before.

12

Going to a Go-Go

Ginger kissed Autumn good night, promised to bring her home something, and left her contentedly watching *Cinderella* with her catnapping grandmother. Autumn hadn't even asked why she was so dressed up. Ginger decided she wouldn't reveal to her baby daughter that she was going out to a club. Knowing how close Autumn was to her father, the child might blurt it out on the phone the next time he called. No, she'd tell Mr. Montgomery of her outing when the time was right.

As Kim and Ginger traveled downtown, both were silent.

Kim knew something had opened inside her heart. It was a strange experience she hadn't felt since she was a child. Was it guilt? The guilt of knowing that what she was doing with her boss was wrong no matter how she tried to push it out of her mind?

Sensing that Kim needed some time to sort out her own thoughts, Ginger sought comfort in the view of the mainland shore between Belle Isle and downtown. The gently falling snowflakes cascaded to the ground, making a feathery cushion that blanketed the earth. As they drove, the delicate frozen ice crystals appeared larger, like feathers bursting in a pillow fight, creating a veil around their vehicle.

It was cold. Winter cold. Kim turned up the heat a notch, and caught the look of serenity on Ginger's face. "Pretty, isn't it?" said Kim, trying to clear the air.

"Yeah. I love the wintertime." Ginger sighed, snuggling deeper inside her black wool cape. "Twenty inches could fall and it wouldn't bother me. Most people are scared of driving in this kind of weather. But after ten years of driving alone on the highway to Champion Motors five and six days a week during my first marriage, I've gotten to be a fairly good driver. The only thing that bothers me is the ice." She shook her head, stretching, extending her pumps to feel the heat on her toes.

"Look over there," said Kim, pointing to an old warehouse. "That's where Randall lives. Entrepreneurs have converted warehouses and small factories into loft condominiums around here. Some were remodeled into taverns and nightclubs." She saw the sparkle in Ginger's eyes even in the darkness. "Remember I told you how Randall's loft apartment was decorated?" Ginger nodded slowly, recalling the conversation about her friend. "Girl, his loft is laid. He might be there tonight. Maybe we'll stop by la—"

Ginger held up both her hands. "Wait a minute, Kim. I agreed to go out to a club, though I've never been before. And you and Mama both know I don't usually go out by myself. Going to the club is stretching it a bit—but I could use a little diversion right now. I've got a lot on my mind. But going to some man's apartment is altogether a different situation."

"Okay, okay, girlfriend. And you're perfectly right. You're a married woman—I'm single." Her voice rose an octave. "Seems like I've been single forever."

Her cousin suddenly seemed older than her years. Ginger had never considered that Kim wanted to be anything but single. Sure, she and Bill loved each other, but she'd confided in Ginger on numerous occasions that she loved her freedom. What had happened lately to make her change her mind? Something was bothering Kim. She always appeared to have herself together, cool, calm, and collected. Nothing ruffled her feathers. But tonight her cousin's mood hinted at something that required further investigation.

The Renaissance Center, lighted and glistening, was the focal point of downtown. Hailed as "The glass canister set," the Westin Hotel, the tallest building in the Renaissance, dominated the city's waterfront skyline. The observation deck atop the Westin surrounded the rotating Summit Restaurant. From there, the seventy-second floor, Detroit spread out in a vast green-and-brown checkerboard of flattened smokestacks down to the river. On the water's other side, verdant southwest Ontario could be seen.

As they turned down Jefferson into Greek Town, the restaurant district, the scent of roast lamb and *saganaki* filled their nostrils. They turned to each other, smiling, admiring the swarm of well-dressed people walking the streets.

"Damn, it smells good," said Ginger, turning in a 180-degree arc trying to capture everything, recording the sights and sounds, the laughter of people having a good time. It seemed as if they had entered a different place in time. The architecture of the buildings was impressive. Some had been renovated to be more modern while others captured the romantic designs of the Greek culture.

"Can we eat first? Mama cooked steak and potatoes for dinner, but for some reason, I'm starved." Ginger felt younger than she had in years. It was as if she were Cinderella, out for an enchanted evening. But in her case, there was no Prince Charming—Jackson. A sadness crept over her as she wished she were sharing this time with the man she loved.

"I know just the place. We'll eat at Fishbone's. They serve Cajun food, and it has an indoor waterfall that's the largest in the United States," said Kim, steering Ginger toward the building spelling out the name in red neon.

Ginger paused outside the door to admire a couple and an accompanying party of loved ones who were celebrating around what looked like an anniversary cake. The party was framed in the full-length picture window at the front of the restaurant. Jackson and Ginger's anniversary was just three weeks away. Maybe she'd surprise him and make reservations here.

*   *   *

"Your résumé is impressive, Dr. Little." He flipped the pages, pacing the floor, looking up every now and then, reading the excellent references from hospitals and head psychiatrists whom she'd worked with over the years. He could sense she was tense.

"Thank you, Dr. Harris. I hope everything meets with your satisfaction." Sheila Little stood nervously in the middle of the room, trying to appear calm, not wanting him to know how badly she needed this job.

Bill motioned for her to have a seat. "Please excuse the mess. We're running a little behind schedule." Her rich, chocolate brown skin was smooth and unlined. He noticed faint creases of indentation on the bridge of her nose. Probably reading glasses, he reasoned. Her hair was fashioned in a casual pageboy, which added to her youthful appearance. Short, manicured nails were coated with clear polish. She wore a plain taupe midcalf coatdress with dark brown alligator pumps and matching purse. Everything bespoke a seasoned professional.

"You're planning on opening by the fifteenth of May, right?" She looked around the office cubicles. Although they were renovating an existing building, there was still a lot of work to be completed, he explained. The building had been vacant for some time and had been the target of numerous vandals. All the plumbing had been ripped out. The wiring needed to be replaced in several of the rooms. The shiny green and gray unit housed at the end of the building, he told her, was a newly installed furnace. Crunched paper cups and potato-chip bags circled the barrel trash can—careless shots from workers trying to imitate Michael Jordan's long shot.

"Even if I have to hire an additional crew, we'll be good to go in less than eight weeks. It's important to show people that we can and will be operating in a timely fashion. I deplore excuses." Sheila nodded as he went on. "I want to earn the respect of the community by showing it the staff's dedication and commitment to excellent service."

"We want the Black dollars circulating in our city, spent in our city," she stated, smiling. Her respect for this man was growing by the minute. He seemed truly dedicated.

"My sentiments exactly," agreed Bill. "We also want the residents of our city to seek out the services of Blacks. Black businesses must court Black clients. Impress upon them that the programs we provide for our patients and families are equal to, if not better than, the treatments in neighboring White clinics. We have to let our patients and their parents know that money spent in Black businesses strengthens our community as a whole."

"I agree. Black liberation doesn't come merely from doing business. We need a collective effort, as much as cultural. A self-sufficient community can spawn its own power base, and it will gain respect from even its most hostile enemies. And we all know, 'The only thing power respects is power.' "

Sheila felt a little embarrassed by her enthusiasm expressed so openly to a man she'd just met. But somehow she felt comfortable with him.

They talked for hours about their ideas. Bill was surprised that most of her goals mirrored his. After their third cup of coffee, from the small pot used daily by the workers, they had shed the formalities of Dr. Harris and Dr. Little and were calling each other Bill and Sheila.

Sheila smiled easily, slightly embarrassed. "I don't usually talk so much." He had been so easy to talk to. They had so many ideas in common. He hadn't discussed anything personal, but there was no hint that he was married, or engaged. So she assumed he was single.

Bill was sure they would work well together. His warm smile mirrored hers as they put on their coats to leave.

"Ginger, you look gorgeous in that dress." Kim stepped back and appraised her as they handed their coats to the attendant. "And a mini—mmmmmmm—what's gotten into you, girl-friend? You going through the change?" She chided Ginger.

"As a matter of fact, Sierra picked out this dress for me," said Ginger proudly. "She told me it was about time I kept up with the new fashion trends." Out of habit, she smoothed her hair, feeling for the strategically placed barrette.

They chose a table near the dance floor. A few couples slow-danced on the lighted platform. Strobe lights of red, blue, and green flashed radial patterns along the walls, ceiling, and floor.

Kim was whisked off to the dance floor a few minutes after their drinks arrived. Ginger looked around the room, checking the ratio of women to men. The women outnumbered the men at least four to one. Probably no one would ask her to dance under the circumstances, but panic began to set in. What if someone did ask her to dance? Would she look stupid refusing them? Oh, Lord, she thought. Why did I agree to go to a club, knowing I don't dance? I can't expect Kim to baby-sit me all evening. Maybe I should just—

"Excuse me, miss. Would you care to dance?" A devilishly attractive man approached her table, his hand extended to take hers. Instead, she shook her head, issuing a polite no thank you. Kim was watching, hoping Ginger would take a chance and go for it. The gentleman was gracious, and when he turned to ask another woman to dance, she quickly accepted him. They were all dancing to Oleta Adams's "Get Here."

Damn, I love that record, thought Ginger. It wasn't as if she had to fast-dance, hoping that she wouldn't mess up. It was a slow record—and slow dancing was easy. Even though Jackson hadn't taken her dancing in years, they would slow-drag to an oldie in their bedroom sometimes. And when the feeling hit them, they'd slow-dance nude, beginning their foreplay standing, instead of lying down.

"Ginger!" said Kim, almost out of breath. "Why didn't you dance?" She filled her lungs with smoke, blowing it out between pants.

"You know what, Kim?" said Ginger, leaning across the table. "You need to give up those cigarettes. Hardly anyone smokes anymore. Haven't you heard? They're going out of style."

Kim tapped her cigarette against the rim of the ashtray. "Touché, my dear. Maybe someday I will. You know how many suits I could've bought instead of paying for these expensive-ass sticks of tobacco?"

"A lot. I nagged Jackson to death until he quit. Almost two packs a day—Marlboros. Everywhere in the house, red, black, and white crumpled packages. Filled ashtrays stinking in our room. The ceiling above his recliner had turned yellow. I made him smoke outside."

"Mama makes me do the same thing. Sometimes, I sneak in my room, if I'm desperate. But she's got a nose like a beagle, and since Daddy's been sick I kinda feel guilty upsetting her any more than necessary."

"How's Uncle Ollie doing?"

Behind the veil of smoke, Kim's eyes darkened. "Mama called me at work today. The nurse said he's stopped talking."

So that was why she was so upset earlier. "I'm sorry, Kim. Mama told me that she and Aunt Jewel talked the other day. She's worried about Aunt Jewel, too. She said she didn't sound like herself."

Kim brushed off a young man rocking to the beat of Janet Jackson who wouldn't leave until she agreed to dance before the evening was out. "Ginger, I don't know what I'd do if both of them got sick. How can I take care of them and work? I have to work, somebody's got to pay the bills. Sure, they've got some savings, but not much."

Ginger thought *she* had problems. She'd heard the horror stories about how they treated the elderly in those homes. It was terrible. The nursing homes that had good reputations were so expensive the average working person couldn't afford them. Kim made an excellent salary, but Ginger knew that would put a strain on her.

"Kim, I think we're jumping to conclusions here. Uncle Ollie is going to get better, and Aunt Jewel is—"

"Kim. I didn't expect to see you here tonight," came a voice from behind her.

As she turned around, the familiar scent of Calvin Klein's Eternity for Men was in the air. She looked into a pair of beautiful turquoise eyes, and grinned. "Randall. Have a seat. I'd like you to meet my cousin, Ginger."

"The one you talk so much about?" He bent down to shake Ginger's hand and smiled. "Hi. I'm Randall Pierce." He pulled out a chair and sat next to Ginger.

And I thought Paul Newman had the prettiest blue eyes I'd ever seen on a man. Lord have mercy, Ginger thought. "Hi, nice to meet you."

"You're planning to sell real estate, right?" She nodded, still staring. "Kim said you'll be working at the Century Twenty-one office downtown."

Her voice, normally deep and husky, sounded more so as she answered him. "Yes, but only part time."

"In the beginning," said Kim. "I'd bet money she'll be on full time by the end of the year."

Ginger shrugged her shoulders. "Maybe by next year if the housing market stays steady like it has been."

"It's like a lady's dress," said Randall, glancing down at her silken, golden thighs, "it can only go down so low, it can only go up so high." He returned his gaze to Kim, as she gave him a sultry smile.

Ginger dropped her eyes, not wishing him to read her thoughts. How could she be thinking these kinds of thoughts? And about a White man too. If Jackson ever thought she was looking at a White man he'd—

"Do you sing?" asked Randall, breaking her musings.

"No. No I don't."

"Your voice is so deep."

Kim and Ginger exchanged smiles. "Trust me. I can't sing a note."

Kim asked Randall to tell Ginger about his apartment as Kim excused herself to dance with the young man who'd been by their table earlier. Studying them from the dance floor, Kim saw that Ginger was smiling, sipping on her second spicy fuzzy-navel cocktail. She had guessed that when Ginger and Randall finally met they would instantly like each other. She was pleased that she'd been right.

Bill didn't understand her friendship with Randall. Kim assumed it was because Bill had little patience with White people. He couldn't think that there was anything sexual between them, could he?

Later, as they walked to Kim's car, Ginger was bubbling over with excitement. "I had a great time. Thanks for remembering I had an early class. I guess that last drink clouded my memory."

It was just past midnight; the icy stars glittered outside. Ginger glanced up at the starry sky, wondering what Jackson was doing at this exact hour. Was he sleeping, or out on the

town as she was? She couldn't bear to think of him smiling
into some woman's face, dancing cheek to cheek, feeling the
warmth of another's body pressing against his.

"I guess Bill couldn't make it." Kim buckled her seat belt
and started the ignition.

Ginger heard the sadness in her cousin's voice. They both
sat quietly, thinking their own thoughts, as Kim entered the
freeway and drove toward home. Ginger had really enjoyed
her evening with Kim. But now, feeling the chill of the
weather and knowing a cold, empty bed awaited her at
home—she began to have worrisome fantasies about Jackson's evening.

"Kim?"

"Hmmmmm?"

"You think Jackson's out with someone else?"

"Ginger, that alcohol must be kicking in real strong about
now." Kim took a quick glance away from the road, to study
the solemn face and glazed eyes of her cousin. Trouble was,
she was feeling a bit melancholy tonight herself—wondering
what Bill was doing. Funny, she'd never worried about him
before. "Listen to me, Ginger. You're everything that Jackson needs in a woman. You don't have to worry about a
thing."

"I know it, and you know it. What worries me is, does he
know it?"

13

Reach Out and Touch (Somebody's Hand)

Tears flowed down her bronzed cheeks as she sat next to her husband seated in his wheelchair. Jewel was crying because Ollie had responded once, and she, Katherine, and Kim had been there for an hour. "Honey . . . please. Can you say my name, Ollie?" asked Jewel. Her voice was soft and soothing.

He began to cry too, tears overflowing his red-rimmed eyes. He willed his mind to move his lips. If she only knew how hard he was trying to speak. But he could only stare, his mouth barely open, slightly curved upwards on the left, creasing his smooth face.

The back of Ollie's wheelchair rested against the window. He shifted his eyes from his wife's lowered head, her wrinkled hand cupping her mouth, and focused on the shuffling elderly man being escorted by the nurse down the hall. He pitied him. He pitied himself. He pitied all the old-timers who could only look back . . . look back. . . .

A wisp of wintry air seeped through the green canvas curtains onto the back of his neck. Kim wiped her father's damp face and kissed his moist cheek as she pulled up the collar of his striped terry-cloth robe.

Kim swallowed hard, and willed back the tears that threatened to fall. She put her arm around her mother's shoulder, shaking her gently. When she glanced into her aunt Katherine's face, Kim could see that she, too, was crying. Jewel composed herself, then asked Kim and Katherine to give her and Ollie a few moments alone together. There was something important she needed to tell him.

Ollie glanced down at his lower body, silently praying for some kind of evidence that he was still a man. That all of his body hadn't withered away with age and time. But his penis was nowhere to be found. His manhood had recoiled like a snail. That's how it will look when I die, he thought.

Jewel formed Ollie's hands into a steeple, and she held on tight, bowing her head and closing her eyes. "Lord, I need you to bless my husband. He's a good man, Lord. You asked for commitment of our lives to you; we've been faithful Christians. You've been generous to us over the years, Lord. And I know this life that we claim as our own belongs to you and is only loaned to us to manage for a while. But please, Lord—grant us a few more years together. Heal him. I know only you can." She kissed the tips of his fingers, placing them back on his lap.

She saw the hopeful look in his eyes, and a soothing calmness flowed through her body. "Listen to God with your mind; listen to God with your heart. Listen to God speaking to you, and God will be with you. See God in all those you love. Touch God in them and let them touch you." She smoothed his moist cheeks lovingly. Rising, she bent down to kiss him on the mouth.

"Sweetheart, you're going to get better, I know it. I love you, honey. I love you so much." Her voice drifted off as she met his eyes. She began to think what their years of marriage had been like. Looking into his eyes, still youthful and clear, she felt the rapid beating of his heart, then put her arms around him.

"Is everything all right in here, Mrs. Lee?" called a nurse from the doorway.

Jewel looked into her husband's eyes and smiled. She

turned, tears of pleasure streaming down her face. Her heart was so full of love for him. "We're fine . . . just fine."

The celery-green floor in the nursing-home waiting room shone like new money, its layers of wax buffed to perfection. Worn beige sofas lined the walls. A black metal magazine rack rested against the receptionist's counter. Unlike the bland drapes in the patients' rooms, cheery green, beige, and peach floral drapes graced the windows. The morning's sunlight poured in through the off-white sheers. A triangular coffee table wedged in the corner was covered with paper cups, plastic spoons, a basket filled with packets of sugar and Cremora, and a commercial-size aluminum coffeepot.

Katherine and Kim headed for the freshly brewed tank, mixed their cups to suit their taste, and sat hands apart on the sofa. "At least the coffee's good," said Kim, resting her head back against the wall. "Aunt Katherine, I just don't know what to say to Mama anymore. Daddy's getting worse and worse."

Katherine rocked back and forth, smoothing her knees with her large hands. "Sometimes it's better to say nothing."

As Kim rose to refill her cup, Katherine handed her hers. "I could use a cold beer, but since there seems to be none available, I'll settle for a second cup. Puts lots of cream in mine," Katherine added.

Kim turned to face her aunt, a worried expression on her face. "Aunt Katherine," she heaved, her large breasts rising and falling slowly, "I'm worried about Mama, too."

"Why on earth—"

"Wait 'til I tell you what she was doing when I got home last night. She . . ."

"Didn't you and Ginger get home around twelve-thirty?" Kim nodded. "And Jewel was still up?"

"Up and painting."

"Painting."

"Painting her bedroom with the heat all the way up to a hundred and five degrees."

"What!" exclaimed Katherine, nearly choking on the hot liquid.

Kim sat back, folding her arms on her lap. "She was stark naked with a plastic trash bag over her with a hole cut out in top for her head." A gasp echoed from Katherine. "I said, 'Mama, what you doing up this late painting?' She said, 'I'm getting the room ready for Ollie to come home." Okay, I thought to myself, I can deal with that. 'Why is the heat up so high, Mama?' I said. She said, 'It was cold in here.' I said, 'Mama, why don't you put some clothes on then?' She said, 'I don't want to get any paint on 'em.' "

"Bless her soul. This past year has been harder on her than I thought."

"I finally coaxed her to bed, after reminding her how tired she was going to be when we came to see Daddy this morning. She'd forgotten about the visit today." Kim sighed deeply, exhaling an abundance of pent-up air. She bit her lower lip until it throbbed like her quickened pulse. "Do you think I should take her in for a complete examination?"

"It wouldn't hurt," said Katherine in a concerned tone. "I'll tell you what—give me a few days. I'll call my doctor at home and see if he can recommend a good doctor. She's complained to me on more than one occasion that she was unhappy using Ollie's doctor. Under the circumstances we should find another for her."

"Aunt Katherine?" Kim asked slowly. "Do you miss Uncle Lewis a lot since he died? I know it sounds like a dumb question, but I've wondered how long a time period a person grieved over a loved one."

"It all depends on how much they happened to love that person. Lewis and I loved each other, but not like your mama and daddy. They've shared the kind of love rarely experienced by two people." A shamed look fell over her face. "I didn't have that with Lewis."

"I'm sorry, Aunt Katherine."

"I've learned a few things in my lifetime. Most of which I wished I'd known before I married Lewis. Deciding who you marry is the most important decision you'll ever make. Because marriages are meant to last a lifetime, like your father and mother's. When they don't, your children, your neighbors, society, and all the world suffer. They say it's never too late to heal an injured relationship. God knows I tried everything I knew how to keep Lewis's and mine together." Tears formed in her eyes.

"You know, Kim," she said, dabbing her eyes with a tissue, "Ollie and Jewel have real love. The kind of love that stands the test of time. You remember that love affair in *Pretty Woman*?"

"Yeah, that was great. I could watch it over and over again. I loved it. Why can't life be like that?" said Kim dreamily.

"Because love stories in movies are just figments of someone's imagination. They're only single moments in time. Real love in a marriage or relationship works when you make the transition from falling in love to being in love."

Was that where she and Bill were? Still falling in love, but not yet feeling the commitment of being in love? A vision of love, was that all that her and Bill's relationship would turn out to be—her vision?

Her mother insisted that what makes the difference in a relationship and binds two people together is a public commitment. An official document. Men and women will always differ on the expectations, negotiations, and transformations in a marriage. But when you commit to marrying someone, it proves you're willing to go that extra mile to make sure it works. Well, she was not ready for that yet.

After bathing the boys and reading them their nightly bedtime story, Mae Thelma allowed herself to luxuriate in a steamy bubble bath, filled with the sweetness of jonquil-honeysuckle crystals. She relaxed in the solitude of her private little pool until the insides of her fingers crinkled like dried prunes.

Her evening had come to a jarring end because of a shouting match with Robert Earl over the phone. She wound up crying, telling him she'd pray for him. That was all she was able to do. He'd fired his latest court-appointed attorney, and they were running out of options.

Couldn't he just once think about her? Her loneliness. Needing someone to hold her. To love her. To whisper sweet words in her ears. She'd worked herself to death every evening, cleaning everything she could, so she'd be too exhausted to feel the desire in her young body.

She flipped through the pages of her Bible until she came to the passage she enjoyed reading:

> Let him kiss me with the kisses of his mouth: for thy love is better than wine. Because of the savour of thy good ointments poured forth, therefore do the virgins love thee.
>
> Draw me, we will run after thee: the King hath brought me into his chambers: we will be glad and rejoice in thee, we will remember thy love more than wine: the upright love thee.
>
> I am black, but comely. O ye daughters of Jerusalem, as the tents of Kedar, as the curtains of Solomon. Look upon me, because I am black, because the sun hath looked upon me: my mother's children were angry with me; they made me the keeper of the vineyards; but mine own have I not kept. . . .

Yet, instead of seeing her body lying nude next to the caramel-skinned body of her husband, his straight, jet black hair brushed back close to his head, she saw the rich dark chocolate skin of a man with cropped wiry hair smiling slyly at her through large white teeth.

> . . . His left hand is under my head, and his right hand doth embrace me. I charge you, O daughters of Jerusalem, by the roes, and by the hinds of the field, that ye stir not up, nor awake my love, 'til he please.
>
> Set me a seal upon thine heart, as a seal upon thine arm: for love is strong as death; jealousy is cruel as the grave; the coals thereof are coals of fire, which hath a most vehement flame.
>
> Many waters cannot quench love, neither can the floods drown it, if a man would give all the substance of his house for love, it would utterly be contemned.
>
> . . . Awake, O north wind; and come, thou south; blow upon my garden, that the spices thereof may flow

out. Let my beloved come into his garden, and eat his pleasant fruits.

Mae Thelma closed the black leather book, smoothing her long fingers along the shiny gold-edged pages. Lying outstretched like an angel on the bed, using the Bible under her head as a pillow, she prayed for forgiveness for the adulterous thoughts that were so vivid in her mind. So real. But when she lifted her head upwards for guidance, her eyes shut tight, and the vision of a tall, dark male reached out his hand, beckoning her to come . . . come to him.

That Sunday, Ginger had a dinner party with Mae Thelma, her boys, Kim, Bill, Katherine, and Autumn. Kim had pleaded with her mother to stay home. Jewel assented, adding that she was a little tired from church this morning. By the time Kim left home at three-thirty that afternoon, Jewel had fallen asleep on the couch, the Bible perched on her lap.

Dinner was a success, thanks to Katherine's succulent turkey and dressing. Surprisingly, Mae Thelma's boys weren't any trouble at all. Bill had spent time telling them stories after they'd finished dessert. Jackson's name had also been mentioned a lot.

"I'm glad that's over, Mama," said Ginger, flopping down at the table. "I thought they weren't ever going to leave."

Katherine urged Ginger to rest, placing a cup of hot Lipton tea before her. After putting away the dinner leftovers, Katherine joined Ginger, selecting a glass of Pepsi over a cold brew.

"Given up alcohol, Ma?" said Ginger, lifting an inquisitive brow.

"Just tired of beer for the time being. Haven't given it up. Just had enough." Katherine remembered hearing the preacher say today, "Save us Lord, not from *ourselves*, but for *ourselves*."

Katherine had gotten up for the early-bird service at 7:00 A.M. Ginger could never manage to get the kids ready on Sunday before ten-thirty. The congregation was quickly growing, and it was difficult to get seats at the 11:00 A.M.

service. "Does this have anything to do with you and Aunt Jewel going to church this morning? You had an odd expression on your face when you came home. Is something wrong, Mama? Your asthma isn't acting up again, is it?"

Katherine shook her head. "No to all three questions. As far as church goes, I enjoyed the service. It was uplifting. For me as well as Jewel. Funny how the pastor knows just the right words to comfort you, and Jewel seems better."

Autumn walked up behind her mother and hugged her around the neck. "Mommy, are the kids coming home tonight?" she asked with hopeful eyes.

Ginger reached her arm around, patting her baby on the back. "Yes, baby. They should be home around eight." She looked at her watch; it was barely six-thirty. She searched her mother's eyes for help.

"Autumn, you wanna do Granny a big favor?" Katherine patted her thigh, urging Autumn to take a seat. A smile beamed across the girl's face, her two pigtails flopping like wings. "Granny's clothes are downstairs on the ironing board."

"I know, Granny, you want me to pack your suitcase for you. You going home today, huh?"

"Yep, Granny's catching a ride back with the kids' father when he comes so your mommy won't have to drive seventy miles to take me home." She kissed her granddaughter on the forehead. "We don't want to tire your mommy out before your daddy gets home, do we?"

"No, Granny. My daddy said he's bringing me something special back from his trip." She turned to look at her mother. "When is Daddy coming home, Mommy?"

"Tuesday, baby. Remember the days of the week you learned at Sleepy Hollow. Today is Sunday—"

"Tomorrow is Monday, and the day after that is Tuesday." She unfolded her fingers as she counted the days. "That's three days. Daddy'll be home in three days with my present." She drew a large circle with her hands. "And Daddy says it's big." She jumped off her granny's lap and hugged her mother, rubbing noses with her mother and kissing her mother's buttery cheek.

"I know how to pack your bag, Granny. I helped Daddy

pack his bag. He told me I was a big girl—and big girls can do everything. Right, Mommy?" Ginger smiled sweetly at her daughter and patted her narrow buttocks before she skipped off downstairs.

"Ginger, I declare that girl looks so much like her daddy, I'd swear he spit her out. The only thing she took from you is her keen nose."

"Leave my baby alone, Mama," said Ginger, blushing. "She does have the cutest little button nose, doesn't she?" Katherine nodded as she finished the last of her Pepsi. "She's been asking me when she's going to get a bridge like mine and the rest of the kids. She doesn't like that little button in the middle of her face." Ginger and Katherine both laughed.

"Time. When she's ten years old, she won't remember ever not having one. Remember when Christian's and Jason's noses sat on their faces like that?" Katherine said knowingly.

Ginger thought fondly of her boys' small noses, and how she'd wondered if they'd ever resemble hers and their father's. Katherine had assured her, no child was born with a keen nose like hers, they had to grow into their schnozzes. But then Sierra was born, pale as pie dough, fire red hair, and a sharp, pointed nose, complete with a bridge, and Katherine had had to eat her words. "Yeah, I remember, Mama."

"Well, this baby ain't no different. Autumn's got to grow into it. Yes sir, she's got the same fine line of baby hair outlining her face, full lips, and a tall narrow body just like him. Them hard legs of hers remind me of a young colt, just learning how to walk."

Ginger thought of Jackson's nude body as he stepped from the shower, his firm body glistening as he toweled himself off. She smiled, shaking her head slightly, recalling how the soap suds ran along his hairline at the base of his neck. He never seemed to remember to rinse the soap from his hair. Standing behind him, she would wipe away the suds, her eyes feasting on the beauty of his physique as he shaved.

"Don't talk about my baby's legs, Mama. Jackson's got terrific legs—and so will she."

"Sure, sure," said Katherine, rising to clear the table.

Ginger followed her into the kitchen. "Mama, do you think Kim's been acting a little strange? She was so quiet today—and when he wasn't taking time with the children, so was Bill. Something's wrong." She reached in the cabinet, searching for her vitamins, which weren't in their usual place.

Katherine reached around Ginger, opening the cabinet next to her. "Is this what you're looking for?" She handed her four brown bottles. "Ain't nothing wrong with them two that a good night of screwing won't cure."

"Mama!" Ginger counted out the vitamins in her hand, gulping them down with water.

Katherine wasn't paying her any attention; she was looking in the refrigerator. "So they had an argument—everybody does." She kicked the door shut with her foot after she tucked a bottle of Colt 45 under her arm.

"I thought you gave that up for today?" said Ginger, looking into the refrigerator for something to snack on that wasn't fattening. She settled for a bruised golden Delicious apple. Cutting off the brown spots and rinsing it clean, she joined her mother, who'd already consumed half the bottle of cold brew.

Katherine eyed her daughter as she belched loudly. "That sneaky-looking Mae Thelma is who you should be concerned about." Ginger's eyes bugged out as she studied her mother's I-bet-I-know-something-you-don't face. "Every time you mentioned Jackson's name, that sanctified whore feasted on every word, like he was the main course, instead of the turkey and dressing piled on her plate."

"Mama. She's so nice. This is one time you don't know what you're talking about. That's Jackson's cousin's wife." Her mind retraced the conversation at the dinner table earlier. When she thought about it for a minute, Mae Thelma did seem a bit interested in hearing about when Jackson was coming back home. No. She was saved. She wouldn't even think of looking at another man. Especially Jackson—would she?

"I don't give a damn how saved and sanctified she is. She's still a woman." Katherine took another swig of beer and wagged the bottle in Ginger's face while she continued. "I asked her when her husband was coming home from jail." Katherine gave Ginger another one of her knowing looks.

"Mama, you shouldn't have done that. Mae Thelma doesn't like to mention it to other people. I hope you didn't say anything in front of Bill?"

"Do I look like a damned fool to you?"

"No, Ma."

"Tact. Something you don't have. Tact." Katherine sat back in her seat, sipping on the last of her beer. "Gonna be a while before he gets out. Her ass should be getting plenty hot by the summer, you mind what I'm saying."

"Isn't it obvious she knows how to pray? She carries that Bible with her everywhere she goes."

"Don't mean diddly shit to a young woman in heat. Pretty, too."

"What about *older* women in heat?" asked Ginger, seeing her mother's body tense.

Katherine creased a fold in the waxed paper to keep the air from getting into the rest of her crackers. She lifted her robust frame from the table, glaring at her Ginger. "You know, if you had an ounce—"

"Granny," called a sweet voice from the hallway. Autumn came in with a big smile on her face. She grabbed her granny's hand, using her tiny body to pull her from the room. "Come see."

Katherine softened her features into a smile. She rolled her eyes at Ginger as she left the room hand in hand with Autumn. Just in time, before she cussed out her daughter. Something she really didn't want to do, knowing how much Ginger was missing Jackson, and knowing how insecure she was feeling about her hair. And Mae Thelma sitting there earlier looking like a Greek goddess with enough hair for Rapunzel. Katherine saw Ginger staring at the younger woman's hair with such envy in her eyes, she almost couldn't stand it.

Although Katherine's daughter had lashed out at her, the problem was, Ginger was right. Her ass was getting a might overheated lately, and she planned on doing something about it. Soon. Point was, a horny bitch could always smell another bitch in heat, and Mae Thelma's scent was evident to Katherine even through all that sweet-smelling honey-suckle.

14

The Tracks of My Tears

Ginger and the children huddled around the television set in the family room. Channel Two news was on, and Ginger sat watching patiently as they waited for Jason to end a phone call to his girlfriend so they could have a family discussion.

"See, that's him, Mama," said Sierra, pointing to the handsome face on the screen.

Ginger turned her head to watch the good-looking young man in his late twenties who was anchoring the six o'clock news. His striking gray eyes caught Ginger's attention, and she was certain he must have had the same effect on her daughter. His Hershey's light-chocolate skin resembled Sierra's. A tad light for Ginger's taste, but great-looking all the same. "He's cute, Sierra."

"Cute," butted in Autumn. "Mommy, Ivory Michaels's superfine."

"If you say so." Ginger turned toward the doorway—what was keeping Jason? Anxiously she looked at her watch, it had been almost—

"Here he comes, Ma," said Christian, hearing the sound of footsteps.

"Yo, Ma, what up?" called Jason, from across the room, drinking orange juice from a quart bottle.

"I hope you bought that juice from work, and it didn't come from the refrigerator. I told you about drinking from the bottle."

"Chill, Ma. I brought it home with me," he said, flopping down beside her on the couch. Autumn and Sierra still sat mesmerized by the articulate figure on the screen. Jason smiled as he watched his sisters' attentiveness to the set. He'd seen them many a night, agog over this man on television who looked like a sissy to him—his hair was too straight, nose a bit too pointed, and his lips were too narrow for a Black man. He couldn't possibly shoot any hoops with those well-manicured nails of his. Nope, pure fag, thought Jason.

Christian was busy eyeing the female co-anchor, a woman who looked like Liz Taylor. Even had the same first name. Elizabeth Guest. Big boobs that strained against her tight silk blouse. He hoped it wouldn't be long before he'd be joining his brother with a list of conquests. He turned his attention back to his mother.

"—anyway, that's what I hope to be able to do within the next year, if everything goes as planned," said Ginger, looking around at their inquiring faces after she'd explained about her plans for changing jobs.

"I'm all for it, Ma," said Jason, The other three chorused a yes, nodding their approval.

Ginger stood, pacing the floor in front of them. Turning down the volume on the set, she was amused to see the unhappy looks on Autumn's and Sierra's faces. Well, Ginger thought, if a handsome anchor was the only way to get them to watch something informative and mind-stimulating, instead of the endless music videos they watched on BET, so be it.

The problem was, when Jackson found out about their crush on Ivory Michaels, all hell would break loose. He was so old-fashioned. He'd already told Autumn she couldn't have a boyfriend until she was sixteen. Autumn had confided in her mother that she already had a boyfriend in nursery school. He slept beside her every day at nap time, and they ate lunch together at the picnic table. How romantic, thought Ginger, wryly. But judging from the moonstruck look she'd seen on her daughter's face, it was.

"I'm hoping that the four of you will keep the house clean for me, until . . . until I can convince Jackson to get a house-keeper." Her voice lowered. "Perhaps it won't be too long. Anyway, I'm hoping that you, Christian," she said, pointing at him, "can fry chicken for me, once or twice a week."

Christian had learned to fry chicken well over the past few months. He'd watched his mother so many times, waiting for her to lift the crispy wings from the bubbly golden grease as his mouth watered in anticipation. He'd decided he could imitate her cooking skills. One evening when Ginger had worked twelve hours, Christian surprised her and had the chicken fried and hot when she got home. Sierra had reluctantly made a salad. Autumn had made Kool-Aid.

Ginger quickly added, "I plan on adding to your allowance, Pie Face." That got an eager response. "Fifteen a week." Christian tucked his bottom lip, sucking merrily as his mind did a quick calculation of the monthly benefit. If the increase lasted for a while, by the end of the year he'd have tucked away quite a sum. Close to three hundred dollars would be added to his other stash. Yep, he hoped this would last awhile.

"What can I do, Mama?" asked Sierra. "I can clean real good. But I can't cook nothin' but pancakes."

Ginger hugged her daughter, patting her on the head. "I don't see anything wrong with eating pancakes every once in a while for dinner, do you, Autumn?" The little girl shook her head no, eagerly agreeing. Autumn's favorite food happened to be pancakes.

"Yo Ma. You know I can't cook," said Jason, bouncing his basketball on the polished tile. "I don't want to learn how either. My wife gonna cook for me. That's a woman's job." He looked at Christian, giving him the fag sign.

"No it isn't. When a woman works, everybody should help with dinner."

"Not in my house," muttered Jason under his breath.

Autumn cradled Suzy and stood beside her mother, taking her hand. "I'll help you, Mommy. What you want me to do?"

Ginger whisked her up in her arms, hugging her and kissing her on her brown cheeks. "You can help Sierra make the salad in the evenings and butter the biscuits. How's that sound?"

"How much more do I get on my allowance, Mommy?" asked Autumn eagerly.

"Five more dollars a week. Is that okay?" Even though Autumn was much younger than her other children, Ginger didn't want her to feel left out by not getting a weekly allowance. She genuinely wanted to help. Ginger also noticed that her math skills at school were sharper. Counting a few silver coins, a crisp dollar bill, worked wonders in math computations.

Autumn tried to figure out exactly how much more that would be, when added to the three she already got. She looked at her small fisted hands, slowly lifted one finger at a time, and silently counted under her breath, until Sierra kicked her.

"That's ten a week for you, Sierra. Is that okay?"

Her eyes lit up like two candles burning inside. She leaned forward on the sofa, managing at last to tear herself away from the glances she'd been stealing at Ivory Michaels. "I can buy me a new outfit next week. When do we start, Mama? Do we get our extra money this week?"

"Yes, starting this week. Mama's got classes this week and next week. I can help you guys for two weeks until I start working in the office at the beginning of next month, then you're on your own. How's that sound? I want to make sure you're doing everything just right, so Jackson won't fuss, okay?"

"You're excused, Jason. I just want you to remember that this is a secret we're keeping from Jackson. I don't care how you feel about women's lib. You're still just a child to me, even though you're doing other things." She gave him a naughty stare. "If you know what I mean?"

He gave her a smile, picking up his basketball as he stood. "Ma, don't get me wrong. I want you to quit your job at the factory. If I can help around the house—" he stopped bouncing the ball, tucking it under his muscled arms—"that is, on the days I don't have to work, I'd be more than happy to pitch in." He kissed his mother on the cheek.

"Thanks, Jason. I'm sure I can figure out something for you to do and work around your schedule." An unpleasant thought was nagging at her lately. She hadn't remembered seeing Jason do any homework lately. "Jason, have you been keeping up with your studies?"

"I got it covered, Ma."

"Sure?" She stared deeply into his eyes, looking for a quick glint of betrayal. She detected a split-second hesitation while his eyes caught up with the lie.

Jason nodded a yes, slowly, as he fingered the sparse hairs on his chin. Trying to skip the subject, he said, "I'll do what I can to help, Ma."

Instantly, the phone rang as if summoned by Jason's guilty conscience. "As a matter of fact, I already got it worked out." She gave him her best imitation of one of his smug smiles as she picked up the phone to answer.

"Hello."

"Hey, girlfriend."

"Kim. How's Aunt Jewel?"

"I don't know. She hasn't spoken a word to me since I came home. I've tried to get her to talk. But she won't answer me. She's been in her room lying down for the last two hours. I know she's not asleep, she keeps tossing and turning."

"Let her be, Kim. She's got a lot on her mind, with your daddy not being able to talk and all. Just give her a little time, to be by herself. That's all she needs."

Kim began crying. Short, panting sounds reached Ginger's ears. "Kim. Take it easy. Everything's going to be okay. Don't take it so hard. You know how much your mother loves you."

"I know," she whispered. "Bill and I got in an argument over the phone while I was at work today. He hasn't got time for me anymore. Couldn't you tell Sunday? He left after he told the little kids stories."

"You've told me how busy he was with opening the clinic. It's got to be a strain on him, Kim."

"Yeah, yeah. But what about the strain on me? My father just had a stroke. My mother and I arguing every other day, about nothing. Just plain nothing. Even Randall turned on me today. I can't take too much more of this bullshit." And my boss fucking with me at work, she wanted to add, but didn't. Things were getting too hectic at work. The new girl, Brenda, was screwing up everything in the office, and George Cameron had blamed Kim for not training her correctly.

The other girls in the office were whispering among themselves, saying Brenda wasn't qualified for the job and was causing them constantly to make excuses to their clients for her ineptness. Ordinarily, Kim would have taken up for any other sister they tried to put down, but in this case they were totally correct in their assumptions. They hinted at her being qualified at other things. Kim was sure she didn't need any training in the other department because Cameron hadn't looked at Kim in a sexual way since Brenda was hired.

"Kim, why don't you call Mama and talk to her. You two seem to be able to get along so well. She'll know how to deal with Aunt Jewel." She paused. "Promise me you'll call her?"

"Sure, I'll call. Ginger—"

"Yeah."

"I'm thinking about quitting my job." Kim blurted out quickly.

"What?"

Randall walked into Cameron's office without knocking. It was past office hours, and he'd been waiting for the last person to leave before approaching him. "What the fuck!—"

"Excuse me, Mr. Pierce," said Brenda, Picking up her bra from the desk, she quickly unstraddled herself from Cameron's lap. She gathered her blouse, clutching it to her bouncing nude breasts, and made a beeline to the door. She looked back at Cameron before closing the paneled entryway.

"I told that stupid bitch to lock the damned door," Cameron muttered under his breath. "And what the fuck do you want?" he asked, zipping up his pants. "I've just about had it with you busting in my office anytime you damned well please," he said, walking around his desk.

Randall took a seat on the burgundy leather chair facing the desk even though he knew he hadn't been asked, and probably wouldn't be. "So that's the reason you hired her. I should have figured it out sooner and saved her the embarrassment. Not that I give a damn about catching you. I've caught you before with other women. I'm tiring of you fucking over my Aunt Sylvie." Reaching inside his breast pocket, he lifted a toothpick and placed it in the corner of his mouth, chewing mildly.

"And by the looks of it, she's getting a little fed up with your indiscretions, too." Randall jutted the toothpick upwards with a flick of his tongue.

"Why, you little bastard . . ." Cameron snapped, standing in front of him.

"If I were you, I'd sit down." Randall stood, his six-foot frame towering over the short man. He swung his raven ponytail around until it hung perfectly down the center of his back. "You weren't planning on hitting me, were you, Uncle?"

Cameron stepped back two steps, resting his buttocks against the back of the desk. "Hell no, what's a piece of pussy between family? You want a piece? She'll fuck you if I tell her to . . . and she's damned good," he added, walking around to sit in a leather padded arm chair. "Or," he said, sarcastically, "would you rather have one of the delivery boys?"

Blood rushed to his face, but Randall remained cool, refusing to stoop to this level. He smiled smugly to himself, sure that the cocky son of a bitch's days were numbered.

15

My Guy

Closing the door of his apartment, Randall dropped his keys on the kitchen counter, tossed his briefcase on the bar stool, then hung his black cashmere coat in the front hall closet. After pouring himself a glass of Chardonnay, he relaxed in the raspberry suede armchair next to the stereo system.

Extending his long legs, Randall leaned his head back. His Adam's apple strained tight against his tanned skin as he stared at the ceiling while dangling the fluted wineglass carelessly in his right hand. The beauty and serenity of his surroundings, the quiet peace of being alone, made him feel wonderfully tranquil.

Anchored against the west wall was a white lacquered ladder leading up to the loft bed he used primarily for romantic evenings. Dozens of bright pillows splashed color against the blue walls. A wet bar and private bath provided all the necessary furnishings for an evening of lustful indulgence.

He'd painted his apartment in eight shades of blue: royal Hawaiian blue, midnight blue, heavenly blue, Scandinavian sky, royal blue mist, empress blue, cornflower blue, and federal indigo blue. A royal blue sectional chintz sofa accented the mix of his beloved blues. Clouds, painted as though they were billowing in the wind, wafting like sails without need of a boat, were scattered along the twelve-foot-high ceiling and along one wall that had floor-to-ceiling windows.

Large ferns and palms, placed throughout the huge great room, sat on sculptured pedestals. Beautiful paintings framed in antique gilt covered the remaining walls. Anyone visiting his home for the first time would know that Randall was a connoisseur of art. His many treasures included priceless sketches as well as paintings by obscure but interesting artists.

Randall had been obsessed with collecting since the age of twelve. He'd started by going to yard sales, garage sales, antique malls, buying and repairing what he'd found there. He'd found a few minor treasures for as little as three dollars. But with the proper repair, and the perfect frame, the small investments became attractive works. His collection now, at age twenty-four, totaled almost two hundred pieces.

He spent several hours each week restoring his paintings, rematting, reframing, and cleaning them. He learned how to glue torn canvas together, to retouch paint and work chipped paint back onto the paintings. A waterfall oil painting that he was especially fond of had had three layers of paper glued to the back of the original. He'd spent twelve hours removing the paper and glue before reframing the painting.

He took his empty glass to the sink and walked into the bedroom, peeling off clothes along the way. A black iron canopied bed was placed strategically in the center of the huge room on a pedestal of three powder blue carpeted stairs. Silk brocade pillows in cream and dusty pink, trimmed with silk tassled fringes, layered the top half of the bed. Yards of ecru chiffon were casually draped over one corner of the iron canopy, puddling like fresh cream down the steps.

Filmy ecru chiffon drapes framed the floor-to-ceiling windows on either side of the massive fireplace. A Chinese rug clung to the thick, silver blue carpeting. The whir of the ceiling fans overhead at each end of the airy hideaway lent a Mediterranean touch to the formal bedroom.

Combing his fingers through his thick hair, Randall studied the painting he was working on. He walked around the easel tilting his head to see various angles, then placed the wooden tip of the elongated black brush between his teeth and squatted.

He sat there for almost twenty minutes before finally acknowledging to himself that the concept he'd envisioned wouldn't work. The background of the canvas was painted black, echoing his mood, but the essence of the scene that he wanted to convey still eluded him.

The clock in his work room read 10:40 P.M. It was late, but the thought of sleep was far from his mind. So was the thought of going to bed alone. Hesitantly, he dialed a number. When the phone rang and he heard a strange voice uttering hello, he quickly hung up.

A few minutes later, he found himself still staring at the phone. Wondering if he'd accidentally dialed the wrong number, he dialed again. Balancing the cordless phone under his chin, he sipped more wine, covering the easel with a drop cloth.

"Hello."

"Hello," he said, listening for the familiar voice.

"Was that you that called a few minutes ago and hung up?"

Tightening the caps on the tubes of paints, he answered casually, "Yeah, it was me. Who was there?"

"My uncle is here from New York. You could've asked," said the voice defensively.

"Can you come over?" Randall pleaded. "I know it's late, but I need to see you. I miss you. It's been a while."

"Whose fault is that?"

Randall paused, falling back on the cozy sofa, slowly drawing in several deep breaths before answering. "I wanted commitment from you. Is that too much to ask?"

"Look, I've missed you too. But I won't let you force me into making a decision I feel we'll both regret."

Randall felt the heat stirring in his pelvis. He rubbed his growing erection as he spoke into the receiver. "Just come over tonight," he begged. "Is your uncle—"

"He just went to bed. He'll be asleep soon—can you wait?"

He reached inside his pants, extracted his penis, and massaged the outer skin in gentle downward strokes. A faint gasp escaped from his mouth. "Not long."

"I love you—you know."

"I know. Hurry," said Randall, forcing his voice to sound calm.

Running down the aisle, Ginger checked her watch, hoping it was a tad fast. Two minutes and he'd be there. Hurry, hurry, she told herself—you can walk faster than this. Skipping up the escalator stairs in twos, she dropped her purse and keys on the conveyor belt as she quickly walked through the large arch of the metal detector. Bzzzzzz.

"Can you step over here please, miss?"

"Damn," she muttered to herself, "I don't have time for this shit today."

The airport security personnel asked if she had on anything metal, and she assured him she did not. He nodded for her to pass through again. Again the buzzer went off. Several people behind her, also in a hurry, were becoming impatient.

Stepping to the side again, she cursed under her breath as the attendant asked her to remove her coat. She obliged him grudgingly, and he put the coat through the machine—no buzzer. He examined her critically.

Then she remembered. Reaching in the back pocket of her blue jean skirt, she removed a key. She'd tucked the key to her locker at work in her back pocket after Veto had used it to get her coat and purse so her boss wouldn't notice she was sneaking out early. The security man looked at the key and waved her on.

She attached the iron key to her key ring and bounded down the aisle to the designated terminal. Checking her watch again, she looked around, and noticed the gate to the plane was closed. Hardly any of the waiting-area seats were occupied. Panic started to set in. It was just 9:47; she couldn't have missed him. His plane was schedule to land at 9:40. Ginger ran to the desk to inquire.

"Miss?" she said, panting as she placed her hand over her

throbbing chest, "has flight three-o-three arrived?" Her eyes were fixed on the plane taxiing toward gate number Fifteen A.

The flight attendant pointed to the schedule of incoming planes behind her. "That flight was delayed on the layover in Chicago because of the inclement weather. It's not scheduled to land in Metro until eleven fifty-nine A.M."

Damn, what am I going to do for two hours? Ginger wondered in irritation. After a visit to the newsstand, she placed her purse on the vacant seat beside her, balanced her large cup of piping hot lemon tea on her crossed leg, and took out the *Detroit News* from her purse. She began reading the cover story.

"Hi, baby," said Jackson, bending down to kiss Ginger on the mouth. A large package bundled with brown paper crackled noisily as he hoisted it higher on his hip. "I wasn't expecting to—"

"I called Little Bubba last night and told him I'd pick you up. Surprised?" asked Ginger, eyeing the enormous bundle. Flight arrivals being announced over the speakers and the hustle and bustle of crowds of people uttering hellos and "I love you's" added to the noise of the terminal. They were eager to get home.

As they walked past the escalator leading to the baggage area, Ginger started to get on but Jackson pulled her back short. "Luggage won't be in until this evening. I'm not coming back out in this weather; I'll get it tomorrow."

"You going to work in the morning?" asked Ginger, trying to match his long stride. She eyed the parcel again, waiting for an indication of who it was for, but received none.

"Nope. I called in and took two more vacation days. I got a few things I want to do around the house. Something wrong, baby? You're so quiet all of a sudden."

"No, nothing's wrong," she lied. She couldn't take the suspense any longer, and blurted out, "So what's in the bag?"

"Something for my baby." Me, she thought, smiling. "I hope *she* likes it." *She?* "It's a life-size Raggedy Ann doll."

Outside, Ginger's face grew rigid as the cold air slapped

her cheeks. The snow was coming down heavily. They headed for their truck, searching the parking lot for their vehicle, which was indistinguishable from the other snow-covered automobiles.

"It's over here, Jackson," Ginger hollered. Her toes were beginning to freeze solid through the leather soles of her boots. Taking the keys, he opened her door and tossed the package on the seat. Then, he wrapped both his arms around her, kissing her softly on her icy lips. Brushing the snow from her hair, he stopped to kiss a single snowflake from the tip of her fluttering eyelash.

She embraced him lovingly, dismissing her temporary jealousy about the gift for Autumn. She knew it was childish to feel so needy for his affection, but she was unable to help herself. She had missed him terribly. He was here now. Home. She probed his hazel eyes, seeing all she wanted to see—love.

16

Back in My Arms Again

"Ooooohhhhhhh Lord, that's it baby. Ahhhhh," said Jackson, moving his lithe body sensuously above Ginger.

"Let me wipe some of the juice off," said Ginger reaching
for the tissue at the head of the bed.

"No baby, leave it." Jackson panting, as he accelerated his
pace, planting fiery kisses along her arched neck. Reclaiming
her lips, he feathered his tongue in and around the warmth of
her sweet mouth.

Repaying his tantalizing kisses with a soul-reaching massage, she met his body's rhythm, instinctively anticipating
his thrusts. She felt him inside her deeper and deeper, until
she herself was aflame with desire, shuddering in her own
realm of passion.

An essence of dark musk from a group of scented candles
permeated the room. Melodic love songs flowed from the
Nite Mix for lovers program on the console. Flickers of light
bathed Jackson's darkened flesh, his silvery sweat glistening
like morning dew on a tender rose.

He groaned as the walls of her passage tightened greedily

around his throbbing member. It was as if she were draining him, weakening his defenses, as she gripped and released, gripped and released, until he exploded in ecstasy.

Jackson lay back, exhausted, utterly satisfied, but not spent. He'd gained his pleasure three times and yet his erection gave no evidence of fading. His large organ stood at attention, as Ginger shook her head in dismay.

"What's got into you?" she said, still trying to catch her breath. She knew he had missed her and expected their sex would be stimulating, but my goodness gracious, she hadn't imagined their union could reach the crescendo it had tonight. Yet, time and time again, he'd proven he could take her to a higher level, taking her to a world where their two souls could meet and rejoice in the harmony of their bodies.

Propping himself up on his side, his lustful eyes traveled the course of her body. He stroked her thighs with his dampened palms, saying huskily, "You ain't been that juicy in a long time." His eyes begged for more, but her face, shining in the candlelight, glowed resistance.

"And you ain't stayed that hard in a long time either." She blushed. She kissed him tenderly, outlining his full lips with her tongue, before whisking off to the bathroom. Jackson's mouth had fallen open, and he was already emitting a faint snore by the time she returned moments later.

She checked the time. A giggle stuck in her throat.

Turning away from the clock, she straddled her husband, washcloth in hand. He was awakened by the soothing cleansing, as Ginger washed beneath his testicles, around, up and down his stiffened organ, inside his firm thighs where their dried love juices were still evident. Satisfied he was thoroughly soaped, she returned with a rinse cloth. Steamy smoke wafted from the piping hot cloth as she continued the ritual he loved.

"Ohhhhhhh, baby," he said in reverie, "that feels soooo gooooood!" He fell asleep seconds later as she stroked him until all the heat had left the cloth. She nibbled at his tiny dusky nipple, then covered his naked body. Clicking off the music and blowing out the candles, she disposed of the cloth in the bathroom, and went to do a last-minute inspection of her sleeping children.

Making the arc around the circular stairway, she checked first on Jason, sleeping with his window cracked open, the cold February air cooling his half-nude body. She shook her head as she closed the door. Why he never caught pneumonia was beyond her.

Christian was the exact opposite, snuggled up tight with his comforter, floating on a dream on the clouds of six fluffy pillows that surrounded his angelic face.

Entering the girls' room, she heard the faint sound of the music playing from Autumn's Fisher-Price portable radio resting next to Sierra's ear. As Ginger clicked the Off button, Sierra's eyes opened wide. "Mama," she said sleepily, "I heard Autumn peeing. She snuck some more pop after you and Monk went to bed."

Ginger turned on her heels, to stare at the small form in the matching brass bed. Autumn's butt was raised high in the air, her narrow face pressed against Suzy Scribbles. Damn! I forgot to tell Sierra to remove her comforter, she chastised herself. Usually, Ginger would remove the beautiful white eyelet comforter and replace it with an old quilt from the shelf in their closet. The comforter was so thick that it wouldn't fit in the drum of the washer and had to go to the pound cleaners. After five previous cleanings, which caused it to lose its fluffy fullness, she had no recourse but to remove the comforter nightly.

As Ginger lifted Autumn from the soaked bedding, the child clutched her doll-baby by her golden hair and hugged her mother with her other free arm. Ginger carried her to their bathroom after grabbing a change of pajamas. Turning on the light, she had to laugh to herself when she spotted the large yellow stain on Suzy. It was a wonder Suzy didn't speak up, saying, "Autumn, you pissed on me," but Suzy hadn't been able to talk in a while. Well, I'll be damned, Ginger thought, the doll's batteries got wet, and that short-circuited her voice box. Wait until she told Jackson!

"You don't understand how I feel, Randall," said Kim, sitting on the edge of her desk.

Randall came up behind her and began massaging her shoulders. "You're tense, you know that? You shouldn't get yourself so worked up. I'll talk to Cameron for you. Maybe I could—"

Her shoulders stiffened at the sound of footsteps in the hallway. She relaxed when they passed her opened door. "Don't bother, Randall. I don't think it'll do any good. Besides, I'm a big girl. I can take care of myself." She elbowed him in the ribs. "You should know that better than anybody." Reaching up, she stroked his unshaven face. "And what's the deal with this Don Johnson look?"

He turned to look at her. "I'm letting it grow out. Like it?"

"Sexy. Yeah, sexy. I wish Bill would grow one. I like a beard on a man." She slowed her voice. "Feels good down here," she said, pointing toward her crotch. They both laughed. Randall placed his arm around her shoulder just as Kim looked up to stare into Bill's face.

"Am I interrupting something?"

Kim jumped off the desk, trying to assume a professional air. "Bill, you know Randall."

Hesitantly, Bill extended his hand. Randall placed his large hand over Bill's, innocently placing his right hand atop Bill's shoulder. Bill's cutting glance prompted Randall to remove it immediately.

Randall plowed his fingers through his hair nervously. "I guess I'll leave you two alone." He turned to address Bill. "I hope to see you again sometime, Bill."

Not saying a word, Bill stood staring at Kim as though she were naked. She wore a black double-breasted coatdress that stopped roughly four inches above her knees, a bit longer than her usual attire. Clad in black silk stockings, designer black suede pumps, she wore only one dangling silver earring, with a half-carat diamond stud in the other. Distinctly chic, distinctly sexy.

She opened her mouth to speak, and stopped short as Bill threw the bouquet of flowers he'd held behind his back onto her desk and walked out. She caught up with him in the hall, and begged him to please listen. She hadn't done anything wrong. He'd known about her friendship with Randall from the beginning. He couldn't possibly think—but the coldness he showed her proved otherwise.

She returned to her office and sat at her desk mummified,

scanning the screen on her computer. The words jumbled together into a large black blur. Bill and she had been dating
just under a year, yet it seemed like only yesterday she had
told Ginger how much in love they were. Funny how one remembered only happy moments. In order to cope with the
pain and anguish of the present, you had to let it go and just
remember . . . remember when just a few months earlier their
love was sweet, ever so sweet. . . .

"You won't believe it, Ginger. You just won't fuckin' believe it," she'd sung into the phone.

"Tell me. I could use a good laugh about now. We haven't
talked in a while. I miss talking to you."

"Don't be so downbeat. Anyway, Dr. Bill told me he
loved me tonight."

"He'd told you that before. . . ."

"I know, I know, but that was before and this is now. I
didn't' believe him the first time he told me, because we
hadn't, you know—"

"Yeah, I know," said Ginger wryly.

"Uh-huh. But girlfriend, I believe him this time. I really
feel we have a solid future ahead of us. I think this is the
closest I'll ever come to having the right man in my lifetime.
I don't plan on blowing it."

"And have you been faithful?"

"Honey, Dr. Bill's been throwing down on a regular basis.
He can't get enough of this juicy pussy."

"Kim, do you have to talk so dirty?"

"I'm only talking to my cousin, what's wrong with that?
As I was saying, honey . . . this pussy is a cross between a
Hawaiian pineapple and an overripe mango—Mr. Bill thinks
he's entered tropical paradise."

Ginger had laughed at her cousin's description of her luscious body. She was consumed with her sexual abilities. Ginger had liked Bill immediately after meeting him at her
aunt's house. He didn't seem anything like Kim's other
boyfriends. Maybe that was what attracted Kim to him. They
say opposites attract. Here was the prime example.

"Wait . . . wait . . . I forgot to tell you, as soon as I think Dr.
Bill's romped around heaven long enough, I wrap my legs

around his back, lock my ankles, and start sucking on that dick like a plunger in a toilet, using my pussy muscles to suck every ounce of cum he's got in him."

"Uh-huh. And while you're performing your ass off, when do you come?"

"I get mine, honey. I want to make *sure* he gets his."

"I was always told it was supposed to be the other way around," Ginger had said, slightly amused.

"Girlfriend, when a man leaves my bed, he knows he's been laid, thoroughly."

"So that's why you have a swarm of dates lined up at your doorway every Friday night?"

"Don't be catty, Ginger. I didn't say I had the best ass in town—just in the top ten—and I've got enough sense to know you can't get a man or keep a man with just sex."

"You coulda' fooled me. I thought you thought you were going to screw your way to Beverly Hills. All you ever talk about is sex. Correction—that was until you met Bill."

"He's really brought about a change in me. Quite frankly, Ginger, before Bill came into my life, I was starting to get bored with sex."

"You, bored with sex?"

"Yesssssirreee . . . me, bored with sex. Imagine. That's why I know he's special. He started with a totally different approach than all the others, and the killer is, that he wasn't even faking about not wanting to have sex with me right away.

"You know after we made love, I got a good look at his body. He's really got a nice firm body. Not too muscular."

Ginger interrupted her. "I thought you loved those biceps?"

Kim continued, "I did until lately. I used to like big penises too. But I've found out firsthand that Oscar Mayer wieners can be made to feel like Eckrich beef Polish sausages with proper guidance."

"Kim!"

"I swear, he's only five foot seven inches tall, weighs almost a hundred and fifty pounds, but that small piece of leather is well put together. The next time I see that commercial 'Where's the beef,' with that little old White lady in it, I'll be thinking to myself, If she hadda got a hold to this

USDA choice Black Angus beef of Dr. Bill's, she'd know where the beef was. Yep, Ginger, I think I've finally grown up."

"My, my, Kim. Somebody's been praying for you, girl."

"You know, I just thought of something. Is it all right if I go to church with you and Jackson and the kids Sunday?"

"Anytime, Kim."

"Truth is, I want to get married in the church and I've got to start visiting a church on a regular basis, or join one, before I can ask the pastor if I can have my wedding there."

"Lots of people get married in churches they don't belong to. Has Bill asked you to marry him?"

"No, but I think he will. For some reason I can't explain why, I feel the need to have what my parents share—you know—that closeness. Might even join the church too, like Mama and Daddy did."

And now Kim's hopes and dreams of a future together with Bill were like a bittersweet memory.

Like the twilight fringe of the moon floats the dust of stars, and lovers soon to be dust soon become dreams. Dreams are wishes wished silently; desires held inside, visions of tomorrow's yesterdays, fantasies we hide.

Kim's eyes filled with tears as the image of Bill marrying another woman sneaked into her thoughts. She pulled her eyes away from the computer screen and rested her head on her folded arms. Tears poured from her heart. All the emotions that had built up from her father's illness, her mother's odd behavior, and Bill's rejection collided like a tidal wave.

Randall peeked inside her office, but seeing the uneven rise and fall of her hunched shoulders, backed slowly away, allowing her privacy.

Early Wednesday morning Mae Thelma made a telephone call. She managed to catch Jackson before he left the house, explaining that she needed to talk to him about Robert Earl. Mae Thelma told Jackson that she'd spoken to Robert Earl and he wanted to know if Jackson would come over and let his car engine run every now and then. He didn't want the battery to die. That request from her husband, luckily, gave her the excuse for asking Jackson if he would teach her to drive.

Jackson extended an invitation for Mae Thelma to ride along with him to pick up his luggage. He'd give her a few driving tips along the way.

"That was a mighty fillin' dinner Ginger cooked Sunday," said Mae Thelma, looking at Jackson's handsome face as they sped along the freeway toward Metro Airport. "I was so hungry my navel was ticklin' my backbone. Didn't know these women from the North could cook good ole down-home food like us southern folks."

"Yeah, she's a pretty good cook," said Jackson appreciatively. "Only thing she can't cook good is egg custard pies." He clasped the steering wheel tighter, weaving the truck between the slow-moving traffic. "The filling is good, but she can't seem to get 'em thick enough."

Mae Thelma tucked that little information away for the time being. It would be helpful later, when she chose to use it. "I been apraying day and night for Aunt Hattie and Robert Earl. I was glad to hear that she came through her operation all right."

"Thank you, Mae Thelma." He uttered a short sigh. "Seems like your prayers were answered for my mama, but not Robert Earl. Little Bubba told me last night he was sentenced to four to seven years in Jackson."

"Was. Monday morning a week back." Her eyes were calm and clear; she'd cried for days wondering what she and her boys were going to do. She'd counted on him beating the case, and assumed he would be home before spring. Now she had to find another plan for her and her two sons' future.

"You were right to ask, Mae Thelma. You need to learn how to drive. Don't make no sense to have that car sitting in the garage catching dust." He patted her on the arm. "Don't you worry none, by the end of next week, you'll be good enough to drive in the Indy Five Hundred."

He gave her a smile that left her heart aglow. As she felt the tender magic of his hand touching her, she longed to have his arms around her. For several moments, she studied the richness of his smooth chocolate skin, inhaling the clean scent of his cologne, his full lips, dark and luscious as ripe blackberries.

Sitting beside him so close and alone, she felt the power of his attraction. His muscular body, his sexy voice, his intelligence and maturity all spelled Mr. Wonderful. Mae Thelma rehearsed over in her mind one of her favorite passages from the Bible, which she'd hope would soon bear truth, as she looked into his eyes:

> How fair and how pleasant art thou, O love, for delights! This thy stature is like to a palm tree, and thy breasts to clusters of grapes. I said, I will go up to the palm tree, I will take hold of the boughs thereof: no also thy breasts shall be as clusters of the vine, and the smell of thy nose like apples; and the roof of thy mouth like the best wine for my beloved, that goeth down sweetly, causing the lips of those that are asleep to speak. I am my beloved's and his desire is toward me.

She smiled as his hazel eyes met hers for a brief moment. He handed the parking attendant the toll and walked around to open her door. Her long, loose hair was entangled in the seat belt. As she worked to free her tresses, Jackson reached over to help. Mae Thelma felt as if each hair on her head was a living, breathing tentacle of sexuality as Jackson manipulated the silky lengths with his large hands.

She flapped her lashes as though she were about to take flight, uttering a polite thank you when he helped her down from the truck. Her heart stopped short as his breath whipped across her cheeks. At that moment she knew, knew that she needed a man . . . this man.

"I'm sorry to bother you, Aunt Katherine," Kim said, wiping her reddened nose, "but . . . I knew you'd understand." She wept into the phone. "Bill came into the office today, and saw me and my friend Randall together . . ."

"And?"

"Aunt Katherine, we're just friends, nothing more. Randall was consoling me—his arm around my shoulder—just trying to make me feel better. My boss, Mr. Cameron, and I have been at odds lately." Her voice trailed off with embarrassment. "That's not completely true," said Kim feeling the need to confess and rid herself of the guilt she felt.

"What, you and Randall?"

"No, Mr. Cameron and I." She pressed her balled fist in her mouth, as tears crowded her eyes. "Aunt Katherine, I feel like killing myself, I've been such a fool!"

"Kim!" Katherine shouted into the phone, "I don't ever want to hear you talk like that again! Do you hear me?"

"I'm sorry. I didn't really mean it. I feel I'm being punished . . . punished for the wrong I've been doing." Her words came faster as she spat them out quickly before she could snatch them back. "I should have stopped, I should have resisted, I should have been stronger, I should have—"

"Kim, what are you saying?" Katherine was now concerned.

Kim spoke in an almost childlike voice. "I sometimes feel that it would be easier on everyone concerned if I just wasn't around."

Katherine understood so well how she felt. Sometimes life just dealt you a bad hand. Yet she'd never entertain the thought of taking her own life. Her life was consumed with loneliness when she wasn't with Ginger and the kids. There was nothing for her to do all day. No one to talk to. No one to complain to about her pains and ailments. No one to cook for. No one to love . . .

"I've been having an affair with my boss for the past three years." There, she'd done it. It was out in the open. She heaved a sigh of relief and, closing her eyes, told her aunt about her indiscretion.

"I was weak, Aunt Katherine. It hadn't happened since I met Bill. I promised myself in order to earn the love from Bill and, hopefully, his proposal of marriage, that I wouldn't continue the affair. I truly love Bill. Though he deserves better—I'm not ready to give him up. It's become more and more apparent to me since my father's illness that I want what Mama and he have. All the screwing around and all the men I've been through, trying to avoid a commitment, has stopped. I should have been running toward a relationship instead of away from one."

"Kim, honey. Don't judge yourself too harshly. Everyone makes mistakes. Lord knows, I have. Do you think I don't have a past that I'm ashamed of? I've done some things in my lifetime that I wouldn't dare tell my kids, and wouldn't want them to find out about either. Even though they're all grown, they still wouldn't understand."

"You . . . Aunt Katherine?" said Kim, amazed at her candor and frankness.

"Yes, me. You got part of my blood running through your veins. We're creatures of nature. And nature intended for us to be sexual. We don't always choose the right mate, but we choose by instincts and survival. Sometimes you get caught up in the web of lust and adventure and you don't even wish to escape."

"That's how it was with Mr. Cameron. I was the adventuress scheming to win a higher position in the office, climbing the executive ladder ahead of my colleagues, looking down on them as though they were fools, doing it the hard way—while all the time, unknowingly, I was being finessed by a skilled con man, hip to what I was doing all along. I ended up being the usee instead of the user."

"But you've learned?"

"Yes, I've learned the hard way. Bought sense, instead of borrowed sense, like my mama used to say." She smiled at the thought of her innocent mother, but it quickly faded when she admitted it would kill her if she knew her daughter was nothing more than a high-class whore.

"I don't care how he threatened you, Kim. If I were you I'd change my job. You're educated, and Jewel's shown me all the awards you've received from the firm."

"Mama showed you my awards?" Kim asked incredulously.

"She might not talk to you as much as you would like, Kim, and she's just too overprotective of you, but she's proud of you. Always has been. She knows she's too critical of you, but she thinks she's too old to change her ways, electing to just be silent. Be still, as they say in the church."

"Be still. I've heard her say that before. Just be still."

Be still, and know that I am God: I will be exalted among the heathen, I will be exalted in the earth.

Stand in awe, and sin not: commune with your own heart upon your bed, and be still. Selah.

But if ye shall do wickedly, ye shall be consumed, both ye and your king.

He that is unjust, let him be unjust still: and he which is filthy, let him be filthy, still: and he that is righteous, let him be righteous still: and he that is holy, let him be holy still.

Why do we sit still? Assemble yourselves, and let us enter into the defended cities, and let us be silent there: for the Lord our God hath put us to silence, and given us water of gall to drink, because we have sinned against the Lord.

O thou sword of the Lord, how long [will it be] ere thou be quiet? Put up thyself into thy scabbard, rest, and be still.

Katherine uttered the verses from the Bible. A heartfelt sigh escaped her trembling lips.

"Aunt Katherine," said Kim amazed. "I didn't know you could recite the Bible."

"My neighbor, Lavern Washington, is a pastor, has been for the last thirty years. He's recited those same words to me so many times when I came to him begging for forgiveness of my sins. Now I know them by heart—I get down on my knees and pray. Pray for understanding and guidance." She was silent for a moment with her own prayer.

Why aren't you listening now Lord, listening to my silent prayers? she prayed silently. *Help me through these troubled times of my life, Lord. And dear God, please my niece to glorify your name and cleanse her soul and heart of her sins*—*Thank you, Jesus. Amen.*

Kim was comforted.

17

Your Precious Love

Sitting at the desk in her bedroom, Kim studied the silver-framed pictures that covered her dressing table. Old photographs her mother had given her. One was of her parents when they were married in 1939. She smiled, admiring their clothing. Her mother looked especially youthful at the tender age of eighteen wearing a beaver coat with a large raccoon collar, her hair done up in crimps and spit curls haloing her narrow face. She was beautiful.

The aged black-and-white pictures had faded to more of a burgundyish brown color. Her father wore a herringbone three-piece suit that fit him more snugly than he would have liked, as he had told her on several occasions. His strong, proud African features were plainly as handsome at twenty-one as they still were today at seventy-three.

When she arrived home from work Kim found her mother in her bedroom, asleep in her rocking chair with the Bible facedown in her lap. She wore an old blue tattered house-dress, with a pink fringed shawl covering her shoulders. Fluffy yellow slippers were half on her bare feet. As Kim turned to leave, the scent of a dozen fresh roses overpowered the newly painted room, and she wondered who had brought them.

Kim had brought home dinner for the two of them, planning to surprise her mother with some of her old favorites. After talking to Aunt Katherine, she realized she needed to spend more time with her mother. Dinner at home for a change would be a start.

She'd stopped at Erma's Soul Food Restaurant on Six Mile Road to pick up her order of turkey and dressing, collard greens, macaroni and cheese, potato salad, candied yams, and a single order of peach cobbler, with a scoop of French vanilla ice cream on the side.

After she spooned the steaming food from the foam container into two china dishes, she placed their meal on the dining room table, then poured sparkling water into two iced glasses and arranged her mother's favorite silverware on a folded linen napkin. Standing back to admire the setting, she felt everything was just perfect.

The cozy dining room was filled with treasures from an era of long ago. The walls were painted a rich antique white, red brocade drapes were tasseled and tied back over lace sheers on the double-framed window, blood red carpeting covered the floor of the modest little house.

The cherrywood dining furniture gleamed elegantly from years of polishing and loving care. Kim lit two candles on the table, then placed a large floral arrangement on the buffet.

"My Lord, Kim, what have you done?" Jewel exclaimed as she was being led into the room by her daughter, who was doing her best to suppress her excitement and not spoil the surprise.

Then in a voice that appeared to issue forth from some sequestered cathedral, Jewel said the customary grace. A polite amen brought the prayer to a whispered close. And Kim felt the healing begin.

"So that's what happened, Mama," said Kim, laying her head on her mother's lap.

Jewel smoothed the back of Kim's head, feeling more

content than she had in years. She swayed her upper body
back and forth as if in concert with an old spiritual.

"Do you believe in the Lord, Kim? Do you want to be
saved?"

"Yes, Mama. But I've sinned. Will God ever forgive me?"

"He that believeth and is baptized shall be saved. Get on
your knees and pray to Him, and He'll hear, for God is gracious, 'cause the Lord knows your heart. Trust in his words:
'If my people which are called by my name shall humble
themselves and pray, and seek my face, and turn from their
wicked ways, then I will hear from heaven and I will forgive
their sin and I will heal . . .' "

"You're going to be proud of me," Kim told her mother.
She promised to pray every night, get baptized at the church
her mother and father belonged to, go to church faithfully
every Sunday, stop fornicating with Bill until they were married. Ouch! That last one was tough.

"Been knowing Bill for a while. Didn't like him first off."
Jewel smiled, pausing. "But that was around the time Ollie
had gotten sick, and I didn't cotton particularly to anybody's
company thereabouts."

Kim pulled herself up on her knees, looking like a five-
year-old child with her eager, wide-eyes half-stance. "But
you liked him, didn't you Mama?"

" 'Course I did," Jewel answered, blushing slightly. "Perfect gentleman he is. Make a right fine husband. I'm sure
your father would app—"

"Approve?"

"Yes," she said. Yet Jewel kept it to herself about Bill
coming to see her that morning. He had given her a beautiful
bouquet of white roses. They'd talked and talked until almost
noon. He'd confided in her that he planned to ask Kim to
marry him soon, but wanted the approval of her and Mr. Lee
beforehand. Jewel told him there was no need to approach
her husband, because he was unable to communicate, but
they were as one, and she felt she could speak for her husband under the circumstances.

"He hasn't asked me to marry him yet, Mama. But I'm
hoping he will, despite what happened today. I feel it in my
heart." She stood, giving her mother's hand a pat. Kim was

enjoying their conversation. She went over to the sofa and sat down, propping her elbow on the arm, resting her forehead in her hand. "I want a marriage like yours and Daddy's, Mama," she said respectfully. "Tell me what to do, Mama. I've never felt like this about a man before. I'm scared."

"No need to be scared. Be happy. Be still." Jewel closed her eyes as she continued rocking, a peaceful expression on her face. "When I first saw your father, I knew I was in love. It was love at first sight for both of us. Eternity shone in our lips and eyes, bliss in our brows bent. Two people have to see each other for the first time at the same time, or it doesn't work. It worked for us, and I've been a happy woman ever since. You know what it feels like to really be happy with a man?" She opened her eyes slowly, gauging her daughter's response.

Kim was spellbound by the loving glow she saw on her mother's face. She shook her head no, as her mother continued. "When a woman's truly and completely happy, when she talks she sings, when she walks she dances. When you're thinking about how much you love that man, you envision a beautiful sunset, an old love song, with heaven only knows what thoughts to keep it company."

Kim listened and saw a side of her mother that she didn't know existed. She was compassionate, caring, and bore so much love in such a frail body that Kim was overwhelmed with affection.

Jewel shook her head, remembering when they'd taken Ollie away; the strength being pulled from his eyes was more than she could stand. "Those first few weeks after Ollie was gone I couldn't bear to be without him. I dreamed of him lying beside me day and night, breathed the scent of him on my pillow"—her eyes closed again, inhaling, as if the scent still lingered—"just a breath of him. I savored those precious moments as if they were the last gulps of oxygen in an airless world. But the anguish of the moment of truth is devastating. The anguish finally leaves, but the echoes remain." She whispered the last few words into the stilled air, which was filled with silence.

Kim looked up into her mother's tear-streaked face. "The only other time Ollie and I have been apart was when I was in the hospital having you." She choked on her words as Kim wiped both their tears with the soft fringes of her mother's shawl.

"I love you, Mama," said Kim, hugging her around the neck. "I'm sorry for the selfish way I've been acting. Will you ever forgive me?"

Jewel placed her hands gently on Kim's shoulders and looked her steadily in her cherubic face. A fresh stream of tears blinded her eyes and choked her voice as she said, "No, I want you to forgive me."

"Wha—"

Jewel silenced her, pressing a tender finger over her warm lips, "I, too, am guilty of being selfish, more so than you. I was lonely. So very lonely. Missing that physical touch from your father, a simple hug, a kiss, a quick embrace, or maybe just a little emotional support. But not realizing, and not knowing, until Katherine . . . yes . . . your wonderful Aunt Katherine enlightened me. She told me all those feelings and all those needs could be and should be shared and felt with the other person that I loved dearly . . . my daughter."

Kim broke down on her knees crying tears of joy that dropped like petals into a pond. She was ready for love.

Everyone was seated, waiting anxiously in the family room, when Jackson entered like Santa Claus carrying a large black plastic bundle on his back. He passed out the small items first that were wrapped and tagged with everyone's names. There were burgundy T-shirts for the entire family, with their names embossed on the back in glossy white lettering, and the state of Mississippi outlined on the front.

Having received her gift the day before, Autumn sat content with her Raggedy Ann doll tucked on her right, and a naked Suzy Scribbles on her left. Her mother had taken Suzy's clothes and washed them, though Autumn couldn't understand why. Her eyes darted back and forth to the laundry room, waiting to hear the buzzer from the dryer.

Ginger opened the large box for Autumn, who didn't seem to be interested in the two Sunday dresses that were fit for a little princess. Ginger could tell by the furrow in her brows that she was still mad about Suzy's clothes. Ginger didn't want to hurt her baby's feelings and remind her that they smelled of strong urine from at least two drenchings.

Jason's box was empty, except for a card inside explaining that his gift was in the garage. He quickly went out to find it, leaving the others tearing open boxes, with wads of wrapping paper and ribbon cluttering the floor.

Christian was relieved when he saw a chemistry set containing 101 experiments. It was the biggest one he'd ever seen. Feeling himself almost a man, too old for kisses, he extended his hand, giving Jackson a macho handshake and thanking him.

Sierra was getting nervous; her gift was the last one in the bag. Jumping up and down with excitement, she managed to tear open the paper. There was a deep shiny black box with large bold red letters on it. Layers of white tissue paper covered three elegant girl's party dresses, each one prettier than the next, trimmed with tiny seed pearls and Victorian lace.

"Jackson, they're beautiful," said Ginger, totally surprised at the quality of the fabric and his ability to select such exquisite clothes.

"I know what you're thinking." He sat down beside her, placed his arm around her shoulder, and whispered in her ear. "My sister Shirley went shopping with me. She picked out the dresses for Sierra and Autumn."

"You done good . . . you done real good," she said nodding her head, smiling at the euphoria on Sierra's face.

"I haven't forgotten about you." He walked through the discarded empty boxes and retrieved a tiny box hidden at the bottom of the plastic bag. Resting on one knee, he placed the box in her hand. He pressed his lips against hers, then gently covered her mouth with kisses. Her heart skipped a beat at his touch. A loud chorus of throats clearing interrupted their embrace.

"Man . . . Jackson." Jason came in, elated. "Thanks a lot for the basketball rim." He hugged Jackson around the shoulder, then shook his hand. "I've got the tools out to hook it up, but I can't find a Phillips screwdriver. Do you know where one is?"

Ginger shook her head while opening her gift. Jackson

kept tools in the garage, which also housed an impressive work station. But his tools were not stored neatly in the drawers and cabinets. Wrenches, screwdrivers, pliers, channel locks, sockets and ratchets, and hammers were strewn carelessly in kitchen drawers, under the kitchen-sink garbage disposal, in the furnace room, under the sink in their bathroom, next to the satellite unit in their bedroom, in the exercise room where the burglar alarm system was mounted, and in the west Florida room where the kids kept their bikes in the winter months. Consequently, he could never find the right one when he needed it. He walked out with Jason to look for the screwdriver.

Ginger draped a black down coat over her shoulders and ran out into the blistering cold. Jason was busy with the snow blower, plowing away. Placing her arms around Jackson's waist as he stood on a ladder, she hugged him, burying her face against his firm buttocks. "Thank you, sweetheart. I thought you'd forgotten about me."

He eased himself down the ladder, tilting her head back, planting a series of kisses around her face. "How could I forget about my baby." He took her hand in his, admiring his purchase. "You like it?" And before she could answer, he said, "Now, if you don't like it, the jeweler assured me that I could send it back in the mail."

"Sweetheart, I love it. I really do. But didn't you spend a lot of money?"

"Our anniversary is in two weeks. I figured I'd kill two birds with one stone. You don't like the clothes I pick out for you anyway, so what else could I buy?" She shrugged her shoulders, extended her left hand, and admired the exquisite diamond ring.

"You remembered our anniversary . . . that's sweet, honey."

Jason, completing his task, put his arm around his mother's shoulder and lifted her arm to appraise the gift. He nodded his head. "Nice." He placed his balled fists in the center of Ginger's back, guiding her back toward the house. "Now get, Jackson and me got some work to do."

Jackson winked at Ginger as she reentered the house.

Looking back over her shoulder, she noticed the work Jackson said he planned on doing inside the garage hadn't been touched. What had he done all day today? She'd have to remember to ask him later.

"Who's leading, honey?" Ginger asked, leaning her head over Jackson's shoulder on the back of the recliner.

"Detroit." He stuffed a handful of popcorn in his mouth, spilling several kernels onto his lap. "They shut down Jordan; he's hardly scored. I thought you were gonna watch the game with me."

"I'm almost finished washing the girls' hair. It's almost halftime anyway. I'll be done in a few minutes. Want me to bring you anything back from downstairs?" she asked, walking toward the doorway.

"Bring me up a Diet Pepsi," he called after her.

Later that evening, Ginger and Jackson sat sipping Christian Brothers brandy and ginger ale as the final seconds of the game ticked away. James Edwards was the high scorer with twenty-one points, one more than Michael Jordan's paltry twenty, to lead the Pistons to another victory as they edged closer to their second championship.

"Sweetheart, I meant to tell you something before you—"

Jackson placed his drink on the coffee table in front of him and turned toward his wife. Placing his hand on her shoulder, he removed the gold barrette, easing the bobby pins from her french twist, freeing her hair. "See . . . I've known for a while, Ginger." He ran his fingers through her thinned hair and cupped the back of her head, bringing her face close to his. "I just wasn't ready to see you get upset again. I know how much it hurts you to lose your hair."

Ginger's eyes filled with tears. "You know . . . and you didn't say anything?"

"Ginger, try to understand. This is something that happens to you that I'm powerless to help you with. I can't blame anyone for your pain. I can't go out and buy you something to replace something that's broken. I can't fix it with tools. I can't beat the shit out of somebody that's hurting you . . . and I can't screw away the pain."

"Jackson . . . I'm going to be all right this time. I'm not

going to feel sorry for myself, I just want to be sure that it doesn't bother you. I know you keep telling me it doesn't, but for some reason, I feel like I'm letting you down again every time it happens."

He stroked her hair lovingly. "Ginger, I know it's not your fault. Stop blaming yourself for something you can't control. Hell, I know it won't be easy. But try to remember, I'd feel the same way about you even if your hair never grew back. I'm in love with what's in here," he pointed to her heart. "Hair doesn't make a person or a woman attractive."

"What about Mae Thelma? She's got beautiful hair. Tell me you don't admire all that hair. I know how much Black men love long hair. Go ahead, tell me you don't think it's pretty."

"Sure, it's nice. But I'm not in love with her, or her hair. I'm in love with you—bald or otherwise. Now shut up and let's get in the bed."

She gave him a side glance, leaning her body against his. "I thought you said you couldn't screw away my pain?"

He lifted her chin with his fist, kissing her as lightly and tenderly as a feather stroking her lips. "Don't plan on screwing my way, just planting a few seeds is all."

"Not tonight. Romeo. I'm menstruating."

"Damn!" He snapped his fingers, then pulled her close to him while whispering in her ear, "I just want to hold you in my arms." He kissed the top of her head. "Is that all right with you, baby?"

She nodded and held fast to his waist, pressing her head into his chest, knowing he was her heart and soul.

Bill lay in his darkened bedroom, listening to the soothing voice of Luther Vandross. The station was playing a medley of his love songs. He listened for some time until he felt the anger rising in him again at the thought of the woman he loved in the arms of another man. How could she? And a White man—she knew how he felt about the White race. He sipped his drink; the bitter taste of straight whiskey burned his throat.

As he reached across the bed to change the station, the

phone began to ring. "Hello," he said, turning on the bedside lamp.

"Bill . . . can we talk?"

The relaxing alcohol suddenly reversed its effect as he jolted up, making him feel as though he'd drunk a pot of black coffee. "What shall we talk about?" he asked cynically. "Shall we talk about your flirtation with a White man, or should we talk about your screwing me over?"

Kim swallowed her pride, stifling a nasty retort. "Bill, it wasn't like that at all. I've told you repeatedly about my friendship with Randall. We went—"

"Who the fuck is Randall? He's just a man—just like me. Would he want to see his woman in the arms of a Black man? Hell no!"

"Nothing happened, Bill. I swear it didn't. I've been upset at work lately. My boss—"

"What about my problems, Kim? Don't I deserve any respect?" he asked calmly.

"I respect you because I love you," she said, swallowing a sob that rose in her throat.

He pulled himself up, swinging his legs over the side of the bed. "Kim, I just can't accept this so-called friendly relationship you have with Randall. We've discussed this before—my feelings haven't changed."

Kim remembered an article she'd read describing the attitudes of single men toward single women. She hadn't believed Bill fit into that category. These men felt that women were less honest and dependable, less considerate, supportive, and sensible—and even less moral—than women saw themselves to be.

Kim had laughed when she read it, knowing the man she loved couldn't possibly fit into these categories—after all he was a psychiatrist, he knew the spiel—and yet he couldn't accept her innocent friendship with a White man.

"I think it's important that you trust me, Bill. Trust me to be able to befriend a man, no matter what color or race he may be—knowing that I can and will be true to you, regardless. Allow me some freedom to be myself."

"I need a woman I can believe in, Kim. A woman I can

trust, a woman I can hold up on a pedestal, and know . . . know that she's putting my interests first."

"Bill, I have the same needs. I need a man who believes and trusts in me. That isn't so selfish, to think that in today's world that both egos need to be stroked occasionally." She paused to let that last statement sink in. "Yes, I need my ego stroked too, Bill. I know who I am. I know what I am. I know what I can be to you. I know I have a lot to offer to a man, and I know what you are to me. I'm willing to give some of myself to you, but not all. I need to build up my own self-esteem before I can be so generous I put your interests first. I'm also guilty of being selfish as most people are, because you have to have a *self* before you esteem it."

"Exactly . . . I feel we should see other people, Kim. I think it would be for the best."

18

My World Is Empty Without You

Exactly seven days later, Kim found herself nearly in shock at Henry Ford Hospital. Unable to sleep, Kim had awakened during the night and noticed a fragmented pale blue light streaming beneath her mother's door. It was 3:47 A.M. Jewel lay on her side facedown, wedged between the bed and the wall, semiconscious, mumbling incoherently. Her right hand curved like a bear claw. Jewel's mouth curled into her cheekbone. Her fingers were stiff, immobile. Jewel made a valiant effort to shake some feeling into her stiffened hand as her daughter lifted her limp form. Kim quickly checked her faint pulse and called 911.

Kim's mind was numb. Unable to deal with the shock of seeing her mother so helpless, she waited for the ambulance in a trancelike state, cradling Jewel's body, until the paramedics whisked Kim and Jewel into the ambulance.

Katherine, Kim, and Ginger paced the waiting rooms nervously. They took shifts going downstairs to bring up fresh coffee. It didn't look good for Jewel. She had hidden the fact that she'd been on blood-pressure pills. Along with the added stress of her husband's deteriorating condition, it was too much pressure for a woman her age.

Jewel looked tired, defeated, as she lay in the hospital bed in the intensive care section. Katherine and Ginger did their best to console Kim. But how much could a child take? Her mother and father were both hospitalized. The prognosis for both was bleak.

Ginger called Kim's office and explained her absence. Randall sent an exquisite floral arrangement, though he was unable to deliver it himself. Mr. Cameron had him working a double shift, picking up Kim's workload. But Randall promised that somehow he'd be there tomorrow to give Kim and Jewel his love.

Jewel died less than forty-eight hours after being admitted. Kim was in denial. Katherine and Ginger pleaded with her to call Bill. But Kim wouldn't hear of it—she needed time alone to think. And she didn't want Bill to come back with feelings of pity. She couldn't take that now. How much more could her heart bear?

"Mama, did you remember to get Uncle Ollie's suit out of the cleaner's?" Ginger asked.

The family had received a terrible shock. Jewel Lee's untimely death was deeply felt by her friends and neighbors. She'd been an icon of the community. Kim was taking it hard, and couldn't be consoled by her father, because she thought he hadn't been able to understand what was going on, or refused to accept it. But she was wrong.

Katherine and Ginger had gone with Kim to make the arrangements for the funeral. Then Katherine had assured Kim that she and her daughter would handle everything for the wake, and told her just to take some time alone by herself.

Katherine didn't bother to answer Ginger. She kept going to and from the kitchen, placing the dishes of food in groups of salads, vegetables, casseroles, meats, and breads. She'd set up a separate dessert section along the buffet. There were so many cakes, pies, and cobblers that there was hardly any room for the main dishes. Steam rose like a ghost, clouding the kitchen windows, as Katherine removed the domed top of the roasting pan. She placed the chicken, stuffed with cornbread and savory sage dressing, in the center of the dining table.

In the living room, Ginger's eyes scanned the tables, making sure there were enough ashtrays and sufficient Kleenex throughout the crowded room. Unfolding the last of the chairs they'd rented, she stopped short, her eyes focusing on the family picture above the fireplace mantel. How lovely they all looked, Uncle Ollie and Aunt Jewel seated, handsomely dressed in white suits with Kim behind them, smiling, her elbows resting along the chair and her chin pressed against her steepled hands.

Ginger pulled a tissue from the box on the mantel, dabbing her eyes as they clouded with tears. The sound of her mother's voice broke her mournful reverie. Passing through the living room into the kitchen, she shook her head distastefully, discarding the balled tissue in an empty garbage can.

At every wake Ginger had attended, she always wondered how people could work up such an appetite after someone had just died. Food was the farthest thing from her mind, no matter how tastefully it was displayed.

"Hold still, Mama, I almost got it." Ginger pulled the two pieces of fabric together on the slacks as Katherine sucked in her breath. The older woman's coffee brown makeup was running down her sweaty face as she wiggled into the tight garment. In the old days, one of Ginger's three other sisters would help fasten her mother into her clothes, tugging, pulling, pushing, until finally she was dressed.

After years of guzzling Colt 45s, Katherine had developed a beer belly. Therefore it had become extremely difficult for her to get into anything other than sweats without the support of whichever daughter was available at the time.

Katherine's ritual consisted of ten minutes of struggling into two girdles, first one, then another on top. Next she slid into her hosiery, fastening them with the straining hooks. Then she'd sit and rest for five minutes, catching her breath, wiping the perspiration beneath her arms, around her forehead; the sweat between her legs wouldn't dare fall under double layers of rigid rubber.

Rested, she'd ease into her blouse or sweater. Next, ten to

fifteen minutes of fluffing her thick, chili-pepper coiffure.
Rest again. Then, after retouching her makeup, she would
slide into her slacks. That was where the girls came in.
They'd strap her in with two diaper pins to keep her pants
up, and a shoestring attached on each end of the waistband,
tying it into a bow. Rest again.

Sometimes they'd get up enough nerve to ask her how she
was going to pee with all that stuff on. She'd tell them she
wasn't going to drink any beer, just take teeny-weeny eye-
drops full of whiskey.

"So after all these years you managed to get on the girdles
by yourself, but you still need help with the diaper pins and
the shoestrings?" Ginger asked, kneeling beside her mother.

"Shut the frig up," said Katherine, puffing away.

"Mama, have you ever thought of just buying bigger
pants?"

Katherine rolled her eyes at Ginger, ignoring what she
considered a stupid question. "Where on earth is Kim? She
should've been here by now." Katherine glanced at her wrist-
watch, sucking in her stomach as Ginger worked old magic
with the strings.

"You think she's all right, Mama? It was so sudden, Aunt
Jewel dying like that. I'm worried about Kim. They'd just
started getting along so well. This just wasn't fair." Her
voice was light and soft as it trailed off. Just then the doorbell started to ring. "I'll get it, Mama. You finish up here,"
said Ginger, hesitating a moment to swat her mother's sweat-
beaded forehead with a tissue.

"Hi sweetheart." Ginger hung Jackson's jacket in the front
hall closet as he trudged into the kitchen carrying a brown
grocery bag of noisily clinking bottles.

"Hi Granny," he called out to his mother-in-law as she entered the room. Placing fifths of whiskey, gin, rum, and
vodka along the kitchen counter, he scoured the cabinets for
an ice bucket, leaving each door wide open as he moved to
the next.

Reaching underneath a cabinet next to the sink, Katherine
took out the insulated bucket and put it beside the soda.
"Pour me a quick one, will you Jackson?" Turning toward

the cabinets again, Katherine caught him with her eyes, gesturing at the double row of plastic cups.

She'd known from the beginning that Jackson loved her daughter, and wholeheartedly approved of their marriage. It hadn't taken her long to figure out he was a bit selfish. But no man was perfect. Ginger had yet to find that out, and though she would never admit it, she was a bit selfish herself.

Kim finally made her entrance a few minutes later with her friend Randall in tow, to thank her aunt Katherine for all her help organizing, cooking, and setting up the food.

Jackson kissed Kim in a brotherly manner as he offered her his condolences. After shaking Randall's hand, he excused himself to join Ginger greeting the guests in the living room. He whispered in her ear as Ginger reached in the closet, searching for an empty hanger. "What happened to Bill? Is Kim going out with that White guy in the kitchen?"

Ginger turned. "You mean Randall?" Jackson gave Ginger a knowing stare. "He's a friend of hers from work."

From the dining room the subtle clamor of roaster lids being lifted and replaced could be heard over the polite conversation of the men and women who'd come to pay their respects. Closing the closet door, Ginger rested her back against it. She smiled warmly at the guests as they passed, carrying their plates piled high with food. "Can I fix you a plate, or did you eat already?" Ginger asked Jackson, trying to change the subject casually.

"Nothing." He turned to walk away, looking so *bad* in his black cashmere turtleneck, black denim jeans, and black lizard cowboy boots. "I'm going to call and check on the kids." He shouldered a path through the crowd as Ginger stood, clenching her fists.

She hated when he dismissed her like that. Ever since he'd returned home from Mississippi, he had been acting a little distant. She thought he was angry because of the time she was spending away from home, showing clients properties, working in the office. They still rode to work together every morning and evening, but their conversation wasn't as spontaneous as it used to be. He, deep in thought, she with a million things on her mind, resenting yet also appreciating the silence.

The kids were doing a wonderful job cleaning the house. Sierra had learned to cook a few dishes, Christian's fried chicken was just as good as hers, and little Autumn learned to make a mean tossed salad. Jason pitched in when he could, working around his hours at the grocery store and the hours he put in serenading his girlfriend.

"Ginger, are you feeling okay?" asked Kim, a worried look on her face.

Ginger quickly pulled herself together. She'd tuned out the people and the conversations that were going on around her. Here she was muddling over some insignificant spat that she and Jackson had, and Kim, who was carrying the weight of losing her mother, caring for her convalescent father, and breaking up with the man she loved dearly, was trying to console *her*.

Ginger smoothed the back of her cousin's tapered haircut. "Sure, I'm just fine. But not as fine as my cousin, sporting this new hairdo." She spun Kim around, admiring her new Halle Berry look.

Kim forced a strained smile. Outwardly, she appeared and looked normal, lovely in fact, in her stunning taupe lace tea-length dress. However, the tears that had rained inside her body had dried, leaving permanent cracks and crevices of pain in their wake. Feeling as if her world was being turned topsy-turvy, her thoughts were caught up in a trap of mirrors and echoes.

Bill sat quietly in the back, watching as the family entered the church. A hushed silence fell over the pews of mourners. Their faces reflected the sympathy and sorrow they felt over the untimely death of a cherished soul. Kim, tall and proud, pushed her father's wheelchair down the aisle, pausing at the casket, allowing him a final view of his deceased wife.

Two weeks had passed since they'd seen each other. Bill hadn't realized the time had passed so quickly; he'd submerged himself in his clinic, working as much as twenty hours a day. The date of Jewel's obituary brought the reality of their separation over the past two weeks into focus. He

felt the pulse quickening at his temples as a whisper of
Kim's cologne floated past him. Memories of their times together flashed before him like the quick clicks of a camera.
How he missed her. How he needed her. He was wrong not
to answer her repeated calls. Wrong to try to find solace in
another woman, whom he cared nothing about. When Kim's
calls had ceased, he had become worried, panic settling in.
And then he learned of her mother's death.

At that moment Randall entered, and the usher directed
him to be seated on the left. He squeezed between two heavy
women eagerly moving purses and Bibles and fanning themselves like girls at a debutante ball. Kim saw him and
seemed pleased by his arrival.

Katherine, Ginger, Jackson, and their four children sat beside Kim and her father in the front pew. Directly behind
them were several rows of elderly women dressed and
gloved in white, wearing vibrant purple sashes diagonally
across their chests with the words EASTERN STAR etched on
them in gold lettering. Since the age of eighteen, Jewel Lee
had been a member of the Eastern Star women's organization, the women's auxiliary of the Masons, to which Ollie
was pledged.

There were no other family members, Kim being an only
child and her mother having outlived her own small family.

Beautiful floral arrangements were everywhere, sent by
Ollie's friends in the Masons, by people at the newspaper office he'd retired from eight years earlier, by the Eastern Star,
and by several friends and neighbors. Kim had gone to the
flower shop to order a spray of white and red roses with radiating patterns of exotic green foliage that spiraled into a subtle bouquet. A white band with *To my loving wife* embossed
in gold lay across the floral arrangement, which covered the
entire expanse of the casket.

Tears ran down Ollie's cheeks as, closing his eyes shut, he
drifted on the memory of their love and life together. He
loved her. Jewel was his heart. He knew when you've been
wildly and deeply in love with someone, you don't stop loving them just because they've died—you keep on loving
them, until you join them in the floating Avalon above,

where the love of God and the love of a loved one prevail for eternity.

Kim reached over to take her father's hand in hers. Though he was still unable to speak, she read his thoughts in his eyes, shared his pain, understood his loss. She held her tears in check as the pastor read the eulogy and while the choir sang; softly in the background, Mae Thelma led them in her spiritual soprano.

A beautiful, inspired church song always moved Ginger. She listened carefully to the words, and something stirred inside her. Unconsciously touching the wig she wore, she thought about her hair loss, and her eyelids released the pain. Ginger felt the tears brushing her cheeks. Felt the words soothing her body like a breath of fresh air. She rocked from side to side with the rhythm of the music, the comfort of the words that she was certain could heal.

Katherine, also moved by the song, felt the tears trembling at the corners of her eyes. Reaching inside her purse for a tissue, she looked up as Mae Thelma completed her song. The dreamy look Mae Thelma had given Jackson might have gone unnoticed by most of the mourners, but not Katherine Lee. She hadn't missed a beat. She'd read the woman's intentions months ago, during dinner over at Ginger's.

Raising her hands in the air, Ginger broke down crying, surrendering to a power stronger than she'd ever felt before. Joy . . . she felt the joy from God manifesting and internalizing within her. She felt Jackson's arm around her shoulder, comforting her. Looking up through tear-stained eyes, she inhaled the clean air flowing through the church windows.

Jackson stroked Ginger's shoulders, pulling her closer toward him. He felt something stir within him as he watched Ginger's outpouring of emotion. He'd never seen her act that way before, he thought, looking into her eyes, which were glazed and dreamy, as if she'd experienced a metamorphosis of sorts. She was still crying softly, clutching the handkerchief he'd given her over her mouth.

But when he overheard Ginger asking the Lord for forgiveness of her sins, his eyes became misty as the realization hit him full force; he knew that Ginger was grieving over the loss of her aunt, yet he also knew he had just witnessed his wife surrendering to the spirit of the Holy Ghost.

"Kim, please, let me try and explain."

Opening the door for Bill, she paused to listen to the soft, refreshing May shower that sounded almost polite as it began to fall. She felt an aura around her, the presence of her mother's spirit surrounding her, moving through her, warming her from within.

Kim smiled warmly at Bill as she sat in her mother's chair, rocking gently to the comforting words that echoed in her mind and heart: "Create in me a clean heart, renew the right spirit within me. . . ."

Bill was amazed at the peace and serenity glowing in her eyes. A vision of beauty by anyone's standards, she sat before him without any makeup, her hair brushed casually in an asymmetrical bob. She wore a chenille nightgown that hid her feminine curves, yet never had she looked so beautiful to him.

Flickers of flames danced around the logs in the fireplace. With a *swoosh* a white-ashen log broke in half, disrupting the peace, kicking up puffs of white flakes just as a split, knotted stump fell forward.

"Kim," said Bill, turning away from the fire, "I been thinking a lot about us lately."

"Us?" said Kim timidly. "We haven't been an 'us' for quite some time."

"I'm sorry for not returning your phone calls. I should have—"

"It's not necessary to explain. I totally understand. I saw you with your friend at the restaurant—remember?"

"She works for me at the clinic, Kim. It's purely a platonic relationship. Nothing more," he lied.

Kim stared into the warm, tranquil fire, a peace filling her as she picked up the pace of her rocking. "As I said, it isn't necessary for you to explain. I wouldn't compromise my right to choose my friends—or become your convenient whore anytime you felt you had a few hours to spare. No—I won't fall prey to that kind of relationship. I've accepted our breakup."

"Kim. I was wrong," he said, his eyes pleading. "It isn't about compromise, it isn't about convenience, it isn't about sex. It's love." He moved to face her on his knees, taking her warm hands in his. "I love you, Kim. Will you marry me?"

Funny. Those were the words she had longed to hear only a short while ago. Yet today they provided little comfort. Yes, she loved him, wanted him. In her heart wanted to marry him, still. But this was not the time. Since her mother's death, she'd made some important decisions, definite plans, and he wasn't part of any of them.

"I can't." She withdrew her hands quickly, as if he had tried to steal something from her.

"And I can't accept that, Kim. We both know we love each other. I'm sorry for the things I said. I'm sorry for trying to control who you talk to, who you befriend—I'm sorry, and guilty as hell for not spending enough time alone with you," he apologized. "What more can I say?"

"That you'll understand when I say I need to make some changes in my life. In me." She looked into his eyes, searching for understanding. "I need to be alone with myself, to find out what I'm all about." She felt an energy, a strange power guiding her forward, toward the light. Turning her head slightly, she looked up above the fireplace at the image of her mother.

Ollie moved his left arm from beneath the covers. He fingered the back of his gold wedding band, feeling the scratches imbedded in the smooth surface. Time. Worn. A reminder of their union, of their love. Through the open window, he could see the stars twinkling in the purple darkness. Closing his eyes, he said a prayer for his beloved: "Though the world may try its best to keep us apart, our love will transcend time, sweetheart. It was written long ago in the stars that our love would be born; just as night leaves the sea, it was fated to be. In the heavens high above, where dreams flourish and flower, it was written that our love would grow stronger each and every hour. So always remember, Jewel Kimmery Lee, as Venus is mated to Mars, so are you to me. It was written in the stars that you and I will always be."

19

Just My Imagination (Running Away with Me)

The morning sun streamed through the bathroom windows. Ginger poured the powdered milk into the gushing water and caressed the opalescent pool with her fingers. Before the tub filled, she reached into the linen closet for the box of brown bottles left over from her Body Shop business. Jackson had voiced his displeasure over and over again about the abundance of soaps and oils she kept in their bathroom. She knew he didn't care about the space; it was just his way of reminding her of yet another failed business attempt.

Truth was, when she'd closed the booth in the trade center, she had no idea how long all the bubble bath, shampoos, lotions, and oils would last. Unbeknownst to Jackson, she had given her mother, Kim, and a few friends at work bags of the leftover stock. She'd kept what she figured their family of six could consume in a year's time.

She added rose oil, the oil of rose geranium, and a few drops of peppermint to the milky water, then turned off the tap. Walking into the sitting room, she selected a single red rose from those she'd taken after her Aunt Jewel's funeral. She placed the red bloom along the rim of the tub. She pulled the two remaining roses from their stems, one white, one red, and placed them inside her Bible, pressing the covers tightly together.

Moments later she stood naked before the opaque pool. Removing the petals of the red rose, she dropped them one by one onto the surface of the tranquil water. She slipped off her wig and eased into the center of the petals. Her head back, she took a deep breath, inhaling the cool, minty scent of peppermint, the heady fragrance of the rose petals.

She trained her mind to allow her body to become weightless, letting her arms float to the surface as her fingers relaxed and opened. Lifting her head, she massaged both temples with the tips of her fingers, then rested her bald head against the cool porcelain. It had taken only two short months for her entire head of hair to shed. Willing herself to be strong, she'd endured clumps of hair falling from her scalp, filling the comb with strands of dark auburn.

Lifting a velvety petal to her nose, she breathed the scent, allowing her thoughts to drift to the peacefulness she had felt in her heart yesterday at church. She was sure her patience and faith in God would enable her to endure any and all afflictions that lay before her.

"There you go again," said Ginger, sneaking up behind Jackson.

"What?"

"Planting those collards too close together." She stood at the edge of the tilled garden. Each year he planted a small patch of vegetables behind the garage. Although their yard was three-quarters of an acre, he refused to cut up a piece of his precious yard. He took pride in the well-manicured lawn, which resembled lush, green carpeting. Wouldn't let the kids have a dog because it would dig holes and patches around the doghouse. They'd begged him for years, until finally they gave up, and settled for a pet turtle.

Stopping to assess his progress, Jackson scratched his head. He wondered why he hadn't noticed it himself earlier.

They *were* too close together. "Damn," he said, taking the hoe and digging up the delicate plants.

"Kids up yet?" he asked, wiping the sweat from his forehead. Leaning against the hoe, he stopped to sip his frosted can of V8 juice, which sat on the windowsill of the garage. A pair of beige cotton gloves hung from the back pocket of his stone-washed jeans.

"I'm giving them another half an hour." She looked at her watch, squinting her eyes against the glare of the sun. It was just twenty-five past eight. "Why don't you ever wear these?" She touched the cotton fingers flapping against his buttocks in the brisk wind. He shrugged, finished his drink, and offered an expressive belch.

"Talked to Mama last night," he said, smiling.

Ginger stiffened as that old feeling of competition returned. She said a quick prayer, asking God to take these selfish feelings from her heart. "What about?"

He rested the garden tool against the brick siding. As his strong arms encircled her waist, he brushed a gentle kiss across her forehead. "I'm proud of you, baby. I told Mama about you getting saved yesterday. She's praying for you. I told her about—"

Ginger stiffened, "You didn't tell her about my hair, did you?"

"Baby, don't be so sensitive."

She withdrew from his embrace, nervously fingering the curls in her wig. "I just don't feel like I have to explain why I'm wearing a wig when we go down there in July."

He went back to making furrows in the ground, setting the bell pepper plants along the two outside rows. "Baby, you can't tell you've got on a wig. Anybody would think that it was your own hair. And Mama isn't going to mention it to anybody."

She knew how much faith Jackson put in his mother's prayers—knew his mother wouldn't tell anyone. Secretly, she'd thought of calling Mother Montgomery herself to ask that she and the saints of the church pray for her, yet each time she picked up the phone to dial the number her insides turned queasy. Would she ever get over this jealousy and competitiveness with his mother? Had she actually been saved yesterday to prove to Jackson that she was just as good as his mother was?

Ginger hadn't expected that being saved would be so easy, but it had been. Acts 16:30 to 31 of the Bible said that if you believed in the Lord Jesus Christ, you would be saved, and she had, and was reborn.

White petals from the trio of blossoming apple trees bordering the bricked patio blew softly in the wind, scattering across the yard, sprinkling the garden as a choir of robins fluttered through the branches.

Ginger brushed the petals from Jackson's hair, kissing him on the back of his neck. "I know she won't, honey. Thanks for asking her." She cupped his derriere, removed the gloves from his pocket, and pulled the large mitts over her manicured nails. They worked together, planting the remaining trays of vegetables, hosing them down afterwards, standing back to admire their handiwork.

Sitting on the stone bench of the patio, Ginger leaned her back against the brick wall to soak in the morning sun. "Jackson?" asked Ginger, hating to broach the subject, but knowing it had to be said.

"Yeah," said Jackson, straddling the lower wall of the patio, tilting his head to study the back of the fountain. "Damn. I can't figure out why the water won't come out." He scratched his head, holding a socket wrench.

"I have to go in the office for a few hours today." She saw his stern expression, and tensed.

"I thought we agreed right after your aunt died, you'd take this weekend off."

"It's just for a few hours, Jackson. I'm showing a house in Indian Village Monday to a client. I've got some paperwork to do for the homeowners. I won't have time to prepare all the documents after work Monday, and check the figures, before the appointment is scheduled."

Jackson's temper flared. She was hardly at home anymore. Spent very little time with the kids, and their time together consisted of quick romps in the sack late in the evening, and she had to wake him up from his sleep to get that. "Do what you have to do, Ginger."

"Sweetheart, I know I haven't been home as much as I'd planned. But I've worked out a solution."

"I'm listening." He'd taken off the fountain handle and was coating the inner threads with lubricating grease.

A broad smile beamed across her face as she spoke. "I figure if I drove my van to work, I could come home early and put in the hours at the office, be finished by two or three, and have dinner started by the time you sit down in front of your Westerns."

"You're going to be able to do all that? Drive to work, work at the office, cook dinner, and take care of me?" He shook his head, sighing deeply, as she eagerly nodded yes to all four questions. "Is selling real estate that important to you?"

Over the past seventeen years, Ginger had begun work daily at five in the morning. She usually finished by ten-thirty or eleven in the morning, and would pick up a book and read, or talk on the phone until it was time for Jackson to get off work at two-thirty.

"Yes, Jackson it is. I'm good at it, too. You'll see." It was her ticket out of that plant. She felt it in her heart, could see herself successful, and prayed nightly for the victory. A ticket to salvation. God only knew how much she needed to be free to live a normal life like other people did. Like her clients did. Getting up at seven or eight in the morning, watching the eleven o'clock news at night. Simple pleasures people normally took for granted.

"Do what you gotta do," he said, still straddling the short wall. He didn't like it, but he knew that Ginger needed to keep her mind off her hair. Even though she tried to shrug it off, like it wasn't bothering her this time, he knew she was hurting. He saw the pain each morning as she put her wig over her smooth head, and every night when she put it back on the Styrofoam stand.

Studying Jackson as he sat on the wall, Ginger decided he looked like a cowboy on his rearing horse. His jeans and shirt were grimy with the dirt of the garden and splotches of grease from the fountain, his hair was matted and speckled with white petals, and salt-and-pepper whiskers shadowed his unshaven face. And yet the musky sweat coming from his body smelled like a whiff of provocative perfume. The power of his hazel eyes drew her in like magnets. Her cowboy. Tonight they'd ride into the sunset together.

"What you daydreaming about, Ginger? You look—"

The sound of motorcycles from more than three blocks away caught Jackson's attention. He listened intently to clamor of the approaching machines. "That's Mr. B," said Jackson, leaning toward the blaring sound.

"How can you tell?"

"By the sound—Mr. B's riding a Yamaha. Sounds like a little car with a small engine in it, like a Fiat." Hearing the tone of the next bike, he said, "That's Ramsey's Honda." He saw her questioning look, and explained, "Sounds like a Yugo." Next, a louder sound. "That's Ves driving his Honda. His bike is older than Ramsey's, pipes are almost burned out . . . louder." A smooth, even sound hummed behind the trio. "That's Little Bubba." Still the questioning look from Ginger. "He's driving his new Harley. A Harley has a two-stroke engine."

"That's different from your Kawasaki?"

"Yeah, all the other bikes, Hondas, Yamahas, Suzukis, have four strokes. Try to listen to the sound of the exhaust pipes. Mine is a two in a two . . . two cylinders going into the left side and two cylinders going into the right side of the exhaust pipes. Some bikes are four in one . . . all four cylinders going into one pipe out the back of the bike . . . see . . . listen. . . . My Kaw sounds heavier."

He smiled to himself as he thought about the Harley. He wanted to trade in his Kaw and buy a Harley, but he didn't want to broach the subject to Ginger. She'd bought his Kawasaki as a surprise after his special-edition Kawasaki LTD had been stolen from the ethnic festival downtown.

He went on explaining to Ginger as the bikes rounded the corner. "A Harley has a unique sound. It can be distinguished as far off as it can be heard. The wind carries the sound."

An "oh" was all Ginger could manage to answer as the male members of Jackson's Production 10 Motorcycle Club approached their driveway in single file. "Hi Mr. B., Ramsey. Hi Ves, Bubba . . ." greeted Ginger, still amazed that Jackson had guessed the order of the bikes correctly.

Ginger walked toward the house, knowing without being asked that five cold ones would be more than welcomed. Minutes later, she sat a six-pack of beer on the patio table. They each thanked Ginger for the cold brew. Jackson had turned on the stereo system he'd installed in the garage, tuning it to 1400 FM, the blues station. He'd backed his black-and-gold Kawasaki from the garage stall as his friends stood around appraisingly. It was their ritual to check out the condition of each member's bike at the beginning of bike-riding season.

Ginger went back into the house unnoticed. She knew they'd be out there for hours, talking, laughing, reminiscing about the Kentucky Derby they attended each year, the first weekend of May. Jackson and Ginger were unable to attend this year with the other members and their wives. Jackson's boss had put in a request for Jackson to be put on a special team that was being formed to help eliminate millions of dollars of waste in the plant. Jackson was elated that he'd been chosen. Though the timing was bad, he'd happily agreed to join the pilot project.

Pausing to take a final look at her Black cowboy, his long body leaning against his metal horse, Ginger smiled to see him enjoying himself.

Looking outside her patio window, Katherine watched the man cutting her lawn. He wore a tank top and she could see his muscles glistening with sweat. She had only spoken to him over the phone, when he'd agreed to come by Saturday after he finished his mother's yard.

Katherine glanced up at the clock above the refrigerator. The sound of the mower had awakened her; it was early. Stretching her arms above her head, she sank her fingers into her thick head of hair, feeling the coarse edges. *Shit!* Her scalp was still wet; her head had gotten sweaty last night, dreaming about Jewel.

Moving to the refrigerator, she poured herself a generous glass of beer. As she turned on the radio, she thought of her sister-in-law. Jewel, just seventy years old, had been thirteen years her senior. Though Jewel hadn't looked old, she'd aged since Ollie had got sick. Little by little, her vivaciousness had been drained from her. She'd given up. Katherine had felt months ago that Jewel was the one who needed medical attention. Ollie would make it. Even though he'd had a temporary setback and lost his power of speech, Katherine still saw the fight in his eyes. He hadn't given up, as Jewel had. She knew that sooner or later, Ollie would garner the strength and find the courage to free himself from the cocoon that sheltered him from life.

Kim had been a pillar of strength throughout the whole ordeal. Katherine was proud of the stamina and tenacity shown by her niece. Kim had inherited Ollie's stamina, Katherine's intelligence, and Jewel's looks. A helluva combination. She was going to be fine, just fine.

Katherine consumed her second glass of golden spirits and looked again through the patio windows at the handsome man, sweating profusely now, as he filled the tank with gasoline. She contemplated her next move. Figuring she had at least a good hour and half before he'd be finished, she rushed upstairs to put her plan into action.

"Whhhhhew. Thank you, ma'am," said the young man. He drank the cold lemonade in three gulps. The sweat from the glass ran down his neck, along his Adam's apple, as he tipped his head back.

Katherine watched in awe. Up close, his muscles were even more impressive. He was taller than she expected. Probably six-one, six-two, she figured, lowering her gaze from his uplifted arm, hesitating at the bulge nestled against his thigh.

"Why don't you stop and rest a minute? You're not in any hurry, are you?" said Katherine, holding down the brim of her straw hat against a quick gust of wind.

Intrigued by his stories of Vietnam, she listened intently as he filled her in on the last fifteen years of his life after he returned home from the Service. His name was James Cotton, but all his friends called him Cotton. He'd contracted a severe case of quartan malaria and was sent back home to the veterans' hospital. There, he was diagnosed as also having a disease that affected the nervous system.

The government had sprayed this orange *mixture*—Agent Orange—over the area where the soldiers were fighting. It was used as a defoliant, to kill leafy plants and trees that provided cover for the Vietcong. But the plan had backfired, and the government knew it. Thousands of American soldiers were affected by the spraying and were subsequently sent back home.

Cotton was involved in a lawsuit against the government because it turned out that the military knew about the side effects all the time, and chose to ignore them. He was bitter about risking his life, fighting in a war he didn't believe in, and coming home to spend twelve years cooped up in a facility that made him feel more like a prisoner than a war hero. Not being able to hold down a full-time job, he'd started mowing lawns in the summer and shoveling snow in the winter. It was just pocket change, but his lawsuit would be coming up in court soon, and he could purchase the truck and tools he needed to really make some money.

Katherine immediately felt a kinship. He sounded mature, was moderately handsome, and, if she'd read correctly between the lines, was looking for a woman. Katherine shimmied the bodice of her sundress down, with the finesse of an old pro at work, to show the fullness of her caramel breasts, and ran her hand over her long, thick head of red hair, which men seemed to love to touch.

Near dark, she and Cotton had moved from the backyard to Katherine's living room. After consuming two quarts of beer, they were laughing like two old friends. She showed him around the house. He was impressed with its large basement. It was done in knotty pine, had a bar similar to the one he'd seen in the Red Shingles, a spot everyone in Port Huron frequented on the weekends. He stopped short to stare at the huge workroom. There were drawers, compartments, and pegboard sheets of paneling for hanging tools, and tables bearing impressions from the weight of table, hand, and power saws. A carpenter's paradise.

She sat in front of the bar as he mixed and poured them drinks. She wondered if he could be in love with a woman his age. What did love have to do with anything, anyway? Not a damn thing, in her mind. Not a damned thing. He looks like he belongs here, she thought. And judging by the signals he was sending her with his body and his mind, he thought so too.

"You sure this is what you want to do, Kim?" asked Randall, closing his hairy, tanned hands around hers.

They sat at a small table near the window, awaiting their dinner, going over Kim's plans for her future. Kim had called Randall late Friday evening after Bill had left and asked him to join her for dinner tonight. She'd selected a small, out-of-the-way restaurant that she knew hadn't made it onto his list of the "in" places to dine. She was ready to make some changes in her life.

"I have little choice, Randall. I can't keep working with George Cameron. He'll end up firing me. Then where will I be." She withdrew her hands, leaning back in her seat. "No, I think it's better that I make a clean break and quit. I typed out my resignation this morning. He should receive it by Monday. I sent it registered mail."

"Then it's settled. Where do we begin?"

"Then you'll help me?" asked Kim excitedly.

"What are friends for?"

Kim smiled at the Black couple seated in the small dining room, who had been eyeing them since the moment they arrived. Hadn't they seen an interracial couple having dinner before? There were three other tables occupied by two women, a single male, and a young child and grandmother, none of whom seemed bothered or interested.

While they ate, Kim agreed that during the four months she needed to wait to qualify to be a licensed broker, she would shop for her office equipment. She needed two computers, a fax machine, a copier, and a laptop computer. Randall tallied up the figures for the purchases, giving Kim a quizzical look.

"Are you sure you have enough money for all this, and to live on until you get on your feet? I told you, and I mean it Kim, I can make you out a check—"

"I've been saving money for years, Randall. Taking risks

with my investments, and they've worked out. I'm not saying I'm loaded, but by no means am I near needing a loan." She added thoughtfully, "But if it becomes necessary that I do, you'll be the first one I'll come to."

"Have you thought of a name yet?"

"Jewel Investment Services, Inc.," she said proudly.

"Has a rich ring to it, doesn't it?"

"About as rich as this dessert we're eating. How do you like it?" She frowned. His expression mirrored hers. She lifted the fork from her plate, chocolate filling running through the prongs. "This Mud Pie is just like it reads, muddy." They laughed together, enjoying each other's company, making jokes about Cameron, whom they both had reasons to dislike.

"So, you've decided to call it quits with Bill?" asked Randall, getting serious.

Pushing her dessert plate forward, she tapped her flamingo-pink sculptured nail along the edge. "I've decided to try celibacy for a while. I don't have time for romance right now. What's important is helping my father to get well and opening my business. I've tried it the easy way, and it hasn't worked, the only road left is the uncertain one—which I'm traveling alone."

"You're on the right road, Kim. You're heading in the right direction. Just don't plan on making too long of a journey alone." He leaned back, extracting a toothpick from his suit pocket. "Believe me, there will come a time, and it won't be very long, when you'll feel the need to connect with someone, emotionally, spiritually, and sexually. Someone to share your most intimate thoughts, feelings. Someone to laugh with, cry with, someone you can put your faith and trust in, someone you can lean on for understanding." Randall's turquoise blue eyes looked into Kim's, expressing a pain he was helpless to hide.

"You two still haven't made up?" Kim asked with sympathy.

"No," he whispered. "He doesn't want to make a commitment. Claims I'm suffocating him, he enjoys his freedom." He issued a halfhearted laugh. "Can you believe he tells me how much he loves me, has never loved anyone as he does me. Yet, he won't come out and admit he's gay."

"Are you willing to do that, Randall?"

He squared his shoulders, sitting up proudly. "Yes. I've given it a lot of thought. I'm not embarrassed about who I am or what I am. Why should I hide it?"

"You shouldn't." Leaning across the table, Kim caressed his arm. The young couple turned up their noses like they'd sniffed something foul in the air. Kim boldly kissed Randall on his cheek, ruffling his smooth raven hair, before she sat back in her seat, glaring at them.

It was late, and after a long day—she had even played Scattergories with the kids—Ginger was exhausted. But seeing the smiles on their faces was worth it. Jason, who had gotten a rare Saturday evening off work, had opted to break a date with his girlfriend and stay home. He was making the girl suffer, a control tactic a friend of his had hipped him to. As Jason explained the mechanics of dating to Christian, Ginger watched her younger son's obvious admiration of his older brother's worldly wisdom.

Ginger kissed each of her children good night as they continued playing. She reminded Jason they had church tomorrow, and they'd all have to be in bed by eleven. Hearing their moaning and groaning, she left them. They turned their conversation back to the game at hand.

"Hey, sweetheart. You miss me?" she called in to Jackson as she changed into her nightgown.

The room was flooded with light. Warm gusts of wind blew in through the open windows behind the sofa, billowing the curtains into poufs of bishop's sleeves. Soft music rode along the waves of fresh air as Jackson studied the loose pieces of metal spread before him on layers of newspaper. "Hmmmmmm," was all he managed to say, as he contemplated the gear mechanism.

On the weekends after a hot shower, Jackson loved to work on small objects in the comfort of his bedroom while he watched television or listened to the radio.

"What you doing, honey?" She sat beside him on the sofa. Scooting her body close to his, she fondled the back of his head and felt the dampness in his hair. He'd just taken a shower, and wore only a pair of red undershorts.

"The gauges on my bike weren't working right. The speedometer wouldn't move past thirty." He smiled smugly to himself. "I was doing at least eighty on the freeway this afternoon."

"Honey, don't you think you and your friends are getting a little too old to be speeding?"

He gave her a devilish look, moving his eyes in the direction of the bed, at her, then finally at the bulge building between his legs. He smiled at her seductively. "Got any complaints?"

He had a way of looking at her, of lowering his eyes and staring intensely for long periods of time until she was unable to resist him. "Not a one, honey," she said, contemplating the passion that his eyes suggested. "I see you've got on some nice music for a change. It's soothing, isn't it?"

"Yeah."

She reached over, massaging the length of his bare thighs. "When we're in bed, and you turn on the soft music you know I love, why do you act like it kills you to listen to it sometimes? I don't understand why you don't like listening to anything other than the blues and news."

He pulled back the insulation, exposing the cable, and looked at her. "You know the reason why I've got this station on?"

She shook her head, looping her arm through his, trying to coax him into paying her some attention and putting his toys away.

"I took some screws off the back of the radio to see if they would match the ones missing from the speedometer bracket, and now this is the only station I can get."

"Sweetie, you listen to that news station all the way to work and all the way home—"

"I like to learn something about what's going on in the world."

"If you read something other than the sports section in the newspaper, you might learn something."

"I can't learn nothing listening to music."

"You can learn sensitivity."

He gave her another seductive smile. "I've already got that."

"Who told you that lie?" They laughed together as he pushed aside the speedometer and guided his wife to their haven of pleasure. . . .

He rode her as long and hard as an adventurous ride on his Kawasaki, and they lay happy, breathing heavily. "You get enough?" he whispered, stroking her buttocks as he pulled her against him.

"I could stand a longer ride, that is, if you're up to it, old man," she kidded.

He lifted up the sheet, proudly displaying his growing erection. "Must be all that V8 juice I've been drinking."

Stepping from the shower, Mae Thelma toweled herself dry, lavished her body with lotion, and strolled into the bedroom stark naked. Turning off the lights, she lighted a scented candle and placed it on the nightstand near the bed.

She turned the dial on the bedside radio until she heard a soft, soulful tune. Swiveling her legs from beneath her, she lay back, sinking her head into the soft pillows. She cupped her large breasts, stroking the fullness with the curve of her thumbs. Her dark areolae peaked as she felt a warmth flowing through her body.

It had been so long since she felt a man's body lying next to hers. Felt the warmth of his love melding with hers. Her breathing became short at the thought of him. She arched her buttocks, drew up her knees, stroking the soft folds of flesh. Flickering her slender fingers across the hard jewel of her womanhood, her body writhed beneath her. She felt the moistness coating her fingers as she offered her body relief from months of celibacy.

Opening and closing like a shell, she felt the throbbing, throbbing, throbbing of her passion, grabbing in need of male penetration. Her fingers worked fiercely, faster, frantically, until at last, with a sweet sigh of relief, she felt herself relaxing, uttering a cry of pleasure.

As she cleaned herself with the white cloth, she felt anger slowly rising from the pit of her stomach. She knew that once a young girl became a woman, that feeling of needing a man and loving a man, sharing the intimacies that transpire between them, was meant by God to be experienced for life. Not just a temporary thing. She'd tried to be faithful in God's eyes, prayed for strength, yet her needs were as great as ever. She was a woman, and she had a woman's needs.

Tears sprang into her eyes, tears of guilt and shame from knowing she desired the comfort and love of a man whose golden brown eyes seemed to visit her in the darkness.

20

Oooo Baby, Baby

The double doors were pushed open wide. Dozens of hangers lay bare, pushed together in the right corner of the closet. Large brown cartons filled with clothing lined a complete wall of the modest bedroom. Smaller boxes taped and labeled with a black Magic Marker read: *Shoes, Hats, Lingerie. . . .*

"Don't touch that, Autumn," said Ginger, taking the silver frame from her small hand. Kim and Ginger sat on the floor going through Jewel's cedar chest. Autumn sat in front of the round dressing table, looking into the mirror.

Kim put an arm around Autumn's shoulder, explaining, "That's my mommy, Autumn." She pointed to the man standing next to her. "And that's my father."

"Don't look like Aunt Jewel or Uncle Ollie," said Autumn.

Kim kneeled down beside her as Ginger continued removing the quilts packed neatly inside the xyloid trunk. "They were just married, sweetheart. Mama was eighteen, and

Daddy was twenty-two." She smiled at the picture, closing her hand over Autumn's. "Don't they look handsome?"

Autumn nodded. She knew her great-aunt Jewel had died not long ago. That was why her mommy brought her over, to help Kim go through her mommy's old things. She wanted to ask Kim how come Uncle Ollie wasn't coming home to live with her now, but something told her to just be quiet. "Your nails are pretty. My mommy doesn't have that color," observed Autumn, studying Kim's beautifully manicured nails.

"Would you like to paint your nails this color?" asked Kim, smiling at Autumn. "There's a bottle on my table in my room down the hall." Autumn scooted off the chair and was halfway out the door before she peeked back around to look at her mother.

"Is it okay if I paint my nails, Mommy? I won't make any mess."

Ginger took her little hand, escorting her to Kim's room. She placed old newspapers over the rectangular table, stacked two pillows on the chair, and tied an apron she'd found in the linen closet around her daughter's neck. Then she planted Autumn in the center of the cushions and handed her the opened bottle of flamingo-pink polish.

"Thanks, Kim. She's getting a little bored. I was hoping she would fall asleep until we finished."

"The kids gone for the weekend again?"

"Um-hum. Left yesterday. Jackson's at home watching the Pistons and Bulls playoff game, so I didn't want to ask him to watch her. He can't stand being interrupted when the game is on. What time is it?"

"Almost eight."

Walking over to the dresser, Ginger turned on the small radio to News Radio 95. "The game is almost on. Might as well listen to it. Haven't listened to George Blaha over the radio in a while." She sat down, crossing her legs in front of the mounds of quilts. "You don't mind, do you?"

Kim shook her head, as she focused her eyes back on the photograph. "You think I'm doing the right thing, Ginger, giving Mama's things to the Salvation Army?"

"Yes," said Ginger, patting her on the back. "You'll never wear them. It doesn't make sense to hang on to articles of clothing when someone else who's needy could be making good use of them. Now . . . her old costume jewelry is another matter altogether."

"I just don't get it, Ginger. One day you have on a man's suit and tie, and mannish, wide-rimmed hats, then flashy sparkly dresses, jeans and T-shirts." She threw her hands into the air as she continued. "Then the next thing I know, you've changed again into flared peasant skirts and Cinderella blouses, or romantic ankle-length period dresses . . . and now you want antique jewelry. . . . I can't figure out your style."

Ginger smiled and winked at her. "That's what style is."

"Point taken. The jewelry's yours." Kim sat back, looking pleased, and said, "Got a surprise for you."

"What?"

"I want you to list the house for me. I've decided to sell it."

"You did?"

"After the attorney, Mr. Hammond, read the will, I was shocked when I found out Mama had left me quite a bit of money."

"You told me you knew how much money your parents had saved."

"I know I did. But Mama had this money in her maiden name: Jewel Kimmery Kramer. Her attorney had been paying the taxes on the principal for the past twenty-five years. She put the money my grandfather had left her in an account when she was pregnant with me. Hadn't even told my father about it. She told Mr. Hammond to make a high-risk, long-term investment, because she planned on giving the money to her son or daughter when they were married." Tears welled in Kim's eyes as she looked at her ringless fingers.

The fans' cheers and screams seemed inappropriate and Ginger struggled to find words of comfort to ease her cousin's pain. Kim's decision not to accept Bill's proposal of marriage might not have been the correct choice in Ginger's mind, but knowing that Kim rarely made important judgments without carefully weighing the pros and cons, she kept her opinions to herself.

"Your father will live to see you walk down that aisle one

day soon, Kim—and your mother will be seeing you through his eyes," said Ginger seriously.

Kim gave her an appreciative smile. "We can't sit here all day, chatting like two old women. Let's get busy." She paused to regain her composure. "Thanks, Ginger."

"Thank you for giving me the privilege of listing my first home."

"I figure . . ." began Kim, and launched into the details. There was a vacant loft apartment being remodeled in the building that Randall lived in downtown. She'd given them a deposit, and planned on moving by the first of July, when the renovations would be completed. The apartment was in the right location for her in-home business, and close to the nursing home she was moving her father to. The new senior center had a new treatment program that had just been introduced by a resident physician.

"Oh my goodness!" Ginger was surprised to hear the crowd cheering the Pistons' victory over the Chicago Bulls.

"Are you that excited over the Pistons winning?"

Ginger jumped to her feet, heading for the door, then spun back around. "Yes, but we've been talking for hours. I haven't heard a peep from Autumn."

Kim followed her down the hall, peering over Ginger's shoulder as they observed Autumn sleeping peacefully at the dressing table. Two bottles of opened polish lay before her. She'd found Kim's box of press-on nails—and pressed all ten over her tiny fingers. Slivers of pink were visible around the edges, and the generous coat of shocking red polish made them resemble vampire claws.

Ginger and Kim could only laugh.

Ginger felt the picture of success and supreme satisfaction painted inside her head, like God's paintbrush when he created the earth and stars. She couldn't have been more pleased at this moment of her life; she was in heaven. She knew that there were better things still to come.

Jackson had suggested that they go out and celebrate after she'd closed on the home in Indian Village. It hadn't been a large commission because someone else had listed the home, but it was a start.

Admiring Ginger's buttocks bouncing provocatively in the supple silk jersey fabric of her form-fitting dress, Jackson opened the glass door of Fishbone's of Greek Town, at 400 Monroe Street, as Ginger passed before him. He gave the maître d' the name for their reservations, and a short time later they were seated next to a beautiful waterfall.

Sitting down, Ginger felt as though their table were situated in the open air of a veranda. The atmosphere was naturally so romantic, just like a picture-postcard she'd seen of a warm scene of two lovers at Niagara Falls on their honeymoon. The fresh zest of approximately six thousand gallons of water per hour rushing down variegated columns of Mediterranean marble over a hundred feet high was entrancing.

"Come on sweetheart, let's make a wish," said Ginger, rising from the table and raising her voice above the thundering force of the multitiered waterfall.

The lighted pool was filled with glittering waves of copper and silver from other well-wishers hoping their dreams would also come true. Closing her eyes, Ginger felt a cool breeze brushing her face, and threw several copper coins over her shoulder. She wished for a successful career in the real estate business that would allow her to quit her job next year.

Jackson wished for good health, and the opportunity to get the transfer to Mississippi and move his family back home. Several engineers in Mississippi were retiring in two and a half to three years, and the company planned on replacing them with a transfer from another facility. Jackson hoped that engineer would be him. He had all the qualifications the job required, and the seniority that would almost guarantee the lateral move.

"Here's to you, baby, and to many more closings," said Jackson, lifting his glass to hers. Clinking their glasses together in a salute, he with a flute of whiskey and water and she with sparkling cider. As he drank, he eyed her appraisingly. *So this is where you and Kim went while I was away?* he thought but did not say. Instead he asked Ginger, "Who'd you say told you about this place?" An innocent smile came across his face.

It was a small world. One of Jackson's cycle checkers, who worked for him at the plant, had clued him in the moment he returned to work that he'd seen Ginger and some fine chick in Greek Town. He'd noticed them from the window of Fishbone's as he was on his way up to the nightclub, and saw the two of them later that evening upstairs, mingling with the older set. Jackson was mildly perturbed that Ginger hadn't mentioned she'd gone out. What bothered him was the fact that the cycle checker had told him how good Ginger looked in her minidress.

A minidress! Ginger knew his views on appropriate attire, and apparently while he was away, she'd chosen to ignore them. No respectable woman, married and with children, wore minidresses unless she was looking for something, he insisted. Women who stood on the street corners at night, the kind of women who wore clumps of makeup at night, stockings with unsightly runs—they wore those short skirts.

The young man had assured Jackson that Ginger hadn't danced with anyone. And that he saw them leave by twelve, *alone*. Jackson wouldn't trust Kim alone with his ninety-year-old grandfather. He'd bide his time, catch Ginger off-guard, and find out how the rest of the evening went. And he knew just how to get her to talk.

Ginger stiffened. All her jubilation of the evening disappeared as she tortured herself with the idea that he knew she'd gone out but was keeping it to himself. He couldn't possibly know, could he?

"Kim," she said nervously. "Kim told me about this place." She looked around the room of people seated at other tables, trying to avoid his piercing stare. "Don't you"—she stopped as her eyes rested on a familiar face—"like it?" Ivory Michaels. The newscaster. Before she could bring her head back around, their eyes met, and he smiled casually.

Jackson leaned back in his chair, missing nothing. "Yes, it's nice." He raised an eyebrow, then picked up the menu to study the spicy Cajun entrées.

Ginger already knew what she wanted to order and closed the plastic-covered folder, scanning the restaurant a second time. At seven-thirty on a Saturday evening, the popular bistro was filled to capacity. The constant shuffling of feet moving to and from the waterfall sounded like the hoofbeats of cattle stampeding over a prairie.

"Jambalaya . . . mmm," said Jackson amusingly. "Pecan trout, alligator, smoked whiskey ribs, crawfish étouffée and cat—"

"You should try the catfish, honey. It—" She caught herself. "Kim said it tastes like butter."

Ginger still felt a little uneasy having to keep something from Jackson, but she knew he'd take it the wrong way if she confided in him that she had been lonely and upset about losing her hair.

She knew that Jackson's desire for her was still as strong as ever. When they were in bed together, he made her feel as if he worshiped her body and couldn't get enough of seducing her, but that wasn't enough to make her feel attractive. His approval in the bedroom was no measure of her self-worth, but apparently he seemed to think otherwise.

She wagged her bare foot over her crossed leg under the table, until it touched the leg of his pants. Arching her foot, she traced a path along his thighs, ending at his crotch, grazing the bulge in his pants with probing toes.

Judging by the slow seductive smile forming across his face, she knew that later, no matter what the evening entailed, they'd surrender to their silent obsession.

Ginger continually scanned the room. She noticed Ivory Michaels's ominous stare once again since their eyes met earlier. Ivory continued his lynx-like gaze until Ginger turned away. He reminded her of one of those poor little rich boys who was bored with his toys and needed something new to play with.

Though internally Ginger felt somewhat inhibited, outwardly she projected her best. Sexy and confident, she emanated warmth and vitality.

Ginger noticed the impatience in Ivory's date's attitude as his gaze shifted from her to the other woman. Ginger was a woman who offered a challenge, something Ivory's date was undeniably lacking.

"Ivory?" said the woman, trying to break into his thoughts.

Pulling his attention back to her, he turned to address the business at hand. "You were saying, Elizabeth?"

"Has something or someone else caught your attention?" asked Elizabeth Guest.

He touched her jet black hair across the table, looking into her violet eyes, "Away from you, my dear?" There was music in the question.

Jackson licked his lips, tasting the last of his Bourbon Street bread pudding, just as Ginger popped the last crumbs of her Key lime pie into her mouth. "Mmmmmmm. Good, isn't it?"

"Next time I'll have the pecan pie for dessert."

"Next time. You mean you want to come back?"

"This is just like home. I gotta bring Mama here next summer when she comes up."

Why did he have to spoil the evening by bringing up his mother? Everything was going too well. Couldn't they have a moment together without his mother's name being brought into the conversation? Didn't he realize how upsetting it was to have him constantly mentioning his mother, even during their private moments, which she felt should be shared by just the two of them? God knew her mother-in-law had done nothing to warrant such feelings, yet Ginger was powerless to control the resentment she felt in her heart.

Mae Thelma stared up, mesmerized by the heat of the flickering flames as another explosion rocked her house. Red, blue, and yellow sparks circled the brick bungalow as smoke poured out of it.

She stood next to the neighbors she'd known for the past nine years, who cried for her and issued their prayers of thanks that her sons had been away and no one was hurt. No one but Mae Thelma knew the truth—that she had secretly started the fire. And that this was precisely why she'd sent her boys away to a church member's house for the weekend.

"Oh my Lord," said a voice from the crowd, watching the engulfing flames spread.

Mae Thelma's small house sat on a corner lot. There was a larger home adjacent to hers, but fortunately it wasn't touched by the fire. The firemen worked feverishly to contain the blaze.

Tears streamed from Mae Thelma's eyes. But they were

tears of joy, not sorrow. A woman standing next to her, mistaking their source, hugged her shoulders as they stood watching the firefighters try to save the little house.

Going to be butterfly mornings, and wildflower afternoons, thought Mae Thelma. In her heart, she knew she was treading on the thin side of evil. For the time being, she had to be still, patient, and humble.

It was as if someone had snapped off the lights and, frozen in time, the stars were gazing down, their moonlit reflections gazing up. In the quiet of the night, probing eyes were watching her, while one pair of eyes was watching over all.

Mae Thelma thought back on the sermon the pastor had preached at the Thursday evening service:

"God wants for his people to be all that they can be. A seed. It starts as small things, and ends up a big thing. A thorn is another place that resists change. A thorn is hard and resistant to the seed needed for growth.

"The soil is nothing without the seed. One without the other is nothing. The soil needs the seed as much as the seed needs the soil. The soil is the word of God. We must be rooted in the soil. We cannot realize our spiritual growth without the word of God. Giving you power, strength, and guidance."

Mae Thelma thought about the seed and her personal growth in the Lord. She'd felt as if the pastor had been talking directly to her. It was time for a change. She felt it in her heart, her body, her soul. Staring at the flames, she knew she'd done the right thing. It was time. Time for her. Time for her children, and time for *him* to learn that there were some people put on this earth to care for other people, and there were some people who needed to be taken care of. Jackson needed that from her.

She kicked a pebble near the firelight with the toe of her house slipper and smiled to herself. Soon, she thought. Soon, there would be seeds planted, and the growth of the richness of her fertile body would be the evidence of the changes and growth being sowed by their union.

21

I'm Gonna Make You Love Me

"Kids okay?" asked Jackson as he hung his suit in the closet. Standing in his ribbed cotton T-shirt and briefs, his dusky physique seemed the perfect embodiment of male beauty.

Turning her focus away from his body, Ginger took off the red dress. "Fine." She thought of Ivory Michaels and Sierra's unwavering crush on him. Ginger had seen him again on the six o'clock news, and noticed his co-anchor, Elizabeth Guest, was back in her spot. She had been on leave for the past four months because of a notorious scandal. They were rumored to be having an affair.

Ginger told Sierra that she'd seen the two of them at the restaurant where she and Jackson celebrated her closing. Sierra asked a million questions. How did he look in person? Were his eyes as gray, or were they more blue? Were his eyelashes really that long? Was his hair naturally wavy or was it from a Jheri-curl kit?

Sierra was disappointed when Ginger admitted that she hadn't gotten close enough to answer most of her questions. Her view of him had been partially blocked, but she had to admit to herself that he was extremely good looking in person despite his fair complexion.

Ginger smiled to herself as she entered the sitting room. To her dismay, Jackson was thoroughly engrossed in *Rio Lobo,* featuring John Wayne—one of Jackson's favorite heroes.

The sound of a six-shooter banging away on the television wasn't exactly the musical score Ginger had in mind as the denouement of their evening. Nevertheless, all the grunts, snorts, rumbles, whistling, and cackling seemed to hold Jackson's attention, thwarting her efforts to create a more romantic atmosphere. She went down to the kitchen.

Jackson joined Ginger downstairs as she prepared hot tea. He filled a thermal quart jug of ice, topping it with a generous splash of Diet Pepsi. "Oh, I see we gave up on our V8 juice." She angled her head slightly, glaring at him. "Perhaps my man has traded sex for horses."

He walked toward her, passion in his eyes. With the sleek movements of a tiger, graceful and carefree, he whisked a cool kiss across her cheek, winking seductively as he climbed the stairs.

Suddenly, from above the stairs, came a slow voice inviting her to hurry and join him. Guessing the evening might be taking on a whole new aspect, she fixed her cup of tea and went quickly up the stairs.

He always took everything so slow. Ginger admired that in Jackson. He was so methodical in everything he did. She knew he had absolute control over her in the bedroom, though she often tried to deny it. She tried desperately to emulate his cavalier attitude, but it just wasn't in her.

Kicking the door shut behind her, the darkness and quiet turned her apprehension into anticipation. She heard him moving . . . no, she felt him stirring in the bed.

"Baby," his voice summoned caressingly.

"I'm coming, sweetheart." She knew that in a few short minutes that was exactly what she'd be whispering in his ear. Resting the mug on the coffee table, she clicked on soft pink nightlights on each side of the headboard. Ginger hesitated for a luxurious moment to sachet her body with sweet jasmine before joining Jackson in bed. "You forgot to turn on the music, honey."

He reached for her, caressing her naked buttocks beneath her gown. "When did I need a stereo to make beautiful music to your body?" His tongue swept the soft column of her neck, trailing kisses along the nape, up and along the bare side of her face.

"You don't," she whispered, closing her eyes. Her fingers trailed the long expanse of his thighs, luxuriating in the softness of his flesh. She toyed with the tight curls that coiled around his manhood, hesitating to touch his throbbing member. Her breathing quickened as he shifted his pelvis, causing his enlarged penis to graze her inner thigh.

"Ummmm, you smell good. It's been a while, baby," he said, aligning his body next to hers and kissing her moist lips with heated passion. His kiss deepened as his probing tongue sweetly claimed hers. Ginger welcomed him into her mouth, teasing him with ravenous strokes of her tongue, and tasted the Pepsi sweetening his mouth.

As their bodies lay together, Ginger's hand automatically reached for the vehicle that she knew would take them on a tumultuous journey toward heaven. And knowing that the intimacy from years of being together, caring for each other, and knowing each other, would take them even higher.

"Let's take it slow tonight, baby. I want you," he said, kissing her tenderly, "to want me," and added huskily, with another sonorous kiss against moist lips, "to want you."

"Just what I had in mind," said Ginger, guiding him to lie on his back. Then she reached into the nightstand for a small vial of oil.

Leaning over him, she dropped dots of sweet sandal oil over his naked flesh. Now, straddling his long form, her knees touching his, she floated her hands over the surface of his chest. Using the fingertips of both hands, his skin glistened as she gently massaged in the silky oil.

With feathering, butterfly carresses, she carefully, artfully, began traveling down his body with soft brush strokes until she felt him yielding. Then, leaning over his torso, she pulled firmly with her right hand, drawing it toward his chest, and paused just before reaching his nipple. With her left hand she pulled his warm flesh toward her, again ending at the hairy circle of his dark nebula. She continued alternating with both hands lower and lower, dissolving thought into rhythm, until only the rhythm existed.

"What you doing to me?" asked Jackson lazily.

"Loving you, baby."

Still kneeling over him, she continued the magical pursuit of arousal with her lover. In long, flowing, overlapping strokes, Ginger worked her way down methodically from shoulder to hand, inhaling the scrolling sweet sweat emanating from Jackson.

Raising his forearm, she held his hand palm up, and kissed it slowly, attentively, as if she were blessing it. She enclosed his wrist in her other hand, and massaged the interior of his hand. With the side of her thumb she created small circles, then larger ones inside his palm. Next, with his palm against the palm of hers, she matched her fingers with his, then slid her fingers upwards toward his fingertips, massaged and stroked the sides and insides of his fingers. She could feel the heat circulating, his pelvis articulating her message. After kissing the tip of each finger, she took each digit slowly into her warm mouth, and sucked.

Jackson shuddered with pleasure.

Carefully, she released his arm, then lowered her head farther down Jackson's quivering body. Ginger's tongue toured Jackson's abdomen with wide, wet strokes, down, down, until it touched his navel. She pressed her tongue inside the hollow of his stomach, alternately blowing into and kissing it. Her mouth and hands traveled from navel to nipples and back again; sucking, biting, licking, gripping, squeezing, kneading the supple skin.

"Oh—yes," Jackson murmured.

"Close your eyes, and tell me your deepest fantasy," said Ginger, now stimulating his lower torso. She tugged and pulled at his crotch hairs with her teeth, coming close to, but not touching, his burgeoning tower of manhood.

"Mmmmmm," he said sultrily. "To have an orgasm that lasts ten minutes, then being bone-deep inside you, and loving you *all* night long."

"Sounds like we're working on the same fantasy." Ginger said, her eyes melting into his.

Kissing him now, she arched her body to straddle one of his thighs as they embraced. Jackson raised his leg to rub her crotch back and forth, forcing then releasing pressure until he felt the creamy fluid signaling her passion.

Taking the lead, Jackson eased Ginger back onto the bed, glided her knees up, then pushed them open like broken butterfly wings. While softly kissing her, he inserted one finger, a second, stretching her open for the third, inside the folds of her flaming lips.

As Jackson stimulated her clitoris, working his fingers expertly inside her silken casing, Ginger felt like an orgasmic butterfly, her breath like the flutter of wings soaring higher, higher and still higher than she could imagine, until finally, she cried out in painful ecstasy.

Outside, the wind sang through the billowing pines, the delicate tracery of branches brushing against the windows. Then it began to rain.

Sharp cracks of thunder coupled with shrieks of lightning echoed in the sky above them. The rain fell in torrents while they made quiet love.

Moments later, the rain paused, creating patterns of moisture on the windows, tracing, lacing lines of wet trickled down the panes. A small shelf of water buildup formed a ledge on the sill.

Still holding the keys to the melody, Jackson and Ginger embraced each other as if they were stepping inside each other's bodies. Like a mixture of gin and juice, the energy between them flowed from body to body as the suede smoothness of Jackson's penis pressed breathlessly inside Ginger as deep as it would go.

Like a dancer, he was in complete control, but knew how to lose himself in the music. He trained his mind to regulate the rhythm of his breathing with slow, deep breaths. With each stroke of his manhood, more pressing than thrusting, they moved together in concert. Together, with the thunder, the wind, and the rain, the orchestra was building between them. Her body was like music harmonizing with his, the melody, harmony, rhapsody building, and still building to an emotional peak, their consonances timbred. Their pleasure drowned out every sound but the music they heard inside their souls.

Bold with love, Ginger's moist fingers cupped Jackson's buttocks, pulling him deeper into her burning heat, loving him as he loved her. Their melded bodies moved provocatively, hip pressed against hip, gasping, in an accelerated rhythm. And their passion heightened with every crash of thunder outside. Through the pleasure and pain, the wind and the rain, their bodies shuddered. There was rapture.

Outside, the beats of the rain softened, suddenly, then stopped.

"Jackson!" Ginger cried out in ecstasy.

He answered her with electric kisses on her lips before moving onto his knees and bringing her ankles over his shoulders. Jackson gracefully kissed the spines of both her heels while tucking a pillow beneath her buttocks. Their bodies wet with sweat, Jackson easily slid inside her silken casing, and began rotating his hips, accompanied with equal beats of thrusts. Each gasp from Ginger fueled Jackson's desire to satisfy as he angled his hips from side to side, taking care to touch the outer walls of her vagina.

"Am I hurting you baby?"

"No, sweetheart. Please don't stop," Ginger whispered.

Ginger eased her knees up a little closer on Jackson's shoulders. She knew the sensation was heightened for him as she squeezed the muscles of her pulsating vagina. She pressed her thighs together, playing him like a precious Stradivarius.

They came together; she became him, and he became her. And then, she trembled.

Outside, it began to rain . . . again.

"Hello," Ginger said sleepily into the mouthpiece, automatically checking the time. She sat upright in the bed, held captive by Mae Thelma's tearful version of her heart-wrenching loss.

Nudging the peaceful body next to her, Ginger shook and shook, until finally Jackson let go of his dreams and recog nized the urgency of her voice. "What time is it, baby? What's wrong?" he asked, mumbling.

She handed him the receiver, and he listened intently. Swinging his legs over the side of the bed, he picked up the phone and walked to the window, staring out into the darkness. As he placed the receiver back onto the cradle, he let out a deep breath.

Ginger followed behind him as he dressed. "You want me to go with you, honey?"

"No, you stay here and get the upstairs bedrooms ready. Wake up Jason, and ask him to help you." She could see his brain racing, thinking, yet all the time he was moving as slowly and gracefully as a leopard. Pausing at the door, he blew her a kiss, giving her a sweet, church-door expression. Suddenly, she felt a stab of fear.

As she turned the door to Jason's room, she stood stock still, praying silently to God to erase the jealous thoughts that were playing through her mind. Mae Thelma was saved and sanctified, wasn't she? She didn't have to worry about that gorgeous woman coming into her home and trying to steal her man as her mother had warned, did she?

She reflected on the pastor's message last Sunday. His words rang in her ears:

"If you do not love your fellow man that you have seen, how can you love the God whom you have not seen?"

She pushed the bad thoughts from her mind as she willed herself to do God's work and execute his will helping those in need.

As they slid beneath the covers, Jackson reached over and kissed his wife tenderly. "That was sweet of you, honey, to get those clothes for the boys. Thank God they weren't home tonight. They're going to need them when they come tomorrow." Pulling her close to him, her buttocks fitting neatly into his abdomen, he lined her shoulder with kisses.

Her body tensed.

"Ginger? Something wrong?"

"No. Nothing." She pulled the covers tightly around her shoulders, warding off further affection. "How long do you think they'll be here?" Her voice was filled with trepidation.

"It don't look good. The entire inside of the house is burnt. I don't know too much about fires, but if the insurance company decides to repair it instead of paying her off, it's gonna take months to get it in livable shape."

Months? "Oh. Well, we have plenty of room. They can stay as long as they like," she lied. God, she hated lying like that, but if he knew how she truly felt, he'd accuse her of not being saved. Lord knows she was trying as hard as she could to be humble and serve the Lord the best she could. God willing, she'd make it through the next few months.

Ginger tossed and turned all night, seeing visions of Jackson running his fingers through the long silky tresses that were Mae Thelma's only care, as she lay before him, nude.

Mae Thelma smiled smugly to herself. She was in his house. Looking around the modest surroundings of the maid's quarters, she knew she wouldn't be there long. It paled pitifully in comparison to Jackson's beautiful bedroom suite. Soon. Soon, she'd be walking through these double doors, her toes sinking into the plush peach carpeting, and reclining onto the king-size bed, awaiting the loving arms of her man.

With her right hand, she rubbed her inner thighs, running her finger through her waist-length hair until the silkiness feathered the peaked nipples of her full breasts. Reaching down, she placed her fingers between her legs. Imagining that those fingers would soon be replaced by the warmth of Jackson's manhood, it took only minutes for her to climax.

Ginger awakened in a cold sweat, as a pain, sharp as steel, stabbed at her heart. A small choir of birds chirped noisily outside her window. Wrapping her housecoat around her, she tiptoed downstairs. The first light of day streamed through the leaded windows . . . the outside world was wet and still, as dew clung to the grass. Delicate wisps of fog blurred the landscape.

She sipped her tea, talking to herself, trying to shed the ludicrous images that had held her from a sound sleep. Sighing, she leaned back in her chair and listened. Outside the breakfast room window, the little birds had gathered in the rosebushes, sparrows singing sweet and loud, bold bluebirds interrupting their melody.

Something in the house stirred, and she listened quietly as the unfamiliar footsteps spoke. Knowing the kids wouldn't get up this early, nor Jackson, she decided the only person treading down the back steps had to be . . . Mae Thelma!

22

I Second That Emotion

Why are you whispering?" asked the voice over the phone.

"Because she'll hear me if I speak any louder!" said Ginger, peeking around the doorway of the dining room. Tapping the receiver with the tips of her nails, she hesitated before continuing their conversation.

"Who in the hell is the *she* you're talking about?"

"Mama, it's Mae Thelma. Her house burned down the other night. She and the boys have moved in with us for a while."

"Ahhhhhhh shit. I smell trouble. What did I tell—"

"I know. I know, Mama. But there's nothing I can do about it right now. I think Jackson is trying to test how saved I am."

"Two women in one household, with one man—"

"I get your point, Mama. But I really think it's going to work out all right. We talked this morning, and she's offered to cook dinner and clean for me while I work at the agency. No need for the kids to keep doing all the work when she'll be here all day."

"Next thing you know she'll be doing the rest of your wifely duties." Like fucking your husband.

"I'm due at the agency in a couple of hours. I'll have to leave her here all day with Jackson. I don't think he's planning on going anywhere today. You know he watches——"

"... his Westerns all day, I know," finished Katherine bitterly. "I hate to tell you I told you so, but I told you months ago that that Cleopatra-looking bitch was after your husband. You mark my word."

"So haven't you been down lately?" asked Ginger, already knowing the answer.

"Didn't the kids tell you about James?"

"Yeah, they told me. But I wanted to hear about him from you. He's young, right?"

"Forty-three." Katherine waited to hear the quick intake of breath before she continued. "I'm tired of old-ass, decrepit men with one foot in the grave and the other one on a banana peel, smelling like mold."

"Mold?"

"Damn right. Moldy and stale. I bought James some cologne. What's the name of that cologne you bought for Jackson?"

"Calvin Klein's Eternity for Men?"

"Yeah, that's it. Smells like heaven on a young man. Wouldn't smell like shit on a old-ass motherfucker laying on the couch with three coats of Ben-Gay liniment on his body." They both laughed, and Katherine felt that Ginger had relaxed a bit. How could she tell her daughter that if it was her husband, she wouldn't let a female fly next to him for too long, let alone a woman?

"Mama?" Ginger's voice changed almost instantly. She worked her fingers nervously through the curly wig. "My eyebrows are coming out." She held her feelings in check as she waited for her mother's scolding about feeling sorry for herself.

"Ginger, I know it's hard." Katherine tried to suppress the pity in her voice. "But you've been through this before."

"I feel different somehow this time. It's not the same as before. I've never lost my eyebrows, only my lashes. I've got a bad feeling, Mama, and I don't know what to do about it."

"You been back to the U of M hospital?" She heard a garbled yes, and knew Ginger was holding back tears. "And they don't have any new treatments?"

"Uh-uh." Walking into the dining room, Ginger opened the french doors to let the wind blow across her face. The oriental garden she'd recently planted next to the patio was breathtakingly lovely. Tiny explosions of colors from exotic flowers filled the huge garden, against an emerald backdrop of cherry hardwoods and shrubs. Laburnum, sweet white alyssum, wispy white wisteria and clematis climbed along the brick walls.

Reaching beneath the cap, she loosened the hooks of the hairpiece as she felt the pressure of an oncoming headache. "Did I tell you I closed on my first house last week?" She angled her body in the doorway, to listen for the kids.

"Got any spare change for your mother?" asked Katherine, only half-kidding. James Cotton was costing her more than she'd anticipated. Sure, the thrill was worth it, but she couldn't discuss with Ginger the needs and habits of a young man trying to make his entrepreneurial mark in society. She just wouldn't understand.

"I didn't list the house, Mama, so my commission was pretty small. But I'm putting some of the money aside for Jason's graduation party. It'll coincide with his eighteenth birthday next June." She went on to explain to her mother about all the plans she made for an outdoor party on the patio, with rented palm trees and ice sculptures—it was going to be beautiful. After all, it wasn't every day your first child graduated.

They talked for a while longer about the other three children and how well each of them was doing in school—except Sierra. But Ginger left that out, knowing her mother had so many plans for her oldest granddaughter. After watching Carol Ann-Marie Gist from Detroit win the crown in the Miss USA pageant in Michigan, she'd told Sierra that someday she'd win it, too. If Katherine knew Sierra was almost two years behind in her reading level, she'd be praying right along with Ginger.

The sound of aluminum pots being set on the stove alerted Ginger that someone was in the kitchen. She looked in to find Mae Thelma, her hair flowing down her back like shimmering black diamonds. She's never worn her hair down before, thought Ginger. She is never without her trademark halo hairstyle.

"Figured I fix breakfast for the family. They'll be up soon. It's almost nine," said Mae Thelma in her southern drawl. She continued on about her business, extracting eggs, bacon, sausage, grits, bread, and jam from the cabinets and refrigerator. Ginger nodded and went back to her conversation in the dining room.

"She must be planning on feeding an army with all the food she's got out. Them women from the South cook so much food for breakfast, 'bout time they finish it'll be time to cook dinner. That's why they're always so tired—they live in the kitchen—right where their man wants them," Ginger said.

"Hold on a minute. Think about it. Most of the women in the South have got nine, twelve, and fourteen or so rug rats running around the house." Katherine paused for effect. "They get more business than the average woman. Lord knows when they're in church smiling and thanking the Lord, it ain't just about the moving service the pastor just preached. Silently they're thanking the Lord for what that man did for 'em last night, and praying he'd able to do the same thing tonight." As she and her mother laughed and chided, the sound of sizzling bacon reminded Ginger that someone might be listening in the kitchen.

"Mae Thelma, I'll be home around two-thirty. I'll cook dinner myself, so you don't have to bother with that. You've got a million other things to do trying to get the kids settled." Ginger pounded up the back stairs, missing the woman's forced smile, which turned into a thin flat line as Ginger rounded the corner of the stairwell.

With her back resting against the kitchen counter, Mae Thelma pondered her next move. Ginger didn't realize the kind of woman Jackson needed. If she did, she wouldn't be running all over town like a harlot, instead of being home to cook and clean for her man. Mae Thelma had overheard Ginger laughing about southern women. She'd soon be surprised about a southern woman's expertise in satisfying her man. One day soon, that's exactly what she planned on serving Jackson for dinner, a piece of juicy, ripe, Mississippi mud pussy.

"So how you getting along with your new houseguests?" Kim asked timidly. She blew a plume of smoke toward the ceiling.

"Getting on my nerves." Ginger answered in an iron voice. She walked around Kim's loft apartment, admiring the newness. The smell of freshly painted walls and the strong aroma of ammonia penetrated her nostrils as she admired the view of the city. The afternoon light filtering through the window was soft and diffuse. "Your apartment is great."

Grinding out her cigarette, Kim joined Ginger beside the window. As she gazed around her apartment, she said. "It is nice, isn't it? I can't believe how quickly they finished the remodeling. Almost a month early."

"I wish my client would stop shuffling his feet about buying your property and sign on the bottom line, so I can get our money."

They walked around the apartment, discussing decorating ideas. Kim selected the loft upstairs as her bedroom. There was another room, partially decorated, for her father. The largest bedroom, near the front of the apartment, was the only completely furnished room. All the office equipment had been delivered, including comfortable leather seating for prospective clients.

"Randall ordered all this for you?" asked Ginger, turning on the desktop computer.

"Yep. Best friend you could ask for." Kim relaxed on the black leather sofa, crossing her legs. "He helped me to get my certification from the International Board of Standards and Practices for Certified Financial Advisors, and set me up with a Rolodex of clients. Some of whom were my best clients who generated most of my bonuses at Pierce-Walker."

"He stole 'em?"

Kim nodded with a smile on her face. "I deserve it. I've

given that company years of dedicated service. And made them a helluva lot of money. They won't miss a few clients."

By the time Kim left the securities company, she had accumulated light-years of special training in a short period of time. She had learned firsthand under a seasoned professional with more than twenty years' experience how to serve clients and advise them on the financial opportunities that best met their needs.

"You had an eight-hundred number put in?" said Ginger, admiring the state-of-the-art office furnishings.

"It's relatively inexpensive. But in the business world, it's a must. Black business owners have to be ready to be available and accessible for the expanding world of customers. We have to think national. It's not enough these days to just do business in Detroit or New York."

"I'm impressed, Kim. Seems like you've got yourself together, business-wise. So how's your love life going?"

"Don't have time," she said flatly.

"Bill hasn't called again?"

"Several times." Ushering Ginger back into the family room, Kim showed her a batch of forms. Ginger shuffled through the papers with an inquisitive expression on her face. "I've been accepted at Wayne State Law School. My classes begin in August. Bill met with me to help select which classes I should tackle first."

"How on earth do you plan on starting a new business and going to school?" said Ginger, amazed.

"Unlike you, I don't have any children. I can do whatever I want, whenever I want. My father is doing better, but it'll take two to three years of structured physical therapy before he regains his speech and learns how to walk again." She shrugged her shoulders. "Meanwhile, I plan on making the best use of my evenings by attending law school. I figure in four or five years I'll have my degree."

"What about the securities business?"

"By that time, I hope to have hired three or four assistants to do the work for me. I'll be their boss, like Mr. Cameron was mine." Just thinking about that bastard made her ill. Randall had filled her in on his last visit. He said that Cameron and Brenda were still thick as thieves, but everyone in the office knew the relationship was purely sexual. Brenda had gotten a little better at performing her secretarial duties, and apparently at a few other duties, too.

"You're not trying to reestablish your relationship with Bill?"

"I still love him, if that's what you want to know. I feel he still loves me, but we agreed to take our time in trying to pick up the pieces. A lot has happened to both of us." Kim poured herself a glass of wine. Respecting Ginger's decision to abstain from alcohol, she offered her a chilled glass of raspberry sparkling water. "How about you? Is working two jobs hindering Jackson's and your X-rated rendezvous?"

"Jackson's not as attentive as he used to be. Having Mae Thelma around sort of takes the spontaneity off our lovemaking. Every time I turn, everywhere I look, she's in our face, in our room, asking me questions, asking Jackson for a favor. Can he go down to the insurance company with her? Can he drive with her to go and see Robert Earl?" Her eyes grew dark with indignation.

"Have you talked to Jackson—"

"I've told him I think Mae Thelma intentionally tries to interrupt our personal time together. And I've told him time and time again over this past month and a half how much I resent another woman cooking day and night in my kitchen."

"Aren't you happy not having to cook?"

"No. Most women want to cook for their men. Sure, it was nice in the beginning. But enough is enough. I've explained to Mae Thelma I appreciate her helping out, but I would prefer to cook my husband's dinner, thank you."

"And?"

"And she went and cried to Jackson, turning the whole conversation around, so I'd look like the guilty party, and he believed her. Told me that she needed to keep herself busy. But this is the killer." She searched Kim's eyes before continuing. "I've started having dreams about another man."

"Who?"

"Ivory Michaels—"

"The anchorman on Channel Two?"

"Yeah." She released a bushel of air. "Seems Sierra's

given up her crush on him and set her sights on Robert Earl Jr., and I've picked up the fantasy."

Ginger prayed nightly over her constant misgivings over Mae Thelma. Her heart was in a quandary. "God don't like ugly" were the words that constantly flared up in her brain when devilish thoughts about Mae Thelma's ulterior motives entered her mind. Ginger thought she'd be nice to Mae Thelma. After all, she hadn't done anything wrong . . . yet.

Trying to relieve herself of the guilt she felt, Ginger invited Mae Thelma to go to the Parade of Homes in Shelby Township. It turned out to be a great idea. Mae Thelma loved it. She'd never seen homes so fine in her thirty years.

Fourteen beautiful homes priced from $250,000 to $750,000 were dramatically decorated and furnished with expensive custom furniture. There was a home to suit any lifestyle: split levels, ranches, Colonials, quads, contemporaries, Cape Cods, and even an English Tudor that rivaled Ginger's house.

As they drove home, bubbling with lively conversation over everything they'd seen, Ginger felt at ease with Mae Thelma for the first time. Was it because she'd finally managed to get her away from her husband for half the day?

Ginger had frequented the Parade of Homes Showcase over the past ten years, and she never left the event without several new ideas she could implement in her home. She'd taken pictures of small embellishments that she could imitate herself.

When they drove up to the house, Jackson had all the kids lined up in the backyard. He held two freshly cut switches in his hand. Ginger and Mae Thelma looked at each other totally bewildered, and hurried toward the unhappy group.

Tiny tracks of mud were all over the dining room rug, ending at the opened french doors. All the smaller children had denied that they'd done it. Knowing Ginger would be livid about the dirt, Jackson took the necessary steps to insure that it wouldn't happen again.

It began to rain, so Jackson hauled the kids to the downstairs family room. No one had uttered a word, each protecting the other, until Autumn finally spoke up. "Robert Earl and David Earl did it, Daddy." She felt the tears sting her eyes as she thought of the chastising she'd get from Sierra later that evening when they were alone. She'd promised Sierra she wouldn't tell on her boyfriend. But Daddy had said he'd beat all of them until one of them told whose muddy footprints were all over Mama's white carpeting.

Ginger stood in the doorway of the dining room, hands on hips, shaking her head at the mess that lay before her. She stormed upstairs, clenching her fists, as Mae Thelma stood mute.

The sweltering heat of July passed with no further misbehavior on the part of the unruly boys, especially after Jackson had given them the whipping that everyone agreed they needed. They'd acted almost like little angels ever since.

"I'm so glad to see you," said Ginger, hugging her mother, who had surprised them with a visit. She extended her hand as she gave her mother's lover a perfunctory once-over. "And you must be James? It's nice to finally meet you." She thought she'd choke on those words as she smiled falsely. He barely looked thirty, he was so skinny. And to think he was almost twenty years younger than her mother.

He clamped a callused, bony hand over Ginger's. "Just call me Cotton. Everybody else does." He gave her what he seemed to think was an award-winning smile. Ginger thought he looked like an oversized rat smiling with beaver teeth.

After the introductions, Jackson and James carried their bags into Jason's room. Jason had tried to hide his disappointment at having to give up his room for the weekend, but Ginger overheard him complaining to Jackson. He figured since he was the oldest, Christian should have had to give up his sleeping quarters. Jackson agreed and popped him a twenty-dollar bill for his troubles. Jason didn't voice another gripe.

"But Mama, he's so skinny," said Ginger as they mixed a large tossed salad.

"Haven't you heard? Skinny men have long dicks." They giggled like two college girls until Mae Thelma interrupted their musings.

"Need any help, Mizz Lee?" Mae Thelma asked, her words pouring out slowly, like warmed caramel.

"No thank you, honey." Katherine kicked Ginger's leg and took a sip of her Lauder's scotch on the rocks. "We can handle it just fine," Katherine said, imitating Mae Thelma's southern drawl.

Mae Thelma did a quick turn, her hair swinging behind her like a whip, and pounded up the stairs. Ginger felt so good she almost wanted to take a sip from her mother's tumbler. From the expression on Katherine's face, it was evident that she was not fooled by the other woman's manners. The duel was on.

Mae Thelma sat down on her bed, shed her shoes, and stretched out her legs. She mulled over the snide looks and sharp retorts Katherine had given her throughout the day. So that's how it is. May the best woman win, she thought.

She recalled her encounter with Jackson last night, while Ginger was away showing a home. Timing it perfectly, having figured out his daily schedule and habits by the sounds outside his door, she had gone up to ask a question.

Reaching for his robe, Jackson had stood before her, clad only in his white cotton briefs. Their eyes met and held. Neither moved. Her eyes spoke the secret of secrets. She couldn't take them off him. Then and there, she knew that he knew she wanted him. Cooler than the quickly passing dusk when the heat of the day is silenced, she left him to ponder the encounter.

She'd lain awake all night, listening. Waiting. Hoping. Praying he'd climb those stairs and profess his need. Her heart pounded at the thought of him lying beside her. Loving her passionately. Desperately. Releasing the desires she'd seen in his eyes. Knowing it had to come.

While she waited, she opened an old book and read a song by Genevieve Tobin and William Gaxton, which inspired her to write him a letter, explaining her feelings.

Folding the letter carefully, she tucked it beneath her pillow, until the right time when she could share her feelings openly with Jackson. Together, they'd figure out what to do about Ginger and Robert Earl.

"Up to no good, that bitch is, Ginger. I don't care how sweet and mannerly she is. She's full of shit," said Katherine, wagging her hips, her tight pants pressing her buttocks together like two kidney beans.

A few months ago, Ginger wouldn't have believed Katherine's accusations. But lately her cousin-in-law had been a little too bold in her attentions toward Jackson. It was downright disrespectful. Every time Jackson farted, Mae Thelma didn't have to know what he ate!

23

Songs in the Key of Life

Randall stood outside his lover's apartment door, banging on it. He'd spotted the familiar foreign sports car in the allocated parking spot, so he knew he was at home. He continued to knock until he heard someone swearing on the other side of the door.

"What the hell—"

"Can I come in? I'd like to talk to you."

The short smoking jacket barely covered his lover's nudity. Cracking the door and speaking in hushed tones, he said, "Can't you see I'm busy? I've got company. Right now just isn't a good time."

Randall put his foot through the small opening just as the door was being pushed shut. "If not now, then when?" His piercing blue eyes narrowed like slits, and his mouth twisted up as though he were sipping vinegar. He repeated the question, but received only silence and a drop-dead look from his annoyed lover.

"Call me tonight. Around eleven." His eyes begged for understanding as he lowered his gaze down toward Randall's intrusive foot.

Because he loved the man, Randall decided to give him the benefit of the doubt. "*You* call me at eleven. I'll be waiting." Pointedly consulting his Rolex for effect, Randall turned and walked away.

"You're trying to be like Alice in Wonderland, even though one world—the normal one—is obstinately blind to what lies beyond the looking glass," said Randall as he continued working on his painting later that night.

The voice over the phone sounded defensive. "I understand how you feel. I can even empathize with you. But during all the years of our relationship, I've tried unsuccessfully to get you to understand my situation. I don't have the luxury of coming out. Perhaps being gay won't affect your job, but it will affect mine!"

"That's something you've conjured up in your mind. It's the nineties. Society is no longer concerned with your sexual preferences."

"Most of my friends and co-workers have no idea that I'm gay, and I prefer to keep it that way. There are men in my business that everyone assumes are gay, but once that person says it out loud and admits his sexual preference, he confirms a reality that people cannot accept."

"Let me—"

"I haven't been totally honest with you lately. You seem to be comfortable knowing who you are and having society and America accept you for what you are. But, as yet, I haven't come to terms with myself. Every day it's a struggle."

At the beginning of their relationship, he'd told Randall that every now and then he desired the intimacy of women. Though the level of lovemaking and satisfaction didn't compare with how he felt when he was with Randall, he still pursued his quest for the one woman who might convert him.

"You're still seeing women?" asked Randall, hoping he'd deny it but knowing that he wouldn't believe him if he did. Randall knew that a woman's love couldn't possibly compete with the more powerful love they felt for each other. He would have to be patient, and in time his lover would come to realize that his sexuality was nothing to be ashamed of. You had to learn and accept it first within your own heart and mind.

As his lover talked on, Randall began covering up the painting that he knew he'd never complete.

"I told her I'd cook it, Jackson," said Mae Thelma, hoeing the weeds in the garden. Jackson worked the soil on the other end. He'd just finished picking the first batch of turnip greens, and was about to put six more packages of turnip seeds in the ground for a second mess that would be ready to pick by late September.

Sprinkling the seeds, he smiled at Mae Thelma, saying, "Ginger don't burn things too often. I managed to eat it anyway, even though it was a little tough."

"It was tougher than puttin' socks on a rooster. That's how tough it was. And I refuse to eat food that ain't prepared right."

Ginger had insisted that she would cook dinner Friday evening. One of Jackson's favorites. Liver and rice, smothered with onions, and broccoli and fluffy Bisquick biscuits. But problems had arisen at the office, and she was unable to leave as early as she'd planned. Scurrying around the kitchen, frantic about the lateness of the hour, Ginger had thrown pots on the stove as Mae Thelma watched, biding her time, knowing that dinner would be a disaster.

Jackson smiled as he raked the dark earth smooth. He loved gardening. One thumb hooked in the loop of his jeans, he stood back to admire his handiwork. Then panic set in as his eyes scanned to the other half of the garden. "Mae, you moved my collards?" he asked incredulously.

"Feels to me like you had 'em too far apart."

But now they're too close together, thought Jackson. Collards were supposed to be planted at twelve- to fourteen-inch intervals, and she'd mistakenly huddled them less than eight inches apart. What the hell, he thought to himself. Ginger probably wouldn't even notice, she'd been so busy lately.

"It's hot as blue blazes out here," Mae Thelma said, and, wiping her sweat-stained forehead, she went inside.

Moments later, she returned with two tall glasses of iced lemonade. Sitting cross-legged beside Jackson on the grass, she pondered Jackson's attitude toward her over the past week. Retracing her steps, Mae Thelma was sure it had been a week since she placed her outpouring of love in a letter she'd left under his pillow. She had assumed that after he read her letter, he would approach her. Maybe he was waiting until this afternoon. He'd promised to take her to pick out the new appliances for the kitchen that would be installed in her house in a few weeks.

Jackson reminded Mae Thelma of their garden his mother always planted in Mississippi. They planted everything from asparagus to sweet potatoes to zucchini in the red, rich soil of the South. To water it, they used a little pond on their property that was approximately fifty yards from the garden. He chuckled as he remembered all nine of the children passing buckets of water down the line to their mother. It was a sweet memory he would always cherish.

Loving memories of his mother and family always made him think of going back home to the South. Feeling nostalgic, he started humming "Sylvie," one of his old favorites, and after a few notes, Mae Thelma joined in.

Mae Thelma surprised Jackson with her knowledge of Huddie "Leadbelly" Ledbetter. She talked about how Leadbelly had been born to a family of Louisiana sharecroppers in 1888, and became an itinerant musician with a wide-ranging repertory of turn-of-the-century blues, ballads, spirituals, and work songs.

"Remember 'Good Night, Irene'?" asked Jackson jocosely, after sipping a swig of tart lemonade.

"Sure I do. And do you still know the words to 'Midnight Special'?"

"I'll never forget 'em. 'Midnight Special' was one of his songs the White folks prettied up after Leadbelly passed in nineteen forty-nine and tried to claim as their own. He was the first authentic traditional singer to go before the American people and make them aware of the rich folk music that existed down there."

"It's a downright pitiful shame that his songs didn't become popular until after his death. Otherwise he might have realized his dream of becoming 'the nation's first Black singing cowboy,' " said Mae Thelma pensively.

"Girl, how you know 'bout Leadbelly?" inquired Jackson, smiling. Admiration showed in his eyes. "You ain't but thirty."

"My mama told me all 'bout Leadbelly." She sipped her lemonade, cooling her temptation to touch him. "Got aplenty of his albums still stored up at Mama's house. All us kids loved to sit down in the cool evenings and listen to old Leadbelly singing them spirituals. His voice was so relaxing and uplifting, it was enough to make a Mississippi preacher lay his Bible down."

Leaning back on the palms of his hands, Jackson stretched out his legs. There was a kinship about southern folks that was hard to explain to people unless they had been born there. Ginger didn't understand how he felt about home, how much he loved the South. Loved the peace and openness, the freedom of having your own little piece of land, where life was easy and slow. You'd work in your garden, listen to the gospels on the radio, full and satisfied after consuming the fruit of your labors, then go to bed when the sun went down, and rise when the sun rose again. Now that was living. "You ever think about moving back to Mississippi?" asked Jackson.

"Don't everybody want to go home?" She felt the pulse of her heart beating wildly inside her, and was about to blurt out her feelings for him when she heard the padding of oncoming feet.

My, but don't they look cozy, thought Ginger. She clasped Autumn's tiny hand tighter as they walked toward the two lazy gardeners. "Good morning, folks," said Ginger, carefully.

"Hi, Daddy," said Autumn, ignoring Mae Thelma. "You going with us, Daddy?"

Picking her up and swinging her in the air, he kissed her soft cheeks and landed her next to her mother. He gave Ginger a warm kiss on her lips. "Daddy can't go, baby. I promised to take the boys to get a haircut. Then Mae Thelma and I have to go pick out the new stuff for her house. Remember her house burned down?"

"Yeah," said Autumn, casting a sullen glance at Mae Thelma, still failing to acknowledge her presence with a hello or good morning. Autumn had seen the woman putting a red pouch in her daddy's pants pocket. She'd taken it out, found a letter inside that smelled real funny, and given it to Granny because she couldn't read. Granny said she was a good girl, and to keep an eye on Mae Thelma for Mommy. She couldn't wait for them to move. Mae Thelma and her two bad boys.

Mae Thelma took the cue and went back to the garden as Jackson mentioned how good his women looked, all dressed up and fancy.

As Ginger backed out of the driveway, she stopped, remembering to tell Jackson that Little Bubba had called and wanted him to stop by the club. They were having an emergency meeting.

Keys dangling in hand, she tiptoed around the garage, trying not to sink her heels into the soft earth. "Jackson," she called out. "Jackson—" She stopped dead in her tracks as her tan leather pumps sank into the lush grass. That bitch had moved the plants. She had to have done it. As Ginger looked deep into Jackson's eyes, she saw in the smoothness of light flashing the entreaty imploring her silence.

Ginger conveyed Little Bubba's message and turned to leave. A thought came to mind as she glared down at her muddy shoes. "Jackson?" she said seductively, her wide-brimmed straw hat casting a soft shadow over her eyes.

"Yes, baby."

"Are you planning on taking Bronco Billy out for a ride tonight?" The coy look on her face was readily read by Mae Thelma.

Jackson's hairs raised on the back of his neck as he struggled to compose himself. If he had been three shades lighter, he probably would have blushed. Not wanting to create any further problems between the two women, and especially not wanting to infuriate his wife any more than necessary, he added, "Sure, sweetie. A long ride." His voice sounded like a caress as he exaggerated his southern drawl, pausing between each word.

Satisfied with his answer and the embarrassed look that crossed Mae Thelma's face, Ginger walked away. Thank God she had explicitly told that bitch not to do any of her washing. She could cook and clean until she got sick and tired; Ginger didn't plan on anyone washing her husband's shorts and smelling his funk but her. That was all she needed, to walk in on that she-bitch checking Jackson's drawers for semen stains.

The sun had risen early that Saturday morning, but was still low on the horizon. There were long lines of children in all colors and shapes waiting for their turn to enter Detroit's zoological park.

The youngsters wore cheerful smiles and their eyes looked triumphant as Ivory Michaels and his daughter made their way through the park's entrance.

Ivory felt the women's stares on his back as he and his daughter boarded the train at the main station in the front of the zoo. The loud toot-toot of the whistle and shrieking noises from the horn elicited excited cries of laughter from the small children, and they were off.

One of the mothers sitting next to Ivory asked him for his autograph, which caused a swarm of other women to reach over their seats to follow suit. His daughter became slightly annoyed with the invasion of her private time with her daddy.

"You mean it, Daddy?" asked his daughter, her ponytail swinging from left to right as she pulled him away from the small train.

"Let's see," he said. "I was told by my partner that there was a beautiful boutique not too far from here, for little princesses just like mine." He kissed her small hands, flicking a finger across the tip of her nose lovingly.

Ivory thought about the bitter fight he and Elizabeth had had the day before his daughter was due to arrive from California. He'd told her he was ending their after-working-hours relationship. She'd been furious, and left his apartment crying.

He'd grown bored with her, sooner than expected. She was an extremely intelligent woman, which was what had attracted him to her in the first place. It was more of a challenge to date an intelligent woman than an attractive one. And though Elizabeth was both beautiful and intelligent, it was her brain that had given her the privilege of his bed.

His father had been a preacher, and he had grown up with deep-rooted spiritual convictions that somehow had been left behind as he became more successful. Nevertheless, his early Christian upbringing had taught him to respect religious women. He therefore tried to avoid them.

Usually the young women in church were more sensitive than the worldy ones—and would gossip among themselves terribly. Their mothers would encourage him to take them out—to church functions or the movies. After seducing most of the young adult choir and some of their mothers in the church offices, the baptismal chamber, the kitchen . . . Ivory had lost his respect for both the Church and its saintly women. His father had been deeply upset and disturbed when Ivory began to find excuse after excuse not to attend weekday or Sunday services.

At sixteen years old, Ivory had already bedded more women than the average man of forty. Subsequently, the girls had gotten to be a bore, and his sexual desires moved from females to men. It intrigued him to find how some of the older males whom he had admired and looked up to now found him attractive. He had a few serious relationships, before his father found out about it. When he did, he forced Ivory to marry a pretty young girl right after high school, to save face for their well-respected family.

His mother had always told Ivory that God had blessed him with such good looks. If she'd only known what a curse those looks would be for his own self-respect, she would have prayed for a less attractive son.

It hadn't taken his wise, young wife long to learn of his bisexuality. But by that point she was about to deliver their first and only child. She told him she'd keep his secret if he'd give her complete custody of their child. He agreed, and had regretted it ever since.

Single at twenty years old, sex became a job for Ivory, and

he was looking for the benefits. Going to bed meant getting what he could get out of the relationship. His partners had to have something to offer him. Pretty just didn't do it anymore. He'd known for years that any woman could give you an orgasm but that one could make it special. He knew that when he concentrated first on dominating their minds, like an awakening of spirituality, he could essentially control any woman—a woman he didn't have to trust, because there was no need to trust a woman whom he could control.

Yet as he sat watching his daughter enjoying her food, he knew that deep inside he wanted to find the woman who could challenge him, who wouldn't acquiesce to his unlimited "tricks of the trade." He knew he couldn't care about a woman if he controlled her, because if he really loved a woman, he wouldn't try to control her.

After the divorce, his ex-wife had tried everything to hurt him, in return for his hurting her. She took the one thing he loved most in life—his daughter. And, having accepted a job in California, she left the city of Detroit with the blessings of the court when his daughter was at the tender age of eleven months. Over the past five years, he'd been granted summer visitations but missed most of the cherished "first" moments of his child talking, walking, running—moments that couldn't be told secondhand over the phone. They had to be experienced to be remembered and treasured.

Yet there was an unmistakable bond between him and his beautiful daughter, despite their separation. He hadn't missed a single birthday or Christmas, and he'd even sent her the latest Teenage Mutant Ninja Turtles Halloween costume. He wanted custody of his daughter.

As he turned, running his hand down the back of his head, he spotted a gorgeous woman in the company of a little girl—probably her daughter. He'd seen her before. Remembering, he watched as they made their way to the picnic area.

The woman held her head up high like an African princess, walking as though petals of roses cushioned her feet. She possessed grace, style, and a hint of inner mystery.

Watching him watching her, Ginger felt as though a giant orchid were blooming inside her chest, as though each petal were unfolding a provocative fragrance to inspire her fantasies.

"What a lovely name . . . Liberty," said Ginger as Ivory introduced himself and his daughter. The girls immediately found several topics of interest to discuss: dolls, hair, clothes, the animals around them.

Admitting that her ten-year-old daughter had a crush on him, Ginger had laughed and accepted Ivory's invitation to join them. Ivory Michaels relaxed more than he had in years as Ginger and Autumn entertained them with tale after belly-cramping tale of adolescent pranks. Neither Ivory nor Liberty had enjoyed the adversities of sibling rivalry.

As time wound down, no one was ready to end the outing. The girls were both feeling lonely: Liberty was homesick, and Autumn was suffering through one of her sister and brother's bimonthly visits to their father.

"That's interesting," said Ivory, watching the camaraderie between the two girls with pleasure. They were holding hands, standing by the concession stand, as they discussed which flavor of ice cream to order. "It may sound odd, but I've never met anyone personally who worked in a factory," he said, showing his megawatt smile, "and you certainly don't look like the type."

"You know, most people think that the women that work in the factory look like he-shes. They're wrong. There are plenty of attractive, feminine women employed in the automobile plants. Most of 'em would love to have a desk job, working in some air-conditioned bank or office. The problem is most of those jobs don't pay very well." She tapped her newly manicured nails against the picnic table. "It costs a fortune to get your nails done these days, let alone get your hair done twice a month, and clothes! Well, I'm sure you know how much they cost."

The smile again. "So your goal is to make it in the real estate market?"

"Hopefully, I'll have built up my clientele enough by next year through word-of-mouth and networking that I can quit. It's difficult working two jobs when you have four children." And a lazy husband, she wanted to add, but didn't.

"Next year I'll be in the market for a new home. Do you have any business cards on you?"

"Are you kidding?" She handed him three Century 21 business cards with her picture on them. She knew that most of his associates had six-figure salaries and could afford to purchase very nice homes.

Sure, she flirted a little with him. But it was harmless. They chatted like children out for recess. The girls ignored them, venturing over to the neighboring exhibit. As Ginger and Ivory became better acquainted, they realized they had much in common. The same tastes in homes, clothes, food, entertainment, and, most important, similar ambitions to own their own businesses.

Ginger felt giddy with excitement as Ivory bought her an ice cream cone. She studied his relaxed smile as he walked toward her. She knew by the ease of his walk, the sway of his lean hips, that he would give a woman enormous pleasure. She imagined herself in his arms, her face tilted skyward inviting his luscious lips to caress hers.

But she knew her thoughts about the famous Ivory Michaels were nothing more than a harmless fantasy.

There was a voice-over advertisement on the radio pitching a Caribbean cruise. Exactly what he and Ginger needed. But when would they find the time? She was so busy, and happy in her new career. Jackson felt a small pang of jealousy.

Jackson leaned back in his chair, loosening his tie as he studied the revised blueprints of a new sewing unit being set up in the west end of the plant that he and a group of young engineers had just completed. Same old routine. He was bored. Looking around his office, he viewed the bleak surroundings and sighed.

He couldn't stand the prejudice he'd experienced in this job, the promotions he should have gotten but didn't, because he was Black. He couldn't even confide that information to his beloved wife. Someone had to keep things in perspective, and it was his job as a man to provide for his family. So he ignored the bullshit and sucked in his pride, bowing to the reality that he had another six years before retirement. And then he was out of here.

Checking his watch, he saw he had roughly fifty minutes before he could break the monotony of the day and exercise for an hour in the Nautilus facility the company provided for the workers. They figured the employees would be healthier if they had the opportunity to exercise and stay fit. But in most cases, the workers who frequented the health room went to break up the boredom, as Jackson did. He'd do just about anything to get a few hours away from the cement hole, and mocking faces, where he was forced to make a living.

The thud of the door slamming shut behind his visitor sounded like a stack of lumber falling. Bill went back into the bedroom. The thought of the acts that had just transpired left him disgusted with himself.

He had submitted yet again to his weakness. Angrily, he snatched the soiled sheets from the bed, then forced them down the overstuffed hamper in the small bathroom. After remaking the bed, he poured himself a stiff double shot of scotch.

Tonight he'd found solace in a paid whore. His sexual relationship with Sheila had ended days before Jewel's funeral. He had known all along that he still loved Kim, and trying to drown out that love in the arms of another woman hadn't worked. Sheila had been diplomatic about the breakup, and they resumed their professional relationship at the clinic.

He desperately wanted marriage. A wife and child. Bill's own son had died without his knowing he'd been a father. He blamed his misfortune on God then, and still did today. The good Lord, the just Lord, the all-knowing Lord in his greatness had failed to shed any light or blessings on his life. Sure, he'd made it, climbed the ladder of success, but not by the grace of God, rather by the anger in his heart, and a desperate determination to prove to himself that he was worthy, even though the good Lord had seen fit to rob him of everything that was important and necessary in his life.

Though he was a psychiatrist, and understood the human mind in its many functions and facets, the ability to diagnose and cure himself of his guilt and remorse still eluded him.

*   *   *

"Yes, Mama, she's still saved."

"Thank the Lord. And how about you, son? Don't you think it's about time that you came on in?"

"I know, Mama."

"God so loved the world that He gave His only begotten Son, that whosoever believes in Him shall have everlasting life. You believe you can be saved, and filled with the Holy Ghost, don't you, son?" Hattie B. Montgomery asked, her tone serious yet loving.

"You know I do, Mama. Men are happier knowing God," Jackson said, and waited for the answer it would bring.

His mother's relentless quest to bring him back home into the Church, following in the footsteps of his older brothers and sisters, was always part of their conversation. He rocked and listened intently as his mother talked on.

Shuffling through the mound of mail that had just been delivered, he stacked the envelopes, and elected to open a small brown box. "Yes, Mama," he said respectfully, as she continued her spiel.

Opening the box, he was shocked to find a perfumed pair of women's pink lacy underwear with a note attached to the crotch. *Miss Lilly would like to invite Bronco Billy to dine with her tonight, at the O.K. Corral. Be saddled up and ready by eight.*

What on earth was that woman going to do next? She was saved all right—went to church every Sunday, read the Bible stories when she could to the kids, and hadn't touched an ounce of alcohol in over four months. But she wasn't so busy "trying to be a lady" that she'd forgotten how to be a woman . . . his woman.

He smiled to himself, snickering under his breath at the thought of his sexy, saintly wife. There couldn't be another woman like her anywhere. The good Lord had surely broken the mold when he crafted her. She was his lover, and his best friend. He prayed that their love would last forever.

But Mae Thelma thought otherwise as she stood before the mirror in Ginger and Jackson's bedroom, admiring her perfectly proportioned body, clad only in bra and panties. Lying back on the bed, she placed another red velvet pouch beneath Jackson's pillow, sinking her face into the softness, inhaling his scent. The pouch was filled with herbs and potions, blessed by the high priestess in New Orleans, guaranteed to make the intended man or woman fall in love with the holder of the love potion. Mae Thelma was sure it wouldn't be long before Jackson's thoughts and desires were for her only.

24

What's Going On?

Everything that could have gone wrong that day had. The motor on Ginger's power sewing machine at work decided this would be the day for its demise. It had taken the mechanics nearly three hours to replace it. Three days earlier she'd pulled a hangnail from her right ring finger, and it had gotten infected, though she hadn't realized it—until today.

She'd gone to the medical office early that morning to get a pain pill. By eleven, despite a second pill, the pain had worsened and was almost unbearable. Her temperature topped a hundred, and the doctor sent her home. She'd barely driven three miles when she fainted at a stop light, waking from the blaring sound of a motorist's horn. Afraid she couldn't drive the additional thirty-five miles home, she went to the emergency room of Saint Joseph Hospital, which luckily was less than two blocks away.

"But how is Jackson going to get home?" asked Mae Thelma, uninterested in Ginger's condition.

Before Ginger had left the plant, Jackson called the Ford

dealership. They assured him that the cooling system on the air-conditioning unit would be fixed by two-thirty. Jackson told Ginger not to worry and to go home and get some rest; he would hitch a ride home with one of his employees.

"Don't worry, Mae Thelma, he can catch a ride." I don't believe this woman, she thought. Jackson's Bronco was in the shop being worked on. It was the first time in months they'd ridden together.

Ginger climbed the stairs to her bedroom, carrying a freshly brewed cup of hot Lipton tea. The bitch didn't even bother to ask me how my hand was, she railed silently.

The infection was worse than she'd thought. Her finger had to be opened, drained, and stitched. The doctor had told her that most people weren't aware of how severe a hangnail could be if it got infected, hers was one of the worst he'd seen in a while.

After a few questions about what Ginger did for a living, the doctor explained that the chemicals on the body-cloth fabric at work were the primary culprit in such an infection. He gave her a slip for work that said she would be unable to use her right hand for three days. He also told her to return in two days so he could change the bandages and check on the stitches.

If the infection wasn't cleared up by then, they might have to cut off the tip of her finger, the doctor had cautioned. Ginger was given oral medication along with a piercing shot from a needle that felt as though it was five inches long. She would be able to drive home safely, the doctor assured her, in half an hour.

Her nerves were so frayed by the time she got home that she planned on going straight to bed, fearful she would explode at even a well-meaning family member.

The door to Jason's room was shut, but Ginger could hear the creaking sound of mattress springs. To her surprise, after opening the door, she found Jason speaking into the phone. He turned abruptly. The shock of seeing his mother home before twelve in the afternoon was written all over his face.

"What are you doing home?" Ginger fired, checking her watch, although she was acutely aware of the exact time of day. "Aren't you supposed to be at work?"

Jason mumbled a few words into the receiver and hung up. "Me and the two other guys were drinking sodas we'd opened during our break in the stock room, and the manager came in and caught us. Everybody drinks the stuff, Ma, and he sent us home, just 'cause we're Black."

"What!" Ginger used her left hand to massage her throbbing temples. "What have I told you about following the crowd. Being Black has nothing to do with it. You got caught stealing sodas from the store's warehouse, and now you want to blame it on color. You're wrong, Jason, and you know it." This was altogether too much to take in one day. She decided to deal with it later. Right now the pain in her head and right finger seemed to be competing against each other. "Don't you step out of this house today. I'll speak to you this evening," Ginger hollered as she slammed the door of Jason's room.

"What the hell?" said Ginger abruptly sitting up in her bed after a long nap. Sierra and Autumn ran into the room, announcing that Robert Earl Jr. and David Earl were up to something. Something bad. Mae Thelma was nowhere to be found.

Pounding up the back stairs to the third floor, Ginger cupped the back of her head, feeling an oncoming headache. She wanted to get rid of the pressure of the wig against her temples, but ever since her unwanted company had moved in, she never took it off until she went to bed for the night and could lock her door.

"Robert Earl!" Ginger called out, "What y'all doing up here, making all this noise!" As she opened the door to their room, she noticed that most of their toys and furnishings had been turned over, topsy-turvy. The room was a mess. But it was empty. She heard a faint scuffling from Mae Thelma's room and backtracked to it. She opened the door, hearing muffled snickering sounds from behind it. Something scurrying fast and dark greeted her at the door. All she could do was scream as she felt the tiny feet of two mice run across her stockinged feet.

Her clothes stuck to her damp skin, her head pounded

wildly, her heart beat at an alarming rate, and she felt sick to her stomach. She lifted her hand to her mouth, and fainted.

"Ooooooooooh," said David Earl, "your mama ain't got no hair."

"Shut up," said Sierra, frantically trying to pull the curly cap back over her mother's head. She'd sent Autumn downstairs for some water as she valiantly tried to wake her mother.

"I already knew," said Robert Earl Jr. "My Mama told me."

As Ginger awoke, she caught the tail end of his statement. Taking a few deep breaths, she planted her hands on the floor, muttering incoherently to herself. She looked around desperately, then she stood up, screaming. "Get out! You little bastards get out of my house! Now!"

Mae Thelma rounded the staircase, rushing past Autumn, who was trying to balance the overflowing cup of water. "I declare to goodness! What's goin' on in heah?" Her usually immaculate room was in total disarray.

Ginger stood, her arms crossed tightly over her middle, her wig plopped haphazardly atop her head. "You. I want you and your kids out of my house, this minute."

It was getting crowded in the small room. The August heat, along with the heated bodies and tempers, rendered the tiny room unbearable. As Ginger cranked open the window behind the bed, she noticed a small picture of Mae Thelma and Jackson on her dresser.

"Feels to me like you just a might bit upset over your hand today, Ginger. I'm sure my boys didn't mean no harm." She turned to the boys, her eyes pleading. "Now y'all tell the truth and shame the devil. Go on now, tell Ginger what y'all done did, and apologize." They stood stock still, their mouths tightly shut.

"Frankly, I don't want to hear it. It's too late for apologies from them or you either." Ginger moved across the room to stand face to face with Mae Thelma. "Get your boys, and leave. I'll have Jackson bring your clothes over later."

"Where we s'posed to go? We don't got nowheres to go," said Mae Thelma, stammering.

"Go to a neighbor's house. Go to a church member's

house. I don't give a damn where you go. Just get the hell out of here."

"You shouldn't talk like that. Ladies don't talk like that."

Ginger grabbed the cup of water from Autumn's hand and threw it in the woman's face. "You conniving, whoring, sanctified bitch. What kind of lady are you supposed to be, running after my husband like a two-cent whore."

Mae Thelma began crying then, not knowing what to do as the truth of Ginger's words stabbed her. But she quickly recovered, determined that she wasn't going to let this woman upset her plans. She stared blatantly at Ginger's wig, and a sadistic smile came across her face. Taking her boys by the hand, she went down the stairs and left the house, without uttering another word.

Forgive me Lord, but thank you for finally getting this bitch and her brats out of my house. Thank you Jesus, Ginger prayed. She opened all 140 windows in the house, welcoming the fresh air, letting out the stale odor of the unwanted trash that had just left. She forgot about her finger, her nerves, and for the first time in months, felt like herself.

When Jackson came home, Ginger was sitting in the living room, sipping Christian Brothers brandy and ginger ale, her old standby. Christian had agreed to catch the mice that the two boys had let loose in their mother's room.

"I'm nobody's damn fool," said Ginger, sipping her drink, feeling a little tipsy. She rolled her eyes at Jackson.

"You're overreacting as usual. I can't fucking believe you made them get out." He sprawled in the chair, running a hand down the back of his neck.

"That bitch has been after you ever since she and those varmints of hers moved in here. Do you think I haven't noticed?"

"What you talking about, woman? Are you crazy?"

Ginger stood before him, waving her glass in the air. "Let's start with those perfect egg custard pies she was always making for you. You couldn't stop bragging about 'em. And in front of me, like I was invisible. I come home, and you and she are in the kitchen, or out in that fucking garden laughing and joking like an old married couple."

"Ginger, you know—"

"Just wait a damn minute. It don't stop there. I told that bitch over and over again that I liked cooking your dinner on the weekends. Did she listen to me? Hell no. I'd get home from work, and she'd have crackling bread warming on the stove, chowder peas, gumbo, sweet potato pudding, and Lord knows whatever else those fickle-ass southern women cook. And those damn zephry—"

"Zephyrinas," said Jackson, correcting her. Zephyrinas were an old Charleston biscuit recipe named after Zephyr, the Greek god of the west wind, because the biscuits were so light. Jackson had begged Mae Thelma for the recipe for Ginger. But she'd torn it to shreds, hurt over Jackson's obvious admiration for Aunt Jemima reincarnated.

"You embarrassed me, Jackson, with those fucking biscuits. I know how to cook. If I'd wanted the recipe, I would've asked for it." She walked out of the room, going straight to the liquor cabinet in the butler's pantry. He followed her.

"I know you're mad, Ginger, but be reasonable, will you? I can go get them and bring 'em back tonight. Things'll—"

She turned, giving him the coldest look she could muster. "That bitch and her kids can't come back in this house."

"They don't have anywhere to go."

"I really couldn't care less, Jackson. That's not my problem, nor yours either, for that matter. Or have you lost sight of your priorities? I'm your *wife*, and I *said*, I don't want them here." She leaned back against the counter, sipping her drink, feeling really good now as the liquor spiraled through her body. He hadn't even asked about her finger since he'd gotten home. She was hurt, but refused to show it. "You told that bitch about my hair."

Guilt was written all over his face, there was no need for a reply, yet he mumbled out a half-truth. "I asked her to pray for you."

"You had no business telling that bitch about my hair." Her voice cracked as her eyes clouded, brimming with tears. "I don't fucking believe it, Jackson. I don't believe you wouldn't know how much that would hurt me, telling her." She brushed past him, whispering over her shoulder, "How could you?"

Loading up the repaired Bronco with Mae Thelma's possessions, Jackson left the house. The kids watched, saying nothing, as he backed out of the driveway. Mae Thelma had called him at work, sobbing, just after he'd returned from doing his daily exercises. She had given him her version of the incident. He assured her that he'd straighten out everything, and she and the boys would be back home by nightfall.

Though he knew Ginger was right about Mae Thelma's obvious attraction to him, he'd ignored it. Secretly, he'd hoped that Ginger would become jealous and think twice about spending so much time away from home.

And he was disappointed in Ginger. Resorting to using alcohol and cussing like a mad sailor. She had obviously lost her religion in the course of a day, and had not put her problems and faith in God's hands, taking it upon herself to solve them. What the hell was he going to say to Mae Thelma? What the hell was he going to say to his mother? Damn! He screeched down the street, stirring up puffs of dirt, sweating in the scorching heat of the afternoon sun.

Katherine sat perched in the middle of her bed, hugging her knees, staring at the empty pillow, trying to hold back the tears. An empty Lauder's scotch bottle and a drained glass with a quarter-inch of root-beer-colored water from melted ice cubes and whiskey sat on the nightstand beside her.

She'd been drinking all night. Straight liquor, on the rocks. James hadn't come home all night. They'd had a terrible argument. It had started when she'd finished her shower earlier, and she'd slipped downstairs wrapped in a towel, dripping beads of water on the carpeting to surprise him with a thought she'd had while bathing. She was going to propose that they take the poles and spend the night on Black River, fishing, listening to the radio, and making love.

Only she'd been the one surprised. She caught him going through her wallet, apparently in search of money, and they argued. He left, and hadn't returned. Starring blankly in the mirror, she saw the image of an old woman reflected in the looking glass.

Ordinarily after she'd consumed almost a fifth of scotch, she'd be a little tight. However, under the circumstances, her loneliness flowing through her like the river of purgatory, she felt sober as a judge.

The rhythm of her heart beat like a tom-tom, a tear trickled down her face; she lifted her heavy body and stood before the mirror. Was it too late for love? For a last chance at capturing the essence of youth? The youth of her lover had kindled the embers of a flickering flame still burning bright inside her—*still*?

"It's so good to see you," said Kim, hugging her cousin. "I've missed you."

Tossing her briefcase on the ottoman, Ginger plopped down on the leather sofa, exhausted. "I'm bushed. You got any wine?"

Intrigued by this sudden change of character, Kim poured them each a drink and joined her. Sitting across from Ginger, she urged her cousin, "Okay. Come on. Out with it. Something's wrong between you and Jackson."

"How'd you know?"

"I know you," said Kim, turning on the stereo. The melodic voice of Mariah Carey floated through the room.

"You know I've got to get one of those CD players. The sound is better—"

"Cut the crap, Ginger. I said, what's the problem?"

Emptying her glass, she blurted out the ugly scene with Mae Thelma and her kids. She began crying as she confided that the relationship hadn't been the same since she'd thrown them out six days ago. Jackson and she argued almost daily. He complained about everything. The house wasn't clean enough. Dinner wasn't done on time. The kids were being left at home alone too much. The bottom line: He was trying to make her life miserable as he could because of what she'd done.

Kim refilled their glasses. "Girlfriend, I'da done the same thing. Bitch didn't deserve to be in your home in the first place. Aunt Katherine was right about her. I noticed it too, but I didn't say anything to you about it. She wants Jackson all right. No ifs, ands, or buts about it."

"I figure if anybody's gonna do any fucking in my own house, it damn well better be me and my man, and not some bitch sneaking behind my back screwing my husband in my home." Kim and Ginger did a high-five in the air. "Hypocritical, sanctified bitch."

Kim understood Ginger's situation and totally agreed with her actions. What she didn't like was the fact that the battle with Mae Thelma had caused Ginger to backslide in the church. Kim certainly wasn't a saint, but she admired and respected Ginger's dedication and love of the Lord. She hadn't told anyone except her father that she, too, wanted to give her life to God. She prayed and had started going to church when she could, praying for her mother and her father's recovery.

Ginger checked her watch, frowning. Dinner would be late again tonight. What the hell? Things couldn't get too much worse between her and Jackson. She'd eat dirt before she'd kiss his ass and give in, knowing she was right about what she'd done.

The phone in Kim's office rang, and she excused herself to consult with a client. Ginger looked around. Kim had done wonders with her apartment. It was tastefully decorated. Beautiful paintings hung on the walls. Randall, thought Ginger. Kim had a casual style that bespoke sophistication. Her apartment reflected her own personality, something Ginger hadn't noticed until now. Having seen her most times in her mother's home, she hadn't expected Kim to be so different from her mother. A framed picture of Kim, Jewel, and Ollie hung in the center of the brick wall, surrounded by other mementos of her mother and father. The apartment seemed filled with love and affection.

As Kim made her excuses for the lengthy call, the grumbling sound of rock music roared above them. "What in the world—"

"That's Randall. He's gearing up for his party tonight."

"Oh?" said Ginger, tapping her foot by the door as the thought of not going home and having a carefree evening at a party crossed her mind.

"Don't even think about it."

"Why not?" argued Ginger, defensively.

"Because it's a gay party." Kim waited for the horrified expression to leave Ginger's face before continuing. "Randall's gay. I've known it since we've met, but I didn't tell anyone." She changed the carousel on the CD player as Ginger stood beside her, shaking her head in total disbelief.

"I would've never guessed. He doesn't even look like it. Usually I can spot a gay guy in a minute. Well, I'll be damned."

"I'm worried about him. He's come out. He's letting people know he's gay."

"That's supposed to be healthy, isn't it. Kinda therapeutic?"

"Not in his case. He's doing it for entirely different reasons." She glanced upwards toward the uninvited music. "His boyfriend refuses to make a commitment. He'd hoped they could move in together. He loves the guy." Kim shrugged, then sat back leisurely on the sofa.

"And the guy doesn't feel the same way about him?"

"He does—but—he's not willing to admit publicly that he's gay. Randall's gone off the deep end and is dating all kinds of weirdos. Totally unlike himself. Before, he was so selective about who he went out with. Now it's like he's advertising. Anyone who wants some can have some." She mouthed the word *sex,* just in case Ginger didn't get it.

Ginger called home. Jason answered. Ginger was so stressed about Mae Thelma she'd completely forgotten about Jason's incident at work. She explained to Jason that she needed him to order pizza for dinner, and to order Jackson a quart of Diet Pepsi, and regular Pepsi for them. She told him to pay for it, and she'd reimburse him when she got home.

Ginger missed the relief in Jason's voice.

There, that would do it. If Jackson didn't like that, he could go to hell. Maybe she'd bring home a bottle of V8 juice. A subtle hint. After all, the old saying was "If you don't use it, you'll lose it," and she'd couldn't afford to lose anything else.

Smoothing the back of her wig, she thought of Randall, loving someone, as she did, and feeling the brunt of his lover's inability to commit himself totally. Sure they loved you, but only on their terms. She understood why this was unacceptable to Randall, just as it was unacceptable to her. Deep in her heart, Ginger knew she couldn't tolerate Jackson's indifference, lack of understanding, and selfishness much longer.

As Kim walked Ginger to the elevator, she came face to face with Mr. Cameron. She hadn't seen him in months. He said nothing. She said nothing. They each looked at each other with utter contempt.

"That Black bitch!" George Cameron said as he entered Randall's apartment.

"Who is it that you're referring to, Cameron—your indispensable secretary, Brenda? Or the whore you picked up last night?"

Cameron ignored that last remark as he walked around his nephew's apartment. He wiped his nose and seated his stout little body by the bar, pouring himself a drink. "Why wasn't I invited to the party?" he asked between gulps of Crown Royal.

Randall gave him a slight bow. He was dressed impeccably in an off-white silk linen walking suit. Soft caramel leather sandals covered his feet. "Forgive me, Uncle. You might very well enjoy this sort of entertainment."

Cameron poured himself another hefty round. "I'm no fucking faggot. I came here to talk to you before your sissy friends got here."

Randall consulted his platinum watch. "You've got twenty minutes. Say what you've got to say and get the hell out."

Cameron steepled his fingers. He took his time before answering, cracking the joints of each finger as he watched Randall become increasingly uncomfortable. "I'm thinking about sending you to our London office—pronto."

Randall pinched the crease of his tailored slacks, casually relaxing back into one of the raspberry suede chairs. His voice was hard. "We discussed this before. I told you then and I'm telling you now, the answer is no."

A sly smile grew on Cameron's face as he crossed his chubby legs, clasping his hands over his knee. "You see, as of this moment, you have no choice. The papers have been signed, and the ink is dry. You're outta here next week." He rocked back, enjoying the ugly look on Randall's handsome face. How satisfying.

"My aunt—"

Cameron raised an eyebrow as he reached inside his pocket to take out a Tiparillo. "Is gone. Won't be back for four months. Left word not to be disturbed unless it was an emergency." He blew out the match, aiming the smoke at his intended victim. "Guess this doesn't constitute an emergency, does it?"

Randall knew Cameron had timed his underhanded dealings perfectly. He'd gotten Randall first. Randall had hired a private detective to try to get something tangible on his uncle. Sure, his aunt knew he had his whore working right in the office. That didn't matter. The company was making money. She'd left the country, as she did every year, on screwing excursions of her own, either to meet, or accompanied by, one of her paid gigolos.

Randall had hoped that one of these days his aunt would meet a man with a code of ethics and get rid of this egotistical bastard. The irony was that Cameron was fairly well endowed, but he couldn't get it up for his wife. Seemed he only desired Black women. His aunt tolerated their relationship because he'd made her rich in the twenty years they'd been married. Cameron possessed the intellect and the killer instincts that had built their financial corporation to its Fortune 500 status.

Cameron puffed leisurely on his cigar, blowing circles above him, as he watched Randall squirm in his seat. "I read recently that a renowned doctor is on the verge of discovering a gene in gays. He says that you people look for the masculinity in other men that you lack with yourself."

"I don't care to discuss my sexuality with you. It's none of your damned business."

"Oh, but that's where you made your mistake when you openly admitted your sexual preference." Leaning forward, he tapped the silver ashes into a beautifully sculpted vase he knew wasn't an ashtray. As he spoke, he whispered as though other people were in the room and listening in.

"You see, I called an emergency meeting with the board of directors, and they agreed that under the circumstances, we'd send you over to London, where sexual freedom might be more acceptable."

"Believe me, Cameron, you're not going to get away with this."

"I already have. You leave next week." He stood up, checking his watch. "Oh, yeah, you've gotten a promotion. My treat. And you'll be staying at the Regency Hotel in London, in our company suite, until you find a place. There. Only took twelve minutes. That leaves you eight to get all prettied up and smelling fresh for your queer boyfriends." Moving toward the door, he looked around nosily, searching for the bathroom. "I'd like to take a piss, but I wouldn't want to catch anything."

"You son of a bitch."

Cameron pointed a finger at Randall, who lunged out of his chair. "Don't you ever steal another client from my firm and think I'm not going to find out about it. Kim thinks she's gotten away? She's got a surprise coming too. Nobody fucks me and gets away with it."

Randall's party mood had disappeared. Looking around his apartment at his beautiful paintings and furnishings, his eyes filled with tears. How could he leave? This was home. Yet, he knew his uncle had covered his tracks, which left him little choice unless he planned on quitting. He wouldn't give that bastard the satisfaction. He'd fight back. Hard. And when he came up with enough evidence, he'd bury the bastard.

Randall couldn't let Cameron harm Kim. They were best friends. Even from the beginning, when they'd first met, Kim had guessed that he was gay. Yet she never stood in judgment. They'd spend time together viewing paintings at the Detroit Institute of Arts. He'd taught her all about literature, given her a crash course in dining in elegant restaurants and networking, how to get ahead in the financial world.

In turn, Kim had taught him to laugh, mostly at himself. Taught him to dance, to express himself in his painting, helped him to free the voice within, taught him street talk. But mostly she'd helped him understand himself, his guilt, and the feelings that no one else, even his mother before she died, bothered to acknowledge.

He picked up the phone to call Kim and warn her of Cameron's plans. He also told her that he planned to give her the key to his apartment, so she could care for his plants while he was away. He wouldn't give up his home, since he knew he'd be back sooner than anyone thought.

Turning down the lights, he sat in the comfort of his lounge chair, basking in the serenity of his home. Looking up into the ceiling, he let his head fall back as he thought about fate. He let the doorbell ring and ring as he meditated on his revenge.

25

What Becomes of the Brokenhearted

It was almost midday when he drove up to her small bungalow on Elmhurst, but he knew she'd be home, cleaning or working in the house. She'd been gone over three weeks, setting up temporary residence at a neighbor's house. She hadn't even called him at his office as he'd asked her to the night he'd dropped off their belongings. He had left quickly, undeniably embarrassed by Ginger's actions, and promised to check on her and the boys in a few days.

He hadn't come by or called, and he thought now that he should have. Maybe she wouldn't want to see him. He worried that his shirt was not tucked neatly inside his jeans. Took a little more time than usual smoothing down his thick mustache, smoothed back the tight, curly strands of his short Afro, and finally, satisfied with his appearance, proceeded to the door.

Purple and green patches of fireweeds sprang up around the yard, their seeds dangling beneath silken parachutes, floating in the air. After such a disastrous fire, there was an irony in their beauty among the charred pieces of wood and debris that hadn't as yet been removed.

Mae Thelma opened the door as he pressed the bell. Jackson smiled at the beautiful woman who stood before him, an angelic glow on her face. He felt almost compelled to take her in his arms and hold her—just for a moment. Yet he stood stock still as silence fell between them. The sound of gospel music coming from the living room was ignored by both. Jackson hoped the erratic beat of his heart wasn't audible, not realizing that Mae Thelma was experiencing the same thing.

"It's so good to see you, Jackson." She folded her arms, cocking her head slightly. "Now what took you so long to come and see me?" Grabbing him by the arm before he had a chance to think of a suitable answer, she pulled him inside.

"The boys around?" he asked awkwardly. For some reason, he felt he needed someone to be around, to break the tension that was building. Or was he the only one who felt it?

"No," she said, guiding him into the living room. "Robert Earl's sister sent me some money last month so they could spend the rest of the summer in Mississippi with their grandmother. They haven't seen her in a while, and I figured I could use the time alone to get this house organized." A proud smile beamed across her golden face. "It looks pretty good, doesn't it." Jackson nodded. "It's nicer than it was before the fire."

He sat uncomfortably on the plush French Provincial sofa that he assumed was also new. Jackson felt a pang of guilt at the thought of her being all alone for the past month, and he hadn't had the nerve to call and check on her, not once. A young woman with the beauty and innocence she possessed and no man around to protect her was prey for the scoundrels who lived in this lower-class neighborhood. "Have you thought about installing metal security bars, Mae Thelma?"

So he was worried about her. She knew it. All it took was a little time for him to miss her. Just as her aunt Gitty had said he would. "As a matter of fact, I haven't, Jackson. You think I should? These young boys 'round this neighborhood are meaner than a junkyard dog with fourteen suckling pups.

Ain't been raised right 'tall." She untwined her beautiful hair while sitting beside him.

"Been trying to get some of the young mens around heah to do the yard work for me." She shook her head, ruffling her beautiful hair until it cascaded down then around her shoulders as she turned to face him.

He sucked in his breath, feeling a warmth flow through his body—primarily his lower body—as he regarded the magnificent creature sitting beside him. He could sense the suppressed sexuality within her. "You got any Diet Pepsi, Mae Thelma?" He needed something to cool his mind and his unhealthy thoughts.

Her almond-shaped eyes, hooded with dark lashes, lowered seductively, resting on his alluring lips. "Sure. Be right back," she called over her shoulder, swaying her hips just enough to evoke her femininity, but no more. "Anything else you want, Jackson?" Her southern drawl was like a magnet drawing him in.

She'd learned early on that a woman's true desire should be to satisfy the desire of a man. Her aunt Gitty, from the deep Creole backwoods of Louisiana, taught her while she was just a teenager how to control a man. How his desire was not only for sexual satisfaction, but also for the natural passion in the stillness that follows lovemaking. As Aunt Gitty would say, pleasure makes him weak as his limp lingam. And every woman should be willing to submit to the discipline of the looking glass. She should be willing to attract a man by what she has, though knowing, in his deliberate confusion to resist the more human desires of a woman, that it is precisely this superhuman element in her that he pursues.

As Mae Thelma passed the mirror in the dining room, she saw a vision of a seductive woman looking back at her, her lashes dark, her eyes bright, her lips subtly scarlet. Yet vanity was not the reason she stood there. She stepped closer to the looking glass, searching for the face she had before the world was made. For the temptress within her.

By the time Jackson left, the spell had been cast. He'd volunteered to put the bars on the windows, clean the yard, haul away all the trash, and fix the cracked windshield on her car.

He'd neglected to offer his assistance inside her body, inside her mind, where she felt she deserved the utmost attention. But that would come later. She could wait. Time was on her side.

After taking her bath, she perfumed herself, sliding her nude body between the cool sheets, clutching Jackson's picture to her bosom. Her thoughts were of Jackson as she drew her knees up, fantasizing about their lovemaking, fondling herself, with the thoughts of him touching her, loving her, until she reached a climax.

Suddenly, her heart crumbled like a broken eggshell, hot tears streaked her face. Her lips trembled as she prayed to God that he wouldn't punish her for what she was doing. Was it wrong to love a man so much? It was wrong to love another woman's husband. Her conscience was talking to her, but she refused to listen. Was it God speaking to her? If God was everything, and knew, saw, and heard all, was he telling her she was wrong?

Walking around to the other side of his compact car, Bill opened the door and took Kim's hand, supporting a packed picnic basket with the other. He was glad that she'd finally agreed to meet with him. It had been too long. He knew she still wouldn't be ready to renew their relationship, but he felt that it was necessary for them not to lose touch.

A gust of wind ballooned the blanket on the bank near the water while Bill and Kim quickly spread the contents of the basket on each of the corners. The cool breezes from the Detroit River tickled their faces, teasing a smile from each. Belle Isle was beautiful, the weather a pleasant eighty degrees at the approach of August's acme. Near day's end, before sunset, the setting was perfect.

Over the riverbank, oak trees dripped Spanish moss, which floated through the air from tree to tree like restless souls. The spiked flowers of the cattails huddled in clusters lining the shore, swaying in the breeze. The trees on the island, cottonwoods, maples, spruces, and wavering elms, opened their limbs skyward in a sultry stretch.

As they ate cold cuts with hot peppered cheese and crackers, Bill studied the beauty of Kim's face, remembering their lovemaking. When the meal was over, they continued nibbling on grapes, sipping wine from a chilled bottle of 1965 Cabernet Sauvignon.

Bill felt a rush of desire as their eyes locked. He wanted her passionately, wanted to feel the pleasure of him giving her pleasure, but knew that it would have to be her call. When she was ready, she'd make the first move. That was how it had to be, and he accepted it.

Pouring them both a second glass of wine, he waited patiently, taking pleasure in the artful display of Kim's tongue moistening her lips. "How's the wine?" asked Bill. Sunrays boomeranged from his black-rimmed tinted glasses as he turned toward her, then looked away. They were both lying on their sides, looking out into the water. "I'd almost forgotten if you still drank."

"Perfect." I haven't forgotten a thing about you, she wanted to say—the smell of your skin, the texture of your hair, the glaze on your eyes when you take off your glasses. Yet something made her hold back. Folding her arms beneath her head, she lay back, her eyes closed, mulling over pleasant memories.

Flashes of the last time they made love reeled through her mind as if in slow motion. That had been several months ago, and it was wonderful. How she missed touching him, loving him, the ruddy hue of his raw skin after they were done. Tingles prickled along her taut belly, and the tips of her fingers itched to touch, to feel.

As much as she loved him—and she couldn't deny that— she wasn't ready to forgive him for not returning her calls, her pleas begging for understanding. Many a night Kim had parked outside his apartment building trying to build up the nerve to go in and plead yet again, to try to make him understand. And on each of those occasions she'd found Sheila's car either parked or approaching Bill's apartment complex. After nights of spying, Kim felt ashamed, and didn't return again. It was over.

Leaning his upper torso over Kim, he kissed her tenderly, saying, "I love you. Forever. I'll love you forever, Kim, until the end of time." He stroked her cheeks as she opened her eyes, searching his, her mouth agape wanting to respond.

She closed her lips. Closed her eyes. Enraptured by his profession of love, a soft hope blended with apprehension. Her instincts and intelligence told her to hold back a little bit of herself for safekeeping—even as the pulsing of her heart sought another.

Jason started his senior year at the end of August six credits short of the forty-four he needed to graduate by next June. Two weeks into September, Jason discussed his dilemma with his home-boy Mick, with whom he'd played basketball daily over the summer. They both were in the same situation. Together, they made up jokes on the basketball court about school, how stupid it was.

Eventually Jason started cutting classes. On the days he graced the school with his presence, he interrupted the class by continuously letting out gas or laughing with the other students. His Spanish teacher dropped her coffee at seeing fake spiders floating on top. Wads of chewing gum held tacks in place at the edge of his economics teacher's seat. Ultimately, he was caught and sent to detention.

He never studied, and began taking a lackadaisical attitude toward school. And by October boredom had set in. He was out of pranks, and running out of time, which led him to his final act: bringing a toy gun to school. Jason was caught taking the gun from his locker by his science teacher. Thirty minutes later, he left the principal's office, suspended from the Detroit public school system.

Letters were sent home detailing the incident and Jason's suspension. With no response from Jason's parents, the letters kept coming, and Jason found ingenious ways to intercept them.

During the day he played basketball at an out-of-the-way court that most of the other dropouts frequented daily. His girlfriend, Tiara, stopped by during the school lunch hour to try to talk some sense into him.

"I'll tutor you, Jason. We can bring up your grades, together." Tiara was eager to help Jason, buying into the lies he'd told her, saying he was flunking his senior year because of low grades. He was too ashamed to admit that he'd been expelled for something as stupid as bringing a toy gun to school.

Jason kept silent. Getting A's was the least of his problems. When he barely studied he got a B. When he did absolutely nothing he could make a C. But he wasn't ready to tell this young girl with her puppy-love emotions how difficult life could be. Jason leaned against her car, bouncing the basketball as he listened to Tiara, his mind light-years away. Nobody could understand how he felt. Nobody could. . . .

Eventually the school called the Montgomery home directly, and Ginger found out that her son had been suspended from school for an entire month and had lied about it.

Hanging up the phone, she was stunned by her son's deception. Hadn't any of the kids noticed him being home? Why hadn't Christian mentioned anything being odd about Jason's attitude? How could her household be falling apart right before her eyes and she not be aware of it? Had she taken on too much responsibility, thinking she could manipulate two jobs?

Earlier that evening, having confined Jason to his room, after vowing to half-kill him if he left for any reason other than to go to the bathroom or have dinner, Ginger left his room fuming. He would not give her an explanation as to why he'd started a nonstop campaign to fail school. He said nothing. Wouldn't even look at her, just stared noncommittally out his bedroom window.

Ginger spoke to each of the kids individually, and they swore they hadn't known anything about Jason being suspended. After the girls said their prayers, Ginger kissed them on their cheeks, tucking them in bed. She caught Christian closing the door to Jason's room with an "I tried to talk to him, Mom, but he wouldn't listen" expression on his face. But he shrugged his pajamaed shoulders, padding barefoot toward his room.

Ginger, nervously chewing away on a Milky Way, found Jackson downstairs in the family room. "I'm worried about Jason, Jackson. He's never been this rebellious before. He's not exactly setting a good role model for the rest of the kids. And I don't know how to reach him."

"If you were at home more, maybe you would have seen this coming."

The bitterness in his tone stung Ginger as the truth of his words hit home. She didn't try to defend herself, momentarily silenced by the sharp pain of an oncoming headache convulsing from the base of her neck, searing its way up to her throbbing temples.

Sitting next to Jackson on the sofa, she winced as he watched *The War Wagon*, another John Wayne classic. Though she'd seen this Western at least three times—and Jackson had seen it twenty times or so—she enjoyed watching Kirk Douglas. The cleft he'd had put in his chin always intrigued her. Made him sexy, somehow.

During commercials, Jackson constantly changed channels—which got on Ginger's nerves. She elected to go upstairs for two Tylenol and another candy bar while he flicked back and forth. Back and forth. It didn't make any sense. Couldn't he keep his mind focused on one station for more than five minutes? The only activity that seemed to hold his attention for long was sex. And lately they both seemed to be vying for the prize, see who could hold off the longest. It was a Mexican standoff.

The big-screen television Ginger had purchased from her latest commission check was supposed to be a special gift for the kids. However, Jackson had taken it over, much to their heartfelt objections. Why couldn't he watch television upstairs, like he used to?

Mesmerized by the violent action on the set, Jackson uttered a statement that left Ginger reeling. "Let him flunk. Teach him a lesson. You baby that boy too much, Ginger. You've spoiled him rotten."

How could he say such a thing? Who could have been more spoiled by his mother than Jackson was? Let her son flunk, not graduate with his class? Never! He must be crazy. Or think that she was.

Briefly, she ignored his selfish comment, massaging her forehead, and responded, "He's going to have to go to night school, Jackson. I don't know where these schools on the list are."

His eyes hadn't left the television for a millisecond. "I told

you. Teach him a lesson. Let him know that his unapprecia-
tive attitude won't be tolerated. Who's going to take him to
night school every night? It don't let out until ten P.M. You
gonna go pick him up, and get back in the bed maybe by
eleven, and get back up to go to work at three-thirty A.M.?
You're being punished instead of him. Let him flunk."

Ginger was furious, but she held her emotions in check.
She merely said, "I'll handle it myself. You don't have to
worry about my missing time at work, I can make it." I always have, she thought to herself—and felt the pain of being
alone. A part of her refused to accept just how alone she felt,
even though she shared most of her adult life with a man.
Her heart made her speak the familiar words, "Jackson, I
don't want to argue. Let's not argue tonight." Ginger's head
suddenly felt numb. The pain subsided, in its place an ache
in the core of her bosom. She secretly wished there was a pill
in the medicine cabinet full of her prescription drugs that
could cure an ailing heart.

After all the preachings Jackson had given her about how
much his mother had done for him, his sisters and brothers,
how much he loved his mother and respected her, how much
she'd sacrificed, didn't he think she wanted her kids to feel
the same way about her? After all, she was a mother too.
And just because his mother was saved and sanctified, she
didn't love her kids any more than Ginger loved hers. When
you truly loved your child, she thought, religion didn't have
anything to do with it. Being saved didn't make you a better
parent, didn't make you love your child more than the next-
door neighbor loved hers. How could he expect her to give
up on her son, who was only a child at seventeen, when
Jackson, as a man, at forty-three, had yet to relinquish the
apron strings of his mother?

Ginger stared at the clump of clothes in front of the laundry
chute through the mirror as she applied her makeup. I'm not
picking it up. Not today, she told herself. Fifteen minutes
later, Jackson emerged from the darkness in the bathroom,
stretching his arms and squinting his eyes as they adjusted to
the bright light.

Giving her a quick kiss on the cheek, he reached for his

toothbrush. Ginger stiffened as their bodies touched. She rolled her eyes, which he ignored, continuing his vigorous brushing.

Having dressed and checked on the kids, she made herself a cup of tea, and Jackson's coffee, then returned to their bedroom. Peeking inside the bathroom, she noticed the pile of clothes still resting comfortably on the floor. "You ready, Jackson?"

"Yeah," said Jackson, fastening the latch on his watch. He turned out the lights in the sitting room. When he reached for the bathroom lights, Ginger caught his arm. "Aren't you going to pick up your dirty clothes?"

He rolled his eyes, saying nothing, and strolled out of the room.

Ginger turned off the light, quickly skipping steps down the front staircase as Jackson went down the back stairwell. Standing before him as his foot touched the bottom step, she pushed her knuckles into her hips. "I'm tired of picking up after you, Jackson. If I didn't know better, I'd think you were doing it on purpose. Diet Pepsi cans are all over our bedroom. Empty packages of cracklin' are on the dresser instead of in the trash can."

"Is this my coffee?" he asked, moving past her into the kitchen, picking up the warm mug.

"I'm calling a service to come in and clean once a week. This is getting to be too much. And since you don't give a damn about how tired—"

"You had a woman in here cleaning every day. Remember? You threw her out. You had it made. Mae Thelma—"

"Don't you mention that bitch's name in my house." She grabbed her purse from the counter, spilling hot tea on the floor. She paused, turning by the back door. "And since you seem to have such admiration for bitches, consider yourself married to one."

Ginger snubbed the cotton mountain Jackson was building on their bathroom floor. She ignored the soda cans, ignored the crumbled papers all over the room. She supervised the kids cleaning every other room in the house, but left their bedroom just as Jackson left it, a cluttered mess.

Weeks passed before he finally got the message and

cleaned up his mess. However, he hadn't bothered to speak to her cordially. Didn't say hello or good-bye. Just complained when dinner was late.

Ginger grew exceedingly tired of carrying more than her share of work. Taking Jason to school during the week was more taxing than she'd imagined. Her patience with Jackson was wearing thin. She even made an appointment with Merry Maids to come out and give her an estimate on the cost of a weekly cleaning. But knowing this would cause further problems between her and Jackson, she called back and canceled.

Ginger tried to gloss over their problems when the kids questioned her. They wanted to know why Jackson was mad all the time. Why Mommy cried in the bathroom when he was gone. It was getting harder to keep up the pretense of their once happy marriage.

For the sake of her children, Ginger decided to make more of an effort to smooth out the problems she and Jackson were having, knowing her children deserved and needed the strength and stability of a family home. After one unsuccessful marriage, Ginger vowed that she wouldn't let her kids suffer through a string of stepfathers like so many of her friends' children had to. Usually the children ended up the real victims.

Taking vacation time from work over the Thanksgiving holiday, Ginger planned a spectacular dinner for her family. The girls pitched in, cutting up onions, bell peppers, and celery for the cornbread dressing while Ginger juggled pans of hot cornbread and toasted white bread from oven to broiler. Jason and Christian did an exemplary job washing Ginger's antique china service and setting the dining room table.

The windows grew steamy from hours of cooking as the buttery aroma of a twenty-five-pound turkey roasting in the oven and the rich bouquet of desserts cooling on the racks engendered a holiday atmosphere at the Montgomery home.

Jackson smiled at Ginger before seating himself at the head of the table. Two lighted candelabra at each end of the table emitted a pleasant lavender scent. Ginger reached out and took Jackson's hand on her right and Jason's on her left, bowing her head in prayer. And each of the children linked hands in turn, forming a chain as Ginger said the blessings.

This was the catalyst to break the ice between Ginger and Jackson. At Jackson's suggestion they played Concentration downstairs in the family room. Concentration turned to playing Tonk. Tonk ended with several hands of Speed, until Jackson threw the cards in the air, administering his temporary crown to Sierra, who was faster than anybody at Speed.

The warm smile Jackson aimed at Ginger was readily read and accepted. Together, they walked hand in hand up the stairs to their room. They didn't need to say anything else.

Ginger showered and slid into a slinky, black silk nightgown. Perfuming her body with intermittent drops of Red cologne, she carefully restyled her wig more provocatively than she'd worn it at dinner.

"Aren't you cold?" asked Ginger, cuddling next to Jackson's nude body. He lay on top of the blankets, oblivious to the cool of late November. Jackson responded to her question with hot kisses over her neck and mouth until she was breathless. Sliding his hands beneath her gown, he cupped her full buttocks.

"Sweetheart?"

"Yes, baby."

"Do you think I'm fat? I've gained a few pounds."

"Baby, as long as I can lift up this leg"—he backed her buttocks into his stomach, lifted her leg by the ankle and eased on in from behind, proceeding to bump and grind—"I don't care how big you get." The rotation of her hips against his gyrating pelvis made a loud smacking like hands clapping.

Jackson slowed down the pace, easing her leg a little higher, moving in long, methodical strokes. He lifted the wig from her bare head, all the while saying, "You don't need to put this on." He kissed her smooth head, tossing the wig on the dresser. "You're sexy to me, baby, big, small, or bald. I love you, Ginger." Then he eased on in a little deeper, pushed a little harder. The pace of her heart raced, she greeted his strokes with a primal rhythm to match his, and at that moment and for a few moments later, she was ready to believe anything.

* * *

Christmas Eve brought a surprise visit and gifts from Kim and Bill. The twinkle in Ginger's eye at seeing them together again brought a quick explanation from Kim. Bill, however, winked at Ginger behind Kim's back as he hung their coats in the front closet, overhearing the tail end of Kim's short remark about just remaining friends.

Bill declined Ginger's offer of a mug of hot cider and headed upstairs to play the video games he'd brought for the boys. Ginger couldn't help remarking to Kim at Bill's natural rapport with her sons—the boys truly respected and admired him. But when she mentioned what a good father he'd probably make, Kim steered the conversation elsewhere.

Ginger thanked Kim for the presents they'd brought as she placed them under the Christmas tree. And as they sipped on spicy, hot apple cider, they caught up on all the happenings of the weeks since they'd seen each other.

Jackson, Sierra, and Autumn had left earlier that afternoon to pick up Katherine in Port Huron. Knowing that her mother was embarrassed at not having any money to buy Christmas gifts for the kids troubled Ginger. Katherine hadn't known, nor had Ginger, that Jackson had taken matters into his own hands. Knowing his mother-in-law, and how proud she was, Jackson had gone shopping at Northland Mall, bought toys and clothes for all four kids, and had them wrapped and signed *From Granny*.

Jackson, the kids, and Katherine hadn't returned by the time Kim and Bill had to leave. Hugs and wishes for a prosperous New Year were reciprocated. Ginger felt relieved after locking the door behind her guests. Even though she and Kim were blood relatives, she was supremely thankful that Kim had the wisdom and tact not to mention her weight problem.

Katherine, however, wasn't as generous. The second she'd shed her heavy coat, she kidded Ginger about the size of her thighs. The twinkling lights of the tree caught Katherine's eye before Ginger could say a thing. She was sure her mother was secretly counting the presents under the tree with her name on them as she bestowed compliment upon compliment over the lovely decorations.

Ginger handed Katherine an ice-cold Colt 45, all the while eyeing her mother's trimness. Unbeknownst to Ginger, Katherine's young man had worried thirty pounds off her robust frame. Ginger had unwittingly packed on a lean twenty-five. The similarity between mother and daughter in features and proportion hadn't been so close in twenty years.

Ginger took the remarks in stride, relieved to see her mother enjoying herself around her grandchildren. While sipping her beer, Katherine apprised Ginger of Jackson's Santa Claus rescue. Ginger's heart warmed at her husband's foresight.

During January of 1991, Ginger made several appointments with various school officials at the board of education, and begged them to allow Jason back in school. It was useless. He'd committed a serious offense when he'd brought the gun to school, even if it wasn't real. How could a teacher with so many students in a classroom possibly tell the difference between a real gun and a play one? There had been an insurgence of young men bringing real guns to school and teachers were fearing for their lives. After a heart-to-heart with one of the more communicative assistant principals, Ginger finally understood the seriousness of what Jason had done.

By February it was touch and go whether Jason would be able to graduate with enough credits by June. He'd lied to the bitter end to his mother about the classes he'd missed, using the computer at school to print new report cards over the past year. Trying not to get her son into any more trouble, she'd managed to secure an accurate transcript with the help of a friend of a friend, who worked at the school.

One tired evening, on Ginger's way back from picking up Jason from night school, he rolled down the window, hollering at a young man walking down the street. "Yo homie, need a ride?" The young man strained through the falling snow to see Jason smiling gleefully, and nodded yes.

"I'm not picking up strangers, Jason. Especially this time of night."

"That's Mick, Ma. We play ball together. Stop at the corner."

Ginger offered a curt hello, and asked the young man where he lived.

"Where you been, man?" asked Jason.

"Library. Been doing a little extra studying."

"Yo man. What for? You ain't graduating either, are you?" said Jason without the slightest bit of embarrassment for himself or his mother because he might be joining him.

"I'm graduating in June, dude. Me and my dad had an interview in Royal Oak last weekend with the air force. If everything goes okay, and I'm bettin' it will, by August I'll be leaving for the Service. Armed forces don't take dropouts. You have to have a diploma. I found that out when I took the test. Scored real high, but the sergeant said that getting the little piece of paper with my name on it was more important than my test scores."

"Yeah," said Jason, an octave lower. Embarrassment crept into his voice when he said, "So you're bringing up your grades, studying at the library."

"Yeah, man. Working on those credits I'm short, too, thanks to my dad. I got plans. Gonna invest in that Air Force College Fund too."

In the rearview mirror, Ginger could see the conviction in the young man's face. A quick glance at Jason acknowledged that he was having a few conflicting thoughts about being labeled a dropout.

Ginger would never know that Christian had taken Jason aside that evening after seeing the exhaustion on his mother's face and given Jason a little brother–big brother talk. Christian, though naturally quiet, always kept a close eye on his mother. He knew she was under extreme pressure trying to work at Champion Motors, hurry home, and put in an additional fifteen hours a week at the real estate agency. Christian hit home when he made a cutting remark about Jason being so insensitive when the whole family knew their mother was trying hard to deal with the loss of her hair.

Jason respected his younger brother's concern about their mother. And Mick's oration on top of it did a guilt trip on his conscience. That night he tossed and turned for hours, unable to sleep.

What did he have to look forward to? He hadn't listened

when his mother tried to discuss helping him make up his
credits. He had ignored her, tuned out her and everyone else.
And after hearing Mick's remarks about how his father
helped him get his senior year together, Jason was jealous
that he was unable to confide in *his* father about his problems
and his future after school. But how could he tell his mother
that at seventeen years old, he still needed quality time with
his father? Unsure whether he'd appear disloyal to his
mother or Jackson by mentioning his father, he kept these
feelings to himself.

Valentine's Day brought a small box of Godiva chocolates
from Jackson. Ginger had pleaded with him not to buy her
anything sweet. Flowers would suffice . . . but he didn't heed
her advice. Stuffing a chocolate truffle in her mouth, she
struggled to ward off the self-pity that creeped into her mind
on a daily basis over her hair loss.

Worrying over Jason, and trying to pretend she wasn't
tired when she felt exhausted, had her nerves on edge. Her
only comfort was succumbing to the temptation of black
cherry ice cream or milk-chocolaty Mars Milky Ways. Often.

February ended with broken promises of dieting. By the
end of March, further procrastination forced Ginger to take
her weight loss more seriously. Her breathing was labored.
Occasionally she felt sharp pains in her heart. She sought out
the advice of her physician and he assured her she was as
healthy as a moose, that the pains were probably gas, but he
insisted she needed to shed some pounds. Thirty-two pounds
heavier than her normal weight, she was back to being one of
the butt sisters.

Jackson had laughed one evening as she exited the
shower, telling her that her buttocks had so much cellulite it
looked like she'd been sitting on a pile of rocks. Ginger hadn't
laughed with him. She was angry and reminded him that last
night while he was huffing and puffing, he *still* managed to
get her leg up.

During the next week, Ginger forced herself to start a
daily jogging routine through the subdivision. Speckles of
silently trickling snow blanketed dormant green. Dressed in
sweats, she braved the cold weather, preferring the intoxica-

tion of fresh air to the confines of the house. Occasionally, when the roads were coated with snow or ice, Ginger opted to use Jason's exercise equipment downstairs in their basement for an hour. By day eight, she'd elevated her daily trek from one and a half to three miles.

Stepping onto the scale, nude and still wet from the shower, Ginger was amazed that she'd lost only two pounds. All that work for just two pounds! She felt like quitting. However, Ginger refused to admit to herself that she hadn't changed her eating habits sufficiently. She wanted instant gratification as much as any overweight woman.

Tears streamed down her face as she threw another too-tight suit on the bed, adding to the mounds of clothes that threatened to topple over onto the floor. She wouldn't feel sorry for herself. She just wouldn't. Involved in sorting through the racks of clothes in her closet, Ginger hadn't noticed that Autumn was standing beside her.

The young girl, filled with wisdom beyond her years, had noticed her mother's anxiety. "Mommy?" asked Autumn innocently.

"Yes, sweetheart," said Ginger, trying to remain calm, but screaming inside.

"I was watching television downstairs, a commercial came on. You know what it said?"

"No, baby," said Ginger, impatiently. Quickly, she inserted her diamond stud earrings in her ears as she studied an outfit carefully, then held it in front of her, the threat of tears not far from the surface.

Following her mother into the bathroom, Autumn studied Ginger struggling into a charcoal gray flared skirt, the waistband almost four inches from closing. Autumn looked up into clouded eyes. "It says you don't have to be slim to be sexy."

Ginger bent down to hug her daughter. A smile beamed across her face, as she closed her eyes. "I know, baby. And Mama appreciates you telling me that." She kissed her on her warm brown nose. "Thank you, sweetheart." Autumn rubbed her nose back and forth across her mother's before she left the room.

Chastising herself for letting it all get to her, she slipped

into the unconstructed sack dress—which made her look like
a fifty-pound bag of potatoes—that she should've put on in
the first place. Sucking in her gut, she pulled a pair of smoke-
gray pantyhose over her heavy thighs. The crotch didn't quite
meet hers, and the waistband slid down midway to her hips,
but she had no choice. It was time to go.

Taking a final glance in the mirror in the foyer powder
room, she fluffed the bow in the royal blue, black, charcoal,
and white print scarf, clasped it with her favorite silver-and-
black antique pin, slipped sterling silver hoops through the
second holes in her ears. Twirling her black leather swing
coat over her thick frame, she nervously patted the back of
her store-bought hairdo. It would have to do. She was showing a property in twenty minutes, and the client had been re-
ferred to her by Ivory Michaels.

"Mr. Deiter?" asked Ginger, walking toward her client as he
engaged the alarm on his black BMW. The custom silver-
and-gold-studded wheels glistened, even as smoky storm
clouds embroidered the bleak sky.

He nodded rather stiffly as Ginger offered her hand.
"Hello, Mr. Deiter. I'm Ginger Montgomery."

"Mrs. Montgomery." As they shook hands Edward Deiter
outlined his ideal home, letting her know right away that price
wouldn't be a problem.

Though it was only five o'clock, Ginger felt uncomfortable with her new client. He was good looking, well dressed,
and arrogant as hell. The information she'd compiled on him
was impressive.

He headed an advertising firm, making well over six figures. He was a divorcé, but needed a large home for personal
reasons. The Boston-Edison area or Indian Village subdivision were the only localities he was interested in.

Throughout the half-hour tour of the home, he barely took
notice of the impressive architecture.

Edward insisted on seeing several other homes in the area
that were for sale. Ginger, tired and with a million other
things on her mind, hadn't noticed that most of the homes he
wanted to see were vacant. She had keys to most of the prop-

erties. The ones she didn't, they walked around, peeping through the windows so he could get a feel of the structure.

By seven-thirty, she'd had it. "I'm sorry that you haven't found a home you like, but it's late. I'll check the listings tomorrow and see if there are any new ones in the area you specified, and I'll call you." Why wasn't his girlfriend with him? she wondered. No man could pick a home out for me.

"Remember the second home we went in, over on Boston?" asked Deiter.

"The Maximillian estate? You didn't like—"

There was an odd look in his eye. "After touring so many of these historical homes, I believe that one seems to be in better shape. Just need to see the furnace room and check the alarm system." He raised his elegantly ringed hand before she could protest. "Trust me, ten minutes tops. If everything's in order, I'll make an offer in the morning." He flashed her an award-winning smile, looking like an older Denzel Washington.

Slipping on her black leather gloves, she picked up her briefcase from the impressive foyer of the mansion. After a quick computation, she realized that the commission on the Boston Street home would be a hefty one. What the hell— ten minutes would generate almost five grand for her bank account. "Follow me, Mr. Deiter. It'll be my pleasure to show you the home again."

The homes in the historical subdivision off Edison Boulevard were stately mansions, built in the late 1880s and early 1900s, many by lumber barons or industrial tycoons.

The night wind howled, and dried leaves matted against the black iron fence and scraped the sidewalk as if they were metal. Ginger discounted the uneasy feeling she had as she unlocked a set of massive iron gates, then unlocked a set of solid wood carved doors. The home was always kept partially lit. And flicking on the remaining lights, Ginger failed to notice that Mr. Deiter casually locked the door behind them.

He assured her there was no need for her to go down to the basement. He'd check the furnace, and meet her back in the family room in five minutes. While he was gone, Ginger admired the beautiful house. Roughly twelve thousand square feet, the palatial home was a sight to behold. There was even an indoor pool and sauna.

The last owner had updated the left wing. It was breathtaking. Two hand-painted murals of panoramic Roman scenes graced the ceiling and the rear wall. Gold leaf adorned the harps being played by chubby cherubs. The polished marble floors glistened beside the matching carved interior columns. Ginger would have loved owning a home of this magnificence, but the upkeep alone, utilities, and separate buildings for the maid and butler would run two thousand dollars a month. Definitely out of her income bracket.

Glancing at her watch, she pursed her lips. He'd been gone almost fifteen minutes. Damn! *I should've said no,* she chastised herself. Jackson was going to be pissed if she got home after nine! But as she started to turn, she felt the pressure of cold hands on the back of her shoulder. Her body immediately tensed. *What the hell—*

His chin pinned down her crown, pushing her head into his chest. When Ginger felt his pelvis rotating against her buttocks, she screamed. "Stop! Don't do this! Please!" she begged as his hands roughly explored the softness of her body underneath her coat. She struggled to disengage him. Crouching in a half-stance, she wiggled, pulled, pushed, and tugged until she was free of his grasp.

"Don't fight it," he said, walking steadily toward her as she retreated backwards. "I know you want it just like I do. You've been coming on to me all evening." He grabbed the collar of her coat with such force that her heels left the ground.

Ginger felt her legs weakening, threatening to betray her efforts to fight back. His breath felt like hot coals against the hollow of her neck. "I'm sorry if you've mistaken my politeness as a come-on." She spat the words out through gritted teeth. "I'm married, Mr. Deiter, and my husband is expecting me home." Why had she worn that stupid sack dress? If she'd had on slacks his hand wouldn't be pushing between her thighs. She could feel the sweat beading on the top of her bald head beneath the wig.

The protection of her tight panty hose temporarily blocked his fingers. She sighed with relief, but as her body relaxed for a half second, he took advantage of her limp posture. Putting his right leg between hers, he pushed hard. She lost her balance and fell backwards onto the marble floor. The wind was knocked out of her. She opened her mouth to scream again, but terror froze her voice. He was tearing off her panty hose with one hand, pulling off her spiked heels with the other, even as she kicked wildly at him.

Sweat poured down his face. His movie-star-handsome face was distorted, ugly with rage. "Shut up." He slapped her. Bright red lipstick smeared across her face, tears covered her cheeks. Ginger's eyes grew large with fear. Even though the room was lit, the big house sat back almost two hundred feet from the street, and no one would notice any disturbance even if they happened to drive by. No one would hear her screams. No one could help her.

"Please, don't," she whispered. Something warned her to be quiet. She'd heard that rapists like to hear their victims beg. It turned them on even more. He slapped her again, and she felt the taste of blood oozing from her lips. *Oh, God, someone help me! Please, Lord, someone help me!*

"Don't fight me. I'm tired of playing games." Lifting himself up on his knees, he loosened his belt and unzipped his pants. The brown irises of his pupils were dilated to their full extent. His head moved back and forth in a wild frenzy.

Just then, she saw tiny flecks of white powder under his nose. That was what had taken him so long. He pushed his hands between her bare legs and grabbed the waistband of her briefs, ripping them off in one quick motion. Her hairless crotch seemed to peak his interest momentarily as he stroked the perimeter of her vagina.

Inside, she was quaking with fear. Yet she knew she had to do something. Her eyes scanned the room for something to grab. Something to fight with. Her shoes were across the room. She had no weapon. He took her hesitant hand and placed it on the swell of his penis, prompting her to massage his hardened organ.

Time was running out. He reached inside his pocket and sprinkled white powder carefully along the tip of his manhood. "Kiss it," he said in a commanding voice. Oh, Lord, she couldn't do that. She hadn't even had oral sex with Jackson. He thought it was filthy, and that only whores lowered their heads below a man's waist. Tears of helplessness streamed down her face. How could she have been so stupid?

"No," she said, with the last drop of dignity she could muster. She thought of Jackson and her kids, and her own self-respect. "You'll have to kill me first." Her words were as deadly as snake venom, as she swallowed the scalding bile that filled her mouth.

Unimpressed by her threat, he raised his hand and struck her again and again. Her head thumped against the cold marble. The tight cap of her hairpiece fell back a few inches, but didn't come off. When she tried lifting her head, pain engulfed her, causing her upper body to fall back, as if in slow motion. A ton of bricks replaced the dome that normally resided there.

She felt as though she were inside a mausoleum: the coldness of the marble, the eerie quietness inside walls built a foot thick. I will not die here, she commanded herself. She willed her mind to concentrate.

Her body wouldn't respond, but her brain was still active. She knew what she had to do.

Edward Deiter still straddled Ginger's inclined body. A snarl scowled across his face. "Play time . . ." he growled.

Ginger's survival instincts came into play when she realized that it was going to be her life. Three years earlier, the women at work had been encouraged to participate in a seminar on rape prevention. After several reports of young women allegedly being raped in Champion Motors' salaried and hourly parking lot, the company took preventative action.

She was surprised at what came out of her mouth. "Let me help you," said Ginger, turning into the aggressor. She shimmied down the remnants of the scraggly pantyhose. She hadn't taken her eyes off his for a moment. He was stunned by the change of events. "Do whatever you want." She spread her naked torso wide open. Ginger spoke in the huskiest voice she could conjure up. "Yeah, you suck my pussy first, then I'll suck you till you ache. I guarantee, when I finish working over your dick, it'll feel light as a feather. You got what it takes, swinging between your legs. . . . I like that. You can fuck me till I'm dry. You can suck me till I'm yours. We can stay here till the moon turns full again." His excitement paled, and she continued her ploy: "Come and get it—ease on in." Seductively, yet seriously, she concluded in a husky voice, "Just don't hurt me."

Deiter reared back, words escaping him, obviously unprepared for her submission.

Ginger knew she had him, and she honed in on her prey like an animal ready for the kill. She sensed his next move like a predator. His body suddenly went as limp as the pliant penis between his legs. It was time to make her next move.

Quick thinking had saved Ginger from being raped by Deiter. Seconds after his face registered a forlorn, Deputy-Dog look, she didn't hesitate, karate-kicking him in the nuts with her knee. As he howled in pain, she unfastened the antique pin from her coat. The elongated stem was as deadly as a knife. With the precision of a swordsman she lurched forward, lancing, crisscrossing his face with deep gouges, until blood splattered in her eyes. He screamed, falling backwards, unable to defend himself from the strength of a woman out of control.

Grabbing her pumps, purse, and keys, she ran from the house and Edward Deiter in her bare feet. Now, through swollen eyes, immediately locking the doors and windows inside her van, Ginger released the downpour of tears as she started the ignition. The nightmare was over. Ginger's heart did double beats as she sped away.

Still frantic when she stopped for the flash of yellow, she rocked back and forth, waiting for the light to change. Turning on cue, she was stunned to see a young man and a woman in the next car staring at her disheveled appearance. The pain of embarrassment was accompanied by the throbbing pressure of blood clotting at the curve of her lips, which, Ginger was shocked to see after looking in the mirror, were swollen to double their size. Looking straight ahead, she pushed back her shoulders and held her head high, ignoring any and all who happened to look her way.

The vision in her left eye was cloudy as the van moved of its own volition. A freeze frame of Edward Deiter's snarling face appeared before her. Feelings of anger, humiliation, and guilt flooded her. Having no idea where she was going, questions pierced her brain like arrows: Did it really happen? What's wrong with me? Did I ask for this? Who's going to believe me? What did I do to deserve this? The questions wouldn't stop.

With bruises on her illusions, she mechanically parked at the emergency lot of Detroit Receiving Hospital. After the doctors had taken pictures and patched her up, she found herself forty-five minutes later discussing the incident with a social worker.

She was shell-shocked. Mrs. Beverly conveyed to Ginger that most husbands would have a difficult time adjusting to someone abusing their wife. She then reeled off case after case of similar situations. Knowing Jackson, Ginger knew her husband would have a problem seeing the attempted rape as it was. He would distort it until he made her feel guilty. Ginger couldn't take that. Not now. She had enough problems. So she gathered her things, telling Mrs. Beverly that she'd contact her if she decided to prosecute.

Exiting the hospital parking lot, the simple decision of whether to turn right or left caused Ginger to panic. Tears trembled in her eyes, but wouldn't fall. People walking down the sidewalk cloaked in bright streetlights barely three feet away seemed like black shadows, almost illusory.

She made a right onto East Canfield Street, with no idea where she was going. Steering with her left hand, Ginger nervously tried smoothing down the wrinkles of her dress with her right. Reaching in her purse, she rummaged for a tube of lipstick. She swung her van over to the curb, stopping to look in the mirror, applying fresh lipstick and blush. After combing out her curly wig, she looked back into the mirror, seeing a disguised Little Orphan Annie, then turned away. No amount of makeup could repair her swollen eye, nor the gash on her mouth.

The mere thought of Jackson's reactions to her face and clothes caused Ginger to make a drastic decision: She had to make her attempted rape look like a car accident.

Finally the tears came. Why couldn't she be honest with him? Why wasn't she being honest with herself?

The truth was, Jackson couldn't handle the truth, and she

knew it. Ginger felt a sense of fear, helplessly in love with Jackson, and hopeless in trying to make Jackson understand how weak the foundation of their marriage was. Physically they were strong. Intellectually they connected. But emotionally? The ability to communicate and understand each other's feelings without condemnation was totally lacking.

Knowing all this, Ginger was determined to salvage what they did have. Undeniably, she loved him through all his faults and through all of hers.

Moments later, blinded by tears, Ginger drove her minivan into a tree less than a mile away from the hospital. Bracing herself before impact, she felt like one of the dummies in the safety belt commercials as she lurched forward.

Dazed, she lifted her head from the steering column. Red and blue flashing lights rippled over her arms and legs. Ginger felt herself slipping, losing consciousness. She willed back her weakness as she heard doors slamming and the oncoming footsteps of two police officers.

"Are you okay, ma'am? Do you feel you need to go to the hospital?" asked the first officer, blinding her with his flashlight. The other policeman, after Ginger acknowledged that she was coherent and not in any serious danger, went back to the patrol car to call a tow truck.

"Can I see your license and registration, ma'am," said the officer in a perfunctory tone.

"Sure," said Ginger, trembling as she pawed through the glove box. There were no more tears left. She'd cried all she could cry—she had to pull herself together.

While he checked out her papers, Ginger assured the officer that she had taken some medication earlier, then suddenly blacked out. Since the odor of alcohol was absent from her breath, the officer believed her story.

"I just want to go home to my family, sir. These are superficial wounds. I don't want to trouble anyone. I just need some rest, is all."

The other officer poked his head in, unstrapped Ginger, and guided her in a gentlemanly fashion to the backseat of the squad car. When all three were seated in their squad car, the first officer told her, "It's procedure to take a police report." In an effort to reassure her, he added, "You'll need it for your insurance company."

They offered to drive Ginger home, and she readily accepted. She couldn't have prayed for a better alibi to substantiate her story than two concerned police officers safely seeing her home.

As they headed east toward Palmer Woods, Ginger decided never to tell anyone about the attempted rape. Especially Jackson. He'd make her quit. She refused to let one out-of-control client destroy her dreams. Even if it meant carrying around so much guilt.

26

Fingertips

Nightly, Ginger tumbled wildly in her sleep, resting only when Jackson awakened and held her close in his arms. It was like turning an old movie reel; over and over again, she played the scene with Mr. Deiter in her mind. What could she have done? How could she have prevented it from happening? She wanted to place the blame on someone. Something. Prayer hadn't done any good. It was as if God had temporarily turned his back on her. In her heart she knew that the power of God within was greater than the pressure of the troubles around her. Yet, somehow, that knowledge couldn't comfort her.

When, only days after the incident, Ginger found another note from Jason's night-school teacher hidden in his shoe, she was in no condition to react calmly.

Ranting and raving as she ushered him downstairs, she cursed Jason for lying. Cursed him for not being honest about his grades and truancy. Ginger's hands shook uncontrollably. She felt as if all of her strength were crumbling.

Jason sat on the sofa quietly, until she had vented most of

her anger. He wasn't used to seeing his mother so out of control.

"Why don't you listen to me sometimes, instead of hollerin' all the time?" Jason asked. He lowered his head as he whispered the words he later wished he could have called back. "You love Christian to death. You don't love me."

Anger filled Ginger's voice. "What did you say?"

"You don't love me." His voice began to swell with conviction. "You don't even try to understand me when I tell you I need to talk." Tears welled in his eyes. "You're always so busy, yet you seem to always find time for Christian when he asks."

Ginger put her arms around her eldest son and held him. Tight. Tears of pain streamed from her eyes. There was no denying it—the truth in his words. "I do love you, Jason. Talk to me. Make me understand."

His large hands cupped the invisible air as Jason and Ginger sat on his bed, side by side, both needy in their own right. Both needing comforting. Both wanting to reach out and touch, to touch an emotion and hold on to it, and just feel . . . feel the comfort, feel the love, feel the understanding.

The music played low on his stereo, while outside the spring winds gave a frustrated howl, stroking barren branches along the window pane. Jason paused, and looked deep into his mother's solemn eyes. He said, as painlessly as he could, "I miss my family, Mama. The one I grew up with . . . with Daddy."

Ginger turned her head to shield the pain that penetrated her body like cancer. She'd known it would come to this. Jackson was an okay stepfather, but he saved most of his fatherly affection for Autumn. She'd seen the hurt in her boys' eyes more than once, and chosen to ignore it rather than confront it. Yet she'd known all along how deeply Jason felt about his own father, Michael Carter, and truly there is no substitute for a man who unconditionally loves his *own* son.

"I haven't spent much time with Daddy since I've been working." His pause was longer this time. "Sierra and Christian go to Port Huron every other weekend. They see Daddy all the time." His voice quivered as he uttered his emotional stance. "I love him too, Mama. Can't he make time for me, sometimes? I'm his oldest son." Tears streamed freely down her son's handsome face.

Brushing away his tears with her fingertips, Ginger said, "Your daddy loves you, Dink. Just as much as the rest of the kids. I'm sure he thought that giving you your space as a teenager meant more to you than spending weekends with him."

Shaking his head vehemently, Jason replied, "It don't, Ma. I love my family."

Ginger was so proud of her son at that moment, as she shook her head, slightly in awe. She forced herself to sit erect, trying to hold her emotions in check. "We'll handle this. Together. Just trust me, Jason. Trust me." Cupping her arms around his muscular shoulder, she pulled him close.

The next morning, Ginger made an appointment with a therapist at Mount Carmel Out-Patient Child Psychiatry Center for herself and Jason.

The first meeting went smoothly as she explained her son's problems. Ginger tried valiantly not to reveal her own problems. Dr. Fielding was so genuinely caring, yet also professional, and was easy to talk to. Ginger was almost unable to hold back her own personal anxieties.

Dr. Fielding explained to Ginger that after a divorce, one child in particular would feel the trauma of the split family. But each child was different, and must be treated accordingly. Some children would be more needy than others, no matter how strong a defense they tried to project to the contrary. He cited examples of children who took years of therapy to adjust to the separation of their parents. Some never recuperated. He helped Ginger to understand that when a child truly and deeply loved both of their parents, it was hard for that child to choose between them.

Ginger remembered that the judge had mentioned, during the divorce proceedings, that when a child reached the age of fourteen in Michigan, he could petition the court, with the aid of the noncustodial parent, for change of custody. The thought of her son wanting to go and live with his father or his father pursuing custody of his son terrified Ginger. She couldn't bear the thought of splitting up her children.

*   *   *

April and May proved to be difficult months in the Montgomery home. In the two months since the attempted rape, Ginger dropped weight like a hammer. Flashbacks of that night seemed to be overtaking her senses. She couldn't control if or when the flashback would occur. Guilt overwhelmed her, guilt at not being in control of the situation, not reading the obvious signs. How could she have been so stupid?

She'd changed the scenario of that night so many times that she felt as though she were losing her mind. But she kept it inside. The fear. The hurt. The humiliation. The shame. It propelled her to function without thinking, yet caused her to break down into a state of helplessness at a moment's notice.

Ginger was constantly on guard, never knowing which feelings would surface. Her nerves were shot. She lost twenty pounds, twenty nervous pounds that looked like thirty-five on her short frame. She'd told so many lies to Jackson, she couldn't keep track of them. Lies about her weight. Lies about not being able to sleep at night. Lies about her short temper. Lies about not wanting to have sex so frequently. They were catching up with her.

It was as if she were sleepwalking through the next few months of her life. Trying to rationalize what was happening to her as she tried to readjust. Praying for a sense of normalcy. Trying to cope with Jason.

Dr. Fielding had even called in Michael, Jason's father. He felt that his support was needed. Secretly, Ginger thanked God that Dr. Fielding's infinite wisdom had told him that Jason wasn't getting the nurturing from his stepfather that he so severely needed. The few sessions that Michael spent with the therapist seemed to help Jason's attitude, and his grades began reflecting it.

That Friday before Memorial Day weekend, the counselor of Ferndale High School called to speak to Ginger about her son's final test scores. Jason had passed his GED requirements with flying colors. Even Christian, in all his quietness, became a bit more vocal, constantly voicing his praise for Jason's game-winning slam dunks.

Knowing now that his graduation was assured, Ginger

began preparations for the big event on Wednesday, June 19: Jason's eighteenth birthday and graduation party.

Ginger had kept Jackson at bay with his constant questions about her sleeping problems and quick loss of temper. It wasn't easy. But Ginger managed to curtail his constant prodding with news of her latest closings. Money. Lump sums of money seem always to distract most people from their problems. Nevertheless, Jackson wasn't buying it when Ginger informed him that Michael Carter would be at the graduation party.

Jackson was as furious as Ginger was serious about involving her son's father in his graduation. Ginger reminded Jackson that he was the one who'd suggested that allowing Jason to flunk would teach him a good lesson. Now that the tables had turned, and Ginger's son *was* graduating with his class, Jackson only vaguely remembered the conversation.

Katherine called, offering her help to Ginger, knowing she was strung out with her job and real estate ventures. Ginger declined, saying she had everything under control. So on Saturday, the eighth of June, one of the hottest days of summer, when Katherine showed up unannounced, Ginger wasn't surprised, but relieved. Her euphoria over the party had waned after Jackson had refused to attend.

Her mother noticed right away that Ginger wasn't herself. "Baby, sit down and rest a bit. You know I can handle everything. Just relax." Yet Katherine knew from the glassy look in Ginger's eyes that she hadn't heard a word she'd said.

Ginger sat in the kitchen hearing her mother talk to her as though Katherine's voice were an echo. Occasionally she would nod, when she heard a break in Katherine's speech pattern. Throughout the week, Katherine made last-minute arrangements that she knew Ginger would approve of. She called caterers, gardeners, even went shopping with Jason for his graduation suit. Katherine and Ginger's tastes were similar, and it wasn't hard for Katherine to re-create each detail Ginger had reiterated the year before about the party.

At three o'clock on Sunday afternoon, the sixteenth of June, Jason Carter would walk across the stage at Ferndale High School to receive his diploma. He would be wearing a navy blue cap and gown and the new navy double-breasted suit his grandmother had helped him select. Christian, Sierra, and Autumn had chosen the cream shirt; gold, cream, and navy paisley tie; and size-thirteen navy Florsheims.

Ginger, Katherine, Christian, Sierra, and Autumn had all come early. They sat two rows back behind the nervous graduates-to-be. Jason waved and smiled intermittently at his family until his name was called. No one had inquired about Jackson's absence.

Sitting a row behind them, Michael Carter proudly video-taped his eldest son's graduation, from start to finish. Later, he offered Ginger a copy of the video. Ginger awkwardly accepted, since Jackson usually videotaped all the family occasions. Michael offered to bring the copy to Jason's graduation party.

No one but Kim knew of the bitter argument between Ginger and Jackson about Michael coming to his own son's graduation party. Ginger was ashamed to broach the problem to Katherine. She knew what Katherine's response would be: "Don't you let him intimidate you into spoiling your son's graduation party! His father has the right to be there. This is a time in Jason's life that he'll never forget. It's up to you, Ginger, to make it special for him."

Two days before the party, Ginger broke out in hives. The medical technical diagnosis was urticaria. Her skin resembled a bland piece of lumpy rubber. Katherine did her best to get Ginger to take a tablespoon of Epsom salts to counteract her symptoms. Katherine knew that Ginger's daily habit of ingesting Lipton tea only added to the progression of her ailment.

The weather was as close to perfect as party-perfect could be. Early that morning, Katherine turned on music inside the three-car garage. She felt festive. The neighbors had been forewarned. There would be a graduation party going on at 1935 Berkshire Drive that afternoon, and well into the night. Katherine hadn't felt this good in years. Her firstborn grandchild had graduated. What a blessing! Out of money, but not of hope and love, Katherine felt as if she were blessed with the riches of a queen because she knew that some people have plenty to live on, but nothing to live for.

The stage was set. The theme, a Hawaiian luau. Twenty-two white-clothed card tables were similarly decorated. The color scheme, emerald and avocado greens, mystic jade, rich yellow-golds, petal-dusk pinks, and bright, titanium white. Floating orchid candles were the centerpieces. Later that afternoon, a fresh orchid would garnish each table. Prodigious palm trees were rented and bordered the party area. A cabana covered two of the long buffet tables. Beautiful bone china, sterling silver flatware, and linen napkins were rented to complete the ambience.

Much to Jackson's annoyance, Ginger also rented the Palmer Woods Association pool for the entire day. And Katherine, in her genius for party-planning, convinced her to complete the Hawaiian atmosphere by renting four palm trees to grace each corner of the pool. Ginger couldn't help but admire her mother's tenacity after rushing off early Saturday morning for the coup de grâce: fresh water lilies, floating lazily atop circular accompanying pads in the pool.

Katherine wiggled her toes through the sand on the west side of the acre lot. Five truckloads of beach sand were dumped onto plastic sheathing carefully laid to protect the grass. This was another argument Ginger had won. Katherine shook her head slightly, partly from the pride of her daughter for sticking up to Jackson for her son, and partly from what Ginger had suffered internally in doing so. It was clear to her that Ginger could only bravely pretend that she was happy.

Katherine's three other daughters, LaWanda, Gwen, and Sherry, had arrived late the day before. They brought gifts for the girls, and money for the graduate. After exchanging pleasantries and catching up on old gossip, they retired to the third-floor bedroom quarters.

Turning her head toward an indistinct sound, Katherine noticed that Jackson had awakened. He was headed toward the back of the garage. After a few moments, the smell of lighter fluid was in the air. It was time to start the fire for the spit. A whole pig would be roasted with a large apple in its mouth.

Time. Almost out of time—Sierra and Autumn were ready early, wearing their floral bathing suits and grass skirts to greet the guests. Between them, they'd practiced a Hawaiian dance with Kim's help.

Two weeks earlier, Ginger had made and frozen several dishes, refusing to have the desserts catered. Two roastpans full of peach cobbler. A commercial-sized tray each of blackberry cobbler, apple crisps, cherry crisps, and an oversized round centerpiece dessert of latticed fresh pineapple pie.

Katherine sweated profusely as she took extra care in each small detail. She sprinkled handfuls of sand along the salad table, giving it the casual effect as if you were at a beach. The top halves of pineapples were layered to look as if the branches were extending outwards. Easter grass was strategically placed around each miniature palm tree that graced the table beside the candle decorations. Scrutinizing each decorative attachment on the outsides of the watermelon baskets, she added a few grapes here, a couple of cocktail umbrellas there. Green, purple, and red grapes, watermelon, melon, cantaloupe, cherries, kiwi, pineapple, and papaya were chilled separately in a sparse amount of natural sugar overnight. Later, the mixture would be placed inside the carved-out watermelons. Moments before the party a drop of lemon flavor would be added to the fruit baskets, along with a splash of 7UP, and each would be carefully sprinkled with a soft touch of powdered sugar.

"Mama, is Ginger all right?" asked LaWanda as she whisked a chilled vegetable tray toward the patio. "She seems a little distracted."

"Keep an eye on her. She's been under too much of a strain lately." Katherine kissed her baby daughter affectionately on the cheek, and steered her toward the door.

"Granny! Granny!" hollered Autumn. "Where's Mommy? The people are starting to come."

"Can you go upstairs and check on her for me, baby? I think she's putting on her makeup."

Fighting back tears, Ginger willed herself to think only of her son. She would get her strength from his happiness. His smile was all she needed. Feathering the strands of her wig with a pick, she gelled and spiked her hair to look like Tina Turner's.

The floral dress she'd selected nearly a month ago seemed to swim around her slim frame. Layering several strands of Hawaiian garlands around her neck, she doused perfume on her neck and slipped into her sandals.

"Hi, baby," said Ginger, bending down and fluffing Autumn's bangs. "Is Kim here yet?" Autumn shook her head no. Hand in hand they walked downstairs.

"You did good, baby," said Katherine as Ginger and Autumn walked into the party scene. The glitter of colored lights illuminated her pupils as the dusk complemented the setting. Various-sized gifts toppled over the sides of the table. Colored envelopes with prickly bows were scattered among the pretty packages.

The guests needed coaxing to eat. They were so overwhelmed by the beauty of the presentation of the food, they wouldn't touch it until Katherine led the way.

"Jackson hasn't spoken to me since Michael arrived," said Ginger nervously. Ginger eyed Sherry laughing with Michael as she spoke.

Katherine hadn't missed a beat. Sherry had been drinking too much, and Katherine was keeping an eye on all four of her girls to make sure things ran smoothly. Tonight, she remained stone sober.

It was nearly seven-thirty. The main course was heartily eaten. Seventy-nine guests were eager to sample the sumptuous desserts. Ginger received a number of compliments on her rich cobblers. Some weren't satisfied until Ginger promised to stick the recipes in with Jason's thank-you notes.

"I guess Kim couldn't make it," said Ginger, scanning the crowd. Katherine was about to speak when their thoughts were diverted by a vision in gold, emerging from the crowd, escorted by Jackson.

Mae Thelma, in a skin-tight buttercup-yellow sundress, smiled a sultry smile. Her hips moved like a swan over a silver lake as she made her way through the crowd toward Ginger and Katherine.

"That bitch should be outlawed wearing a dress like that! She'd stop traffic down Woodward Avenue," said Katherine in a jealous tone.

When other women stopped to stare at another woman,

you knew the woman was *looking good!* Heads turned, and
turned back. Some in envy, some in awe. Graceful folds of
silk jersey flowed generously from Mae Thelma's midthigh
to the bend of her knee. Three piped strips crisscrossed her
back, exposing moist, fresh, golden flesh. Fresh yellow and
white baby's breath arched lengths of wavy, luxuriating jet
hair, pinned to the side, swaying easily alongside her left hip.

"You look lovely, Mae Thelma. It's so good to see you,"
said Ginger, giving her a quick kiss on her left cheek.
Katherine ignored her and rolled her eyes in Jackson's direction. "Help yourself to anything you'd like." Ginger angled
her hand toward the buffet tables of food.

"I'm hungry as—"

"Ma!" said Jason excitedly. Water streamed down his
neon pink swimming trunks, swirling and curling over his
muscular, hairy legs. "The party's great. Everybody's having
a good time." He was nearly out of breath. "Everybody said
this is the best party they've ever been to." Jason hugged and
kissed his mother, oblivious to all standing near.

For that moment, that single moment, Ginger knew, she
knew. Mae Thelma could have walked in there stark naked.
Jackson could have screamed at the top of his lungs about
the grass. The sand. Anything. Ginger felt a moment of
peace. A second of total, absolute respect for being a mother.
She'd done her child good. She'd made him happy. She'd
made him proud.

Jason's love and respect for his mother. Her love and respect for her child. Was anything in life more important?

"Mama," said Ginger, near tears. She wrapped a protective
arm around Katherine's shoulder, and the tips of their heads
touched, softly. Ginger's eyes followed her son as he disappeared into the crowd. "Turn up the music. Let's show these
young folks how to do the Funky Butt." Throughout the
evening Ginger caught glimpses of Christian dancing. He
was obviously enjoying himself tonight also. She smiled quietly, and felt good.

Sherry had gotten halfway high as the depth of darkness
descended into evening. Drifting toward Michael, she flirted
with her ex-brother-in-law.

Michael, no fool by any means, read the signs and quickly exited, stage left.

Katherine nearly dragged Sherry into the downstairs bathroom with her right hand, balancing a cocktail glass of ginger ale on the rocks with the other. Careful that none of the other guests could hear the mother-daughter confrontation, she whispered harshly, "Are you out of your mind? I saw what you were trying to do with Michael." Sweat crinkled the edges of Katherine's thick red hair.

"No harm done," Sherry stated as she plopped her small frame, fully clothed, on top of the toilet. An awkward smile spanned her face. She tried to dismiss the disheveled young woman in the mirror, but the same face kept creeping back into view. The last few years had aged her. It showed. Too many men. Too many late nights, two too many kids. She was thirty-five years old, but felt much older. Crow's-feet extended beyond the black mascara under her thin lashes. Dark circles shrouded vanishing cheekbones beneath layers of foundation.

Katherine slapped her. "I overheard you asking Ginger about her wig. How could you be so callous? Have you lost all respect for yourself? For your sister?"

Fury and guilt exclaimed in her eyes. "I simply gave her a compliment—"

"By saying 'I actually thought that was your hair!' "

Sherry looked away shamefacedly. "Besides, I've heard Ginger make jokes about her hair before. Why can't I?" Barely audible, Sherry added, "I didn't think it bothered her anymore."

A low commotion outside the bathroom caused Katherine to cut her sermon short. She glared wildly into Sherry's face, honing in on her point. "Let her make the jokes. How could you possibly know how she feels? Have you ever lost all your hair?" Katherine's voice wavered. Sherry knew she had pushed her mother to the limits. Sobriety edged itself into reality. Being high was no longer a viable excuse.

Sierra was full of cheer when she told her mother, "Mama, Dink was so nice to me today. He showed me how to float on my back at the pool." She shook her head in disbelief. "Even in front of his girlfriend," she continued.

Ginger and Sierra worked together putting away the food as the crowd thinned. Gwen hadn't lasted but a couple of hours at the party before she feigned a migraine headache. Living in London for so many years, it was difficult for her to adjust to Michigan time.

After Gwen was safely upstairs, Katherine confided in her three other daughters that Gwen's marriage was on the rocks, that it was the time that her husband was spending with his other woman while Gwen was away that was giving her the headache.

Jason peeped his head over the refrigerator door and looked down at Ginger as she made room on the bottom shelf. "Me and the guys cleaned up the pool area, Mom. Jackson told us not to bother with the yard, he'd do it tomorrow."

"Thanks sweetheart."

"Have you had anything to eat, Ma?" Wrapping an arm around her waist, he gave her a worried look. "You've lost too much weight already."

"She looks pretty," Sierra objected.

"I'm fine." Changing the subject, she asked Jason to take Autumn upstairs and to awaken his grandmother. They had both fallen asleep on the couch in the living room.

Sierra closed her small hand over her mouth, chuckling. "Wouldn't it be funny if Autumn peed on Granny?"

Ginger tore a piece of aluminum foil and wrapped the contents of the watermelon bowl. "I truly don't think Granny would laugh. She'd probably whip her butt."

Through the leaded windows, Ginger watched Jackson taking down the graduation banners taped to the front of the garage. She wondered where Mae Thelma had gone to. Sherry, LaWanda, and Katherine had done their best to make her feel uncomfortable during the party. Jackson was angry at all of them.

Ginger and Jackson hadn't talked to each other during the entire night of the party. Their fight was a silent one. Yet there had been no malice in Ginger's intentions. She simply invited her son's father to his son's graduation party. Jackson made her feel like it was a betrayal.

Later that night, when the last candle was blown out, single fragments of sand sluiced across the pavement, signifying that the evening was over. The party had been a huge success. But Ginger felt like a failure. She needed comfort from her husband. Wanted to empty the burden of the guilt that flooded her consciousness about the attempted rape. She wanted his love and understanding. She needed him to wrap his arms around her and say that everything would be all right.

Nearly an hour had passed since everyone left, and Jackson still hadn't come inside. It was 3:00 A.M. Closing her eyes, Ginger tried to relax in a hot bath laced with jasmine oil. Then suddenly, her attempt at tranquillity reversed, she felt a tremoring sensation as if she were slipping down a smooth, irresistible current, and gravity was pulling her body down lower, lower. Soon the water covered her face, then suddenly darkened like ink. She was immersed in darkness. Alone. Isolated.

Frantically, she began kicking. Faster. Harder. Unbearable seconds passed. Her eyes squeezed shut tighter. She was afraid that if she opened them, it wouldn't be just another bad dream. Water splattered onto the carpeting. Then it splashed across Ginger's face, causing her to sit up abruptly.

The beating in her heart thumped loud. Her eyes opened wide. Suddenly she felt ice cold. Her teeth chattered as she reached for the bath towel. Slowly, her body crumpled to the floor. Her fingers felt the damp carpeting as she realized what had happened.

Somehow Ginger willed the courage to pray. During the past months she hadn't opened her Bible. Had this rapist, who'd almost stripped her of her womanhood, also stripped her of her belief in God?

She prayed for her children. Prayed for Jackson. Prayed for her mother, her sisters, her brother. Prayed for Kim and Bill. There was even a small prayer to help her to forgive Mae Thelma. Ginger remembered the pastor saying that God portrays himself as standing outside the door of our hearts waiting to be invited in so that this sense of intimacy can be renewed.

He was close. She could feel the warmth—through her body. Ginger opened her heart, and said, "Please, help me, Lord. Please!"

27

Everyday People

Katherine phoned Ginger every day for a week after Jason's party. A mother's instincts were never wrong. Ginger hadn't been her usual self all weekend. She'd been too defensive, too moody. Katherine couldn't put her finger on it, but something was wrong.

Loneliness. Such an empty word. It was what Katherine detected in Ginger's sad eyes, and the feeling she felt herself since Cotton had left. How could she help her daughter when her own life was in constant need of repair?

The drapes were drawn, keeping out the gleam of a young sun in the darkened bedroom. A light air of musk wasn't evident to the room's only occupant. A glowing blue-gray light from the television illuminated the queen-size bed. Katherine, in yesterday's starched pajamas, lay on her side watching Bette Davis—on TV. She'd watched this scene nearly a hundred times, and yet, each time Bette growled "Fasten your seat belts. It's going to be a bumpy ride," Katherine couldn't help but smile.

This morning, however, Katherine was bathed in sweat,

crying into her third jumbo glass of Colt 45. Tears blended with the sweat of her soul. The bitter taste of beer felt desert dry in her throat, and the empty bottles around the room left an unpleasant odor.

Wiping her eyes with the back of her hand, she burped and gave Bette Davis one last look before flicking off the television set. Hell, she thought to herself, I could play that scene.

Jackson felt stymied. He'd laid all the traps. Even used Mae Thelma to make Ginger jealous, yet nothing was working. He couldn't understand it. In one instant, she was vulnerable and ready to do anything to please him. But before he could fully implement his plan, she changed. At the turn of a dime, Ginger appeared to be as strong willed as the devil himself. She wouldn't budge. Just sat there steaming, ready to charge into an argument. Yet the more she argued, the more she defied him, the more he loved her.

Mae Thelma was a good woman, but she belonged to his cousin. One thing Jackson respected was another man's woman, just as he'd hoped other men would respect Ginger belonging to him. Reality was reality. Men these days just did not respect another man's woman as being *his* woman. They felt that they could just *cop* at any time.

Jackson knew that Mae Thelma had been reared in the Church. Basically, she was a good woman. She'd just been left alone a little too long, so young.

As the warming of a Michigan June closed, the heat of July lifted the Montgomerys' spirits. They were going on vacation. Sierra and Autumn looked forward to the yearly trek to visit their southern cousins. Christian landed his first summer job. Ginger and Jackson agreed it was okay to leave the two boys home for a week or so.

Since graduation and with consistent therapy, Jason had made giant strides in his self-esteem. This would be his first test of trust. But the confident look in Jason's eyes as he shook Jackson's hand good-bye assured them that they needn't worry; the house wouldn't be vandalized and he'd make sure Christian was home at a decent hour while they were away.

Driving south on I-75 into Toledo, Ohio, Ginger still hadn't been able to shake the blame she felt about that night with Edward Deiter. Why hadn't she given him an earlier appointment? Why hadn't she questioned him when he asked to see the same house again, one he barely gave a second glance to at the first showing? Why? When did the pain and guilt stop? Would the minute details of that horrid night ever fade so the healing process could begin? Her blank stare reflected her mood as acre after acre whizzed by.

"How much longer, Daddy?" Autumn asked. Interstate 71 carried them through Dayton and Cincinnati. Ginger knew in the beginning, having asked Jackson that same question while traveling through Cincinnati: It would take hours before they reached Kentucky.

Going to Mississippi is turning out to be more punishment than fun, thought Autumn. She whined, "It's hot. Can't we stop for some ice cream?"

Ginger kept her thoughts to herself. Jackson was one of those men who refused to stop when driving long distance. Everyone suffered. He was in a race against time, unrelenting in his quest to make it to his destination in record time. Probably so he could brag to his friends how quickly he'd made it from Michigan to Mississippi. Never mind the inconvenience to the passengers. That was of little consequence.

"Jackson, can't you stop at the gas station up ahead and get the kids a cold drink? It's at least ninety degrees outside," she begged, finally.

"There's more than a half a tank left," he said, pointing at the control panel. "I'm not stopping until it's time to fill up."

Seventy-five miles later, in the city of Louisville, Kentucky, they managed to stop for a reprieve at the service station. Although Ginger had brought sandwiches, fresh fruit, potato chips, and iced pop in the cooler in the back of the Bronco, it was always the ice cream or Popsicles the kids wanted on the thirteen-hour drive.

"Do you want me to drive, Jackson?" asked Ginger. They'd just changed highways in Nashville, Tennessee, from 65 south onto 40 west, and taken 40 into the northeast corner of Jackson, Tennessee. She knew he was tired. She also knew he thought she couldn't read the signs changing freeways and would get them lost if he fell asleep. Telling him time and time again that she could read a map never seemed to suffice. "It's just one more highway, Jackson." She exhaled deeply. Looking over her shoulder at the kids asleep in the backseat, she wished she could join them. "Highway forty-five in Corinth, Mississippi. Then Booneville, Baldwin, and then home into Guntown."

His lids were heavy. The white strap T-shirt he wore was stuck to his back against the hot seat. He said nothing in answer to Ginger's request, just glanced at his watch a few times. It was nearly 7:30 P.M. Pulling over to the side of the highway, he still hadn't said anything.

In two hours and twenty minutes, they would be at his mother's house in Guntown. "Don't drive over sixty-five, Ginger," Jackson said as he moved the girls over on the back bed of the truck. "Wait!" He lifted the cool sheet draped around Autumn's butt. "You think she needs to pee one more time?"

"No," said Ginger, pulling onto the highway. A service station was nowhere in sight, and she didn't like her child peeing on the side of the road. Ginger never could make Jackson understand it was all right for a man to urinate on the side of the road, but somehow it wasn't quite the same for a young girl or a woman. "She can make it till we get to your mother's." She smiled, stepping on the gas pedal. When the speedometer climbed to seventy-five, she set the cruise control. *I hope she pisses all over you,* Ginger thought.

The week did seem long, but the kids had a good time, despite the 102-degree heat. Ginger and Jackson argued throughout the seven-day excursion, especially about the fact that Autumn peed all over him and they had to make an unscheduled stop at a gas station so Jackson could change his clothes.

He'd left her alone while he went off with his friends. She had nothing to do. There was always a horde of people at his mother's house, but Ginger never could remember which ones were family and which ones were friends. Their faces became one big blur as she patiently waited to return home to Michigan.

On the final evening of their stay, Jackson's mother took her aside. It was the first time Ginger and Hattie B. had ever had a talk—alone.

"I was pregnant with my seventh child when he left," Hattie B. told her. "There was no money to feed my other youngins, so I had to move back home with my mama. I'd heard that my husband Jim was in Wisconsin, then he'd settled in Chicago. He sent money home every now and then. Not enough for us to get by, though. Came home a couple times a year. Gotten me pregnant with the two other chillerins while he was passing through. Times was hard then, but we had each other, and the good Lord found a way for us to make it.

"Yes, Lord. My chillerins come up rough. But they was always thankful for what they did have." There was a contented smile on Hattie B.'s face. A proud smile as she rocked back and forth in her rocker, remembering the good old days. "Me and my oldest chillerins made crops for a living."

"Made crops?" asked Ginger, feeling her respect for this woman grow with each word she lovingly spoke.

"Picked cotton. The kids would give me half of their earnings, and keep the other half. They never wasted any money. They 'preciated what little we did have. After I delivered my ninth child, Jim stopped sending even what little money he had bothered to send home. That's when I started weaning myself off from him. He wanted me and the chillerins to move out to Texas with him. Said he'd send us the money to move"—she let out a short laugh—"I told him no."

"Why didn't you go with him? Jackson said he was a minister."

"He was. Been saved most of his life, but I couldn't tell after I'd delivered my last baby girl. He'd changed. Couldn't trust him. He'd stayed away from me too long. This was home. I was raised here in Mississippi. Life here always been good for me and my chillerins. Even when I was a child, White folks around here always treated us good. We all's just like family. When integration came, Guntown was about the best place to be. Didn't have no problems with the folks down here. No, Mississippi is home. My chillerin's home. I can't see myself living nowheres else."

"And how did your husband take it, when you wouldn't come?"

"Ahhh, he didn't seem to bother 'bout it 'tall. People would come back and tell me they'd seen him with other womens. Even my nieces and nephews would send word back what he was doing." She stopped rocking, looking out into the still of the night. Listening to the crickets. "He'd backslid, taking up with them womenfolks. But I never did." She paused, exhaling. "He stayed away too long. The love was gone. We was just like friends, the last time I seen him. We didn't sleep together no more then. Sometimes I would say, 'You pay me for my food, ya heah?' He'd laugh.

"Didn't have but a three-room shack, but I was thankful it kept us warm, and we wasn't getting rained in on. Yes, Lord, weren't for the grace of God watching over me and my youngins, we'd a starved a many a day." She raised her hand, giving acknowledgment to the Lord, saying "Thank you, Jesus" as tears formed in her eyes.

Ginger sat back, feeling guilty over the resentment she'd felt for her husband's mother. She was everything he'd said she was, and more. Hattie B. had told Ginger that Jimmy Montgomery had been gone for twenty-eight-and-a-half years before she received a call saying her husband had passed. The call came from his common-law wife in Texas who claimed to have a daughter by him the same age as her baby daughter by him. Hattie B. said the woman refused to take care of the funeral. He'd left her in so much debt that she was eager to shed any more responsibility. Even the cost of burying him.

Ginger went to bed that evening long after Jackson had made his farewells and hit the sack. He was snoring soundly as she slid in next to him. She smiled—now she understood his obsession with bologna. Her mother-in-law had told her how she and the kids looked forward to spending their money buying rag bologna and crackers down at the corner store. Most of their extra money went for buying good food to eat. They had had the best of times, she and her children; even though they were poor, she swore they didn't even think about it. Because you never missed what you didn't have, she always insisted.

Hattie B. taught her children to appreciate what they did have. They'd just sit on the porch and talk, laughing over good times, all ten of them. Crackers and bologna. After nearly thirty years, Jackson's appetite for the good old days hadn't changed. He'd already loaded up the Bronco with ten tubes of rag bologna.

Ginger stroked Jackson's supple thighs, and hugged his waist, waiting on the comfort of sleep. She shook the somber thoughts from her mind that Jackson could possibly be a bit spoiled—first by his mother, and now by her. Yet she couldn't help but wish that she'd experienced the same overflowing love and affection Jackson and his siblings had been blessed with. Even the wealthiest families couldn't provide themselves with the same abundance of love that one woman had the infinite wisdom to bestow upon her children. Did Jackson possess the same wisdom? she wondered as sleep finally overcame her thoughts.

Broad strokes of crimson canvased the blue Barbados sky. Speckled silver studs twinkled randomly in the background, hinting at a Fab-Five debut. Ginger lay back against the chaise lounge on the patio, meditating. Her interview earlier that morning with a counselor at Southfield's School of Interior Design had gone well.

A closed book rested on her lap. Several colorful brochures were stacked on the table beside her. After skimming the contents of the material, Ginger's mind was made up. In a few months, she'd enroll. Champion Motors would pay the full tuition. It wouldn't cost her anything except her time.

"Mom," called Jason from the patio door, "you out here?" He could see the outline of a form, but was unable to decipher who it was.

"Yes," said Ginger, unaware the evening had crept upon her so suddenly. "I'll be in in a minute." Collecting her books, she quickly went inside.

"Where's the kids, Jason?" Ginger asked, locking the door behind her.

"Playing video games in Christian's room."

As Ginger inserted the books and pamphlets into the bookshelf in the music room, Jason tried to find the right words but, fearing the time would never be right, blurted out, "I joined the Service, Mom."

Whipping around as if she'd seen a ghost, her eyes widened. "You did what?"

"I . . ."

"Tell me I didn't hear you right, Jason." Ginger's fingers went immediately to her throbbing temples. "Tell me I didn't."

"I joined the Service, Mom." His voice was adamant. There was no turning back now. It was time to shit or get off the pot.

The room, already small, seemed to close in and suffocate Ginger. She could barely breathe. "Jason, it's only the middle of July. We've got three or four more weeks before you enroll." The blue-green veins in her forehead protruded. Only a few minutes before; she'd been thinking about enrolling in school herself. She'd completely forgotten about Jason. What was wrong with her? She *never* forgot things that were so important.

"I could swear you told me a few weeks ago that you and your father decided the school you were going to when you were there the other week?"

"I lied, Mom." Jason leaned against the arch, fingering the outstretched palm plants bridging the open doorway. "I've been trying to find the words to tell you without hurting you. I knew you'd be disappointed."

There were no more tears to come forth. She was as dry as blue Ajax. They would not cleanse her soul of the hurt she felt, anyway. "Jason . . ." was all she managed to utter before leaning her weight against the wooden cases.

"Mom, I'm worried about you. You've been acting funny lately—"

"Jason . . ." she said, even more slowly than the first time.

Ginger's feet felt as though they were lifted three inches above the carpeting as her son wrapped his arms around his mother. "Trust me, Mom. I know what I'm doing."

Trust you, thought Ginger. I can't even trust myself.

"Remember that night a few months ago when my friend

Mick told me about his father taking him down to talk with
the armed forces?"

"Vaguely."

"I called Daddy. . . ."

"And he thought it was better for you to join the army than
go to college?"

"Listen, Ma, the Service is different now. There's a lot of
opportunities, especially to travel. You know I hate school—
but I know you want all of us to go to college. So I figured,
why waste your money and Daddy's when I can let the government pay for it? After completing basic training, the
sergeant swore that I'd have time to attend any of the community colleges nearby, or enroll at the University of Arizona. Both are just a few miles from the air force base."

"But what if a war—"

"That's just what Daddy said at first. Remember when he
was in Vietnam? He's still getting over problems from that
stuff. . . ."

"Agent Orange."

"That's it—Agent Orange, and that was in nineteen seventy. Daddy said him and a lot of his buddies that went in
when he did in 'sixty-eight are still having problems. He said
if Bush hadn't terminated Operation Desert Storm, he wouldn't
want me to join the Service either. But there probably won't
be another war anytime soon. Anyway, I want to be a pilot,
that's why I joined the air force, not the army."

"A pilot," Ginger said proudly. Knowing her son aspired
to be a pilot and join the air force suddenly made her feel dif-
ferently about the decision. To Ginger, the air force had more
prestige than the other branches of the Service.

"Yeah. Less than five percent of the servicemen fly air-
planes in the air force. They have a special academy for flying. You have to be an outstanding person to get into the
flight program. And it takes five years to become an officer.
You have to have a bachelor's degree to even apply for the
AFOQT—that's the Air Force Officers Qualifying Test.
Their engineering program is envied even by most civilians."

"An engineer?" Ginger whispered to herself.

"I hope to have a master's degree in engineering before
my tour of duty is over."

Jackson was impressed with Jason's ambitions. He sounded just like his mother. "You know, Jason, I always wanted to be an engineer myself. I can help you. . . ."

A few short weeks later, the entire family was at the airport seeing Jason off. "Don't cry, Mama. I'll be all right. I'm a man," said Jason. He stood erect and proud in his air force uniform, ready to board the plane. He hugged Jackson, thanking him for all his patience. Sierra and Autumn cried, but Christian looked on, bored with the whole scene.

Ginger cried like a three-year-old. She didn't care who was looking. Her son was leaving. He wasn't the most perfect child in the world, but he was hers. A part of her wanted him to go and see the world, to grow up. The other part of her wanted to pull him close and shelter him, so no one could harm him. She knew there came a time in every mother's life when she had to let go. But it was painful, no matter how you prepared yourself. It hurt. Deeply.

"You sure you got all your papers, Dink?"

"Ma, don't call me that. Somebody might hear you." He looked around nervously to see if any of his new friends were listening.

She'd called him Dinky Duck since he was three months old. After his delivery, she'd overheard the doctor telling the nurse that he thought that Jason was a trick baby, telling them how pale and homely he looked. Jason hadn't colored until he was a year old. Ginger had thought he looked just like the yellow Tweety bird in the cartoons. The whole town of Port Huron knew who Dinky Duck was—Ginger's baby boy.

Funny how when her child was leaving her, she forgot about the problems she'd encountered only months before. She'd forgotten the arguments they'd had when she made him walk home from night school, how she'd suffered, worrying if he was cold, if anyone had harmed him, until she heard the key unlock the door and he was safely inside. She'd been going to work with two and three hours of sleep, worrying if he understood the lessons she was trying to teach him.

Yes, Ginger had crossed the threshold of motherhood,

when the first offspring flew the coop and there was no turning back. All the years of teaching her child everything she knew and thought he should know would be put to the test—and she worried if she'd forgotten anything, some pertinent piece of information that she wished her parents had given her. . . .

As they drove home from Metro Airport, Jackson was his usual quiet self. He was biding his time. He had decided it was time for him and Ginger to have a serious talk. There were going to be some changes made at home, and it wasn't just because Jason had left.

Dibs were already being made on Jason's bedroom. "You might as well stop arguing about it," said Ginger, looking over her shoulder inside the Bronco. "I've already made plans for Dink's bedroom." She glanced in Jackson's direction, but he was a master of not showing his emotions. She knew he had something on his mind and she would find out shortly what it was.

"I said I'd give you a year. That was up five months ago. I've been patient with you, Ginger. But now you're going to have to quit. That's all there is to it. You can't work two jobs *and* take care of a family." He sat in the lounge chair in their bedroom, flicking the remote control. Jason's flight had been scheduled early, leaving Jackson the afternoon to watch his Westerns.

Ginger felt as if part of her were growing, making giant strides in the business. Yet, the other, vulnerable, needy part seemed to negate it. She was regressing, succumbing to Jackson's needs, allowing herself to believe that his feelings were more important than her own.

Ginger sat in the chair across from him, her arms folded in defiance. Crossing her legs, she glared at him. "I won't let you control my life, Jackson. You have no idea what my needs are outside the bedroom."

Jackson glared at her. "I've been patient, Ginger—"

Standing up abruptly, she blocked the television screen. "No, baby. You've got it all wrong. I've been patient with you. With your selfish, self-centered, self-concerned-ass attitude. How could you possibly know how I feel—what's important in my life—besides you?"

"Move out of the way, Ginger. You're blocking the view."

She stood before him. Building her courage. "Which view, Jackson? The real world as it is? Or your world that you've created just for yourself, your mother, and your daughter? Where do I fit in, Jackson?" Ginger couldn't give in. She wouldn't. It was his will against hers. And she couldn't lose control.

"As my wife." There was a finality in Jackson's voice.

Ginger gritted her teeth, pushing the Off button on the television. Her hands rested on both sides of her hips. She could feel Jackson's fury. "Where's my Emmy, Jackson? Where's the Oscar for my Academy Award performance of perfect wife?"

The quietness of the room intensified the argument. Jackson rose to leave, a knowing smile registering on his face. He knew that Ginger was ready to argue from here to eternity. There would be no compromising.

Ginger blocked the doorway. She knew that when he was dead quiet, his next move would be out the door. She decided to drop the bomb. "I'm quitting Champion Motors."

Jackson stopped dead in his tracks. The smug smile that had been on his face only moments ago disappeared. "Are you crazy woman?"

Her heart beat nervously. She'd dreaded this confrontation but knew it was inevitable. Ginger had decided months ago, before the assault, that she was quitting her job at the factory in January. Knowing Jackson would be furious, she'd tried to avoid the subject until she could spring it on him under the best possible circumstances—perhaps during Christmas. "I can't work in that factory anymore, Jackson. I can't stand it." She felt the pressure of a headache coming, but shrugged it off.

Ginger brushed past him and headed for the sofa. She wanted to snatch the wig from her head to alleviate the pressure but thought better of it. She wouldn't expose herself, raw, as being so vulnerable, no matter what the costs.

"And what do you propose that we do about paying the bills? Or do you think we can take that vivid imagination of yours and cash it in at the bank?" he said, sitting next to her on the sofa.

Ginger fumed, but outwardly remained as calm as he did. "You know we don't need my whole salary to pay the bills around here! We can cut down on a few—"

"No. I'm comfortable with our two-salary income just the way it is." Jackson crossed his legs. Waiting. As though they were playing a game of chess. He anticipated her next move like a seasoned professional.

Ginger felt tears threatening. "You told me you'd always take care of me, Jackson. Didn't you mean it?"

"Two incomes are a fact these days, not a fashionable fad that'll fade by the next season. I'd planned on buying a new bike next spring, and putting on a new roof. That's over ten thousand dollars for cedar shingles on a home this large. *A home that you insisted that you had to have.* How do you propose I do these things with the reduction of your steady salary?"

"What would you do if I told you I didn't want to work anymore, period?" Jackson's mustache twitched slightly as she continued. "There's a lot of men out there whose wives stay at home. They're working two jobs to make up for the loss in income."

"Not me. That shit went out of style when Roy Rogers stopped riding Trigger."

Ginger stood up, looking for her purse. Now she was ready to leave. She ignored the working tension in his jaw and said, "Fuck you, Jackson." The words rolled smoothly off her tongue. It felt good. "I don't need you or the horse you rode in on." She was sowing her oats now. If Trigger broke down the door to their bedroom right at this moment, she'd jump on the back of that bastard and ride the hell out of him until he broke and lay down, groveling and foaming at the mouth as sure as Jackson would do soon. Begging for forgiveness.

Then his words stung in her ears: "You quit your job, like a fool, and I'll separate our accounts." She stood, staring at him for a moment until he turned and stomped out of the room.

School started for Ginger and the kids in September. Ginger missed Jason. Missed hearing him call out "Yo Ma!"

whenever he came home, expecting her always to be there. Each time as she passed his room she was tempted to call out his name. She missed hearing the rap music blaring from beneath his bedroom door and the size-thirteen dirty Nikes smelling up the laundry room.

She mused over the amused smile that would cross his face if she confided to him over worrying about grades. Ginger wasn't prepared for the barrage of assignments that hit from the very first day.

Dressed for success, Sierra and Autumn were excited about school starting. Ginger had spent more on school clothes than she normally did—with her own money, sending a message of independence to Jackson. The girls' chests of drawers were overflowing with jeans, skirts, vests, blouses, sweaters, jogging suits, and matching sneakers.

Having given Christian his equal share of clothing money, Ginger observed that he'd only spent a third on new school clothes. He was probably stashing a third in his bank and spending another third on the video games that Ginger refused to buy. She'd told Christian that the only way she'd invest in video games was if Christian had written and sold the patent himself.

Jackson hadn't come begging, as Ginger assumed he would. Instead he ignored her. When he asked the kids if they wanted to go to the movies, the invitation wasn't extended or addressed to her. When he took them for impromptu outings to McDonald's, she wasn't asked along. Clearly he was also sending her a message of his independence.

Tired of playing games and not knowing how to make amends to Jackson without giving in to his control tactics, Ginger phoned her mother.

But a few minutes into the conversation Ginger was holding back her own problems and listening to Katherine chatter on about the latest strife between her and Cotton. Ginger concluded that Katherine was dealing with enough problems of her own, and kept silent about Jackson.

Kim was hard to reach. And Ginger felt guilty invading her time, knowing how hard she was studying to maintain her 4.0 average in law school. She'd even picked up the phone during a crisis and attempted to call Bill. He was always so wonderful with the kids. And he was constantly mentioned in the *Detroit News* as a mentor for today's Black children, reaching out into the community. But what about his personal needs? thought Ginger. He was busy, she was busy. How long could Bill continue to go along with Kim's farce of a commitment? It was obvious that Kim and Bill truly loved each other, just as in her heart she truly believed that she and Jackson were blessed with a lifelong love.

Her problems, on the other hand, went deeper. The pain of loving Jackson, constantly being challenged in that love, cut like a laser across Ginger's heart. Trying to talk to Jackson was futile. It was his way or no way. No compromising. Their sex life had hit an all-time low, when and if they deemed it necessary to pursue the act. Neither wished to seem weak and let the other know that he or she needed some affection. Needed some love. Each felt the other should instinctively know.

By the end of September, Ginger was suffering, suffocating without Jackson's attention and love. She'd read her Bible faithfully, but felt her faith waning. She couldn't understand or comprehend that, through her faith, there was a message in the suffering. Her temporary suffering would soon lead to a full recovery. To live is to suffer. To survive is to find the message in the suffering—the lesson. It would take time, but just possibly something positive would emerge from all the pain.

September had come to a close. She and Jackson had avoided each other's company for weeks. Ginger over the weeks began putting in more hours at the real estate office, managing to tuck a few more listings under her belt. She closed on a home on the last day in September, but kept the sale to herself. Not sharing her good fortune with Jackson, she opened a private bank account—but kept the book at Kim's apartment.

28

Pride and Joy

By early October, the preseason basketball games had begun. Ginger and Jackson had always enjoyed watching the Pistons games before the start of the season. The excitement over the home team was at an all-time high since the Pistons had won two consecutive championships a few years earlier.

The street leading to the Palace of Auburn Hills was renamed Two Championship Drive. And though the Pistons' hopes to become one of the few teams in NBA history to "three-peat" had not been realized, the city was nevertheless eagerly awaiting a return to the successes of previous seasons.

Jogging around the subdivision, her sweat-soaked T-shirt clinging to her body, Ginger stopped at the corner to catch her breath. She admired the splendor of Michigan's fall leaves. They had turned from deep emerald green to ruby red, a subtle gold, then hardened to a tawny brown and drifted, one leaf at a time, onto the foliage-dusted landscape. It was a beautiful, hushed October morning.

"Hey there," said a familiar voice behind her.

Trying not to look surprised, Ginger stifled the impulse to close her hands over her opened mouth. "Hi," she said weakly. Smoothing her wig, wondering how she looked, Ginger tried to relax. At least she'd put on lipstick and a little blush before she came out to run.

"I noticed you jogging this morning. You look familiar. Do I know you from somewhere?" The Pistons' backup center, Gene Russell, stood seven feet one inch. His trim waistline was inches away from Ginger's eyes.

Ginger was unable to speak. She just shook her head no. For some ungodly reason, she suddenly felt uncomfortable. Nervous. Picking the pace back up, she continued jogging. He followed her. She could feel the heat of his body behind her.

"That's it. I remember where I've seen you," he said, stopping close to their respective turnoffs. He tapped the top of her hat with his long fingers. "A Piston fan." His smile was wide and genuine, and his beautiful white teeth gleamed at her.

"Did my hat give me away?" said Ginger, smiling, feeling slightly more at ease. "My husband and I have season tickets. We sit about—"

"Fifteen rows behind our bench."

Ginger was impressed. She thought he'd smiled to her a few times. But when Ginger had mentioned it to Jackson, he'd told her it was her imagination. There were too many people around them for her to think he was singling her out. But he had, and Ginger always knew it.

"Jackson! Jackson!" she hollered excitedly. "Guess what?"

He and Autumn were outside shooting hoops. Ever since Jason left, Jackson had taken it upon himself to teach Autumn to play basketball. At six, she was the tallest one in her class. Every one of Jackson's six sisters played basketball in school. Two were exceptionally good. Ginger didn't want to spoil his fun by telling him that Autumn had asked her on several occasions to tell her daddy that she didn't want to play basketball. She wanted to play soccer.

Jackson dismissed the relieved look on Autumn's face as

he told her that was enough for today. "I just saw Gene Russell while I was out jogging."

"So?"

"So, we talked for a while, he invited us to a preseason after-five party he's throwing at his house next week."

Seeming to ignore what she'd said, he shot a few hoops as she stood there waiting for his reply. "Why would he do that?"

"He remembered seeing us at the games. I casually mentioned that I sold real estate, and we chatted a few minutes about redecorating. He suggested I could pass around a few business cards. Wouldn't you like to meet the team?" She tried to hide the excitement in her voice.

"I don't know. I'll have to think about it." He left without another word.

Hurt, Ginger picked up the basketball and, though ordinarily not a good shot, sank the basket on her first attempt. He could go to hell if he thought she was going to pass this up.

They arrived at the party at a few minutes past six. The evening air was clean and crisp. Expensive cars lined both sides of the street and the circular driveway. Clusters of beautiful people, impeccably dressed, walked toward the entrance of the grand home.

Inside, a white-jacketed butler showed them in. Portraits of Dr. Martin Luther King, Jr., Malcom X, Nelson Mandela, and Rosa Parks graced the walls of the main hallway. A consummate connoisseur of African art, Mr. Russell also displayed his enviable collection of masks, drums, and artifacts.

Reggae music could be heard from somewhere down a long hall as two young attendants led them toward the focal point of the party. Like most of the women, Ginger couldn't keep her eyes off the decor.

Holding her hand, Jackson gently pulled Ginger closer to his side. Ginger skipped a step to keep up with Jackson's long strides. She strained her neck to catch a glimpse inside each room as they passed by.

"Jackson," whispered Ginger, "do you think Gene Russell would consider giving us a tour of the house?"

"No. And don't ask."

"Why not?"

The small crowd stopped in front of an elevator. Jackson didn't bother to answer as they slowly descended to the lower level. An orchard of spicy scents misted the air inside the small cubicle.

Ginger hadn't realized that she was hungry until she inhaled the aroma of freshly baked bread. Stepping off the elevator, Ginger felt a rush of nerves. She blinked her eyes several times in succession, worrying if the glue would hold. The music blared. Seconds away, a few feet away, famous people would be talking and dancing.

Jackson sensed her hesitation. "You look gorgeous, sweetheart." He kissed her tenderly on the tip of her nose. Surprised, Ginger relaxed when he added, "Even those bedroom eyes."

He'd noticed. Earlier that day, Kim and Ginger had spent hours at Helga's Spa getting pampered. They had lunch, a couple of glasses of chilled wine, and Ginger felt better than she had in months. Kim had convinced Ginger that she needed to have eyelashes professionally applied. They felt natural. The technician assured Ginger that they would not come off or lift at the corners. Ginger smiled, gazing into the mirror. The softness that Ginger felt was missing in her face was back.

Joe Dumars arrived, giving Ginger and Jackson a polite smile and a hello and continuing toward the back of the room. A few feet away stood Gene Russell inside the doorway, smiling that brilliant smile, shaking hands with his guests. And Jackson spotted Isiah Thomas, Bill Laimbeer, and Mark McGuire by the pool table in the background.

Spit-shined cranberry alligator shoes hurt Jackson's feet. Yet, feeling a little cocky in a new doublebreasted navy blue pinstriped suit, he boldly walked over to Gene, Ginger traipsing along with him. A stunned Ginger smiled shyly as Jackson introduced himself and his wife.

Gene Russell greeted them effusively, excusing himself temporarily from his guests. A waiter appeared offering assorted wines in exquisite glassware. Ginger took one, as Jackson and Gene made quick exchanges about basketball.

Gene led them toward the pool table, assuming that Jackson would want to meet the rest of the Pistons.

Even though Gene was a head taller than Jackson, Ginger couldn't have been more proud of her man. He fit in beautifully. Looked positively scrumptious. Mingled expertly with the guys. Jackson's easy smile rested on her for a moment. She could tell he was enjoying himself. Excusing herself, Ginger deposited her empty wineglass on a tray and headed for the buffet tables.

Three exotic floral arrangements tiered a lighted, eight-foot Lucite display. White linen tablecloths dropped to the floor with lace overlays. Hundreds of votive candles huddled atop each table, casting an elegant glow. Prisms of light reflections shone on the mirror displays and sterling silver chafing dishes.

Stunning floral creations were arranged near each entrée. Spicy shrimp sizzled in a bed of fresh scallions. Fresh jumbo shrimp, marinated and dipped in coconut, were served with pineapple or plum sauce. Béarnaise sauce drizzled over strips of sesame chicken.

A station of Norwegian smoked salmon was enticing. Equally tempting was a circular design of Brie amandine.

Standing beside an ice sculpture of Gene Russell's basketball shoes, a chef hand-carved paper-thin slices of roast tenderloin for the guests who stood in line. Others were helping themselves to the seasoned roasted chicken to his right.

A cappuccino and espresso bar held court near the dessert table of pies, cakes, and tortes. Kahlúa, Baileys, and various other liqueurs were a matter of choice, along with chocolate shavings to add to a savory cup of hot cappuccino.

Ginger relaxed near the bar with a tumbler of Martell and ginger ale. Jackson and Joe Dumars were deeply involved in an animated conversation about the Pistons' chances of victory this year over the competitive Chicago Bulls. Ginger hated to interrupt her husband as he artfully executed his version of Michael Jordan's jump shot. Tapping her feet to the beat of the music, Ginger watched the couples dancing, wishing she and Jackson would at least get in one slow dance before the evening ended. She spotted a woman on the dance floor in a deadly pair of Donna Karan black peau de soie pumps with a rhinestone buckle across the instep.

"Enjoying yourself?" asked a seductive voice.

Ginger's eyes rested on his elegantly clad size-fifteen-and-a-half shoes first. She hadn't seen any shoes that big before. At least not in person. Her head fell back as she looked up into Gene Russell's face. Damn, he was cute, with those thick, sexy lips. "Yes. I'm having a wonderful time," she stammered.

He extended his hand. Taking it, Ginger felt like a queen as he executed a half-bow. "Your husband mentioned that you'd like a tour of the house." He smiled again, and Ginger felt her heart turn flips.

"He did?" Ginger was shocked. "I'd love one." Smoothing out her dress as she stood, she clutched her purse. "Lead the way."

As they entered each room Gene explained the renovations he planned. He was especially proud of the complete remodernization of the Euro-design kitchen. Ginger could see the pride in his eyes.

The estate maintained a houseman, caretaker, security officer, chef, and Gene's personal maid. As they made their way back to the party, Gene asked Ginger if she had circulated any of her business cards yet. "A few," she said, glancing at her watch. It was later than she thought—Jackson would be worried. A slight breeze of his opulent cologne invited her to slow down.

When they reentered the party scene "Time, Love, and Tenderness," by Michael Bolton was causing a rush of sentimental lovers onto the dance floor. Ginger felt the warmth of Jackson's eyes on her from across the room.

Ginger moved stealthily toward her lover. As she batted her lashes provocatively, playing the ingenue, Jackson swept her expertly into his arms. A perfect fit. Their bodies moved languidly to a slow dance.

A half-hour later, while driving home, Jackson hinted that he was apprehensive about letting Gene Russell take her all over that large mansion alone. "Was he a gentleman?" asked Jackson.

The night had long since dropped its inky curtain. A million diamonds sprinkled across the heavens above them.

"Perfect." Ginger closed her eyes, savoring the night. Reaching out, she touched him, feeling his warmth. The warmth she felt for him, even when they were apart. Jackson illuminated her world. Was the center of her universe. "Let's make love, Jackson."

"Now?"

She stretched. Her voice purred. "Outside. On our patio."

"You're kidding?"

She touched him. Stroked him softly. Tonight, she thought, would be the perfect ending to an enchanting evening.

That night, their lovemaking had resumed with the fierce passion that had been missing for the past few weeks. Jackson made love to her so completely and fully; she felt as if no man could ever touch her heart and love her the way he did.

Ginger received several letters from Jason. There were even a few pictures of him with a new girlfriend. He sounded happy but made it clear that he missed home. Missed his mother. Ginger cried, knowing how much she'd missed him too.

By the middle of November, Mae Thelma felt as though she was running low on time. She persuaded her sons to call Jackson, telling him they missed seeing him and asking him when was he coming back over to visit.

Mae Thelma couldn't admit to herself that she had reached this mysterious climax of effacement. The humiliation of using her children scorched her to the soul, yet she couldn't stop herself.

She used every conceivable excuse to get Jackson to come over that her mind could imagine. The refrigerator was broken. The bathroom faucets leaked. A cracked window needed replacing in the kids' room. And the kicker: In the bitter coldness at the start of December, the furnace wouldn't work.

Ginger took all of this in stride as she struggled to be nice, keep her cool, and maintain her relationship at an even keel. She wanted to scream.

Sierra and Autumn weren't thrilled when Ginger suggested that they spend a weekend with their grandmother. An inducement of forty dollars apiece to go shopping silenced their protests.

But by late Saturday afternoon, each of the kids had called from their grandmother Katherine's. When was Ginger coming down to pick them up? They were ready to come home. The phone rang again. Shuffling through a stack of insurance papers, Ginger cradled the phone along her shoulder. "Yes?" said Ginger, thinking it was probably Autumn again.

"Hello. Hello," came the nervous voice.

"Yes." Ginger furrowed her brows.

"Can I please speak to Jackson?" came the unmistakable slow southern drawl.

Goose bumps rose on her flesh. Flashbacks of the mice, throwing water in her face, Jason's party. A streak of yellow. The sickeningly sweet smell of honeysuckle. "He's at the basketball game."

"Me and the boys are at the airport. You think Jackson'll be home directly?" Mae Thelma asked.

Determined to start the New Year with the pledge of Jackson's love, Mae Thelma had made a final attempt to secure a stronger love potion from her aunt Gitty, a high priestess of voodoo in New Orleans. The boys had been eager to meet the great-aunt they'd heard so many stories about.

You're asking me what time my husband will be home? Ginger thought but didn't say. This bitch must have more balls than Jackson.

"I have no idea." She slammed down the phone.

Smothered potatoes and onions, Caesar salad, and a three-quarter-inch porterhouse steak were placed before Jackson as he gave Ginger play-by-play events of the Pistons' game against the red-hot Chicago Bulls.

Quietly she listened. Ginger couldn't keep from watching the clock. It had been nearly an hour and a half since Mae Thelma had called. Though Ginger had prepared a hefty dinner just for two, she merely picked at hers, constantly keeping watch as the clock ticked loudly inside her head. Would she call back? Would he go if she did?

Ginger nearly jumped out of her seat as the phone shrilled loudly. "I'll get it," she offered. Jackson, who sat closer to the phone, sensed Ginger's discomfort and picked up before the second ring.

During the lengthy conversation, Ginger cleared their plates. Outside the kitchen window the winter night was as clear as day. Ice crystallized circles of puddles along the street.

She felt her heart slipping, skipping a beat, hearing the anger and tone in his voice, directed toward her. When he hung up, fury was written all over his face. "They've been at the airport for hours!"

"She could have called a taxi," Ginger said softly to deaf ears as Jackson skidded out of the driveway. Warm tears slid down her face. Gathering her purse and keys, she drove to her mother's house in Port Huron. She wouldn't be here when he got back.

When Ginger and the kids returned home late Sunday evening, Jackson ignored her, focusing on Autumn, hugging and kissing her. Ginger saw the hurt in Sierra's eyes as she watched Jackson snuggle his baby daughter. Jackson finally acknowledged his other baby and kissed her too. But the biggest baby of all, Ginger, was left out.

"What in the hell were you thinking about?" Jackson grabbed Autumn's hand. "Don't you ever put your hands on her hair again!"

Turning abruptly, Ginger's eyes flushed with tears.

"Daddy, Mama didn't—" Autumn looked back at her mother, her large brown eyes glossy, as her father dragged her from their bedroom.

How could he possibly think that she would deliberately cause her baby's hair to come out? He hadn't even given her the opportunity to explain. It had been a simple mistake, leaving the permanent on Autumn's hair too long.

Autumn's hair, normally twelve inches long, had broken off badly from being overprocessed. Ginger was panic stricken when she found sections throughout Autumn's hair that measured less than three inches. There was no way she could hide it. Ginger tried to cut it as evenly as she could into a retro-seventies shag style, tried to make light of it to Autumn as she joked to her small child that she'd go back to school after the holidays with a new hairstyle. It seemed to please her.

When the idea of a permanent for Autumn first arose, Jackson had told Ginger he didn't want to put any chemicals in his baby's hair. He'd given in, though, when his sister, who'd called to wish them a happy Thanksgiving, scolded Jackson for being so old-fashioned. Her daughter, Jamara, had been just five when Jackson's sister had permed her hair—and a year later, her hair was fine. Ginger begged her husband to try to understand how difficult it was to manage Autumn's thick head of hair. But the call from his sister was what had made him agree.

Autumn was extremely tender headed, and Jackson had to leave the house when the crying started. He couldn't stand hearing her cry for so long. Autumn's hair was so thick, like her grandma Katherine's, that it took hours of babying before Ginger was finished. "You okay, sweetheart?" Ginger would hear a low sniffle from Autumn, signaling another crying spell, and she'd stop for a moment, then begin again. "Mama's not going to hurt you, baby. I'll be finished real soon, okay?" By then Ginger was exhausted.

The force of Jackson's accusations was like an earthquake that ruminated deep inside her heart's core. Her body trembled. Her hands shook. Falling facedown onto their bed, Ginger cried like a baby until there was nothing left but dry tears.

Ginger's heart, weeping to belong, to be cherished, closed like a shell, protecting the prize, because the heart has its reasons of which Reason knows nothing. Washing her face with tepid water, she toweled her face dry in the darkness of their bathroom. She vowed vindication. With renewed courage she went downstairs to face Jackson.

"I read my watch wrong," Ginger admonished. "I was trying to make her hair look pretty for the Christmas program at church Sunday. I figured a few more minutes and it would be bone straight. You know how thick her hair—"

"*Was*," he finished.

The six o'clock news flashed interviews with last-minute Christmas shoppers who scurried for that special gift outside the Twelve Oaks Mall. Ginger felt raw envy as she heard a husband saying to his wife on live television, "This is it, sweetheart." He waved a perfectly wrapped diminutive package over his heart. Autumn, quiet, sat on the floor in front of her father, clutching her knees.

"I'm sorry, Jackson." Ginger's voice quavered. She could feel the sweat on her nude head beading beneath her wig. "I can take her to the hairdresser's—"

He looked up from oiling Autumn's reddened scalp. "Don't bother. I'll take her." His voice sounded so cold. So heartless.

"I love her, too, Jackson." Ginger's hands shook violently as she massaged her temples. "You think I'd intentionally hurt my baby? You think I want her to feel like I—" She couldn't finish.

Jackson, unmoved, finished Autumn's hair, then patted her bottom, signaling her to get up. Ginger had crossed the line that divided his heart. He didn't want to admit it, but his baby needed him. To him Ginger was too busy working to notice. Ginger had made her choice. She chose a life away from him and the family that he had worked so hard these past years to create. He resented Ginger's drive toward success. Everyone suffered, except Ginger. He'd had enough of her selfishness.

Jackson appreciated economy in words. "Yeah," he said, and, turning off the television, left the house.

Ginger sat in her bathroom nursing a drink, trying to numb the pain in her heart. Did he think she was that vindictive, to make her child suffer, and deliberately cause her hair to fall out? There wasn't a day when Ginger didn't think about her own hair; not a day that she didn't see the horror of her bald head staring back at her. No one knew her pain. No one. Not Jackson. Not her mother. Or even her children. It was as if a part of her had died.

Each day she played the role of a woman in control. She needed the love from her family to strengthen her. To give her purpose, a reason to be strong, to have faith in God and not wallow in self-pity. Having a loved one accuse her of hurting her child—a child whom she'd loved and nurtured since the first moment she'd felt the gift of life growing inside her body—was more painful to Ginger than having an arm severed without anesthesia.

"Who is it?" Ginger called out, wiping her swollen eyes.

"It's me, Mama." Sierra's sweet voice was hesitant, listening for any telltale signs of anguish in her mother's reply.

The sound of her daughter's caring voice was like an arm around her shoulder. "Hold on, sweetheart. I'm just getting out of the shower. I'll be right out." Trying to evoke a perkiness she didn't feel, she flushed the toilet and turned the cold water on over the sink. Splashing the tepid water over her face, she did her best to be presentable for her daughter.

Wrapping herself in her terry-cloth robe, she wound a hand towel around her head, covering her puffy eyes with a cold washcloth. "What is it, honey?" said Ginger, feigning a headache. She strolled into their bedroom and casually turned on the television set, trying to shield her face with the soft cloth.

"A package came for you this afternoon." Knowing that her mother and Jackson had been at it all afternoon, Sierra's instincts had told her to wait. Looking at her mother now, she knew the timing was right. "I think it's from Dink," she said cheerily. Sierra slipped the small, brown, awkwardly bundled package inside her mother's palm.

Ginger handed her back the package, still holding the cold cloth to her forehead. As if synchronized, they sat together on the couch. "Can you open it for Mama?" She could see the return address from Arizona, and knew it was from her son.

"No, Mom. It's addressed to you. Dink would be mad at me if I opened it." Sierra smiled innocently at her mother.

Ginger turned the package over and over in her lap. "What do you think it is, Sierra?"

Sierra merely shrugged.

"He missed my birthday in October. I didn't even receive a card." Ginger's shoulders heaved. The pressure of another disappointment from a loved one nearly overwhelmed her.

"Open it, Ma," chided Sierra.

"You know how cheap Dink is. He didn't even spend five dollars on me for Mother's Day when he was home working at the grocery store." Ginger tried to lift her spirits. "I know it's the thought that counts." She smiled awkwardly at Sierra, saying a silent prayer. Her heart leaped, wishing her prayers would be answered in a matter of minutes. She flipped the small package over again.

Desperate, Ginger tore the brown paper package, then hesitated. "You know," said Ginger thoughtfully, "I really loved that silk rose Dink gave me. It was real pretty."

Sierra kissed Ginger. She sensed that her mother was under a lot of pressure. "Open it, Mom," she said. It had to be the perfect gift. It just had to be.

Inside was a black velvet box. A white folded card, printed in red and blue bold letters read: DIAMOND CROSS OF DEVOTION: TO MOTHER, WITH LOVE.

"Look, Sierra, isn't it beautiful?" said Ginger, holding up the necklace. The light above them illuminated the rainbow prisms of each blazing gem.

"It's lovely, Mom," Sierra said excitedly.

But Ginger hadn't heard a word she said. *I love you Mom,* the attached letter began. *Every time I call you make me feel loved and missed. Thanks Mom. Each night I read the Bible. I pray that God guides my life the right way so you'll be proud of me. I've got a problem I'm trying to break, I don't feel safe unless I'm close to you.*

Ginger pressed her right hand over her heart, feeling the love swelling up inside her. As tender as a baby's touch, she felt Sierra's loving arm circling her shoulder. She read on: *The three red rubies in the necklace symbolize the gratitude, love and devotion that's in my heart for you. Seven white diamonds symbolize all the purity, beauty and love that's in your heart, seven days a week. Seven blue sapphires thank you for the seven days each week you sacrificed that I might have. Always wear this necklace Mom, and I'll always be close to you.*

Tears she had kept welled inside poured down her face like a raging brook. She slid off the couch, onto the carpet, hugging the cross to her chest, hiding her head in her hands.

She felt the warmth of Sierra's arms around her, and easily leaned against her small body.

"Let me put it around your neck, Mama."

Ginger's hands were trembling as she handed Sierra the beautiful necklace. She read the words over and over while Sierra folded back her thick housecoat, placing the cross around her neck. Only God knew how much it meant to her. "Thank you, sweetheart," she said, wiping her eyes on the sleeve of her robe.

Placing her hands on her mother's shoulders, Sierra held her cheek next to hers. "You okay, Mama?"

Ginger patted her hands, rubbing a tear-stained cheek against Sierra's silky skin. "Mama's going to be just fine," she whispered more to herself than to her daughter. "Just fine."

29

Standing in the
Shadows of Love

Dreading the thought of being alone for the holidays, memories of her mother's death, her father's illness, and the breakup with Bill had added to Kim's postholiday blues.

In less than six months, she'd replaced the black leather couch and contemporary accessories with a cozy moss-green velvet sofa with five-inch braided fringe edging the curved base. Solid brass torch lamps balanced each end of the expansive sofa. A matching love seat and oversized circular ottoman were arranged around an eighteenth-century Aubusson rug. Kim took special pleasure selecting precious pieces of Lalique crystal and a diversity of small treasures that graced the polished mahogany tables. Kim felt her mother's presence guiding her in every purchase, encouraging her to transform her spiritless house into a real home.

To this day, she had never regretted her costly decision; Bill had sat on that very couch precisely one week ago, vowing his unconditional love. On bended knee, on the cold marble floor, he slid a emblem of that love on her left ring finger. Kim felt a gentle warming of her heart as she remembered the words he had said:

"Love goes toward love." Bending down before her, he'd placed her hands over his heart. "I love you, Kim. I want you . . . forever." Softly, in a half-whisper, she felt his words caressing her face. "You're the blood in my veins flowing through to my heart. I can't live without thinking about you. I can't breathe without straining to inhale the scent of you."

"Bill," was all Kim managed to say, as she turned her head away in shame. How could she have kept this man at bay as long as she had? She hadn't been fair, and she knew it. What had she been trying to prove? Her guilt produced trembling tears in her eyes. She and Bill were in love, as deeply in love as she believed her parents had been.

"My heart is my truest gift, the most fragile gift that I can offer you. Marry me, Kim. Forgive my selfishness. I've changed. Missing you, wanting you, needing you has been the worst punishment I could have imagined."

"I do love you, Bill. I'm sorry for—"

"Don't," said Bill, pressing her lips closed. "Just please say you'll marry me."

A single tear fell on the edge of her wrist as Kim uttered a breathless yes. Nervously, Bill removed a gray velvet box from his jacket and guided a circle of diamonds onto her finger.

They embraced, feeling the matching rhythm of their hearts. Bill lifted her small body from the couch and carried her toward the bedroom. After crossing the threshold, he kissed her again tenderly, all the while slowly undressing her. He spread her nude body in the center of the bed, tingling her breasts with synergetic sensations. "I want to kiss you low and love you slow," said Bill as their love spilled like wine on precious linen.

A warm glow flickered along Kim's spine as she cherished the memories of that wonderful night.

It was five o'clock, and the winter evening was settling over the city. Kim picked up the receiver on its fifth ring.

"Randall? It's so good to hear from you. Happy New Year," Kim said, entwining her fingers in the curlicued plastic phone cord as she settled down into the deep pile of the sumptuous sofa, pointing her bobby-socked feet toward the warmth of the smoldering fire.

"Happy New Year, Kim."

"Got a scoop for you. Bill and I are getting married next September. He proposed on Christmas Day." She could barely contain the excitement in her voice. Kim reclined, luxuriating in the warmth of the velvet beneath her, a radiant peace settling over her. The rich smell of pine and mistletoe floated throughout the room, to the holiday harmonies rippling softly in the background on the stereo.

"You still there?"

"Deep in thought for a moment. I still can hardly believe my luck. I'm so happy I could scream." Kim remarked to Randall how much Bill and she had grown while they were apart. He could respect her friendships with other men. And she now understood his hectic schedule as a doctor. Solid now, they could begin their lives together. A clean, fresh start.

Her eyes teared up when she told him her father had spoken her name on her last visit, and would be attending the wedding too. "You'll be here, too, won't you?"

"Nineteenth of September? Wouldn't miss my best friend's wedding for the world." Randall could see the pleased look on her face. There was never a doubt in his mind that Kim and Bill would get back together. He only wished he could say the same about himself and his lover.

"I've truly missed you, Randall. The building hasn't been the same since you left. It's so quiet around here. It's hard to believe you've been gone over a year."

"Yeah, I know. A lot of things have changed. Namely, on your side of the border. Three of the board members were fired by my aunt Sylvie. She's taken a more active position in the company since she returned from her winter vacation abroad."

"I'll be damned. I've never even seen her in all the years I worked there. How strange."

"You remember Brenda, the secretary?"

"Cameron's plaything, right?"

"Right. She's missing. No one has seen or heard from her in over two months. Didn't call in and say she'd quit—nor did she tender a letter of resignation." Static over the line from the overseas phone call momentarily interrupted his stream of gossip. "The rumor around the office is during the past year she's had two abortions, and just recently a third—"

"I knew she was stupid, but I didn't think she was *that* dumb. How'd you find out?"

"I made a couple of trips back home."

"And you didn't call me?"

"I couldn't risk my uncle finding out I was there. I stayed at a friend's house. In a few months I'll have enough dirt on Cameron to get him kicked out of the company." He decided this wasn't the time to confide in his friend and admit that his lover had ended their relationship. "I don't want my old job back, though. No. This is where I belong. He'll never know how much of a favor he did for me. I love it here. I've got a wonderful apartment, and I've painted a cityscape of London. It's breathtaking . . . no . . . more like cinematic."

"You're painting again?" Kim said, hearing the emotion in his voice.

"You know me so well. I've even completed the portrait I'd been unable to finish for nearly two years—my greatest accomplishment yet. Maybe one day you'll be able to come and see it. That particular painting and several others will soon be on display in an art gallery."

"A show?"

"Um-hm. They've given me a year to complete several projects that we've discussed for my first opening. Tossed around a few themes . . . feelings, emotions, truth. That's what I want my painting to convey."

"I'm impressed, Randall." Kim's gaze scanned the beauty of her new home. When September came around, Randall would be equally impressed, and surprised. "You've been blessed to have gained a new home and a new career. You're really happy. I can hear it in your voice . . . inner peace."

"Thanks, Kim. I knew you'd understand. And law school? Doing good with your studies?"

"About as well as you're doing with your paintings." Cradling the phone between neck and shoulder, Kim stood before the semifrosted window admiring the majestic wonder below. Smiling to herself, Kim thought of a funny saying she'd read somewhere: "I used to be Snow White . . . but I drifted." Mae West.

Sitting along the edge of the window seat, she felt a slag of cold air streaming through the glass and tucked both bulky wool sleeves beneath her breasts. The old building creaked lazily above, reminding Kim about the vacant flat. "What about your condo? Still plan on keeping it? I could have a friend put it on the market, then ship your paintings and furnishings after it's sold."

"No. I want to keep things as they are. Can't give Cameron an inside track to what I'm planning, God, help me. I want him to think I hate this place, that I plan on coming back home to the States. Let him think his plan is working. His ego feeds on destroying people."

How well I know, thought Kim. Could Randall have known about her and George Cameron's sexual relationship? She was surprised at Randall's reference to a deity. She'd never remembered hearing him mention his spiritual beliefs before. "Your apartment is just as you left it. I've got a cleaning woman dusting it every couple of weeks when she cleans mine—"

"I'll send you—"

"No need. She won't charge me extra. Doesn't want to lose my business. Says my apartment is the cleanest one on her route. Sometimes I take Ginger upstairs to help me water the plants. She loves your apartment. Remember you asked her to come by and see your paintings? It was so long—"

"I remember meeting your cousin at the nightclub a couple of years back. Good-looking and smart. How's she doing anyway? Did she ever make it in the real estate business?"

Monday, January 6, 1992, Ginger quit her factory job, to Jackson's disbelief. She bought a new computer and turned Jason's room into her office. Ginger couldn't keep track of all of Jackson's insults. She just did her best to ignore him.

She enrolled as a part-time student at the interior design school in Southfield. Four evenings a week, and eighteen months later, she would have her designer's license. Ginger preferred deadlines. They drove her forward. Made her focus harder on what she wanted out of life. By the spring of 1993 she'd have her broker's license. By that fall, she planned to open her own real estate firm. Her firm would offer a slightly different service than other real estate agencies in Michigan. Her license as a interior designer would fit perfectly into her new business venture.

Again, Jackson cursed her out. But her vision was clear: To touch her dream. She knew the direction her life and career were heading. One thing she'd learned the hard way: Don't expect your mate to believe in your hopes and dreams. Because to him, that's all it'll ever be—dreams.

At first she felt guilty, chasing the end of the rainbow. Yet she desperately needed to turn the depression she felt into a personal victory, internal happiness. She needed to feel complete without the love of another human being, to know she was complete by herself, by the love and grace of God.

She was somebody: Ginger Lee Carter Montgomery. There was no one else in the world exactly like her, and there would never be another. She was a one-of-a-kind miracle. A unique, wonderful, unrepeatable miracle of God.

Putting her faith and trust in him, she began praying daily and reading her Bible. He would be the positive anchor that provided her with the wisdom she needed and give her the strength to go beyond herself. She must trust in the talents, abilities, and skills that God had blessed her with. And have confidence that those abilities would enable her to grow, make good judgments and decisions, and become the person she strived to be.

By March Bill's clinic exceeded his expectations. The *Detroit News* had been good to him. Even the local Detroit monthly magazines regularly wrote articles complimenting the success of Dr. William Harris's clinic. His programs helped the Black youths whom most had given up on get back on track and back in school. A Cass Tech honor-student dropout-turned-crack-addict who was undergoing drug rehabilitation at the clinic wrote a moving testimonial about how his life had changed. The story was published in the *News* and picked up by a local television station.

*   *   *

Spring sailed on into April, when heaven and sea rolled together as one, and from them blew fresh exaltations of misty blue. Lovely days like this brought Katherine outside, cleaning windows. A bucket filled with water, vinegar, ammonia, and a drop of lemon juice tugged at her arm. The yearly ritual never ceased to bring a fresh feeling inside and out to her brick bungalow. When her work was done that evening, Katherine would treat herself to yet another triple mixture of Lady Clairol. After all, two-inch gray roots didn't look good in any season.

"This feels wonderful. My first pedicure. I should've had it done years ago." Ginger wiggled her toes as pleasure flowed through her body. Her feet, after her breasts, were the most sensitive parts of her body. Jackson hadn't found that out in almost ten years. Two years ago, when she was blessed with the presence of hair, the ten black bristles on each of her big toes seemed to captivate his interest, and make him laugh. He'd never seen a woman with so much hair on her feet before. Ginger had felt slighted, and kept her hurt feelings about her feet to herself.

"You almost dry?" asked Kim, peeking in the booth. Ginger handed the manicurist a five-dollar bill. The young girl smiled and thanked Ginger for the tip as she collected her trays of polish and left the room.

The cousins spent a luxurious morning at the beauty salon, Kim's treat. They discussed the plans for Kim's wedding, went to lunch, stopped by the drugstore and picked up every bride and wedding magazine published, and ended up back at Ginger's house.

After perusing every magazine, Kim still hadn't come close to picking out a wedding dress. She agreed with Ginger that she wanted an ivory gown instead of white. The ivory looked richer. She also had her own reasons for not wanting to belittle the saintly implications of pure white.

Determined to make some decisions concerning the wedding, they both agreed on the color and style of the bridesmaids' dresses. Telling Kim that she was glad she'd asked her to help her with her wedding for the umpteenth time, Ginger bubbled with excitement.

"I always wanted to have a big wedding." Ginger sipped on a glass of wine as Kim flicked through the telephone directory, looking for a banquet hall. "I feel like I've been robbed. Been married twice, and haven't worn a wedding gown yet. You better believe my girls are going to have the biggest weddings I can afford."

"Have you ever thought about you and Jackson renewing your vows and getting married over again on your tenth anniversary?" Kim knew that Ginger had not been able to afford a large wedding with her first husband. And that when she and Jackson decided to marry, neither of their families could afford to fly in from out of state. They had both agreed it was ludicrous to have a big wedding without their families present. So they'd gone all out and splurged on their enormous home instead.

"It's been four months since I quit Champion Motors. I wish I had done it sooner." Taking a delicate sip of wine, she added, "Jackson seems distant. Colder. It's obvious he resents me for not listening to him."

Ginger remembered just last night. She had been working in her office:

"What the hell is this, Ginger?" He'd tapped the entries in her appointment book.

A plastic T-square, three number-two pencils, drawing pens, a block of graph paper, and various-sized templates were scattered arbitrarily over Ginger's desk. It had taken her hours to complete a school project, redesigning a family room to make it more functional.

A tired look registering on her face, she expelled an exasperated breath of stale air. "My appointment book," she had said matter-of-factly.

Jackson rested his buttocks on the side of the desk. "Why is it that nearly seventy-five percent of your clients are men? Not couples. Men. Why is that, Ginger?" His tone was accusatory.

She dropped her pencil, looking up at him. "The men are the ones who usually make the appointments. It doesn't mean that their wives don't accompany them."

He'd slammed the book down in front of her. "You're never home. You're either at school, out showing homes, or at the office. Everywhere but here! You're pushing our relationship too far, Ginger. I won't have it."

Ginger had looked candidly into Jackson's eyes. "When I'm home you watch television and ignore me. Or you find an excuse to leave. Maybe you've gotten comfortable with me being gone and don't even realize it."

"That's bullshit. I enjoy having . . ."

"Sex! I'll spell it out for you Jackson, S-E-X. That's the only enjoyment we seem to find together lately with each other. We forget about our problems. You never want to talk. It's always wait till tomorrow, baby. Problems aren't solved by having sex. Just ignored. The sex isn't enough anymore." She had stormed off before he saw her tears. It just wasn't enough.

The stark reality of that night brought her back to the present.

Ginger couldn't fathom the thought of being without Jackson. Of living without Jackson. It scared her to think that he could possibly be thinking about leaving *her*. She tested her fears on Kim. Tested and detested the ugly word on her tongue. "The way Jackson and I have been arguing lately, we're liable to make it to the *divorce* court before we take a ceremonial walk down a church aisle."

Kim was as quiet as a church mouse.

He couldn't understand why life had to be so complicated. Why Ginger insisted on making their life difficult. Didn't she understand him at all? Was it too much to ask for a few things from life? Just the simple things. Small things. Ginger produced an erotic and narcotic effect on him. That supreme high that had touched his soul, that he had never felt before, and that meant everything to him. In touching those things, their hearts would merge, and they would meet, together . . . forever. . . .

Parking in front of the clubhouse, he locked his bike, pausing to take a final look at his mean machine. The other club members had heard the roar of his engine, and were pouring out of the club to check out the first new bike of the season. Jackson felt like a ten-year-old kid showing off his new bicycle.

Two hours later, he felt as if he'd aged fifty years in the course of an afternoon. The fellows he'd joked with, got high with, bullshitted with, partied with, and known over twenty years seemed to be mocking him. Had they been talking about Ginger?

"Man, he said by the time he stroked her a few times, she loved it. Said the thought of him taking it at first thrilled her. They'd screwed for hours before she left with the plans to meet him again the next week," said Ramsey, slapping Mr. B. on the back.

"Man, I heard she couldn't get enough. Kept begging for more." The murmuring crescendoed, then faded. The joke passed from one man to another, as it crept closer and closer, within earshot. Before the blood hit the crown of his head, Jackson rose from the bar, and stood eye to eye with the conspirators.

"Something funny I should know about?" Jackson's voice was deadly. Maybe it was someone else. How could they know anything about Ginger? Knowing he had to separate his irrational thoughts from his true feelings because they were entirely two different things, he cautiously backed away from the bewildered trio of faces.

Keenly aware of Jackson's violent temper, they all kept silent until Little Bubba called out, "Get on over here, Jackson." He was racking up the pool balls. "It's about time I kicked your ass today."

Giving the group at the table a final roll of his eye, Jackson waved off Little Bubba and left.

With a flick of his right wrist he started the ignition of the motorcycle, then turned up the volume of the radio inside his Shoei helmet. After shading his amber eyes with ebony sunglasses, he sat gunning the engines a little more than usual before riding off.

At the stoplight, he straddled the fully dressed Harley, turning his head slightly toward some children eyeing his bike. His mouth curved into a smile. To them, he must look like a Black Arnold Schwarzenegger—the Terminator outfitted in all black leather. Out of the blue came an angry German shepherd barking noisily, diverting the young boys' gaze.

As the traffic light changed, Jackson sped off toward the freeway. The overcast sunrise was partially hidden by a morning mist. Last night's rainfall was still evident in the silver sheen of the damp grass. Tender new leaves would soon unfurl into clouds of spring green as the fresh scent of April showers lingered in the air.

He'd never forget that night. The evening had haunted him like a bad dream. He'd never quite been satisfied with Ginger's explanation of what happened that night. It was like a bad itch, and he'd scratched and scratched, but he still itched.

He remembered, just as clear as the sky now forming, the scene that night when Ginger returned home more of a wreck than the car was. Something felt strange about her recollection of how the accident had occurred. Said the driver just drove off. After rattling off some obscenities about him probably not being insured and their rates probably going up as a result of a claim on their insurance, Jackson had stifled any questions about why she hadn't called the police on her car phone—or called home.

Jackson rolled the gossips' chorus over and over in his mind and angrily spat at the curb, before weaving his Harley up Mae Thelma's cluttered driveway. Overturned bicycles slowed his taxiing near the porch. Hearing the thunder of his heavy Harley, the boys ran onto the front porch, screaming for a ride on Uncle Jackson's new bike. After giving each a generous tour, he left them outside, goggled eyed, as they touched and inspected every instrument and gadget.

"Sure you don't mind my drinking in your house, Mae Thelma?" asked Jackson, pouring himself a hefty swig of the pint of bourbon he always kept in his saddlebags.

"Now hush yo' mouth, Jackson Montgomery. Ain't nothing wrong with a man drinking. It's the evil thoughts and deeds he does while drinking is the sin." Sinking her knee in the couch, she pushed back her immaculate white curtains to check on her boys.

"Don't worry, Mae Thelma. The two of them couldn't budge my bike. It weighs over twelve hundred pounds."

She felt the rush of adrenaline as she forced herself to look away from Jackson's taut muscles. Unknowingly, Jackson had cast a spell over Mae Thelma. She felt weak to his overwhelming display of force and power.

Mae Thelma basked in this moment with her man. She was free. Alone with Jackson to talk over old times and test her new love potion. She excused herself for a moment, going to her bedroom to rub the potent concoction over her breasts so it would breathe out from her housedress at exactly the right places.

Jackson finished the bottle of bourbon and was feeling mighty sublime. He unzipped his vest and made himself comfortable, eating a plate of collard greens and sliced tomatoes. He assured Mae Thelma that was all he could eat this early in the day, declining the chicken and dumplings and candied yams.

It seemed every time he and Mae Thelma were together, they couldn't help but talk about the good old days back home in the South. He hadn't had a home-cooked meal like this from Ginger in months. As a matter of fact, their sex life hadn't been up to par lately either. Fast, hurried sex. Everything seemed to be hurried lately. He even suspected that Ginger timed him. He'd noticed on more than one occasion her quick glances at the clock. It spoiled his concentration.

Jackson's eyes rested on the swell of Mae Thelma's breasts as she set a tall glass of Diet Pepsi on the table before him. Less than four months ago, during Christmastime, she'd been bundled under sweaters and coats. But the memory of her youthful body at Jason's party in that sinful sundress was soberingly vivid. Now the flimsy fabric of her spring housedress barely disguised her hard nipples. He tried to shake away the sinful thoughts in his mind. She could keep a man sweat-stained hot in below-zero weather. Must be the bourbon, he thought.

Mae Thelma noticed how relaxed Jackson was. Nor did she miss his stare lingering on her breasts. She brushed the front of her dress ever so lightly against his arm. Just to test him. Cleaning the dirty dishes, she watched as he walked back into the living room after handing her his plate. His clothes, the way he wore them, the casual way he walked, seemed to radiate romance. She tore her eyes away as a voice inside her spoke:

"Wherefore God also gave them up to uncleanness

through the lusts of their own hearts, to dishonor their own bodies between themselves: Who changed the truth of God into a lie, and worshiped and served the creature more than the Creator, who is blessed for ever. Amen."

She pushed the thought from her mind, convincing herself that what she was doing wasn't wrong. As Jackson excused himself for a trip to the bathroom, she quickly ran into the living room, extracted a vial from a small red velvet pouch, and rubbed the oily mixture inside his vest jacket. Another voice intervened as her heart pounded, wildly, from fear:

". . . being filled with all unrighteousness, fornication, wickedness, covetousness, maliciousness; full of envy, murder, debate, deceit, malignity; whispers, backbiters, haters of God, despiteful, proud, boasters, inventors of evil things . . ."

She covered her hands with her mouth as she felt trapped inside a possible evil. Yet her aunt had told her that voodoo wasn't evil. The mixture was merely a love potion, a liquid ampule of ori root, yarrow, rosebuds, and other herbs. It would last for years. Only an eyedropper full was needed to guarantee results. It was supposed to bring and promote love. The glass vessel was kept inside a red pouch because red attracts the spirits. She wasn't hurting anyone. What was wrong with going after what you wanted? There wasn't any harm in it, was there?

"You know exactly what I'm talking about. Don't play dumb!" Jackson screamed as Ginger exited the shower.

"I told you what happened." She smoothed Vaseline over her damp skin. "Why would I lie?" She hoped her voice didn't betray her.

The silver spurs of his cowboy boots sank into the carpeting as he rocked back on his heels, crossing his arms. "You're fucking around. Admit it."

She could smell the stale liquor on his breath. At these times, arguing with him was useless. "Fucking around with whom, Jackson? Can you give me the name of my lover?" She walked past him into her dressing room, tying a scarf around her head. She hated for him to look at her bald scalp when they argued. She felt as if he were mocking her. She felt raw, helpless.

"Fuck the guessing games. You're quitting—"

"Don't start, Jackson!"

"Wha—"

"I said, just don't fucking start with this bullshit again. I'm tired of you checking up on me like I'm a child. I'm not giving up everything I've worked for the past two years just because you're feeling insecure. You don't have any proof about anything. That alcohol's frying your brain. You need to put down the bottle and pick up a Bible once in a while— maybe it'll clear your own conscience and evil thoughts." She threw the Bible in his lap as he sat on the chair and clicked on the television set.

"Forget what I said, Ginger. I'm sorry. I just don't like you out in the evenings by yourself."

She stood in front of the television set, having donned her nightclothes, blocking his view. "So where the hell have you been all day?" She was waiting for him to lie. After showing a client a home this morning she'd noticed Jackson's bike in front of Mae Thelma's house.

Later that afternoon, she'd met with Ivory Michaels. Feeling lonely throughout these never-ending arguments, she needed to confide in a male friend. She needed someone to talk to. Ivory wasn't fresh. He wasn't aggressive. Just a good listener, something Ginger hadn't experienced from Jackson over the past months. He just wouldn't listen to her. Just storm off as she tried to explain. Time and time again, Jackson's ear was absent and Ivory's was waiting.

Ginger sensed that Ivory was struggling through problems of his own, yet he never wavered from his Mount Rushmore stature. Week after week he listened, giving her good advice, telling her when she was wrong, egging her on when they both knew she was right. Yet he never suggested that Ginger dissolve her marriage. He encouraged her to forge ahead.

Was that his strategy for getting closer to her? Ginger wondered. On the surface pushing her closer to her man, yet beneath the façade ultimately guiding her closer to him, because of his unselfish nature?

Ivory was leaving for Paris that spring weekend to cover the extravagant wedding of a rich Texan. The amount of money purportedly being spent on the nuptials was unprecedented. Five hundred guests were to be flown in to participate in a weekend of festivities that entailed a masquerade party Thursday night, a square dance Friday afternoon, a Friday night Texas barbeque and finally, Saturday, a candlelight wedding ceremony, followed by a lavish reception and a fourteen-course dinner. Ivory promised Ginger that he'd show her all the pictures when he returned. Maybe she could get a few ideas for Kim's wedding!

Just out of curiosity, after she and her client had concluded their business, Ginger had swung back by Mae Thelma's house and was angry to see that Jackson was still there.

"Down at the club," Jackson responded casually when she asked where he'd been. "We're putting in a fence around the parking lot. Then me and the fellows had a few drinks." He waved his hand like he was swimming. "Move out of the way, will you?"

"And . . ." she said, not budging.

"Hmmmm," he blew out. "That's about it."

"You lying son of a bitch. You were over Mae Thelma's all morning."

"Funny, I hadn't noticed the time," said Jackson in a Clint Eastwood monotone.

During the heated month of July, Jackson found a bank receipt in Ginger's minivan, and was outraged to learn that she had stashed away so much money. He'd intended to find some kind of evidence disputing Ginger's claims about that night. It was obvious she had been hiding something. Some man. Had to be giving her money. And he'd find out who it was.

"Twenty-five thousand dollars! Where in the hell did you get that much money?"

"Commissions," said Ginger flatly.

"And you didn't bother to offer to help put the roof on?" Jackson was torn between disbelief that she'd earned so much money and resentment that she hadn't offered him any.

"If I was *still* at the plant—if I was *still waiting* on you to tell me to go with my instincts, if I was *still* waiting on your blessings, I wouldn't have a dollar." She rolled her eyes at him.

"Still, I am your husband. You could help out."

Her voice, her heart, were bitter. "You could have supported me when I needed it. Instead you turned your back on me. You closed our account altogether. You tried to make me suffer." Ginger felt exonerated. "My bank account proves I'm not suffering one iota, Jackson."

"You bitch." The words sounded louder than Jackson had intended.

Tears of hurt, tears of defiance, tears of pride clouded Ginger's eyes. "I got your bitch mother-fucker." She grabbed her crotch. "Right here." She fought for courage, and it came. "You'll smell daffodils in December before you get a whiff of this pussy!" Ginger shouted, slamming the door to their bedroom.

Ginger moved into her office for the entire month of July. They never made love. And by the time August rolled around, they were more irritable than ever.

Ginger refused to go down South. She told him to go by himself, or take his wonderful baby daughter with him. It had only taken two trips to the beauty parlor before Jackson had apologized about her messing up Autumn's hair. Ginger, however, hadn't forgiven him for making the accusation. She'd just kept silent.

Time was running out for George Cameron. His attempts to reclaim some of the key clients Kim had stolen proved futile. Not one would return to Pierce-Walker no matter what perks Cameron offered to sweeten the deal. Each had made very clear how satisfied they were with Kim's business acumen.

Cameron was close to accepting his loss . . . until he flipped through the late edition of the *Detroit Free Press*, spotting an engagement picture, and read the small article chronicling the wedding in the middle of September of Dr. William Harris and Kim Lee. George Cameron smiled to himself.

Earlier that summer, after reviewing the pictures Ivory Michaels had given her upon his return from Paris, the two cousins finally made a decision about Kim's wedding dress. She'd chosen to copy a gown by Yumi Katsura. A seamstress from Lansing had assured Kim that she could duplicate the design.

The slim-silhouette gown made of lustrous cream silk-satin crepe was accented with matching baroque pearls layering the empire bodice to midwaist. Hand-appliquéd beaded medallions at the apex of the bustline added style and sophistication. Along the front slit opening, the off-the-shoulder neckline, and at the wrists an elaborate lace rose-petal pattern seductively embodied the godly creation. A chapel train of lace provided the finishing touch.

Six bridesmaids would wear ivory opalescent strapless minidresses that were tight-fitting straight silhouettes with hipline peplums accented with a side cluster of handmade silk roses. The male attendants would wear off-white tuxedos with shiny gold cummerbunds and matching ties.

Having read that wearing a veil this year was passé, Kim elected not to wear one. She'd let her hair grow out and planned on wearing it entwined with flowers over a beaded hair ornament, with rows of curled ribbons cascading romantically down the sides and back at various lengths. Ginger cried tears of joy as she watched Kim try on the dress for the final fitting and last-minute details. It was beautiful. She was beautiful.

Five weeks before the wedding, Bill escorted his exuberant father-in-law-to-be from the nursing home and had him measured for a tuxedo. Miraculously, Ollie had regained the power of speech. Afterwards, Bill and Ollie spent a few hours over lunch discussing the women they loved.

Listening attentively, Bill had been impressed with Ollie's words of wisdom for a happy marriage.

"Do you read your Bible, son?"

"No, sir," Bill had said, embarrassed.

"Always be honest. You can respect a man for his honesty. Have a Bible at home?"

Bill nodded yes.

"Do me a favor. Do yourself a favor, and together with Kim, before you marry, take the time and read Ephesians, Chapters Twenty-one through Thirty-three. It explains how a man and wife should treat each other in marriage. It encourages husbands to love their wives even as Christ also loved the Church. That men ought to love their wives as their own bodies, because he that loveth his wife loveth himself: 'For no man ever yet hated his own flesh; but nourisheth and cherisheth it, even as the Lord the church. . . . Nevertheless let ever one of you in particular so love his wife even as himself; and the wife see that she reverence *her* husband.'

"Take the time to become best friends. Laugh together, cry together, pray together and tell each other your secrets. Treat her like she's special every day. Build your future together. Set goals. Not just for money, but for spiritual growth.

"Give her freedom to fulfill her purpose in life, and achieve your own. In doing these things you'll be the best of lovers."

When they returned to the nursing home, Bill was genuinely moved by their conversation. Not having a father to confide in, Bill appreciated Ollie's pep talk. Marriage, picking a mate for life, was important to him. Over the years, several of his friends had entered into their third or fourth marriages.

The stories they'd reiterated about divorce, dividing property, children, and money were scary. Homes and furnishings that couples had so lovingly selected and treasured over years were now bartered and fought over childishly. Hot-blooded love cooled to cold hatred. And the children suffered, unsure whom to pledge their allegiance to. Bill knew that when he decided to marry, it would be for life. He knew that men, as well as women (though most wouldn't admit it), agonized over a failed marriage.

Ginger was so nervous she'd broken out in hives again a week before the wedding. It had taken numerous trips to salons for Ginger to find just the right wig. She'd never been in a wedding party. Although she'd known Kim would ask her to be the matron of honor, it still brought tears to her eyes when she did.

Ginger, Sierra, and Autumn worked together to make matching pearl-and-crystal earrings for each of the bridesmaids. Kim had made Sierra the happiest preteen in her circle of friends by asking her to be one of her bridesmaids. Autumn, sulking because she wanted a fancy minidress too, was given the task of throwing the flower petals. She was too old and too tall to be a flower girl, she argued, but acquiesced after she saw the beautiful dress her mother bought her. And after she was told she'd be able to wear her hair down, she became thrilled with the whole thing. Christian, at a vintage fifteen, couldn't possibly play the part of ring bearer, so they hadn't even broached the question of his participating. Instead, he volunteered to pass out the rice for everyone to throw.

A week before the wedding, Katherine arrived from Port Huron, strangely enough minus Cotton. The rumors of Katherine's tumultuous on-again, off-again relationship over the past year were rampant. Ginger accepted her mother's vulnerability, understanding her need for companionship. She prayed diligently that when she turned sixty, her love with Jackson would be as strong as when they'd first pledged it. Besides, no one could afford to be without Katherine's expertise in handling important festivities such as these. She was immensely knowledgeable. She didn't forget a single detail of what was expected from each participant in the wedding.

On Saturday morning, the nineteenth of September, the sun rose with a warm glow. The dew loosed its morning smells early on as sparrows chirped busily overhead.

A horsedrawn carriage had been hired, and was scheduled to pick up Kim at her apartment by 12:30 P.M. The wedding was to begin promptly at 1:00 at Saint Michael's Cathedral, six blocks away.

"You look beautiful, Sierra. Mama's so proud of you." Ginger kissed her daughter lovingly on the cheek. Katherine was right. She *did* look like a Miss America. Not usually at a loss for words, Sierra was extremely quiet today. Ginger suspected that Katherine must have whispered in her ear to try not to talk so much. She was constantly telling Sierra to carry herself like the star she would one day become. Sierra, looking and feeling like a million bucks, abided by her wishes this one time.

"Everything all right, Mama?" asked Ginger, nervously checking her watch. Peeking through the door out into the church, Ginger smiled. So far the wedding was moving along fairy-tale perfect. The church was filled to capacity.

"Just peachy." Sweat beaded on Katherine's forehead. Ginger reached inside her purse, then patted her mother's face with a tissue. Katherine looked uncomfortable. She'd gained back the thirty pounds she'd lost last year, and now wore the inevitable two girdles again, squeezing into a dress two sizes too small.

Ginger still didn't feel right about not talking to Kim this morning. Katherine had assured her that everything was fine. Said it was normal for a bride to want her privacy. Kim had lost so much weight recently that her wedding dress had to be altered a second time after the final fitting.

Left unasked and unanswered between mother and daughter were the whereabouts of their significant others. Katherine had no idea where Cotton was, and hoped that Ginger wouldn't broach the subject. And while Ginger knew exactly the whereabouts of Mr. Jackson Montgomery and was sure Katherine had guessed too, she was grateful that her mother hadn't confronted her about it.

At this very moment, thirty minutes before the start of the wedding, Jackson was sitting at home, watching television in his underwear and socks. Taking a large hunk of bologna, he stuffed a cracker in his mouth and washed it down with a half-frozen bottle of Diet Pepsi. He surfed channels with the remote until he found a Western suitable to his mood. *Gunfight at the O.K. Corral*—just the ticket. He hadn't seen it in months. And he'd caught the tail end—the best part. Now this was what he called a party.

A smug smile registered on his face. Ginger had been livid this morning when he dropped the bomb that he wasn't going.

"Don't humiliate me, Jackson," Ginger had said.

"You don't need me. I'll be right *heah* when you get back."

"I need you to be there supporting me, as my husband."

"I can't figure you out, Ginger. One minute you're Miss Executive, executing your life, your money, your time as it suits *you. When it suits you.* Next minute, you're vulnerable, you need *me*, your husband. Why is that, Ginger? Why is it that *our* needs these days only represent *your* needs?"

"You're not being fair, Jackson. And it's obviously too late to talk about it now, so just forget it. I'll go alone."

"No, you started this shit. I'd like to know why you're spending so much time involving yourself in somebody else's marriage when you should be concentrating on working on your own."

"I think you should be asking yourself that question, Jackson."

"You didn't need me to quit your job. You wouldn't listen to my advice. Tell me, Ginger, all those years you worked at Champion Motors—doesn't loyalty mean anything to you? Security? Commitment? Is that how much consideration you'd give to our years of marriage? 'I quit. It's over'?"

"I'll never quit us, Jackson."

"Uh-huh, yeah."

As she stormed off, Jackson reflected on the health of their marriage. Even though their relationship was plagued with problems, he sincerely believed with faith and time, they could make it work. No matter what the circumstances, it was worth it.

Jackson made two decisions: first, to put more trust in God; and second, to go to church with his family. He crossed his ankles, grabbing a handful of fresh popcorn. Next Sunday, the Montgomerys would be sitting in the front pew at church, testifying to their belief in God.

Ginger decided to lie to Kim and Bill, explaining that Jackson had a bad cold and was unable to make it.

Katherine was equally prepared with an alibi for Cotton. Yet she was sure his absence would go unnoticed. It was ironic: Both women would lie to protect their men's reputation, loving their men hard, their men hardly loving. Did either man really deserve this love?

By 12:52 P.M. the cathedral brimmed with carefully dressed guests, whispering. Katherine signaled the organist to begin playing the pieces they'd selected. The soloist Kim had hired to sing "Since I Fell for You" sat on the bench across from the organ. Eight minutes to go. Bill and Kim's father took their places.

Silently as a dream, like a sparkle in a grain of sand, time was running out for Kim's magical wedding, at this moment she was dreaming a colorless dream. . . .

Last night Kim was exhausted, but too hyped up to sleep.

Dark circles shadowed her face, threads of red darted across her fatigued eyes, her skin tone was sallow. After weeks of surviving on three to four hours of sleep nightly, she was determined to get some beauty rest before the big day. Taking her aunt Katherine's advice, she'd acquiesced and ingested four sleeping pills.

Although her mind was somewhat groggy, Kim was sure someone had been ringing the doorbell—then pounding at the door nonstop. She ignored it, until the banging amplified. She assumed it was Bill, excited, unable to keep their promise of not seeing each other before their big day.

Every evening this week, Bill and Kim had entertained each other with their ignorance of the Good Book, then unashamedly communicated their thoughts about it. Kim felt a surge of renewed respect for Bill, adhering to her father's request that they read particular verses of Ephesians together. Tears of grace stood in their eyes as they prayed. It was a kind of epiphany. Rising from their knees, each agreed to wait until the wedding night to consummate their love.

Kim felt a sudden apprehension as she headed toward the foyer and heard the retreating footsteps, then faint rumblings of the elevator doors closing. She hesitated a moment, tightening the sash of her pale blue lacy-silky peignoir before unlocking the door. A large manila envelope had been left outside. Picking it up, she peered up and down the hallway, seeing no one, then locked the door behind her.

The apartment was still as she moved through the family room, past dozens of beautifully wrapped wedding gifts forming a miniature tower. Nearby, an ivory silk gown cloaked a headless, dull gray mannequin. Matching satin slippers loitered around the hem. And a masterpiece headpiece of silk roses, baby's breath, and cascading tendrils of ribbons sat on a small table beside a pair of pearl-drop earrings.

Turning on the lights, she felt the sharp outlines of a rectangle inside the packet; it was an unlabeled videocassette. She placed the cassette in the VCR and pressed Play, smiling to herself. Curious what last-minute message Bill was sending, her eyes locked on the clock over the mantel: 1:21 A.M. But it wasn't the smiling face of her fiancé that greeted her on the screen. The haughty voice of George Cameron stunned her. "Remember me?"

The camera zoomed in closer. His face was dark as the devil's, his eyes frozen in menace. "Did you think I'd forgotten you? You oughtn'tta tried to fuck me over, honey, and think I'd let it slide." He lit a cigar and took his time before continuing.

"You know that cute little Sheila Little was immensely helpful. 'Course I told her I was Bill's former employer and wanted to surprise him tonight. Gave me the date, time, directions, to the hall where your fiancé's bachelor party is going right now while I'm taping. So sit back and watch the main attraction, which I guarantee Bill and his friends won't be able to tear their eyes from." There was a brief moment of static before the scene changed to two nude panting bodies facing each other on an office desk. "Watch it, honey, don't turn it off yet—you'll miss the best part. This is our famous frog fucking position, remember? Gotta love it." He laughed mercilessly. "You just fucking gotta love it!"

She cried, then laughed, tears flowing like wax over her wooden face. Halfway into a fifth of Johnnie Walker she had been willing to accept anything. *Hell, I never was Snow White.*

The mystic shimmer of moonlight through the naked picture windows cast an ethereal glow over Jewel Lee's picture over the mantel. The serene beauty of her mother's soul still shone through her features. Kim could feel it literally filling her. "Thou that believeth that there is one God, thou doest well; the devils also believe and tremble. . . . When he crieth unto me, that I will hear; for I am gracious. . . . If my people which are called by my name, shall humble themselves, and pray, and seek my face, and turn from thy wicked ways, then I will hear them from heaven, and I will forgive their sin, and I will heal. . . ."

For a moment, she felt a glow of hope in her heart, before the devil stepped in to laugh at her. Filled with guilt and self-loathing, she turned away from her mother's surrealistic portrait in shame. Her life, her world, her pain, weren't worth saving, living, suffering. She was fighting against the devil for her soul and losing. Hours passed and minutes drowned throughout the night.

Removing the prescription bottle from the medicine cabinet, she mechanically swallowed a handful of Seconal, washing it down with straight scotch. Turning out the lights in the bedroom, she sat on the edge of the unmade bed nursing her drink. Alone in the darkness, she strained to hear any sounds of life. There were no birds singing, no floorboards creaking, no one else breathing. The alcohol felt like embalming fluid seeping through her veins as she fell into a deep sleep.

Kim wanted to sleep forever. But images of her mother, father, Bill, and their beautiful wedding pressed against closed lids. Cold waves of apprehension plagued her brain. Numbness creeped into her muscles. It reached down deep into her toes, her fingertips, penetrating every pore.

She woke late that morning, aching all over, soaked in sweat. The barbiturates and alcohol hadn't worked.

Kim felt as if she were half in and half out of a dream, unable to escape. Now, in slow degrees, she felt the courage to break the barrier binding her soul from freedom.

Searching inside the closet for her father's gun, her body seemed to move in reverse. As her fingers touched the cold steel, she felt the shadow of death descending upon her. Suddenly her world turned black and white in the midst of dust and shadows. One moment in time, one moment before the deafening crack, shattering the calm of the closet.

Felodesefelodesefelodesefelodesefelodesefelodese; it rang like a melody. . . .

Envisioning her mother's face, hearing the soothing voice talk to her one last time, she felt as if her heart were bleeding, then placed the gun to her head. Her spilled blood ran like wine, raining, staining precious lace. We dream as we live, as we die, alone.

"For whether we live, we live unto the Lord; and whether we die, we die unto the Lord: Whether we live therefore, or die, we are the Lord's."

Double-zero seconds. Showtime.

"Mama, something is wrong. I feel it. Kim wouldn't be late. . . ." Ginger's heart pounded as she met the worried expression on Bill's face. "Where the hell is Kim? She should've been here by now."

30

Reach Out, I'll Be There

Bill pressed his forehead on the white sheets, in near shock. Below him, Kim lay unconscious in the intensive care unit of Henry Ford Hospital. The prognosis was touch and go. But the team of doctors in the emergency room said that Kim was lucky she had used such a small pistol. She might not have made it to the hospital otherwise. However, the angle of the bullet's entry suggested she might not regain all of her memory, if in fact she recovered at all.

"Mama," said Ginger, horror still in her voice, "is she gonna make it?" They stood watching Bill fight for Kim's life through the glass casement. He hadn't left her side since they'd wheeled her into the emergency room.

Telephones rang endlessly outside the small cubicle. Nurses and doctors swished by hurriedly in their starched whites. Gurneys screeched by noisily, bumping and scraping against automatic doors, leaving black scuff marks along the aisle. The whooshing and beeping sounds from the respirator willing Kim back to life made Ginger dizzy.

"The mystery of death is God, just like the mystery of

birth is God. Trust in him, Ginger, and pray for Kim. She's gonna make it," said Katherine, her voice strong and filled with conviction. But even as she prayed for her niece, she knew in her heart that the Bible was clear on the taking of life. What had prompted Kim to do such a thing?

Katherine had elected Ginger to clean up Kim's apartment. Bill was grateful. He'd been swamped with messages from the clinic, even though he'd placed Sheila Little in charge of the small hospital, much to the chagrin of the other male psychiatrists. She was more than capable, and their short-lived romance had done nothing if not assure him that she was trustworthy. Meanwhile, he kept a day-and-night vigil with Kim, going home only to bathe and change his clothing.

Nearly a week after the incident, Ginger hired a cleaning company to come in and clean the carpeting. Even after they'd finished, however, shadows of bloodstains were still evident. The answering machine was full of messages—at least five from Randall. Ginger did her best to call and calm the well-wishers who knew Kim was in the hospital, though the family wasn't disclosing the nature of her illness. They explained that Kim had fainted from exhaustion and was recuperating in the hospital. It was a believable story. Most of her friends knew about her going to law school and running her newly formed financial corporation from her home, while preparing an elaborate wedding. They understood and pledged their services if needed.

Ginger managed to contact one of Kim's friends, Mabel, who still worked at Pierce-Walker, and hired her part time to keep Kim's business from folding. Next, she contacted Wayne State University and talked to Kim's professor, who said Kim might have to take an Incomplete if she missed too much time. He was very upset that his A student wouldn't be back for a while, having nothing but the highest praise for his young protégée.

Katherine stayed at Ginger's for a week, watching the children and doing the chores that Ginger was unable to do while getting Kim's affairs in order. Secretly, Katherine counted her blessings for the excuse. Detroit Edison had disconnected her electricity back at home. Being a proud woman, Katherine couldn't tell her daughter that she only had three dollars to her name until she received her Social Security check in two weeks.

Something struck Ginger about her mother. She seemed older. Different. And it wasn't just because of Kim's comatose state. It was personal. Slamming the cabinet doors, Ginger was seething as she moved around the kitchen. Tired. Hurt. She'd been through hell the past couple of weeks.

"Telephone, Ma," said Christian, who held his breath, catching the authoritative voice on the other end.

"Yes," said Ginger with a what-is-it-this-time? tone in her voice. Leaning over the snack bar in the kitchen, she rested her elbows on the lavender Formica.

"Mrs. Carter, I'm Detective—"

"Mrs. Montgomery, thank you."

"Sorry. My name is Detective Ritz from the Thirteenth Precinct."

"Has Jason gotten in trouble again?"

"Ma'am? I'm not sure who Jason is, but I assure you—"

"Then why are you calling me?" Ginger said, venom in her words.

"Your daughter, Sierra Carter—"

Ginger's body sprang erect like a Slinky. "Sierra. Yes, that's my daughter." Her words jumbled. "Yes. I'm her mother. I don't understand."

"Slow down a moment, Mrs. Montgomery. I'll just take a few minutes of your time. I need you to bring your daughter down to the Thirteenth Precinct to discuss a complaint filed against her and three other young girls."

"What!"

"The complaint was filed by Mr. and Mrs. Noble. The parents of Candice Noble."

"I still don't understand, Detective Reese."

"Ritz. Detective Ritz. If you could bring Sierra down at around three-thirty Friday afternoon, I'm sure we can clear all this up." He hesitated, then said, "We're taking depositions from the four other girls as to the amount of damage done to the Nobles' home." He gave Ginger a quick assessment of the damage.

Ginger mumbled something to the detective. The word

damage stuck out in her mind. She felt damaged, but how would the detective know that?

Sierra, her petite little baby. There must be some kind of mistake. Sierra wouldn't dare do any of those things the detective described.

The Nobles had filed a complaint against five girls who entered their home without permission, allegedly cutting up and destroying two outfits of Candice's, a pair of orange leather jeans, and a rainbow-colored sequined slack outfit. The kitchen and downstairs bathroom carpeting were flooded by stopping up both sinks. Eggs were broken all over the kitchen carpeting and Ajax was strewn everywhere.

Sierra and the girls faced four counts: two counts of breaking and entering, one count of malicious destruction of a building, and one count of petty larceny.

Ginger thought she was losing her mind. Her twelve-year-old daughter might be placed on probation for a first offense. When Ginger called Katherine to explain what had happened, Katherine was speechless. Ginger hadn't expected her mother to be so upset. She cried so on the phone that Ginger began crying herself. Afterwards, Ginger ran downstairs, her breathing still ragged, and tossed a frozen roast in the sink to thaw for dinner.

"Hey, baby," said Jackson, pinching her buttocks and planting a wet kiss on her lips.

Ginger stiffened. Jackson hadn't been this pleasant to her since the wedding. She was certain that he wanted something.

"Just in time," Jackson finished. Yanking the last can of V8 juice from its plastic harness, he shuffled through the cabinets, making himself a tuna sandwich with onions.

Anger shot from the tips of Ginger's toes to the crown of her head. She slammed the cabinet doors shut. "It looks like a hurricane's been through here." Her teeth razored against each other as she attempted to control it. "Can't you ever close the damn doors around here?"

He rolled his shoulders back as though he hadn't heard a word she'd said. "Baby, I've got half the garden picked. Think you could wash and freeze those first, before I bring in the rest of the collards?" Peeking into the refrigerator again, he picked up a bunch of grapes from the colander, dropping them one by one into his mouth.

Ginger spun around, her eyes ablaze. "I don't fucking believe you can possibly think I have the time or the inclination to blanch and freeze vegetables after all I've been through. Did it ever occur to you that your wife might be tired?"

Jackson caught himself before calling her lazy. She knew it was time to pick the vegetables. Each year they always put away the garden for the fall. He hadn't told her to take on all the added work of Kim's business. Why couldn't Bill handle it? Kim was his woman. Jackson wanted *his* woman to take care of *his* business at home. And if she couldn't, he knew a woman who would. "Don't worry, baby. I'll take care of it," he said.

Ginger had turned her back, pretending to take her vitamins as she geared up for a confrontation. But then he surprised her. Changed the rhythm. Had she heard him right? Okay, bucko, I got your number. They hadn't made love since all the ruckus had started. Nearly two weeks. They never went that long when they weren't mad at each other. That was it, he wanted sex. "Whatever," was all she managed to say before a knowing smile formed on her lips.

Later that afternoon, Jackson caught her just as she was making herself a soothing cup of tea, spiced with a stiff shot of brandy. Coming in from gardening, he was in a good mood. His baby girl had cornered him just as he was clipping the last head of broccoli. "Listen, baby, I got a joke for you. Autumn just made it up this morning. I can't believe how talented that girl is."

"Tell me the joke, Jackson."

"Here's how it goes: 'Your mama so fat, she sat on a quarter and squeezed a booger out of George Washington's nose.' "

Ginger didn't smile. Didn't laugh. Just sat staring at Jackson, watching him keel over laughing. He didn't know Autumn was just mimicking a comedian from *In Living Color* the night before.

"You didn't think it was funny?"

"Not particularly."

"Wait, wait. I got another one for you. My uncle told me this joke twenty years ago, but I always liked it. Hold on. Give me a minute to get it right." He scratched his head, thinking. "Two bulls were ambling along a pasture one summer day, and then, walking up on a hill, stopped to chat under a tree. The older bull was telling the young bull about the facts of life, when the younger bull happened to look down in the pasture and saw a herd of cows. He said to the older bull, 'Let's run down there, grab one, and fuck her.' The older bull hesitated, took his time saying, 'Let's *walk* down and fuck 'em all.' "

Ginger waited a few seconds, then burst out laughing. "Now that was funny. I might have to send a tape of you and your daughter's comedic debut to *Star Search*."

They fell on the floor laughing, releasing the tension that had separated them for weeks. Temporarily, Ginger let her problems roll off her back like water over petroleum jelly. Ginger loved playing the hussy. She got into character, deepened her normal husky voice, gave Jackson a sexy smile and a quick bump and grind of her hip. The heat was on, and they both knew it.

Resting her hand on Jackson's knee, she faced him, the devilishness in her eyes speaking seduction. "Remember how Michael Douglas threw Sharon Stone against the wall in *Basic Instinct*?" She moved in closer, raking her nails beneath the bulge of his crotch. "And remember when Al Pacino threw Ellen Barkin against the refrigerator in the *Sea of Love*? Why don't you throw me against the wall like that?"

Jackson, sweaty from hours in the garden, knew the signals. He threw Ginger against the refrigerator as she had asked, kissing her hard. She winced from pain. A light laugh tumbled from her belly. They both slid down the cool surface of the icebox, laughing, as their lips parted. "Black people don't screw like that." Lying on the kitchen floor, they roared with laughter.

Jackson was back in the saddle. He knew by the pleasure in Ginger's face that Bronco Billy and Miss Lilly would ride the prairie by their lonesome tonight.

When Ginger was finally alone, she basked in the peaceful silence. Sitting downstairs in the family room, nursing her toddy, she let her head fall back as she tuned in Oprah. The kids were riding their bikes through Palmer Park with their new schoolmates. Autumn had grown so tall over the summer; Jackson finally convinced her to join the basketball team. But the swim meets had begun first, and this particular afternoon Sierra had talked her into going to check out the competition. Namely, the boys' team.

"I went inside myself for three years," a voice said from the TV. "I didn't have the power to strike back at people when they ridiculed me."

"The painful part was when people looked at me," another voice added.

"People can be nasty. They give you dirty looks, and you wonder how to respond sometimes when people stare at you." The pain in the woman's eyes was shared by the rest of the panel on stage. Ginger was riveted to the set. "People wonder if it's contagious. They mistake it as cancer. Think you're undergoing chemotherapy treatments."

The only male on the panel talked about a neurolinguistic programming he'd recently listened to by Tony Robbins. He claimed that after listening to and implementing Robbins's suggestions for breathing techniques to cleanse the body, he'd noticed a small growth of hair after four weeks. Ginger wrote down the name and immediately dialed the 800 number when the segment ended for a commercial break.

There were all kinds of information for people like those on the panel who suffered from alopecia areata or its severe type, alopecia totalis. The TV screen flashed the number of the National Alopecia Foundation, but Ginger didn't bother to write down the number. She'd spoken to them on several occasions throughout the years, only to find out that there was still no cure. Just theories.

A dermatologist hired by the Oprah staff discussed the problem of hair loss, explaining that a growing number of Americans suffered from it. Though alopecia wasn't a life-threatening disease, it did threaten the quality of life. A strong person could grow weak as a result of experiencing this mind-boggling disorder. In certain cases it was hereditary. Statistically, twenty percent of the patients who had it found that there was a history of alopecia in their family line. And if tuberculosis and diabetes were prevalent in a patient's family history, some doctors argued that their chances of contracting the malady were greater. Some of his patients confided in him that their first reaction was that God was punishing them.

A woman who'd taken off her wig, tears streaming down her face, moved the audience with her personal experiences. She'd almost committed suicide because she was so unable to bear the pain and humiliation. She felt as if she'd lost all of her femininity. Didn't feel sexual at all. However, during her tearful confession she tried to make the audience understand the difference between female baldness and male baldness. She claimed that men looked sexy when they were bald. And they usually kept their eyebrows, while these women did not.

Ginger thought about how sexy Michael Jordan was with his bald head. Yul Brynner had been another sex symbol. And she had a crush on the bald and sexy Charles Barkley. The woman was right. They all had their eyebrows, and mustaches if they so desired. Ginger touched the smooth surface where her eyebrows once grew. She felt a watershed of tears damming behind her eyes.

A proud, bald Black woman from Detroit who frequented the same doctor Ginger did suddenly jumped into the conversation. She told the audience she'd never felt more beautiful. She refused to wear wigs, because she felt as though God had taken away her hair for a reason. Years ago, she'd had to accept the look on the face in the mirror that showed no distinctive definition, that was devoid of expression without eyelashes and eyebrows. She'd had to reconcile it all within herself, and make adjustments. She pointed out that hair follicles missing in her nose and her eyebrows were there for a reason. The nose hair kept your nose from constantly running. The eyebrows stopped the sweat from pouring into your eyes. These were small things that people seemed to take for granted—until they lost them.

Later that evening, Ginger couldn't shake the painful memories the women had shared with the audience. Still, Jackson hadn't noticed that her mind was elsewhere when they made love. And she couldn't confide in him how she'd felt after watching the Oprah show. He wouldn't understand. No one would.

But she'd bare her soul to Kim during her frequent visits

to the hospital, knowing that her cousin was still in a comatose state, unable to respond. Ginger felt herself weakening. Memories of years of dealing with the trial of being
hairless had broken her spirit, and nearly broken her.

Ginger remembered a night when Jackson hadn't been com-
plimentary about her eye makeup, as he was the night of Gene
Russell's party. Jackson would probably never recollect the
evening, but Ginger would never forget it. Jackson was helping her put on her fake eyelashes before going out.

"Turn around," he said.

"Like this?" Ginger was sweating profusely, something she
didn't ordinarily do. But they were going to the Fox Theater to
see Aretha Franklin. She wanted to look soft and feminine, and
felt that wearing fake eyelashes would give her that effect. She
and Jackson had been in the bathroom for nearly an hour, trying to secure the feathery things.

As Ginger turned to look in the mirror, she caught her
breath, shocked to see the wide-eyed, owl-like expression
they gave her. She tore them from her eyelids, trying to make
a joke of it, hoping Jackson wouldn't laugh. But he did.

Funny, Ginger thought, how relaxed she was being there,
alone, watching Kim's feeble form. Away from the house,
the kids, Jackson, the office, and school, she felt a weird solace. Ginger lifted Kim's limp hand, caressed it tenderly.
Kim still lay motionless, her face expressionless, her skin a
dull grayish brown. Ginger studied the bags of fluid seeping
life into Kim's veins. The clear liquid dripped soundlessly.
She doesn't feel any pain, thought Ginger.

Sweet blossoms of freshly cut flowers filled the small
room. Bill faithfully changed the arrangements weekly,
whether they were wilting or not. Ginger remembered him
saying that when Kim awakened, he wanted her to see the
beauty of life, alive and new.

Bending her head forward, she clutched both hands to her
face, rubbing up and down, down and back, stretching her
flesh. Turning toward the window at her mirrored reflection,
she was repulsed by a woman wallowing in self-pity. Unwanted tears fell, dripping from her lashless eyes.

The tears cleansed her troubled heart as Ginger felt the

splendor of miracles slipping inside her. It was as though God were opening her eyes and explaining why. . . .

Everything in life happens for a reason. And God humbled her by taking something she prized. Ginger thought to herself, I've truly been blessed and didn't even realize it.

For a moment, she forgot all of her sorrows and pain. The color, the fragrance, the sheer perfection of every bouquet surrounding Kim's room somehow seemed more profound, more intense than they had just moments ago. And she came away full of love, knowing. . . .

Before leaving, Ginger kissed Kim on the cheek. Feeling better than she had in months, Ginger laid her head over Kim's heart, cupping her hands over Kim's. Ginger bolted up, stunned. She'd felt a slight flicker in Kim's right index finger.

31

*Run Away Child,
Running Wild*

Near the middle of November, Ginger received a shocking phone call from the rape crisis counselor, Mrs. Ruth Beverly, who asked if she would come in and speak to a victim. The circumstances leading to the rape had been similar to Ginger's. Apparently Mr. Deiter had raped another young woman who now lay in the intensive care unit of Detroit Receiving Hospital, fighting for her life.

Ginger couldn't do it. She'd relived that horrible night too many times, and was just beginning to sleep better at night. She felt the pressure of Mrs. Beverly's plea, but she didn't yield. She had enough problems of her own to deal with.

Her relationship with Sierra was strained because of the impending trial. Sierra's grades, already low, were falling dramatically. And each time she sat Sierra down for a heart-to-heart talk, it ended in screams and threats. Sierra's self-esteem was failing, and so was Ginger's patience.

Classes at the school of design were canceled that Saturday morning. The instructor was sick, but had left homework assignments for Monday's session. Ginger thought of the sick young girl suffering in the hospital. She felt helpless. That could have been Sierra languishing there. She was suddenly ashamed of herself for not offering her assistance. And so by 9:30 A.M, Ginger found herself in the parking lot of Receiving Hospital.

"The girl's been through hell," Mrs. Beverly explained to Ginger. They rode the elevator downstairs from the counselor center to the intensive care unit.

The young girl's name was Ri-Va. She was just twenty-five years old. She'd been walking along Woodward Avenue to her apartment, just six blocks away. Suddenly, a man grabbed her from behind, covered her mouth, and threw her inside his car, placing a paper bag over her face. She caught only a quick glimpse of him. After he parked in a nearby alley, she fought, clawed, and scratched, but her efforts against his overwhelming power proved futile, and he raped her in the backseat of the vehicle.

A few weeks later, she started bleeding vaginally, but was alarmed that the discharge had such a foul odor. And the cramps grew worse. She ran a high temperature and experienced severe joint pain, particularly at the knees.

Running scared, Ri-Va confided her symptoms to her boyfriend. And, after a great deal of hesitation, she described the rape. He was enraged and took her to the hospital, but hadn't been back to visit her since.

Ri-Va was diagnosed with disseminated gonorrhea, and was noted to be pregnant. They performed suction evacuation, because it was an inevitable septic abortion. They initially treated her with Rocephin, prophylactically. She failed to respond. Her blood pressure dropped, suggesting septic shock, and ultimately she went into cardiac arrest.

Three code-blue procedures in ICU had stabilized Ri-Va's condition and she was placed on triple antibiotics—ampicillin, gentamicin, and clindamycin. Despite these efforts Ri-Va remained febrile.

"Ri-Va," said Mrs. Beverly. Her voice was soft, but firm. "This is Ginger. The young lady I told you about." Ri-Va's weakened brown eyes registered the two women. "She can describe the man—"

The head nurse interjected, checking her watch. "Five

minutes, no more." Gloom was written all over her face. Ginger and the counselor nodded their heads in unison.

"It's very important that we find the man that did this to you, Ri-Va. Please listen to Ginger's description of your assailant. I know it's difficult for you, but please try, Ri-Va. Please."

"He was kinda tall. Tall and brown-skinned, a creamy-like brown," said the young woman in quick breaths.

"And his hair?" Mrs. Beverly broke in.

"Neat and short—kinda wavy I think."

Ginger stood in the background, watching Ri-Va struggling over the details. Her small breasts rose, as if she were out of breath, but she continued.

"Big teeth. I remember seeing a mouthful of white teeth when he laughed back at me. He looked like the actor that used to play on *St. Elsewhere*."

"Denzel Washington," said Ginger flatly. The memory of that night jumped before her like a black cat. That this could actually be the same man was now a certainty, and she was afraid. Ginger remembered the tears, the blood, the words he'd said that night: "Don't fight it. I know you want it." Then he'd begun slapping her—

" 'Don't fight it,' " Ri-Va said weakly. "That's what he kept repeating, until he forced my mouth over . . . over . . . " she couldn't finish.

"I know," said Ginger, going to the bed and holding her hand. "Kiss it!" Deiter had demanded. It was all so ugly.

"He drove a black BMW. I'll never forget those gold wheels with silver cylinders in the center. Even though it was dark outside, they still sparkled like black diamonds." Her breathing was labored, and she stopped for a moment.

The silver-and-gold Dayton wheels with spinners on the car in question definitely fit the description of Deiter's BMW. With a definite description of the man and a good description of the car, Ginger was certain it was the same man.

"Will he be arrested?" Ri-Va asked, the question more breathed than enunciated.

Mrs. Beverly looked toward Ginger in piteous supplication.

Ginger wrestled with her emotions. She made no commitment just then, but stared at the shell of a woman lying before her, death summoning.

Ri-Va tried to lift her head up from the pillow. "I wonder if he'll find a hiding place, such as mine, for his escape. God knows I'm not judging him." Her dry, cracked lips turned up at the corners cynically. "I just expect justice. Am I wrong?" She fell back, her face expressing pain, exhausted.

"I'll do what I can," Ginger said, with a small smile directed toward Mrs. Beverly.

Ginger wasn't certain that she would testify in court against the man if Ri-Va didn't make it. The young woman struggled to shake Ginger's hand before they left, and she was genuinely moved by the gesture. Ginger remembered the conviction in Ri-Va's voice when the woman stated that her soul wouldn't rest until Deiter was behind bars.

Tears misted Ginger's eyes as she felt the cantillation of the choir revving up to vocalize the hymn for Sunday's morning's worship service, "His Eye Is on the Sparrow." Her mind traversed the short conversation with Ri-Va.

The rhythm of the spiritual song sneaked beneath her skin, the music flowing all through her body. Ginger was surprised to hear herself singing along:

"Why should I feel discouraged? Why should the shadows come? Why should my heart be lonely—and long for heav'n and home—When Jesus is—my portion? My constant friend—is He. His eye is on the sparrow, and I know He watches me. His eye is on the sparrow, and I know He watches me.—I sing because I'm happy,—I sing because I'm free—For His eye is on the sparrow,—and I know He watches me. . . . "

Though Ginger prayed daily, and read her Bible when she could, she was ashamed that she hadn't been faithful in her attendance at church. She felt guilty, knowing that God preferred "fellowship" among Christians. She knew she could draw strength from other people's testimonies—listening to their trials and how they overcame them.

When she returned home, there was a message from Bill. Apparently Kim showed signs of coming out of the coma. Ginger remembered the slight movement of Kim's finger.

She felt the gift of hope, and the power of being blessed. Her prayers had been answered.

"I'm sorry, Ginger. I can't understand how you can profess to be so tired. You don't work in the plant anymore."

Another argument, another night without sex. Jackson was furious. It was almost as if he had to make an appointment with Ginger for her to perform her wifely duties. This was wearing thin. Ginger hadn't been in the plant for eleven months, yet she complained that she was experiencing more fatigue than when she was working. It didn't make sense.

"I work at the real estate office. Or don't you consider that a *real* job?" said Ginger, thinking of defying him and hiring a service to clean twice a month. After months of begging, Jackson still had not agreed to hire a cleaning woman. Ginger and the kids worked continuously to keep the house clean. Yet the down-home, spick-and-span, corner-crack cleaning that Katherine had taught her would have to wait.

"The mildew in the shower stall is three weeks old."

"You could clean it," said Ginger weakly.

"It seems to me that you claimed to be able to work your business, go to school, take care of the kids, the house, and still make some time for me. That seems to ring in my ears, Ginger. Do you deny what you said?"

"No."

"Then don't renege."

"I need you—"

"You need. You need!" His voice shouted.

They didn't make love. Didn't talk anymore. Just remained at a Mexican standoff, neither one recognizing the other's side. Ginger withdrew. She felt empty. Pressured. Unloved.

Early Tuesday morning, Ginger received a phone call from the prosecuting attorney's office, apprising her of the case against Edward Deiter. Her presence was requested at the prosecutor's office on the twelfth floor of the Frank Murphy Hall of Justice at her earliest convenience.

Ginger's mind flip-flopped between her civic duty and selfish pride. She had only known Ri-Va for a mere seventy-two hours before the girl died, yet she felt an overwhelming compassion for her. Ri-Va hadn't made it through the next cardiac arrest. She'd expired at 7:56 on Monday evening. That could have been me, thought Ginger.

Trying to decide whether or not to testify in court, and needing Jackson's support, threatened Ginger's emotional equilibrium.

With charm in her eyes, Ginger sucked in her pride and surprised Jackson with a late-night candlelit dinner for the two of them. The evening sparked a warm glow, and love was met with love. Then only days later, after making love late one chilly evening in November, Ginger snuggled up close to Jackson and they talked for a while.

Katherine had warned Ginger about running her mouth in the heat of passion. Why didn't she listen?

"Jackson," said Ginger serenely, tucking his arms beneath her nude breasts, " I know I've been a little touchy lately, a bit anxious with you and the kids. Can you forgive me?"

"Anytime, baby," he cajoled. The words behind his triumphant eyes said, "So now the truth is finally coming out." He knew Ginger was ready to bare her soul. The sweet peace of sleep would have to wait, Jackson thought to himself.

Like the harkening of a million angels, she was in a mood of charmed surrender. The warmth she felt in her heart glowed in her face as she turned to kiss him. "I've been subpoenaed to testify in court."

"Why?"

"Something happened to me over a year ago that I haven't been completely honest about."

She finally admitted to Jackson that a client had tried to assault her last year, and that she was almost raped, but she managed to get away. The memory still haunted her. Hunted her down like an animal.

"I need your support in this, honey. It's important. A young girl has died—"

"You've been putting on quite an act, haven't you?" Jackson raised up like a leopard ready to attack. Exiting their tangled bed, his sleek, dark, naked frame pounced onto the floor. He was angry. His sixth sense had warned him that Ginger had been hiding something. "Am I supposed to sympathize with you?" Knowing Ginger had been involved sexually with another man had only been a thought, a feeling, until now. He wasn't ready to deal with the reality of the situation. In his mind he could see Ginger and her lover lying naked in bed together. Her husky laughter coupled with his. The laughter! *They were laughing at him.*

"Understanding, Jackson. That's all I ask. I've done nothing wrong. Nothing!" Ginger pleaded.

The purple darkness of the room hid Jackson from Ginger's vision. On the nightstand, the dead-lock glow of the neon clock reflected his golden cat-eyes, which seemed phosphorescent, adding to his elusiveness. "What a pity," he said distastefully, "to have wasted so much grief—"

Ginger wrapped the cool sheet around her nude body before turning on the night-light. "I wasn't raped Jackson, just assaulted. I knew how—"

Jackson slid into his jeans, leaving them unzipped, his massive pubic hair sprouting over the open V. "You lied to me, Ginger. Why?"

The air in the room was suddenly so heated and so close she could smell her own sweat. Ginger's voice, low, full of hurt, replied, "You wouldn't have understood, Jackson. You would have made me quit, and you know it."

"You lied to me, Ginger." I'll never forget that, he thought.

"I need you to understand how I feel. How I felt then. The nightmares I've had. The months of sleepless nights. I could have been killed, Jackson. I was terrified."

Jackson stood before the bed, resting both hands on his narrow hips. "And my feelings. My trust in you." At that moment Jackson felt an ambivalence growing inside him toward Ginger. What else had she lied about? What other men had she met in the night inconsequentially, and later called it an attempted rape? He hated her for lying. And he needed her. Yet he despised himself for that weakness.

Ginger was devastated by his uncaring response. Fifteen minutes ago, they were making beautiful love, their bodies and hearts comforting, passionately pleasing the other. And now, after acknowledging and confiding in her husband about her fears, something so serious, he turned from her. She forged ahead, hoping her vows of love could penetrate his heart. "Trust in our love. My love for you. You're the only man I ever wanted." *You're the only man I need.*

Jackson didn't hear her moving soliloquy. Didn't hear the conviction in her voice. He remembered the guys at the club laughing. It tore at his heart strings.

"What kind of fool do you take me for? You planned this farce to cover up an argument with your lover. Am I supposed to believe that each time we've made love in the past you were thinking of me? Your heart hadn't connected with your body in the bed for some time, Ginger—I've felt the difference."

Can you feel . . . can you know how much . . . you're breaking my heart with your false accusations? Or is this reverse psychology? Are you trying to make me feel guilty because of your philandering around with Mae Thelma? Am I the victim of your perverse sexual desires to want to control two women? The tears sliding down her cheeks felt like pebbles against her granite face.

Ginger tightened the sheet around her now cold body and stood her ground. "I haven't done anything wrong, Jackson. I have no lover. You're distorting this."

Jackson wasn't moved by her tears. The careful picture he'd painted of his "Queen" was now distorted—becoming ugly. Someone had bedraggled his woman, and she had allowed him to do it. His anger boiled. His temper soared. Jackson's knees dug into the mattress, grabbing Ginger's throat, choking her.

"Jackson . . . don't!" said Ginger, backpedaling away from his suffocating vise-grip.

"You lying slut," said Jackson, slapping her across the face.

Her head whirled around like a gyro. "Stop!" she pleaded.

"You're less than a whore." Hot tears filled his eyes. A low moan escaped Ginger's dry throat when he slapped her again. Instinctually both hands clamped her head; she could feel her left ear ringing. The sound in her ears was like the echo of a seashell. "Don't you have an ounce of respect?" Ginger turned away from him, curling her body in a fetal position. Jackson's voice trembled. "You're the *mother* of my child!"

Ginger tried to speak, the fight gearing up inside her, but that word . . . *mother* . . . caught in her throat. She kept her back to him, hoping that he would just leave. She was disoriented, unable to conjure up the words to make everything right between them.

"I trusted you, and you betrayed that trust. You lied when it was convenient. You willingly had sex with another man." Ginger felt the sharpness on her shoulder as he pulled her passive frame back into the center of the bed. Straddling her, Jackson's right hand again cupped her throat, sinking rough fingernails penetrating, breaking her skin. "Bitch!" he spat out, raising his left hand to slap her once more.

That did it. She was nobody's bitch. Not his. Not anyone's. Her upper torso wheeled up, catching Jackson's palm before impact. "Don't you *ever* put your hands on me again," she hissed. Jackson hesitated, their eyes locking. Snorting, he left the bed without another look, or another word passing between them.

Days passed slowly the next weekend, the nights even more slowly, while Ginger endured fitful sleep on the sofa. By the beginning of the second week, Ginger felt the need to reconcile. She couldn't go on living this way. They were worse than strangers—they were virtual enemies. Someone had to make the first move.

Having rehearsed her entire speech, Ginger was waiting for Jackson when he returned home from work. She made a final attempt to assure her man that she hadn't been intimate with anyone but him. Asking his forgiveness, again, for hesitating to tell him the truth. Couldn't he understand? No, he couldn't. His nose flared wide as if he smelled something foul, his eyes as deadly as a vampire's as he stared at her, then casually walked away.

Ginger endured hours of counseling, spending more time with a therapist who casually suggested to Ginger that her husband accompany her at their next visit. She told Ginger that she would not be able to help her much further without the presence of her husband. Jackson finally agreed after weeks of her crying and coaxing.

When the psychologist tried to explain to Jackson the trauma of a woman dealing with an assault on her person and the repercussions stemming from that attempt, Jackson remained impassive. Barely fifteen minutes passed before he got up and walked out, refusing to return.

They drove home in silence. Hurt and humiliated, Ginger willed herself not to cry.

As he pulled the Bronco to a stop in the driveway, he turned to face her. "I've just got one thing to say. Quit the real estate business." He could see the shock in Ginger's face as he continued in an authoritative tone. "I don't care if you go to work at Kmart. I don't care if you take up sewing wedding dresses again. But not this damned house-selling shit!"

"You're not being fair, Jackson. You know how much work I've put into developing my career. I'm successful, and you know it." Hurt filled her voice.

"I don't give a damn about success. You're my wife before you're anything, and I won't have you out showing men property at all times of the night. We both know what can happen!"

The whirring of the fan from the heater was the only sound inside the Bronco as they both sat mute.

"Jackson—"

He lifted his hands from clenching the steering wheel and pointed a finger in her face. "I don't want to hear it. I really don't want to hear any more about this. I said quit! Quit or—"

Staring him down, ignoring the finger wagging in her face, Ginger knew what was coming next. "Or what, Jackson?" she asked evenly. How could the most beautiful person in the world all of a sudden look so ugly to her?

"Or there won't be a marriage left to counsel. You got a week to make up your mind." Before she could say a word, he exited the truck and slammed the door.

"Fuck you," she said, alone inside the truck.

The next week dragged by. Thank God the kids sensed something was wrong. There wasn't a single argument among them—a miracle in itself.

Ginger's heart skipped a beat each time Jackson passed her that weekend, thinking this would be the time they would sit down and discuss their problems. She was sure he could see how upset she was. But it was becoming increasingly evident that he didn't care, and Ginger was losing her patience.

She couldn't deal with all the pressure. She wrote him a letter, hoping to explain her feelings calmly. Maybe after reading it he would finally understand her.

Didn't he care anymore? Didn't he love her? Or had their marriage been just lust, after all? His silence, and indifference, seemed to answer for her.

"I should have known she was under too much pressure," Bill said to Randall. Bill had just taken a quick shower and was on his way back to the hospital when the phone rang.

"You can't blame yourself," said Randall. "Just thank God that she's alive. If you ever loved her, Bill, give her a chance to explain."

Three days after Kim's attempted suicide, Randall had finally managed to catch Bill at home. Randall sensed that Bill was still uncomfortable talking to him, and tried to keep their conversation short.

Randall wouldn't be able to put all the pieces together until he spoke to Kim, but somehow Cameron had gotten to Kim that night. But Randall was certain he knew what had happened that night. However, this wasn't the time to go into it.

"Whatever might have happened, I'm not ashamed to tell any man how much I love her. Only God knows how much. I appreciate your concern, Randall. The doctors aren't sure when she'll come out of this, but trust me, I'll call as soon as she's out of the coma. I'm sure that's what Kim would want. I promised Kim during Christmas that I would respect your friendship. I mean it."

Several weeks later Bill sat beside Kim's hospital bed, holding her right hand firmly between his. Ginger had mentioned to Bill that she felt Kim's finger's moving weeks earlier, but he hadn't believed her. She was so emotional that he assumed she'd been overreacting. But when he felt her stiffened fingers move in small degrees, Bill immediately jumped up to signal the nurse. He reclaimed both her hands, staring down at her in astonishment. Her eyelids fluttered, then slowly opened. Bill's own breathing threatened to stop, and for one silent moment, they found each other's eyes. That single, frozen moment in time, when just a look of understanding reflected back genuine love. That love reached the dormant recesses of his soul, awakening them. Bill knew he'd never experience a feeling this powerful before. It could only be the power of God touching them both. All his questions subsided. His heart opened for understanding.

The room was dusk dark. Every now and then a crack of flames sent sparks flying inside the fireplace. The fragrance of hickory mixed with oak floated into the room.

Cotton was high, flying high on straight scotch and pussy. There wasn't a better combination, as far as he knew. Weaving in and out, out and in, he wanted to show her how deep he could fill her. How the long, thin shape of his penis would slide around inside her like a hot piston inside a Cosworth engine.

The glow of the fire from the fireplace gave Katherine's naked body an ethereal glow. Though her body was thick from food, booze, and age, no one could deny that she was still a handsome woman. Her Rubenesque curves only added to her sexual mystique.

Beside the sofa, on the mahogany coffee table, stood a stack of bills she'd cautiously counted earlier. Cotton had promised he'd bring his full check home this week from working construction after her threat to put him out for good if he didn't start contributing to the household.

"Baby," said Cotton seductively. "Oooooh that's some good shit."

Katherine wasn't impressed by his compliment. When she and Lewis were first married, he'd told her that "if God made pussy better than hers, he must've left it in heaven." Katherine had believed him. Until time after time she caught him with other women. Obviously there were a few more women Lewis had encountered who were blessed with heavenly pussies.

Cotton didn't know that Katherine had gone down to the construction site and spoken to his boss. She'd taken special care to dress that morning: chocolate brown Stuart Weitzman pumps, three-quarter-length double-breasted brown wool-crepe suit with brushed gold buttons, and a gold satin turban elegantly coiled around her head. Her unruly red hair, curled to perfection, bubbled over her shoulders. She knew she looked classy. And with all the finesse she could muster, she gently persuaded the man to tell her everything about Cotton. His absenteeism, his tardiness, but most importantly the amount of his weekly paycheck. The boss man, Katherine's age, knew without being told the reason for her visit. Katherine left his office with enough ammunition to put her game plan to work.

"Mmmmmm, you know you feel good to me, baby." Katherine rolled her buttocks, tightened, then relaxed her well-trained muscles, sucking him farther into the depths of her aura. She locked her ankles across his back. The suctioning sounds of fluids and flesh competed with the crackling fire nearby.

Her tongue flicked over his shoulder, along his neck, inside his ear. "I want to feel every inch of you," she whispered, as she swiftly rolled him onto his back and straddled him. Cotton's eyes pleaded for sexual pleasure.

Balancing her body on her knees, Katherine's weight was a plus. She knew her body well, and maneuvered it expertly. She rotated, gyrated, and finally exonerated his pulsating penis.

As they lay satiated beside the fire, the heat drying their sweat-soaked bodies, not a word was exchanged between them. Just a moment of repose, while they waited for the return of their normal breathing pattern, each immersed in his own thoughts.

She glanced at Cotton from the corner of her eye. Katherine, master of the game, would play her hand tonight, at all costs.

Waiting and more waiting, and for what—Jackson's forgiveness? She couldn't continue living with him like this. She wouldn't beg his forgiveness again, knowing it wouldn't change things between them. No, she couldn't bear the undeserved humiliation of being slapped, and called a bitch, yet again.

During their estrangement, each time Ginger looked at Jackson, he seemed calm and unmoved. It made her furious. Jackson's coldness toward Ginger had increased, as had her irritation at him because of it. Things couldn't continue this way between them for too much longer.

Ginger had to do something. She tried calling Katherine. There was no answer. She called her psychologist. Just when she needed counseling the most, Ginger had forgotten that her doctor was on vacation. She had no one to talk to. No one to understand her most intimate feelings. Unable to understand the emotional roller coaster that her heart was experiencing, she struggled to maintain control, but lost.

It was as though she were imprisoned in her own home for a crime she hadn't committed. The warden: her husband. It had taken her longer to see that there weren't any locks keeping her captive than she cared to realize.

The November sky bleak and dreary, cool raindrops casually fell. Ginger's mood was no brighter. She had to get away. It seemed childish to flee, but what else could she do? Ginger felt that her judgment was impaired, her self-respect depleting in this weakening state. But now she knew that she didn't have to wait for him to release her; she'd let him see how it felt.

There was no note left for Jackson when he came home that Wednesday afternoon explaining why she and the kids had fled. No explanation to her clients for missed appointments. No excuses to her teacher for missed classes. She simply left without a trace of evidence as to when or where she was or when she'd return. Just simply left.

Ginger stopped at the corner gas station and filled up the van while Christian bought goodies for the kids to snack on. Back on the road, Christian hesitantly asked the million-dollar question: "Are we going to be away for long, Ma?" Christian didn't want to mention his record of perfect attendance. This would be the first time he'd ever missed a day of school.

"Just a few days," Ginger answered, steering the van toward the Jeffries Freeway heading toward an out-of-the-way inn in Novi. Jackson would never think to look for her that far away. "Mama needs some time to figure out a few things."

"Is Daddy coming too, Mommy?" asked Autumn innocently.

"No, baby. Not this—"

"My teacher gave me too much homework," said Sierra, shuffling through the mounds of ditto sheets in her folder. "This must be enough homework for two weeks!"

"You need it, 'cause you never turn in your homework anyway," said Christian sarcastically.

"You better shut up before I pop you," shouted Sierra.

"Yeah, be quiet, pie face," intoned Autumn, "before I tell Mama about your messing with her computer when she told you not to bother it."

"Please don't start, you three. Mama's really not in a good mood." Please God, don't let him have erased the notes on my computer. I won't think about this. I won't. I'll deal with it tomorrow.

It turned out that the kids had a ball living away from home. Dinners in the evenings were an event. They ate at Kyoto's, a Japanese restaurant. Dined at Chi Chi's, a Mexican establishment. Ordered a carry-out dinner from Pizza Hut.

Ginger watched her three children thoroughly enjoy themselves Friday evening as they watched *Friday the 13th, Part VI*. They'd rented six videos, and were saving the last two, horror films, for later that night. Ginger snuggled up to a Mary Higgins Clark novel after the third run of *The Texas Chainsaw Massacre*.

"Come on, Mama," said Sierra, trying to snare Ginger away from her reading, "do the Butterfly with us." Even Christian, shy as he was, joined in, cajoling Ginger to get in on the fun.

Laughing despite herself, Ginger declined.

Sierra, unrelenting, pulled Ginger onto their makeshift dance floor.

"It's like batting a baseball and moving your hips at the same time. The same way you swing your hips—you can do the Butterfly with one hip."

Ginger tried several times until she felt the rhythm. Umph, there it was. "Okay, I got it now," said Ginger, grinding her buttocks. My knee hurts. It's hard doing it with one knee, she thought.

"It's called the Tug Rope," said Autumn, showing her another variation of the dance. "You act like you're pulling rope, then you pull it from the side. If you don't move your hips right, you ain't doing it right." Autumn worked her young hips like a frightened colt. "I think this part is called Ride the Pony."

Ginger admired Sierra's taut buttocks, teasingly suggestive as she performed an Around the World Butterfly.

Autumn, seeing Ginger's stiffness, grabbed her mother's hips and showed her how to Butterfly. Autumn said, "I can make my own dances to my own music."

"Stop stepping on my feet," Sierra screamed, aimed toward Autumn.

Sierra was obviously feeling a little jealous toward her little sister, who apparently was outdancing her. Autumn was doing the Crossover. She leaned her body back at a seventy-five-degree angle and worked her pelvis.

Sierra and Ginger were exhausted. For the first time in months they both agreed on something. It was as though a black cloud had lifted. Ginger didn't want to fight with her daughter. She'd wanted a truce to their unceremonious problems. It had come. Sierra and Ginger hugged, relaxing into one another. No matter what happened, the weekend was a success. Ginger had left home hoping to come to terms with her feelings about Jackson, but unknowingly would return with a renewed respect between mother and daughter—and the laughter, the theater of a dance, the Butterfly.

Ginger, Christian, Sierra, and Autumn returned home Saturday afternoon on a happy note. For four short days, they'd experienced a personal high that had been missing for some time. Somehow, a bridge had been formed among them all, a new awareness, a new respect.

Jackson neither acknowledged nor reprimanded Ginger on their return. He tersely kissed Sierra, ignored Christian, and took his baby daughter aside, pampering her with hugs and loving kisses.

They resumed their sleeping arrangements: Jackson sovereigned in their king-size bed; Ginger suffered on the narrow sofa.

On that first night at home, after endless hours of tossing

and turning Ginger finally felt the exhaustion of sleep creep in upon her. She awoke minutes later startled by what she perceived to be a devil, clad in bright red underwear.

He hissed, pointing a finger in her face. "Don't you ever take my kids from this house. If you want to leave, go! But you leave them here. This is their *home*. Kids don't understand parental problems. You're confusing them. Lord knows what you'll stoop to next!"

Ginger rubbed her eyes, still trying to focus on what had transpired. She hadn't imagined she'd see the devil in the red briefs—the scent of his Old Spice deodorant still lingered.

She'd hoped Jackson would miss her and be willing to call a truce when she returned. She thought that giving him time alone to think, and to miss her, would bring his focus back onto the importance of their relationship. It hadn't worked, though. Their conversation was more strained than ever. He wouldn't even look at her. Blow after blow was sending Ginger into a frenzy. She couldn't cope. But then she realized that she had a last hope: *Maybe he still hadn't read the letter.*

32

Since I Lost My Baby

Hurt blinded Ginger's better judgment, and she confronted him at last. "Jackson, I won't live with you like this. We don't talk. We don't spend time together anymore. You seem to be avoiding me all the time. Didn't you read my letter?"

"Yeah, I read it," he lied. "So."

"So, I thought you'd have some kind of response to my feelings." Her voice was betraying the heart that she so valiantly tried to protect.

"Like I said. So." He flicked the buttons on the remote control, seemingly unconcerned. "Am I supposed to fall down on my knees and kiss your ass?" He looked up at her, his hazel eyes reflecting the glare of the television set.

For a second Ginger was scared. Jackson never treated her with such indifference. Their arguments had never lasted this long. For the first time in their marriage, Ginger truly felt that Jackson didn't love her anymore.

"I wrote you a letter, too."

"You did?" Ginger's voice inflected signs of hope.

Picking up the drink next to him, Jackson took a gulp.

"Where is it? Can I read it now?"

Stretching out his legs, Jackson finished his drink. "Yeah, why don't you. I'll get it." Ginger's eyes followed him as he walked to the closet and retrieved the note from his jacket pocket.

A sneer came across his face as he handed it to her. All Ginger's hopes died when she read the note: *Fuck you, bitch.*

Barely able to compose herself, Ginger sucked in her pride. Undoubtedly, the only thing you enjoy about me is fucking me. I seem to have no other value. Thank you for making it so plain. Refusing to cry, she scanned the note again, and dropped it in the trash can. Her voice dropped to a whisper. "If that's the way you want it, Jackson."

Tears were the last thing on her mind when Ginger turned on the stereo. She'd show him. He'd be sorry. A sultry song floated throughout the silent room. She felt the music flowing through her body like hot, liquid gold, enter her like fine wine. Ginger pretended she was a whore, paid to put on the show of a lifetime. And moving her body to a provocative beat, she began a striptease.

Ginger danced closer to Jackson, naked, spreading his legs open as she stood before him. Her right hand caressed his chest, then she outlined his full lips with the index finger of her left. Ginger layered Jackson's mouth with kisses as he responded automatically.

Teasing the nipples on his chest, Ginger pushed his knees open wider, and softly ran her vagina in a circular motion up and down his thigh. The lips of her sex opened and closed, suctioning his leg, grinding her full buttocks slowly and easily down the expanse of him as her eyes held his.

Next, she moved squarely astride him. With both hands, she massaged Jackson's temples. His head fell back against the sofa as Ginger's hands massaged and caressed his chest, neck, face. When Ginger began stimulating his crotch with her long fingernails, she felt his erection straining against his tight jeans.

Jackson had forgotten about their problems just as she had suspected he would.

Stepping back off his lap, Ginger picked up the tempo of the music as she placed her hands at the sides of her hips, cocking open her legs. She rolled her stomach and hips to the rhythm, tantalizingly.

Turning around, she lifted the curls of her wig from her shoulders, piling them on her head, as she worked her butt up and around and down just inches from the floor and back up again. Ginger felt her heart pounding as she placed her fingers around the soft folds of her vagina, stroking her warm flesh, watching Jackson watch her. Feeling the juices gathering between her legs, she inserted a finger, stimulating her clitoris, in and out. Slowly at first, then picking up the pace . . . faster . . . faster . . . harder . . . until she felt herself surrendering to her own passions. She stopped, regaining her focus, her tongue curled, moistening her mouth as she moved closer to him. Touching him. Feeling his hardness, seeing him enjoy the scent of sex on her wettish fingers while outlining his mouth, then kissing him.

Strange how quickly the human body, the instrument of beauty and feeling, could leave the mind behind.

"I want to fuck you, Jackson," Ginger said in a low, husky voice. Slowly, she removed his clothing, managing to kiss every inch of him in the process.

Jackson's usually sharp instincts misread Ginger. Ginger had hoped he'd see the charade, and refuse. But his need for sex overruled his need for love—and he succumbed.

A familiar recognition passed between them as Ginger and Jackson moved toward the bed. Ginger gently guided Jackson to lie back against the pillows. As if in slow motion, she massaged his enlarged member, then skillfully stroked him, whispering erotic expletives in his ear that at first made him stiffen with surprise. Then slowly, as he relaxed, she felt his love juices oozing over his stiff penis as her fingers slowly traveled around the cap of his engorged organ.

Straddling Jackson, Ginger cupped her hands under his buttocks, lifting him a few inches from the bed and guiding him to match her rhythmic thrusts. Jackson grabbed the headboard of the bed and lifted his taut buttocks even higher, as they moved toward a melodic symphony they both could play by heart.

As her knee dug deeper into the mattress, Ginger gripped the headboard, her perspiring hands pressing next to Jackson's as she arduously rode him until he shuddered and climaxed. But she knew her quest was not over, and continued to ride him, slowly, ever so slowly, until she felt the heat of his sex growing inside her.

Placing her hands above his head, next to the sweat-stained pillow, she kissed him hard on the mouth. Twirling her tongue inside, she tasted his tangy sweetness while moving her buttocks erotically around his hardened shaft. Ginger heard Jackson's shallow breathing as she kissed the base of his neck. The brandy Jackson had imbibed that evening seemed to seep through his glands as he sweated, intoxicating the air above them.

Raising and lowering her buttocks, she grazed the tip of his organ, enticing and teasing him. Ginger knew he was close to his second orgasm. Ordinarily, she would be also. Yet, she knew the role she was playing tonight was not out of love, but out of hurt and vengeance. She had to prove something to herself and to him. And she would, before the night was over.

It had only taken Ginger a few minutes of squeezing and stroking with her vagina muscles for Jackson to climax again.

After returning from the bathroom, she cleansed and bathed his sex with a hot cloth, as Jackson moaned, rolling his buttocks beneath him, his eyes closed. Ginger knew he was thoroughly satisfied, and ready for his traditional exhausted after-sex sleep. But the night was still young, as he would soon see.

She lit a lilac-scented candle and moved toward the bed. Hearing his shallow breathing, Ginger straddled Jackson's long body yet again. Only this time, her head was lower. Slowly, she began to massage his penis. She heard garbled words coming from his semiconscious form. Knowing his body almost as well as he did, Ginger knew it would be a mere three or four seconds before he became aroused.

Ginger began sucking on Jackson's toes, one by one, and continued to stroke him. His big toe curved slightly while she worked her way up his legs, kissing and licking his moist skin. The musky scent of sweat lingered on Jackson's hairy legs, as she ran her tongue swiftly over the slick follicles.

KNOWING 373

Turning him over, she kissed the back of his muscular thighs, working her way up to his buttocks. Jackson sighed, and stretched his long body like a leopard, moaning in pleasure.

Kissing the nape of his neck, Ginger massaged and rolled Jackson's skin along his back and shoulder with quick, circular motions. Stroking the lower half of his body with long traces of her curled toes, Ginger glided herself over Jackson like an octopus, heating up his body with hers.

Jackson's hands reached up around her and cupped her buttocks, grinding beneath her. Ginger then turned him onto his side, sucking on his right nipple, then his left, as she guided him onto his back and climbed on top of him.

Feeling the velvet throbbing of Jackson's stiff organ, Ginger quickened her measured strokes to match his gyrating buttocks, which seemed to have a life of their own. Bending down, she kissed his satiny tip glistening in the half-darkness.

Since he treated her like a whore, and this is what he always said a whore did, she'd show him what a whore could do. She began licking down one side, then the other, following his protruding vein, and around the base, catching the hairs of his sex beneath her teeth, tugging gently.

What the hell was she doing? Jackson had awakened fully now. "Ginger!" he said, lifting his head from the pillow. "Don't, baby. You know—"

Ginger clamped her free hand over his mouth and continued kissing and loving his sex. She knew in her heart that he was enjoying it.

Still feeling the alcohol racing through his veins, Jackson lay back, knowing he couldn't fight the excitement rocketing through his penis.

Gliding her tongue over his sex, Ginger opened her mouth wide to receive as much of him as she could take in, sucking gently. She heard a gasp from Jackson, then continued, at first sucking softly, tenderly, then elevating up and down as far as she could, one hand massaging his testicles, the other splayed across his chest, pressing him to lie back.

Ginger felt Jackson's buttocks moving, and pushed his penis farther into her mouth, then she heard a slow hum in the back of his throat. Ginger performed fellatio along and around Jackson's strained sex, until she tasted the clear liquid lubricating his rigid member. Jackson began calling Ginger's name over and over while twisting his body to a sitting position.

Jackson pulled her head to his mouth, and kissed her hard, tasting the musky film coating her lips. Sweat streamed down both their bodies as they slid near the edge of the bed. Knowing her task was not finished, however, Ginger took control of the situation, disengaging her lips from his. Pushing his legs apart with her knees, she lowered her head and stroked his love muscle. As smoothly as a breath, she again took him into her hot mouth, as she knelt before him at the edge of the bed. Grabbing his buttocks, she pulled him deeper into her welcoming mouth. Sucking. Loving. Licking.

Jackson's clutched her head, gyrating his lips frantically, thrusting himself deeper, farther into Ginger's mouth. Arching his back, Jackson stiffened, straining against his desire, trying to prolong the pleasure that was overwhelming him.

Flicking her tongue around the rim, Ginger blew lightly over his throbbing head, her lips smooth and soft, wide, open and wet. She brushed the top of her tongue over his tiny hole, flicking it in and out, and around.

A slow groan escaped Jackson's throat. He started thrashing his legs wildly. Turning his head from side to side. Ginger held on as Jackson tried to scoot from beneath her sucking embrace, but she held on, suckling him harder as they rolled off the bed.

"Stop, baby. I can't take any more," Jackson pleaded as he struggled to free himself.

That's what you think. Ginger came after him. Jackson was valiantly trying to catch his breath when Ginger flipped him over onto his back. Ginger covered Jackson's body in reverse with hers, curling her toes around his shoulders, pinning him down with her weight. Taking his penis back into her mouth, she watched his toes pointing like arrows as she stroked him.

He was powerless to make an attempt to stop her again. Ginger could hear the cries of pleasure as his body began to shake. She placed her hands beneath Jackson's buttocks, forcing him deeper into her mouth. She could see his testicles stiffening, roaming rampant beneath rows of ringed flesh.

Knowing that his climax was near, she clamped his sweat-soaked buttocks tighter. Ginger continued to draw him into the warmth of her, as Jackson dug his heels into the carpeting, begging her to stop, knowing he couldn't hold back much longer.

"Please, baby . . . don't! Please . . ." Jackson begged.

Ignoring his pleas, Ginger sucked harder, faster, increasing the tempo, until his veins, strained to the limit along the sides of his rigid penis, took on a purple hue. Ginger let her mind take control of her body, focusing all her attention on her fingertips and tongue, and played a synchronized rhythm along the length of his penis, adjusting and increasing the tempo.

Ginger could almost hear his heart beating outside his chest, like the drums that she knew were pounding inside his brain. Then he came, and came, trembling uncontrollably. Jackson clamped his legs together tightly, his body responding to the shattering spasms. Ginger massaged the milky fluid oozing from him, then caught her breath, exhausted, wishing his heart had given out. It would have been just what he deserved.

She let him lie on the floor as he was, tangled in the heap of sheets, his heavy breathing winding down to small snatches of a snore, just as he was.

He'd loved it, just as Ginger always assumed he would. Ginger's sweat mixed with tears as she reached to turn off the music. Hesitating for a moment before she left the room, she stood near the bed, looking down at Jackson, staring at the man she loved and hated.

Blowing out the candle, she took one last look at Jackson. Tears streamed uncontrollably down her face. When his light snoring graduated into a deep sleep, she left him. Thoroughly disgusted, she went into the bathroom to clean herself, knowing that a part of her would never be completely clean again.

Knowing he'd be asleep for hours, she pulled the double doors to close off their bed from the living area of their bedroom and packed a small suitcase. She scribbled a note and taped it on the bathroom mirror. Waking Christian, she told him quickly to pack a bag for a few days, and not to ask her any questions. She'd explain later. After packing a bag for the girls, Christian carried the sleeping Autumn, and Ginger assisted Sierra's drowsy body to the minivan. At first Ginger thought she should go to her mother's, but instinct told her that Kim's place would be a better choice. With Kim still in the hospital, she'd have some privacy. She still had her key, and she knew that Kim wouldn't mind her and the kids staying for a little while.

Later that evening, Jackson felt for her in the darkness, coming up empty, yet feeling the stickiness between his legs and remembering. He couldn't believe what he had allowed her to do. Had he been so drunk that he'd dreamed the whole thing? The clammy feeling between his legs proved otherwise.

Walking into the bathroom, he called out her name. Getting no answer, he turned on the light and noticed the note taped on the mirror.

Anger filled him as he read the cutting words: *It takes a bitch to know a bitch and to show a bitch—fuck you.* He didn't bother to look downstairs. He knew she was gone. Still feeling the effects of the alcohol, he walked naked back to their bed and stretched out in the center without covering himself. She could just go to hell. Fuck her. He didn't need a whore for a wife anyway.

On the tenth of December, Kim finally regained her power of speech, and related to Bill the whole sordid story behind the videotape. She knew what she'd done was wrong, but hoped that Bill could forgive her.

"Kim, I knew about your past before I met you. I'd heard the rumors, but I ignored them. I'm not perfect. And I don't expect you to be. I know from past experience that everyone has some shameful secret they're reluctant to share. And I wouldn't have watched a video of you making love to another man, no matter what the circumstances. I have more respect for you than that." Bill's eyes filled with tears as he hugged the woman he loved. "I want you to promise me you'll never try anything like this again."

"Promise. I love you, Dr. Bill. I can't begin to explain how much," Kim said, her voice still shaky from the medication.

Then, pushing her back to arm's length, Bill asked Kim if she would forgive *him*. Confusion was written all over her face. "For what?" she asked.

"I never told you about my son that died."

Beneath the stark-white hospital sheets, Kim's body stiffened, unbelieving. "You had a son?"

"Yes. Remember the story I told the students at Wayne State about the reasons why I dedicated my life to being a doctor?" Kim nodded, still startled by his revelation. "The child I was referring to that died in the shooting was my son." A gasp escaped Kim's lips. "The boy's mother, Angel, and I were high school sweethearts. She knew my plans to attend medical school. We agreed to wait until I completed my internship before marrying and starting a family.

"But Angel became pregnant just before graduation. Somehow my mother found out, and confronted her. Angel assured me that she'd get an abortion. I didn't know why then, but that's when our relationship started falling apart. Before I left, we agreed to communicate, but my letters and phone calls went unanswered a few months later.

"I found out from my mother Angel had left town, and shortly afterwards, married a man much older than herself. Years later, after her husband died, she returned with her son. After one look at the boy, my mother put two and two together and guessed the child was mine. Angel didn't deny it. But my mother never told me about the boy until it was too late. Less than a month after my son was shot, my mother had a heart attack. I was bitter, Kim. I'd lost my son, my mother, and part of my soul as well."

Now Kim understood Bill's ideas about raising a family, and why he had resented her not wanting any children. But after everything that had happened in their lives, he knew that now was not the time to talk about it. They had come a long way.

Embracing Bill, Kim wept harder than she had in years. Everything was coming together.

* * *

"It's so good to hear from you, Randall," Kim said, cupping the telephone receiver.

"How you feeling?"

"I'm just fine. Thanks for the calls to Bill," Kim answered, looking at the photograph of Bill that sat on the stand near her bed.

"Anytime."

"I should be going home by the end of December. Maybe before Christmas if everything goes well." A wave of guilt made Kim want to explain to Randall why she had been so stupid as to try and take her life. "Randall . . ." she began slowly.

"Listen, Kim we're friends. There's no need to explain. I've always known what went on between you and Cameron. Believe me, knowing Bill, I can understand why you felt that you couldn't tell him. Until now. He's got a fresh attitude about life. Just give him a little time." His voice wavered, enunciating each word carefully. "Time is precious. None of us knows how much time we have in this world. We have no idea how long. But once that time is lost, it's irretrievable."

"Randall . . . ?" Kim felt a lump in her throat. "Can I ask you something personal?"

"Anything?"

"Have you found anyone special since you've been in London?"

"No. Just an occasional distraction from . . . you know."

"You two haven't had any further communication?"

"He's been over a few times. He assures me that he still loves me, yet he's still not ready to commit to what we could have together. I don't believe he will ever come to terms with his sexuality . . . *so* . . . I've tried to forget him. That's part of the reason why I'm not coming back. But there's no one I've met who comes close to what we shared."

"I understand totally, Randall."

Kim was released from the hospital five days before Christmas. After a visit from her father, she'd made a speedy recovery. Ollie jokingly told her that he would probably outlive her. When he actually walked from the doorway to her bedside, it had given her the extra push that she needed. Her father had left her with a word of wisdom for her future.

"No one is so old that he cannot live yet another year, nor so young that he cannot die today. When God wounds from on high, he will follow with the remedy. When one door closes, fortune will usually open another."

Kim rehearsed those words until she knew them by heart. They taught her to believe in the glory and the wisdom of God.

Ginger and her three children had spent two weeks cramped in Kim's apartment before Randall suggested to Kim that Ginger and her kids use his apartment. It was all paid for. The only stipulation was tender loving care of its inhabitants.

Edward Deiter was charged with second-degree murder, rape, and attempted rape. He was arraigned, and a "presentation of evidence" trial date was set, as was a bond in excess of $250,000. After completely draining his bank account, Deiter made bond and returned home.

After rumors of his behavior spread, he was inevitably dismissed from his position as an advertising executive. Unable to seek employment, he eventually lost his home. Piece by piece Edward Deiter's life fell apart. The last anyone heard, he was purportedly living in Indiana with a young woman.

After reading that Mr. Deiter was released on bond, Ginger was afraid to go out alone. More often she took Christian with her on home showings. The girls went only when Christian was unavailable. They enjoyed looking at the homes. It was like a personalized Parade of Homes which they'd frequented with Ginger over the years.

Autumn found friends her age in their condo complex and invited them over to join Sierra's posse. They were starting a dance club. Ginger had to admire her verve. It had taken Autumn to coax the inhibited Sierra to seek out and find some young girls from the sixth grade.

Christian learned the bus schedules, returning to their old neighborhood every few days to visit his friend Benny. They'd known each other nearly ten years, and had formed a strong friendship. Ginger tried talking to herself when the girls were off playing with their friends, and she found her-

self alone. She tried to calm her festering hysteria. You've
seen too many movies, she told herself. He won't harm you.

Jackson was in a period of denial. When he came home from
work, he watered his plants, readied his clothes for the next
day, turned on the television, then poured himself a drink.
Alcohol was his constant companion. It numbed him. Anes-
thetized his feelings for Ginger. When he was sober, his conscience told him he was wrong, should apologize. But when
he was high, his conscience said she should come begging
for his forgiveness. He preferred it that way.

Ginger's heart vacillated between the loving memories of her
years with Jackson and how the uncompromising demands
he made destroyed their marriage.

It was as though the views of equality written in an article
in 1906 had been scripted with the female servant in mind.
When Booker T. Washington was invited to dine with President Theodore Roosevelt, the southerners were outraged.
Seemed the female Negroes' invitation to the White House
was extended merely for their performances—musical that
is. Henceforth, on October 16, the *Nashville American* observed the following commentary:

> The South refuses social recognition or equality to
> Booker T. Washington not because of any hatred of
> him, not because of his respectability, but in spite of it.
> It denies him social equality because he is a
> negro. . . . To accord social equality to negroes of
> Booker T. Washington's stamp would be a leak in the
> dam. It would cause other negroes to seek and demand
> the same recognition.

Would her sons ever see Black men being held in the same
esteem as their White compatriots in their lifetimes?

Yet Ginger also wondered if she, being a Black woman,
could ever gain enough respect from her Black man to be
treated as an individual. She wanted to be a helpmate instead
of a slave, demanding the same value he did. She would not
be subservient and submissive to his limitless demands on

her person merely for entertainment purposes. And she was not his mother, his lover, his friend, his wife, but just a woman. Because that was all she was. Just a woman doing the best she could.

She wished, instead, that a man would come out of the darkness into the light and say, "Baby. Baby . . . let me help you." Those four words, so simple: "Let me help you."

Randall's apartment was the perfect hideaway. Time and care showed in every corner of his home. Constantly surrounded by beauty, Ginger felt alone, discarded. A Picasso lithograph, *Girl Before a Mirror,* graced the wall behind the sofa. A copy of Willem de Kooning's *Woman II* adorned an adjoining wall. A Parisian cityscape and several scenes of rural life, elegantly framed, hung in the foyer.

Depending upon her mood, Ginger could take or leave Edward Steichen's 1928 black-and-white photo of Greta Garbo. The extra-large framed glossy hung on the wall near the kitchen. Passing by that wonderfully expressive face when she made her daily cups of tea left Ginger feeling cold. Unlike Garbo, she truly found no joy in being alone.

Ginger learned from Kim that Randall wouldn't be back. She was astounded when Kim said he didn't want to remove the paintings and have them sent over to London. He'd painstakingly hung each artwork, and wished them to stay that way. Having painted up a storm over the past two years, Randall had decorated his London apartment with canvases of his own. Though not of the same caliber as his treasures in Michigan, he felt as though the loving few he'd created himself were worth more to him than any famous artist's works he'd had the pleasure of owning.

Less than a week after Ginger had written Jackson the nasty note, she began to have misgivings. She felt she hadn't given him the benefit of the doubt. Maybe he'd been drinking too much, clouding his usually sound judgment. One night, while the kids were asleep, she decided to try to patch things up. Surprised to find that he wasn't at home, she drove down to the club, hoping he'd be there with his friends.

Disappointed at not finding him there, she asked Little Bubba, but he told Ginger that he hadn't seen Jackson lately.

She talked to Little Bubba for a while about the problems she and Jackson had been having. They popped a few cans of beer, and he even let her beat him at pool. Ginger knew he was letting her win, but it felt good anyway. As she drove back to her new home, something told her to swing by Mae Thelma's house. By then it was nearly one o'clock in the morning.

Her heart sank to her knees when she saw Jackson's Bronco parked in the driveway. From the street, she couldn't see any lights on. She could forgive him for verbally abusing her. She could forgive the gossip from the church. She could forgive his jealousy over her job. But she couldn't forgive his screwing his cousin's wife. Or any woman, for that matter.

Fuck it, she thought. Jumping out of her minivan, she left it parked in the middle of the street and ran to the house, pounding on the front door. Mae Thelma answered in her nightgown.

"It's late, Ginger," said Mae Thelma.

"Is Jackson here?" asked Ginger, praying that his truck had broken down and that he wasn't inside.

"Mae Thelma," a voice called from inside. Though barely audible, Ginger knew it was Jackson's, and left without another word. That was the final assault. She was through with him.

Ginger stopped by their home, piling up her van with all the clothing she could take. Whatever she couldn't pack in the van, she'd buy, or get after the divorce was final. All her hesitancy about filing had vanished tonight. She'd contact her attorney in the morning.

In the days that followed, Ginger phoned her mother every day. Katherine advised Ginger to take the time and effort to do some serious soul-searching before she filed for a divorce. Katherine asked her if the thought that two different fathers would be standing at the front door to pick up their children for their biweekly visits had occurred to her. And what if something happened to her? Would the children be separated, living in two different homes? Had she thought about which half of the furniture she would keep and which pieces Jackson would want? And did she actually think that, during

their separation, Jackson would allow Ginger to entertain another man in front of his daughter? Could she stand to see
him out with another woman? It was obvious to Ginger after
each of their conversations that Katherine felt she was making a mistake, moving too fast.

School was out for the Christmas holidays, for the kids as
well as for Ginger. She found herself with more time than
she knew what to do with. She couldn't concentrate on reading. Every male character in the novels took on Jackson's
face. When the story gravitated to the sex scenes, Ginger had
to close the book. Jackson's naked body appeared before her
like an apparition. Even the scent of him seemed to linger in
the air. Closing her eyes tightly, she tried to squeeze back the
tears that she knew would surely fall.

One morning shortly before Christmas, Bill and Ginger
transported a nearly healthy Kim back home to her apartment. After he was sure that Kim was safely tucked in bed
and resting comfortably, Bill left to have Kim's prescriptions
refilled, leaving the two women alone to talk awhile.

The scars on Kim's face were nearly invisible now. Her
hair was short, cut evenly to the length of her new hair
growth where they'd shaved it from the operation. She wore
very little makeup, and looked refreshingly beautiful in one
of the new dresses Bill had bought for her.

"You first have to forgive yourself," Kim was saying. Kim
handed Ginger some pamphlets Bill had given her about rape
victims. She'd read them over and over. She had even called
the hot line a few times and spoken to a social worker. It
helped. "When you do, you can go on with your life and
grow, and without even knowing it, you'll forget Edward
Deiter."

Ginger wrestled with the strands of her wig as she chroni-
cled to Kim the whole episode of her attempted rape. She
told her about Ri-Va—her struggle, and death. They discussed Jackson's outrage about the incident. His threats to
make her quit her business. His lack of forgiveness or support, and the loss of trust that ultimately broke their marriage.

Ginger broke down crying. "I don't know what to do anymore. I used to be so sure about everything. Now I'm not sure about anything. I'm questioning myself all the time." She stopped, wiping her eyes with a tissue offered by Kim. "I love that man, Kim. God knows I do."

"I know. I know you do," said Kim with tears in her eyes. She hated to see Ginger upset like this. But she knew Ginger's decision to divorce Jackson had to be hers and hers alone.

The papers were hand delivered to Jackson two days before Christmas. The children seemed to have a sixth sense about their mother's difficult decision. And they'd helped out as much as they could with the transition of moving to a smaller place.

Christian was a sophomore at Renaissance High School and still maintained a 4.0 grade-point average. After conferring on the phone with Jason, who was spending a tour of two years in Germany, Christian had risen to the occasion and put himself in charge of the family. He'd taken the girls aside and handed out the rules and regulations of the household.

Ginger, however, struggled with conflicting feelings. This would be their first Christmas away from each other, and Jackson hadn't bothered to send a card or telephone. He hadn't seen his daughter in weeks. Hadn't asked Autumn what she wanted for Christmas. Autumn was devastated. She tried to hide her feelings from her mother, but Ginger knew better. Jackson had spoiled Autumn since she was born, and hadn't missed a single opportunity to show his love to his only child. Sierra and Christian almost felt guilty as their father picked them up earlier on Christmas Eve to do last-minute shopping. Autumn and Ginger were left alone in the apartment. The hurt Ginger saw in her baby's eyes as she watched the clock, the hours passing slowly, broke Ginger's heart.

Why hadn't Jackson come to get her? Weeping, Ginger fell on her knees without realizing she'd uttered a sound. But Autumn, hearing her mother, ran into the family room. She wrapped her small arms around her mother, and did her best to rock Ginger's stiffened body back and forth, their shared tears blending their pain and prayers in harmony.

33

Where Did Our Love Go?

"You sure you're gonna be all right, Mama?" Ginger cinched the winter-white wool cape snugly around her before opening the front door.

"Damned right." Katherine kissed each of her grandchildren before they scooted out the front door, eager to get in a few snowballs before they headed back to Detroit. Katherine had lost so much weight that she no longer needed shoestrings in her pants, nor either of her famed double girdles.

Ginger hated to see her mother like that. Katherine's life had gone downhill ever since she'd let that younger man enter her life, her home, and eventually her heart. She'd broken down and admitted to her daughter the hell she'd been going through. She was embarrassed to tell Ginger, knowing that everyone had warned her about younger men wanting nothing but money from an older woman. They were right. Cotton had used and abused her for as long as Katherine could stand it. But when the lights got cut off, and she was forced to burn wood in the fireplace to keep warm because the gas company had tired of her excuses months before, she had to make a decision.

"You could come and stay with us until my house gets sold, Mama. Or with Kim?" But Ginger knew before she made the suggestion that her mother wouldn't leave her home. She enjoyed her privacy too much.

"No, baby." Katherine smoothed tawny fingers over the folded bills Ginger had given her to get the lights and gas turned back on. "You still ain't heard from Jackson?"

"Not a peep." They watched the kids enjoying themselves in the snow. It was the twenty-ninth of December. The wind whipped across the white earth. Bubbles and pine needles were trapped in the thin ice coating the sidewalk. Ginger called out to the kids to stay off the walkway before they fell and broke their backs.

Autumn, ignoring Christian and Sierra, stretched out on the ground, swishing her arms and legs back and forth to make angels in the snow. Ginger looked back at the fireplace, crackling with flames. "You sure you got enough wood to last until the utility company comes out?"

Katherine pushed Ginger through the front door. "I got plenty of wood, and boxes of candles." She smiled mischievously, and a glimpse of the old Katherine surfaced. "You young people don't know what hard times is."

Driving from the airport, Jackson turned on the radio news as his mind wandered to the letter that Ginger had written him. It was her final plea before she'd made her decision to leave. Why hadn't he listened?

Why don't you understand that I need you to love me? Why do you make our love so complicated? Do you have to have so much control? You know I love you. Don't ask me to submit totally and lose myself yet again, in the process. Giving up my career that I love, that helps to make me who and what I am. No love is worth that.

I need to be able to love freely and express myself. Yet, I know I need a man in my life. I need you, Jackson. I long to feel you near me. To look at me as only you can.

My head is bald, my eyelashes are gone, I have no eyebrows and I look like another being from outer space, but the person inside of me feels beautiful. The person I know I am, whose beauty is more than looks. My heart and my need to give and express my love to you and my children transcends this body.

Don't you know that God has blessed you with everything that's lacking inside of me? Don't you know that I need you to make me whole. Don't you know . . . don't you know . . .

I love to see you walk from one room to another. I get excited just watching your long legs. I just look and look and feel . . . knowing later that evening I'll feel the petal softness of your skin next to mine.

Yet, sex has always been the strong suit of our marriage. It shouldn't be.

All I ever wanted from you is your respect and love. There is nothing you and I can't accomplish together. No reason we can't be as One. But you won't comply. You make it so hard for me. And what you're really doing is making it hard for yourself. That is, if you really love me.

I deserve the respect of being your wife, your woman. I demand it. Because knowing myself, there is no way I could have possibly imagined that in giving so much of myself to a man I love completely, that I would accept so little in return. I'm ashamed of me, for being so weak. For loving too hard. Too much. If you only knew, yet you do know, how much I truly, and I mean truly, truly love you.

If you want another woman, get one. But I'll tell you now, and it may sound corny, but you'll never, never, ever in a lifetime ever **feel a love like mine.**

My life is important to me. Life is short. I want to be happy. After twenty-one years of being faithful to two men, I deserve more than this. I need more than sexual fulfillment, I need your unconditional love. Otherwise, I cannot remain in this relationship. It's time I put my needs first, because God knows, no one else has. . . .

He turned up the volume on the radio, switching it to a soul station. Mood music. Yes, that was what he needed, relaxing music before he faced Ginger for the first time since she left him. In the beginning, he was bitter. He'd hated her for leaving. For taking his daughter away from him. For making everything they'd worked for together meaningless.

But she'd taken none of the antique furnishings she loved so much. Her office was the only vacant room in the house. And then he wondered.

"Who is it?" asked Ginger, checking the clock in the kitchen. It couldn't be Kim this late. Maybe it was Ivory. He'd called and asked if he could come over and bring a carton of eggnog to share with her. She wanted to say yes, but she worried about the kids waking up and seeing a man in the house other than Jackson. Knowing it was too soon for them to see other men around, no matter how innocent the situation, she put her loneliness aside for their sake.

There was a short pause before a deep voice answered, "Jackson."

Ginger was at a loss for words. He was the last person she expected to see tonight. "Just a minute," she said, her voice losing its drowsy tone. She ran into the bedroom. Out of breath, she retied the scarf on her head, snatching a quick glance at herself in the hallway mirror. She sucked in her breath, and opened the door.

Everything was silent, and yet more silent. Ginger felt a secret sensation between the silent beauty of his lanky frame as he stood outside the door. "Hoped I'd finally catch you in." He smiled. They both felt uneasy, saying nothing as their eyes finally met. Shifting her body, she moved back to let him enter the apartment.

A twelve-foot white-flocked Christmas tree was covered with hundreds of pink blinking lights, which were reflected in the floor-to-ceiling windows. Ginger noticed Jackson's raised eyebrow as he viewed her version of a white Christmas. She'd finally gotten her flocked tree. Funny, it was beautiful. Hating fake trees, he'd always managed to talk her out of it before. An expensive leather golf bag and clubs were the only presents left under the tree. Jackson assumed that Ginger had decided to use golf to network.

I should've known she'd be living in a place like this. Must cost a fortune, Jackson thought. His eyes took in everything, from the raspberry suede chairs to the expensive paintings on the walls. "Nice place," he commented.

Extending her arm toward the expansive chintz sofa, she

offered him a seat. She sat across from him, easing back in the plush chair. "It's a little late, Jackson. Couldn't you have made your visit earlier, when Autumn was awake? She's been asking for you. Wondering why her daddy missed giving her a Christmas present."

If she had been home where she belonged, she'd have gotten her present on time. "I've called you several times, Ginger. You're never at home."

"I didn't get any messages."

A stern look crossed his face before he answered. "I didn't leave any." Avoiding her stare, his short nails made a *whht* sound as he raked his fingers back and forth across the smooth chintz. Then, turning back to stare at her, he rested his outstretched arms along the back of the sofa. "Been home—"

"Mississippi?" asked Ginger, rising to fix herself a cup of Lipton. "Like any tea or coffee?"

"No. I'll have a—"

"Diet Pepsi, I know." Ginger poured his drink, explaining that she kept some around for Kim. She put on a CD to break the silence that had overtaken their strained conversation.

He felt as though he should explain his impromptu trip south, which had caused him to miss his daughter's first Christmas away from home. He told Ginger that his mother had been in a car accident. No one else could get away, because of the holidays, and there had to be a relative present to sign the papers for them to operate.

"How's she doing, Jackson?" Ginger's heart fluttered. She felt the tears welling in her eyes as she thought of not ever seeing Mrs. Montgomery again. For some reason, she always felt that they would get together one day, and Ginger would make up for her resentment of all the years. She would explain that it wasn't because she didn't love her as a mother-in-law, but was simply jealous of how much Jackson loved her.

"As well as expected," Jackson answered, unzipping his leather jacket and cinching back the creases in his black jeans. "I came here to talk about you and me, though, not my mother."

Ginger almost choked on her tea. The cup rattled against

the saucer as she nervously placed it on the coffee table. The disc player changed to Peabo Bryson's "Reaching for the Sky": "Love, it's not the first time for us. We've both been there before."

Ginger felt goose bumps rising on her arms. She said quietly, "What more is there to say, Jackson? You made yourself clear. My career or you." Suddenly her mouth felt as dry as sandpaper as she continued, "As you can see, I've made my decision."

"Love may never come again. I'll be your lover and your friend. . . ." the song continued.

He rubbed his large palms against the rough denim fabric. "I'm sorry, Ginger. I was all wrong. But right or wrong, I don't blame you. I'm sorry. Can't we forgive and forget and start again?" The plea in his voice rocked the doors of Ginger's heart.

"Time, to look ahead and leave the past behind. If it's love you're searching for."

Lowering her head, she avoided his teary hazel eyes. "I'm sorry, Jackson. We've been through this too many times before. It's always the same old thing. You're sorry, we make up, we screw, and then we fight all over again about the same problems we had before we made up. It's a merry-go-round that I'm tired of riding."

"You won't stop the divorce and give me another chance?" Jackson's voice started to crack. His lips trembled slightly as he avoided her eyes, hoping she wouldn't see the tears. He'd almost broken down, given her a peep through the keyhole at his inner man. He left hurriedly instead.

Later, Ginger lay in her bedroom, alone, silent tears streaming down her face. *My arms around my pillow at night should be holding you,* her thoughts told Jackson. *I'm missing you now.*

Robert Earl inserted his key in the front-door lock. It had been a little over three years since he'd been home. The place looked a little newer, a little homier. A pleased smile spread across his face as he walked boldly into the living room, throwing his duffel bag and coat in a pile in the middle of the floor.

Robert Earl hadn't mentioned in his letters to Mae Thelma that he'd be home by the end of December instead of on his original January release date. He didn't believe his wife was capable of adultery. But he'd been gone nearly three years. His gut instincts knew that was a long time for any woman, no matter how saved, to be without a man.

"Mae," he called out softly. "Mae. It's me." Silence. The skin across his chest felt as tight as a sausage casing as he walked slowly down the hall.

Peeking into the boys' bedroom, he saw that they were soundly asleep. Robert Earl Jr. lay spread-eagled on the bed in his Batman pajamas, his mouth wide open. David Earl lay on his side, sucking his thumb, in a fetal position.

He ambled down the hall, stopping in front of the bedroom door that he had shut tightly and locked behind him on many a passionate evening. Slowly, he pushed it open, calling out Mae Thelma's name in hushed tones. He stopped, seeing the slice of golden light coming from beneath the bathroom door. Slowly, he approached it, pushing it open.

Shock and disbelief made him drop his bottom lip lower than gravity could have pulled it. Mae Thelma, eyes closed, sat naked in the middle of the tub, her knees raised and spread open. Red scented candles burned low in the darkened room. Tiptoeing in closer, he saw his wife's fingers probing in and out of her vagina as the other hand fondled her breasts. Her moans became louder as she reached a climax.

"Mae? Mae Thelma, what the hell are you doing?" Her eyes flew open as she let out a brief scream. Her body tensed for a moment before she realized that this was none other than her husband. She turned her head slowly toward him in shame.

But before she could answer, he lifted her wet body from the heated water and threw her onto their bed. Crawling backwards on her elbows and heels, she watched as he stripped naked. He carried his hardened organ like a prize as he stood before her. "This is what you want, ain't it?" He pushed himself into the delta of her womanhood. No foreplay was needed. "Tell me this is what you been needin','" said Robert Earl, stroking and panting as they climaxed together.

Mae Thelma smiled, stroking her husband's face; Jackson's handsome face was receding fast from her imagination. She saw only the handsome face of her beloved . . . Robert Earl Collins, Sr.

"Come on baby!" Ginger screamed. "Shoot, Autumn. Shoot it!" Sierra was grabbing her mother and jumping up and down with excitement as they watched Autumn play her first basketball game. In the gymnasium of Hampton Middle School, Leopards fans cheered the young girls' basketball team on to victory over their opponents, the Jesuit Elementary Mavericks. Katherine pointed out to Ginger how Autumn's hard chocolate legs looked in her red-and-white uniform. Ginger said, "They're going to look just like her daddy's. Gorgeous." Autumn's expression was serious. She ignored the crowd, knowing her family was out there rooting for her, concentrating on the game. Playing the center position, she was the second-highest scorer on their team.

Ginger, watching Autumn dribble the ball, could just imagine Jackson at his first game, watching the other players with the same intensity on his face as Autumn's. She was his mirror image. He should be here now, watching his daughter, thought Ginger.

But Jackson was there, sitting at the top of the bleachers, proudly watching his daughter.

After his last conversation with Ginger, Jackson knew that she still wasn't ready to forgive him and put a halt to the divorce proceedings. Yet in his heart he truly couldn't blame her. He could see now that he'd been a fool. All his doubts and suspicions about Ginger seemed so frivolous now. It was incomprehensible to him, now, how he'd allowed a fabricated conception to corrode their marriage. In truth, he felt he really didn't deserve her love.

In convincing himself that she was guilty of infidelity, he had caused her so much unnecessary suffering. Who could blame her for leaving? But he knew, knew that she would always love him, as he would her. It was almost as though he were being pulled back to her by a force within him.

Nearing the final seconds of the game, Jackson watched his daughter standing on the sidelines listening to the final instructions from her coach before reentering the game. The Leopards and Mavericks were tied at 45 to 45.

The Mavericks were in possession of the ball, but midway down the court, one of the Leopards reached in and stole the ball, then passed it back to Autumn.

Jackson stood up, screaming, "Go, baby!"

Autumn dribbled the ball expertly with her right hand, then her left, toward their basket. The Mavericks ran dead on her trail. On her right was a guard; coming close behind, the center. Unsure which way to turn, Autumn dribbled, contemplating her next move.

"Head-fake, Autumn. Do it like Daddy showed you!"

Autumn spun to her left, then did a head-fake simultaneously with a crossover dribble. On her tiptoes she shot a perfect two-hand set shot, but was pushed from behind and fouled. The ball circled the rim three times, then fell off, as the crowd groaned.

The referee held up two fingers.

Standing at the free-throw line, Autumn planted her feet, took a deep breath, and shot. It missed.

The crowd was on its feet. Everyone screamed.

Autumn turned around to look for her mother. After seeing the victory in her mother's eyes, she turned back around and aimed.

Autumn scored the winning basket of the game. Afterwards, she ran to her mother, overcome with emotion and tears. Watching his child rubbing her nose against her mother's and seeing their unabashed display of love, Jackson realized how much he missed that closeness. He knew he wanted his family together again, no matter what the cost. It was then, as he watched his daughter, stepdaughter, stepson, and wife enjoying a happy time without him, that he decided to make some positive changes in his life.

Jackson tapped the baseboard in the hallway of Ginger's apartment with his gym shoe as he stood ringing the doorbell. Ginger, not even asking who it was, opened the door, beaming with pride.

"Can I come in? I'd like to see Autumn," Jackson said. He heard the sound of Autumn's voice as Ginger pointed to his daughter, who was on the telephone.

"She's been on the phone for hours, talking about the game." Ginger signaled to her popular daughter that her father was here. Sierra ran into the room to hug Jackson before Autumn made her excuses and hung up the phone.

"Hi, Monk." Sierra kissed him on the cheek, jumping up on his lap, wrapping her model-thin arms around his neck. "You should've seen Autumn today at the game. She scored ten points."

"Jackson, do you want a glass of brandy or something? I don't have any Diet Pepsi," Ginger said, poking her head inside the refrigerator.

"No. Nothing. Just want to see my girls."

Christian tore himself away from his Sega Genesis CD when he heard the sound of Jackson's voice. "It's good to see you, Jackson," said Christian, shaking his hand. He seemed so much older to Jackson, having acquired a trim mustache and added a few muscles to his compact physique. "You look like the man of the family, Christian." The words had burned on his lips as he wished he could have snatched them back—yet he was too late. Christian smiled, knowingly, and Jackson felt an inner defeat.

The mood was gay, everyone happy. They played checkers. They played Wheel of Fortune. Then finally, they played Scattergories, Christian's favorite. Jackson, who dreaded going home to their large, empty house, had done everything to prolong his visit. After Autumn had fallen asleep on the couch, Ginger agreed to let him change her into her pajamas and put her to bed, something he hadn't done in a long time. Something he missed. The older kids both bid him good night, Sierra with a kiss and hug, and Christian with a strong handshake and a last-minute man-to-man hug. Jackson was moved by his affection.

Jackson looked at Ginger as he hesitantly took his jacket from the front closet. He saw the tender look in her eyes, and neither said anything. They fell into each other's arms, kissing away months of pent-up desire.

"I love you Ginger. I miss you."

"I know, Jackson." She also knew that she was horny as hell and needed a piece. Yet she missed him, and the companionship they once shared as man and wife. Each day she had died a little more knowing their love was slowly slipping away from them. Ginger missed him more each night, especially when she realized that their last night together might have been just that. She wanted to show him that she wasn't really like that, that she wasn't a whore. But Jackson covered her mouth with kisses before she could tell him.

Jackson ripped Ginger's blouse as they fell into the bed. He whispered he'd buy her a new one as they struggled to free each other of their clothing. "Baby, baby. I need you, baby," said Jackson as he kissed her lips.

"Make love to me, Jackson. Hard. Now." Ginger pulled him down with her into the cool cotton sheets. She clasped her hands over his swollen manhood, massaging it gently, as short breaths of heated desire escaped her lips.

He kissed her breasts, licked the tips until they became swollen and hard, as he rotated his hips to her skillful hands. Thick, clear juice oozed down his penis, coating Ginger's hand. There was no shame or modesty between them. She guided him into her moist softness. A sigh of relief escaped both of their mouths, and Jackson sank deep within her. She arched her back, and drove her hips upwards to meet his. Moans of pleasure were uttered between stolen kisses. As sensual as wet moonlight licking an ocean's naked waves, their premature climax was expected, and welcomed.

Before Ginger had caught her breath, Jackson had already recovered and was stroking her vagina with his fingers. Flicking his fingers back and forth over her quivering clitoris, her tiny jewel began to spread open like a blooming flower. The lips of her vagina were eagerly opening and closing on their own. She pressed her buttocks into the curve of his body, her love muscle grabbed and sucked in the length of him. Her sweat-drenched, smooth vagina, void of hair, rubbed against the curly black mound spreading at the root of his sex.

Surprise registered on Jackson's face when he felt Ginger lathering and cleaning his sex. No words were needed as Ginger finished their special ritual.

"Baby, I think you and the kids should move back home tomorrow. We've got a lot of—"

Elevating her body on her elbows, she swallowed hard. "Do you think just because we had sex that everything is just peachy keen between us?"

"We love each other. What more is it?"

Ginger pounced from the bed, boldly standing naked before him. "Do you think just because we're in love, that that's all there is to a marriage? Ordinary people who love each other divorce every day. It takes more than love—it takes compromise. Love hasn't got a damn thing to do with two people being able to live with each other."

"Ginger. We don't have to do this."

"Do what? Just fuck and make up like we always do? I'm sorry, that doesn't work for me anymore, Jackson. I need to know that you trust me. It's important."

Jackson mumbled something under his breath that Ginger was unable to discern.

"Have I ever questioned you about being at Mae Thelma's house in the middle of the night?"

"What?"

"What were you doing at one o'clock in the morning—having Bible study?"

"Not this shit again," Jackson mumbled. Ginger cried, while Jackson quickly dressed, hollering over his shoulder, "I thought you'd grown up. I see you haven't changed a bit." He walked out of the room and slammed the door behind him.

Ginger fell on the floor, covering her head with her hands, clamping them tightly against the bare flesh covering her brain. "Why, Lord, did you make me love him so much, so he could hurt me so bad?" A silent scream escaped from her mouth, as she cradled herself. Her body convulsed in jagged spasms.

Kim finally made progress with her therapy, having accepted and forgiven herself for her past indiscretions. The therapist told her that the key to getting well lay in forgiveness and loving yourself enough to stop the pain of guilt. She must be willing to look honestly at her life, no matter how sordid.

The therapist also explained that there is a difference between feeling better—which can occur as soon as the physical body heals itself—and *getting* better, which results from systematically and faithfully reapplying simple yet effective mood-control techniques.

Ultimately, united in love and strength, Kim and Bill were able to make plans for another wedding. Smaller. And the slow undertaking of renewing their sexual closeness. Bill had cleaned the ghosts from his closet, admitting again to Kim about his tortured past, when his vengeance against God had begun, after losing his son and mother. He'd gotten on his knees and prayed while Kim was in the hospital. There had been nothing else he could do but pray. He prayed to God that she would make it through the operation and live, and she had.

Bill and Kim's relationship couldn't have been stronger. Her botched attempt to take her life and to hide her shame from the man she loved had turned into a blessing for both of them. Each made a vow to visit church regularly and to give God another chance. Ginger cried openly when she heard Bill's confession about the Lord. She was moved beyond words, and began looking at her own faith—her devotion to God.

For years Ginger wondered, Is God, shaping, molding, or polishing me right now? Am I praising and thanking God, or am I complaining about the process? She was told by her pastor to read II Corinthians 4:17: "Our light affliction . . . is working for us a far more exceeding and eternal weight of glory." It made so much sense. Her heart felt peace. She'd entrusted her soul to a power that was greater than Man.

On Sunday, the seventeenth of January, Kim, Bill, Ginger, and her three children attended Faith Methodist Church and bared their souls and hearts at the rail of the altar, where they confessed their sins and asked for forgiveness.

34

You're My Everything

The New Year brought Jackson, a nonbeliever in resolutions, to affirm that he and his wife and family would be back together soon. He phoned Ginger and the kids each night before bedtime. He told them he loved them and would see them soon. Jackson attended church faithfully every Sunday at the Church of Christ. He felt better. Gave up the alcohol. Started doing work around the house. These were things that Ginger had asked him to do years ago, but he'd never seemed to find the time to do them.

By February, Jackson began to feel his attitude change. He was no longer angry. By the time the March winds hit, Jackson felt a spiritual warmth touching his soul. And now, as April rained in, his heart was open to receive God's blessings.

Jackson felt God's voice at work, at home, in the car, and, unsurprisingly, he found himself saying on that bountiful Sunday morning, "Lord, I'm ready." And the Lord walked right in.

"Hello, Mama. It's Jackson. I was saved at church today."

"Praise the Lord, son. Thank you, Jesus. My prayers have been answered," said Hattie B. Montgomery. Her muffled cries were heard over the receiver. Jackson could hear the tissue crinkling as his mother wiped her tearful eyes.

"Thank you Jesus," said Jackson humbly. His voice broke as he clamped his hand over his mouth, whispering a prayer to himself, remembering the words of God. The words that had saved and sanctified him, filling him with the Holy Ghost.

"Praise God, son. Everything's gonna be fine. Just fine. I know you been having troubles lately. But the Lord is who you take your troubles to. You put them in God's hands. He'll know what to do. You pray. Don't be afraid to get down on your knees and praise Him, son. He'll hear you and answer all your prayers."

Opening the windows, Jackson let the clean spring air flow freely over his face. The sun was hot, the breeze cool. A wave of living sweetness drifted into the room, ruffling the white petals of apple blossom trees below. This was his favorite month of the year. April was like a long-awaited visitor who came to town with his yearly springtime show.

He could see the figure of a bluebird with the sun on its feathers, tilting its head, seemingly observing a man with his head peeping out the window. Stepping back, he inhaled, cradling the phone beneath his chin. "I'm praying for my family, Mama. I know you're praying for us too."

He sat in the chair in the living room, staring at the blank television screen. Usually at this time of day he'd be well into his third or fourth Western. Somehow the tales of the old West didn't interest him now. He was coming face-to-face with the truth: The Dummy Box, as Ginger had called it, had taken so much time away from his family.

Jackson's attention was brought back to his mother by the sound of her voice. "Yes, Lord," said Hattie B., "when the Lord comes to take us to Heaven, when He comes back to claim His people, you have to be prepared. Got to get your reservations. Get your ticket early. And there ain't no discounts either. Yes, Lord, He'll soon be calling us all home."

*   *   *

Exhausted, Ginger fell in a heap on the floor in front of the sofa. Her first golf lesson was over, and by her estimations, it might well be her last. Ginger hadn't guessed that walking around the golf course would take so much energy. Yet the people she'd met at the outdoor clubhouse at the Palmer Woods Golf Club Association were perfectly down to earth and polite. Informal meetings with clients or potential clients were being held all over the eighteen-hole course. It was as casual and natural as the robins taking a cool drink of water from a birdbath. She'd have to learn.

Two weeks later, her friend Ivory Michaels asked her to meet him at the golf club. Ginger had been thinking so much about Jackson lately that she needed a diversion, so she half-heartedly accepted. Driving down Seven Mile Road, she could see her English Tudor home through the sparsely leafed trees in the park entering the subdivision. Since she'd left home, Ginger avoided driving on Berkshire Drive whenever she showed homes in the area.

While they sat drinking beverages after only nine holes— Ginger couldn't make eighteen—she thought of her home again, the home that she and Jackson had shared for nearly ten years. Somehow the painful memories had faded, and her thoughts about the times spent there were only comforting, loving ones.

"It's so beautiful there this time of year, Ginger," said Ivory. He wore short white golfing shorts with three-inch splits on the sides. A white cable-knit sweater trimmed in a front V with burgundy-and-navy-blue stripes covered his navy polo shirt.

Ginger studied his golden hairy thighs. He looked like the kind of man many a woman would imagine as their ideal. "Paris?" asked Ginger. He nodded. "I've never been there," she admitted sullenly. "I always dreamed that one day I'd visit." With Jackson, she thought to herself.

She smoothed the short skirt over her red gingham two-piece tennis suit. Her mother had found the vintage outfit at a resale shop and bought it, knowing how much Ginger treasured clothing from expensive stores, like Saks and Neiman Marcus, that were still in excellent condition, clothing that was lovingly cared for by the previous owners.

Taking Ginger by the hand, Ivory pulled her up, suggesting that they walk along the course for a bit before leaving. When they had reached a secluded area, surrounded by trees, Ivory looked at her and gave her his megawatt smile. His gray-blue eyes sparkled in the midafternoon sun.

He seemed to look right through her, his eyes pooled to an almost silver shade of gray. "I left something there—it's the reason I've decided to move."

"You're moving to Paris? What about your—"

"Job?" He arched an eyebrow as a train of golf carts passed. "I've secured a position at CNN in Paris. Doesn't pay as well. But I'll make it."

"What about your daughter, Liberty?"

"It took me a long time to accept that she'd be better off with her mother. I've been deluding myself into thinking I could be a better parent. I was wrong. She loves her mother dearly, as I did many years ago."

"And you've never considered remarriage?" asked Ginger, walking beside him as they made their way back to the clubhouse.

"You probably wouldn't understand; it was difficult for me to accept it at first, but I'm in love with another man. Since he left, I've experienced a kind of slow death. Truly, it isn't the sexual intimacy that we share that has ultimately united us, but respect." He paused and looked at her for a moment. "With that kind of love who needs marriage," he said ironically.

"He lives in Paris?" Ginger tried hard to keep her balance. Was missing a man making her gullible to the first man she was attracted to? How would she survive out in the world? She couldn't even differentiate between a straight guy and a gay one. And to think that at one time she thought he'd desired her. She even thought for a while that she was beginning to feel something for him. Now she just felt stupid. Wait until she told Kim. She wouldn't believe it either.

"No, he lives in London. Right now the English Channel is going to separate us, because of our jobs. But he just submitted his resignation. He's making a good living as a full-time painter, which is what he loves to do." They stopped and picked up their golf bags at the clubhouse locker room.

"You might know him, he lived here a few years ago. His name is Ran—"

"Randall Pierce," she almost whispered. She felt as if she were a huge balloon, and someone had let out all the helium—slowly. She lifted her chin proudly. "Everyone's life seems to be changing lately. I've decided on making a few myself."

"What's all that noise downstairs, Mama?" asked Autumn. She was perched on the stool behind her mother, removing the tightly bound scarf from Ginger's head as she dialed the telephone. Autumn had elected herself to oil her mother's head nightly. Once a week, she happily cut and polished her mother's toenails. She knew how much her mom loved it.

Ginger greeted Katherine, covered the receiver, whispering to Autumn, "Kim's moving her daddy home in a few days. She and Bill are redecorating his room." They'd shopped together for the small objects before repainting, recarpeting, and buying new furniture. Bill had gotten rid of the hospital bed before Kim came home. The doctors reported that Ollie could sleep in a regular double bed.

The kids had gone for the weekend with their father, so Ginger and Autumn were by themselves again.

Katherine had recently turned sixty-one. And though time had been kind to her, she couldn't admit, not even to herself, that she was breaking. She'd cut her long hair to a fashionable short bob, and changed the color to a bold blondish red. After a strict diet, she'd lost twenty pounds, along with twenty years. Or so she told herself.

No one, especially those who loved her, had the heart to tell Katherine that the new look had actually aged her.

She was ready for a new man. Not too old, though, maybe forty-fourish. She was still Kate. And a warm-blooded woman such as herself couldn't end up in the arms of an old man.

Knowing she needed a change, she accepted her daughter LaWanda's invitation to come to California and help her with the boys. Her two sons had joined a gang, a dangerous one. And because LaWanda worked two jobs, she was unable to supervise them as much as she would like.

LaWanda assured Katherine that she would only need her help for a few months. And by the end of June, she would have saved enough money to buy her family a home and move from their apartment complex, where the gangs prevailed.

Katherine silently vowed that by the time she returned back to Michigan in the summer, she'd be wearing a brand-new husband for the warm weather. So, Katherine, in her reemergence to the beauty and passion of life, her life, decided to give her daughter that time.

"Yes, Mama. Everything's just fine here. Yes, I'm still going to church every Sunday. Giving all my problems to God." Ginger smiled as a calm peace filled her heart.

"I know Christian and Autumn are okay. It's Sierra I'm worried about."

Bending over, Ginger bopped Autumn in the head playfully. She'd slipped and smeared the thick cream over Ginger's eye. "Take your time," she said, grabbing a paper towel from the kitchen corner and cleaning her eye. "They dropped the charges, Mama. Apparently the Nobles just wanted to teach the kids a lesson. Problem is, the parents suffered more than the kids did."

"Praise the Lord," said Katherine, "my prayers have been answered."

"Mama, are you okay? I've never heard you talk like that before."

"Time for me to turn my life around. I ain't getting no younger, you know. LaWanda, me, and the kids all started going to church on Sundays." Then the old Katherine surfaced: "You know they got some mighty fine men in them churches. Probably make a good husband for LaWanda. She needs a man around them bad kids she's got. Can't hardly do nothing with them."

And we won't even mention you looking for a husband too. Huh, Mama? "So I guess you stopped drinking?"

"Can't give up everything right away. It's gonna take a little time, but I'm praying on it. You mark my words, by the end of the summer, my taste for alcohol is gonna be a thing of the past. Strongest thing I'll be drinking is orange and V8 juice."

"Hold on a minute, Mama." She didn't want Autumn to hear this part of their conversation. "Baby, can you go to your room and play with your Barbies for a few minutes, while Mama talks to Granny?" She waited a few moments until she heard the creaking of Autumn's toy box. "I'm back."

"Something wrong?"

"Not really, Mama. You were right about keeping my mouth shut in the bedroom. I blew it."

"What are you saying, Ginger? What did you tell Jackson?"

"About my attempted rape."

"When . . ."

"I told him last year, but it happened two years ago."

"Ginger! Wha—"

"Mama, it's more serious now. A young girl is dead. The same man that tried to rape me, raped her." Ginger told Katherine the entire story, from the accident she staged to cover up the assault to the trial scheduled in two months. Katherine felt the same way as Ginger did, that she should testify.

"I knew something was bothering you Christmas. You can't hide nothing from your Mama. You should know that by now. I'll fly in for the trial."

"Thanks, Mama. But you just left. The sexual assault counselor will be there with me. She's called and assured me that we have a good case. The prosecutor is sure he'll get a conviction. I won't even have to be inside the courtroom—just when I testify."

"I'll be there, Ginger."

"I love you, Mama."

"I love you too, baby."

Ginger said good-bye to her mother. She knew then that no matter how wonderful Mrs. Hattie B. Montgomery was as a mother, no matter how endeared she was to her children, Katherine was Ginger's hero. She was an icon. With all her imperfections, she was just what she needed to be—Ginger's mother. There could be no other.

"See, Mommy? I told you so." Autumn had climbed up on the vanity to look in the mirror, as her mother scooted back, holding a hand mirror in her right hand. Ginger closed her eyes for a second, thanking God for the miracle. Then, opening them again, she adjusted the mirror squarely before her, checking again to be certain. Sure enough, there was a black speckled spiral pattern on the crown of her head. Her body felt as if shooting sparks had ignited inside her.

It had been nearly three years, and up until now, there had been no signs of her hair growing back. With renewed faith she'd tried to accept the fact that it would never grow back . . . and now, now she was jubilant . . . ecstatic.

She cradled her daughter in her arms as they rubbed each other's noses, a chilled little button nose against a toasty, keen one. "Guess what, sweetheart. You've got a surprise coming too."

Autumn's eyes bulged as she turned to face the mirror, possessive arms still curling around her mother's neck. "What, Mommy?" asked Autumn cheerfully.

"Your bridge is coming." Ginger traced a line down the center of the child's angelic face. "See?" She pressed her cheek against her baby daughter's exuberant smile. They turned away from the mirror, hugging each other.

The phone interrupted their happy moment. "I'll get it, Mommy," said Autumn, trying to reach the phone before the answering machine caught it on the third ring, but Ginger beat her to it. Jackson had always changed the recordings on their answering machine, and Ginger never learned to do it right. She felt so uneasy about talking into the recorder that the message would always sound forced.

"Jason! It's so good to hear from you, sweetheart. I miss you." Ginger splayed her hand over her heart, rocking back and forth on the stool as she talked to her son. Autumn took her position again behind her mother, taking more time, carefully massaging her mother's scalp.

"I miss you and the kids too, Mama. I should be home by August. That's the month of the family reunion isn't it?"

"Yeah. I'm surprised you remembered. I didn't mention it that last time we talked. You doing okay way over there by yourself?"

"I'll be bringing someone with me, Mama. Is that okay with you?"

Autumn was begging to speak, nudging her mother's back with the bend of her bony knee. "Sure, sweetheart. Anyone special?" Before he could answer, Autumn grabbed the phone.

"Hi, Dink. I love you, Dink." Her pearly-toothed smile spread across her face as she filled in her brother on the latest happenings in Detroit. The new records, rap groups, teenage talk. Even though she was only eight years old, Autumn had more songs memorized than Sierra did, could dance like a member of the Soul Train dancers—and wiggled and rolled her behind like a Hawaiian hula dancer.

"Tell Sierra and Christian hi for me, Mama."

"I will, sweetheart."

"And tell Jackson I said hi the next time you see him."

"Jackson?" asked Ginger timidly.

"Didn't he tell you I wrote him a letter?"

"No." Ginger's mind raced like a fire engine. What had he said to him? Had Jackson written him back? What had he told Jason about them? Jason was speaking to her, but Ginger couldn't make out the words. When he paused she just said, "Um-hm, yeah."

"Mommy," said Autumn, breaking her thoughts. "You got gray hair on your head." She moved her head closer to Ginger's, her face inches away from her glistening scalp.

I don't care if it's purple, as long as it's hair, Ginger thought. She covered the receiver with her hand. "That's wisdom, sweetheart." She exhaled, her eyes scanning the huge kitchen, where there was a semicircle of cabinets. But unlike her white, high-gloss, painted cabinets at home, these were made of white Formica.

Ginger didn't know why, but she'd never felt comfortable in the kitchen since they'd moved there. She felt odd every time she entered into the ultramodern room. She seldom cooked because the kids preferred pizza and carry-out chicken, when Christian wasn't cooking his still famous fried chicken. It hadn't dawned on her yet that the reason the kitchen looked so unwelcoming to her was the fact that the cabinets were always closed.

After a long pause from Jason, Ginger said finally, "My hair's growing back, Jason. I saw it for the first time today."

Walking out of the real estate office, Jackson clutched the deed to a prime piece of property in Bloomfield that could be renovated into the real estate office Ginger had dreamed of. He hoped it would soon change his life for the better. The quality of his life. A life together with the woman he loved. Jackson even stopped in occasionally to visit with Kim.

Jackson signed up for the real estate classes offered onsite at Champion Motors. After work, he spent two weeks putting in the required forty hours of study before taking the exam. The first time he flunked, and his respect for Ginger grew. He hadn't anticipated that the test would be so difficult. He tried again, and passed. Jackson felt that it was important to show Ginger his dedication toward building a business together, which she'd always dreamed of.

They would open their own real estate agency, and work together. Jackson cashed in his stock, and made arrangements to look at a prime building for an office in Bloomfield Hills. After talking over Ginger's plan for her business with Little Bubba, he realized that she'd really come up with a novel idea.

She'd told him about her dreams so long and so many times that he had them memorized backwards. By the end of the summer she planned to open her own real estate firm: Montgomery's Real Estate & Service Corporation. But, unlike other real estate firms, hers would staff interior designers. Only one in the beginning—herself. More would be added at a later date. And she'd have carpenters, electricians, plumbers, drywallers, masons and painters on staff, as well.

Her business would focus on the Palmer Woods, Indian Village, Rosedale Park, and University area, homes built around 1920 to the early 1950s, homes that would require lots of repair work.

Ginger had told him how many times clients would ask for her opinion about redecorating their old homes and her ideas for updating them. So being an expert in the interior design and decorating business would allow her to help the buyer visualize how the home would look when remodeled, and motivate the buyer to purchase the property.

And since most of her potential clients were two-income families, her business would provide the service of making household repairs the homeowners were unable to do themselves. They'd even come over and change light bulbs on some of the homes that boasted forty- and fifty-foot ceilings, which usually required scaffolding.

Yes, it sounded like a winner—and he'd finally bought into it. Now he had to convince Ginger to include him in her dream.

Ginger tossed and turned in the queen-size, iron-canopied bed. A soft breeze blew through the ecru chiffon drapes under an open window. The embers of the last fire of the season furled from a trace of air seeping down the chimney. Ginger had always wanted a fireplace in the bedroom. The irony was, now she had the fireplace, but didn't have Jackson. How insignificant it all seemed when there was no one there to share it with.

Unable to sleep, she threw back the fluffy comforter, let her toes sink into the plush silvery carpeting, and headed for the kitchen. Filling the kettle with fresh water and putting it on the burner, she placed the teacup in front of the toaster. As she waited for the water to boil, she heard the pelts of rain splashing against the windows, and looked outside at the mournful sky. She felt tired and drained, yet she'd been unable to get an ounce of sleep.

Sitting at the small table, she sipped her tea, trying not to think of Jackson. Yet as hard as she tried to force his image from her mind, his hazel eyes seemed to taunt her everywhere she looked. Shaking her knee, she felt the tears slipping down her face. Looking up, she felt her body elevate, almost by itself. Calmly, she walked toward the cabinets, the tears flowing freer, as a small noise escaped her lips. Her body swerved, snatching, opening, pulling all the doors and drawers in the kitchen wide open. She fell to her knees as his name touched her lips: Jackson. . . .

* * *

The moonlight streamed through the windows, illuminating the canopied bed. As sleep finally came, Ginger snored lightly. Suddenly, her feet scrambled beneath her. She kicked the covers wildly, awaking, a light film of sweat coating her forehead. She reached out for him . . . and he wasn't there. Staring at the pillow where his head should be, she fell face forward into the softness, pounding her fists along the plump sides.

Her heart beat erratically as fear enveloped her. The fear of being alone, without him. Knowing she needed the love of God. But knowing she needed the love of Jackson, too. Knowing she missed all the things that nourished her love for him.

Knowing that when she got into his car, the seat would be pulled all the way back. Knowing that his shoes would be sitting on the middle of the landing every day. Knowing that when she walked into their bedroom in the evenings, that the television set would be tuned to the Western station, and he'd be half-asleep with the remote in his hand. Knowing he'd be there to reach for her in the darkness. Knowing that she needed him pulling her close to him, until they fell asleep—as she wanted him to do now, as she needed him to do now.

Yet Ginger knew in her heart that she had to face the truth: that though she loved Jackson desperately, she'd been unhappy during most of their marriage. And as much as it hurt, she had proven to herself that she could do it on her own, without him.

Jackson flicked on the television set, and the room took on a soft gray glow as the black-and-white movie flashed before him. An old segment of *Gunsmoke*. Miss Kitty sat at the bar, nursing a drink. Her trademark black mole caught his eye as she swirled around the bar stool to face the man in her life, Matt Dillon. Jackson felt a smile down inside him as he remembered Ginger's pet name, Miss Lilly.

Occasionally, Jackson teased Ginger about how sexy he thought Miss Kitty was. Ginger, in turn, thought she'd put on her own wild Wild West show, emerging from the bathroom wearing nothing but a pair of pink cowboy boots, stockings and garter belt, and . . . a holster hung low on her hips, with six-shooters balancing on each side. She'd fired the cap guns, blowing smoke into his eyes, interrupting his bang-bang, shoot-em-up Western. By the time the movie was over, he and Ginger had fired off a few shots of their own. God, he missed her. There was no one else like Ginger. There never would be again.

Knowing this, he never wanted to be without her again. Knowing he'd hear the hoarse, deep tone of her voice every day, hollering and nagging. Knowing he'd find her Lipton tea bags drying in saucers all over the kitchen sink. Knowing she'd burn her cooking half the time. Knowing she'd smell like Shower to Shower powder when she climbed in bed every night. Knowing she'd press her buttocks firmly into his abdomen every night. Knowing she'd give him the core of her womanhood, when he'd awaken her in the middle of the night for a moment of passion. Knowing he needed her beside him now. Only God knew how much he loved her. How much he needed the generosity of her love.

Shielding herself and Autumn from the downpour with a large umbrella as they ran into the church, Ginger smiled at the saints running in behind her. Brushing the silvery drops from their clothing, she and Autumn said thank you to the usher who handed them their Sunday pamphlet with the details of the morning's service.

Ginger was astounded at Robert Earl's invitation to come and visit Hope Memorial Church of Christ this Easter Sunday. Jackson had called Robert Earl, asking a favor. He knew Ginger would come by invitation of Robert Earl and Mae Thelma more surely than if he asked himself.

Ginger loved sitting near the front of the church. Autumn guided her mother to a vacant pew up there, near the stained-glass windows, scooting back in her seat to put a handful of mints in her mouth. They sat patiently, awaiting the beginning of the service.

The pastor stood before the pulpit and spoke to the congregation: "We also want to bid Sister Mae Thelma Collins and Brother Robert Earl Collins Sr. and their boys a farewell.

They're leaving this week. Moving back to their hometown of Guntown, Mississippi. Anybody ever heard of Guntown, Mississippi?

"We ask the saints to pray for their safe trip over the highway. We also want to congratulate Brother Robert Earl and his wife on their new blessings. Sister Mae Thelma is with child." A resounding cheer from the congregation caused Ginger to turn and view the happy couple. But she missed Jackson, who was sitting in the last pew.

Mae Thelma had donned a shimmering white triangle, draped loosely over her head. She wore a modest, white, midcalf-length dress. She'd promised Robert Earl she'd convert to the Moslem faith if he'd grant her a final wish and go to her old church with the family before they left for home. He agreed.

Before the pastor stood before the pulpit, he was already wiping the sweat from his forehead. It was neither hot nor warm. Ginger knew he was fired up for a "Glory Hallelujah" sermon.

"I'd like for you to open up your Bibles to Matthew 27:32. My text to you this afternoon will be on 'The Commitment to the Christian Journey.' " Sweat trickled down his forehead. He started rocking back on his heels, feeling the rhythm.

"And as they came out, they found a man of Cyrene, Simon by name: him they compelled to bear his cross. 'The Commitment to the Christian Journey.'

"The commitment I make is between me and my God. The commitment you make is between you and your God. So I can't look at you and presume to know what you are going through, what you should be doing, or where you should be doing it, or who you should be doing it with. *Mind your own business.*

"All I can do is what God told me to do. If I do what I am supposed to do, it is guaranteed to help. *Mind your own business.*

"Where God put me or what He tells me to do, or how He chooses to use me, it's not your business. So *mind your own business.*"

Ginger looked around at the other members of the congregation, who were all doing exactly the same thing, looking around at each other. But no one said a word.

"What God speaks in my ear is between me and God! Where I am led is between me and God. You can't look at me and decide for me what I should be doing. I can't look at you and decide for you what you should be doing.

"You don't know the load you are compelled to carry. We don't know the decisions you have to make. We don't know the sacrifices you have been required to make. We don't know what you've been through, who you've talked to, or who you have seen. We must continually remind ourselves who you are working for and who you are serving.

"Simon was doing what he had been compelled to do on his journey. Simon in doing what he was compelled, so doing he teaches us something. So what if I have to come behind you. So what if you have to follow me. So what if you seem to walk lightly with empty hands while my steps are heavy and my hands are full. So what if we are called to do the dirty work. So what if nobody calls our names.

"How much more difficult could it be for us than it was for Simon? How much more could we suffer than Jesus suffered? We must keep things in perspective. Jesus was doing what He had been led to do.

"He wasn't just doing a job. He wasn't just out for reward or recognition. He wasn't looking for pay or promotion. He was honoring a *commitment*. He was about to die on the Cross!"

Ginger felt a pain, as if her heart had been seared. Even Autumn was still, absorbed in the pastor's sermon. Somehow she knew that he was saying some truths that she needed to hear. She leaned forward on the edge of the pew, concentrating on his every word.

"What do you really know about the Cross? To you, the Cross is a piece of jewelry, a trinket to put on a key chain, an ornament to put somewhere on a wall, a piece of wood that reminds you of Good Friday.

"To you, it's a hard way to go, it's difficulty in your life, some deficiency, some handicap, some thorn in your flesh, some person you have to put up with, some hardship you must face. This is the cross you know. But do you know what Jesus meant when He said, 'Pick up your cross'? He is talking about shouldering your weight, accepting your share of responsibility, carrying your load, bearing your burden, without grumbling, questioning, or complaining.

"Notice that there is no dialogue between Jesus and Simon. Notice that there was no reply from Simon when compelled to stop what he was doing and carry that Cross. Simon said nothing. He just did it!"

Pastor Washington lifted the folds of his robe, shouting, "Glory! Glory!" The men and women rejoiced, shouting amens. He shook his head from left to right, his face downcast. "Y'all don't know what I'm talking about." The organist backed up the commemorable colloquy with a subtle accompaniment.

A woman stood, clutching her Bible to her bosom. "Glory. Glory be to God." Pastor Washington felt that he was getting through. He continued:

"We need more of the 'Just do it' attitude in the church and in the world. Call a meeting, just do it. Cook the food, just do it. Sing in the choir, just do it. Pray in public, just do it. Be on time for worship, just do it. Tithing, just do it. Shut your mouth, just do it.

"Jesus said pick up your cross. Bear your own cross. He's talking to you. Others see the cross and step over it and keep on going. But you, Christian, you have got to pick it up and bear it. Have you ever handled the cross? Some of us are just now reaching out to touch it. Some of us have been stooped over for years, trying to get a grip on it; we can't straighten up. For some of us, it slips right through our hands. It becomes so heavy that we drop it.

"When it comes time to pick up the cross, sometimes our knees buckle, our determination grows weak, and commitment wavers. The cross is never easy to pick up even with the crowd standing by, and to make the lonely journey to Calvary with it, bearing down on us may be more than we can handle.

"This is where your Simon enters. I must help you. You must help me. I cannot see you struggling and not stop to help. You cannot see me in distress and not offer to at least dry my tears.

"Simon followed Jesus carrying the Cross. On our journey to commitment, follow Jesus. You may not know where you will end up, but follow Jesus. You may not feel like it, but follow Jesus. You may not be prepared for it, but follow Jesus. The call may come while you're doing something that you want to do, but just have faith and follow Jesus!"

Ginger stood, clapping her hands, tears of exaltation slipping down her face. More than half the church audience were on their feet, applauding the sermon. The power of God ricocheted through them and back into the pastor, fueling him to carry on.

"You may wonder why the word *compelled* is used. Simon was 'forced' into helping Jesus. He was not recruited. He did not campaign for the position. He was not appointed or sent. He was forced. The Roman soldiers compelled Simon to follow Jesus. Paul used the same word when he wrote in II Corinthians 5:14, 'For the love of Christ constrains me.' *Constrains* means to compel.

"We, too, are compelled because of the love of Jesus. The Christian journey is a walk of love. We don't do it because we want to, we do it because we love God. And that love compels us. It forces us to do right, to love right, to live right, to act right. To make us love our enemies. The love of Christ makes us commit to the imperative to pick up our cross and follow Jesus."

"Yes Lord," said Ginger, joining in on the chorus of the congregation. Cries of "Amen" and "Thank you Jesus" flowed on the tongues of the parishioners. Each soul stood, eagerly testifying to the power of God filling them.

"Sometimes the Cross will get in our way. Sometimes we want to party, but there's the Cross. Sometimes we want to drink and smoke, but there's the Cross. Sometimes we want to get even, but there's the Cross.

"When we talk about Christian commitment, we are talking about Cross-bearing. Not just any cross, but the Cross of Jesus. When I survey the wondrous Cross on which the Prince of Glory died, my richest gain I count but loss, and pour contempt on all my pride.

"Simon carried the Cross for Jesus, then somebody took it from Simon. Somebody will help you carry your cross. God's got a Simon standing in the way. There's Simon's grace: 'My grace is sufficient for you.' There's Simon's mercy: 'Surely goodness and mercy shall follow me all the days of my life.' There's Simon's truth: 'And the truth shall set you free.'

"When we make a commitment, we can't look back. Whatever you commit your hand to do, do it with all your might, all your heart, all your soul.

"If it's to sing, sing 'til the angels get happy. If it's to pray, pray 'til deliverance comes. If it's to shout, shout the harvest over. If it's to preach, preach them to heaven. Whatever you start out to do, give it all you got."

"Please Lord, help me." Eyes closed, head bent, Ginger prayed with all her might that the good Lord was listening. "I feel, Lord, that I'm imprisoned with golden shackles—I'm not able to give birth to the things in life that I feel are important to my survival. I'm chained to Jackson's promises. Chained to the delusions of his selfish love. Free me, Lord, so that I can soar and fly. Free me of the golden shackles that have entrapped me."

"Keep on going. Take the Cross. There's joy in the Lord. There's power in His blood. There's glory in the Cross," Pastor Washington continued.

"When I am weak, He makes me strong. When I am down, He lifts me up. When I am suffering, He gives me a song.

"I'll bear it, yes I will. I'm going to take it; I'm going to preach it; I'm going to tell it; I'm going to sing it; I'm going to shout it.

"Yes I will cling to the old rugged Cross, and exchange it someday for a crown. *Amen!*"

Drenched, soaked in sweat, the Reverend Washington uplifted his arms to a standing ovation. An exaltation of the spirit. A cleansing of the soul. Shameless tears streamed down the faces of men as well as their wives. They shouted amens and praised the pastor's volcanic sermon. This Easter Sunday, Jesus was surely present in the hearts and minds of those who loved him.

As the service neared a close, Ginger heard the pastor giving the final prayer, blessing the souls in the church and those who were sick at home, unable to attend. Ginger said a special prayer for Ri-Va, then mouthed to herself the prayer she loved: "Thou art coming to a King; large petitions with thee bring, for his grace and powers are such, none can ever ask too much."

Love and forgiveness. If you don't have those two qualities within you, you're missing something, Ginger observed silently. As she watched Mae Thelma and Robert Earl gather their boys and head out of the church, she could see the love they both had for each other. Mae Thelma's face lit up as her husband placed his arm around her shoulder.

The rain had relented outside. And, as if on cue, the sun made its debut, streaming the radiant colors of the rainbow through the windows. A brilliant yellow butterfly with iridescent blues and greens coating its wings fluttered against the clear pane. Autumn tugged at Ginger's elbow. "Mommy, did you see Daddy?"

"No." Ginger scanned the church, her heart suddenly beating wildly. "Are you sure you saw Daddy, sweetheart? The church was pretty crowded today."

"It was Daddy, Mommy. He gave me the sign."

"What sign?" Ginger asked, confused.

Ginger took Autumn by the hand and they ventured out into the crowded aisle toward the back door. "It's our secret code, our secret."

"You keep secrets from Mommy?"

"Sometimes."

When Ginger exited the church, the fresh air kissed her cheeks. The clear sky was an effervescent crystal blue. Walking toward the van, she and Autumn passed budding rosettes of plants circling the ground. Small beads of rain still clung to the tender blossoms.

She hesitated a moment, musing over the clear pink, sweet alyssum. The luscious perennial landscape reminded Ginger that her oriental garden would be almost blooming back at home.

Standing beside the minivan, Ginger and Autumn stood looking and waiting, waving good-bye as friends boarded their cars and drove away. A gentle breeze caressed the folds of her dress. Golden rays of sunlight suddenly painted the air.

Autumn's white-gloved finger pressed into her cheek. "Where is he, Mommy?" she asked adamantly.

"Let's go, Autumn. If he were here, he would have found us by now." Ginger tried her best to hide her disappointment as she suggested to Autumn that maybe they'd call Daddy when they got home.

"I'm sorry, sweetheart," Ginger said, taking her eyes off the road for a second. "What did you say?"

Driving home from the church, Ginger could hear the sounds of motorcycles. She could tell now, without Jackson's coaching, the purr of a Harley from the hum of a Kawasaki or the roar of a Honda. She thought of him, sleek on his Harley. How she missed his wisdom, his knowledge, his maturity, his quiet knowing.

The memory of her last ride with Jackson was as clear as the sky above. She remembered the freedom of holding her head back, feeling the wind blow over her face. Beholding the magnificence of an orange ball merging with the darkening gray sky.

"There's a package in the backseat," announced Autumn, pointing back to a box wrapped in brown paper. "Can I get it?"

"Wait till we get home, baby. We're almost there."

Once they were inside their apartment, Ginger couldn't wait to open the box addressed to her. She could tell the handwriting was Jackson's, and her breath threatened to stop as she tore away at the paper. Autumn had been right. He *was* at church today.

When Ginger opened the top of the box, she found an envelope taped on top of the tissue paper along with a deed to a commercial building. The note read: *Ginger, An invitation to "Miss Lilly" for a private viewing of an old Western.* The Man Who Loved Cat Dancing. *Talk show during intermission. Forgive me for not believing in you—in the strength of our love. I love and respect you. Please allow me the privilege of showing you how much. Again, I love you. "Bronco Billy."*

Tears flowed down her cheeks as she opened the tissue paper. Inside were her worn, pink leather cowboy boots.

There was another smaller note saying: *I know your feet must be tired because you been running through my mind for months.*

Ginger's conflicting feelings tore at her chest. It was more than a loving gesture. But Jackson still didn't understand that in giving her the deed to a property, he'd neglected to allow her the privilege of accomplishing something independently. She knew that she needed to prove to herself that she was capable of creating her own future. Why was it so hard for him to understand that?

Autumn peeked at the scarred pink boots inside the box, checking to see if there was something inside for her, oblivious to her mother's dilemma.

The phone rang, interrupting Ginger's thoughts. She hesitated, knowing it was Jackson. And knowing that nothing had really changed between them.

The ringing persisted. Autumn looked up from the box to see her mommy crying, knowing something was wrong. The sorrow she saw in her mother's face was a mixture of tenderness and truth. Autumn kept silent, and waited.

Scared that if the phone stopped ringing, it wouldn't ring anymore, Ginger picked it up, her smile bordered by a tear. Walking toward the beams of warm light that shone through the wall of glass, she placed her hand over the receiver, holding her breath, and heard a man speak her name. Fear tugged at her heart strings. Taking a deep breath, she exhaled slowly, hesitating once again. "Hello Jackson. . . ."

A single white butterfly floated past her view. Ginger pressed her hand against the window, watching its flight.

Please turn the page
for a sneak peak
from
Rosalyn McMillan's
new hardcover

One Better

Coming in October from
Warner Books

Spice

Children begin by loving their parents; as they grow older, they judge them; sometimes they forgive them.

—**Wilde**

Dozens of cars are lining up for the valet service at the corner of University Drive and Pine Street in downtown Rochester, Michigan. By 8:30 A.M. scores of BMW's, Mercedes, Lexuses and Acuras are being parked by the finest red-jacketed valets money can hire. By 8:50 A.M the lot is packed. Anyone new in town would think there was a party going on. Locals, however, know that 9:00 A.M. is when the five-star, multimillion-dollar gourmet restaurant, Southern Spice, opens for breakfast. Renowned for its superb southern cooking, it is considered one of the finest eating establishments in the States.

The four-story, 27,000-square-foot Victorian mansion which houses the restaurant had once contained sixty-three rooms and twenty-six bathrooms. Its gable roof is covered with decorative tiles in different shapes and colors. The same pattern of tiles is repeated above doorways and over the tops of the many bay windows. The steeply pitched roof, topped with pointed spires and turrets, adds to the Victorian opulence. Inscribed in beige into the brick, "Southern Spice" dominates the grand entranceway.

Once inside, the scintillating aromas from the kitchen have caused many a belly to rumble. Orange and pineapple juice are freshly squeezed every morning. Country-cured ham from Virginia, bacon with the rind on and egg-white shrimp

1

omelets with a tropical citrus butter sauce are some of the house favorites.

There is always something different on a menu that changes four times a year, in concert with the seasons. Southern Spice is elegant enough to serve Russian Seruga caviar, and down home enough to have fresh catfish for breakfast.

It is also a place where the Pistons' Grant Hill and Joe Dumars and legendary superstars like Aretha Franklin and Anita Baker can eat without being interrupted by people asking for their autographs.

"Rosa Parks, The Winans, Mayor Quincy Cole . . . hmmm," Spice said to her oldest friend, Carmen, as she perused the morning paper and sipped her coffee. "There's quite a few more black folks on the list this year."

Taking a break from preparing a celebratory brunch for her elder daughter, the restaurant's owner, Spice, was reading the list of the *Detroit News*' Michiganians of the Year. The list had begun in 1978, and for the third year in a row, Spice Witherspoon's name was on it. As one of the nation's leading restaurateurs, she had received numerous culinary, civic and philanthropic awards over the past ten years. She was especially proud of the fact that her efforts in the community were appreciated.

The two women were two floors above the restaurant in Spice's personal kitchen. Spice stood in the room's center, her smooth black hair pulled back into a pony tail that hung past the nape of her neck. Her tall, lithe body, kept supple by daily exercise, looked ten years younger than her forty-one years, especially shown off in a tight-fitting denim jumpsuit. But her best feature was her eyes. Her deep-set velvet-brown eyes appeared sleepy, but behind this facade of sweet drowsiness she was always utterly present. Spice was robust, in the full bloom of her life.

The left side of the huge room was a well-equipped commercial kitchen with a double glass-door Traulsen refrigerator, a $14,000 French La Cornue range and twin smoked-glass ovens. In the far corner sat a wide butcher's block curio cabinet that held an assortment of All-Clad pots and pans. Arranged along the cream-colored Corian counters above the

2

stained-glass–fronted cabinetry were various sizes of cutlery and the latest Cuisinart and mixers. A long island, with back to back twin black porcelain sinks and a wine rack underneath, was at the center of the room. On the right hand wall was an arched barbecue pit and brick fireplace where at the moment a low fire was scenting the air with hickory. Right next to it, floor-to-ceiling built-in shelves were filled with cookbooks.

By living upstairs in the converted mansion, Spice was able to stay close to work. The kitchen was her favorite room in the two-story duplex, carved and refurbished from fourteen of the mansion's original rooms. As Spice read the paper the aroma of smoking meat brought her mind back over a decade earlier to when her daughters were still in elementary school. Her favorite time of day was when she'd prepare them breakfast and then walk them to the bus stop on the corner.

Her elder daughter, Mink, was the straight-A student, the one with her daily homework assignments always ready for her mother to check and sign. Her younger daughter, Sterling, was another matter altogether. While her grades mirrored Mink's, her priority, even at age six, was always her appearance.

Only David, Spice's now deceased husband, thought Sterling's obsession with how she looked was cute. Everyone else saw it as saying a lot about Sterling's future character. And they were right.

At the thought of David Spice was thrown back to their wedding on June 9, 1972, at the courthouse in Midnight, Mississippi. David, at twenty-six, was eight years Spice's senior. Spice remembered how badly his hands were shaking as they stood before the judge.

"Having second thoughts?" she remembered asking him.

There were tears in his eyes when he answered her. "Of course not. I love you."

David had known that when she agreed to marry him, she hadn't been in love with him. With two small children, she had needed a husband, security and a home; David offered all three. And together they had worked to open Southern Spice.

Five years later, the clientele of the restaurant had doubled. They were serving two hundred and fifty customers at each seating. By then, her feelings had changed. Both Spice and David had been working eighteen-hour days for the three years that the restaurant had been opened. Spice was the head chef then, and David had to manage everything else. One evening, Spice looked at David cleaning the kitchen after the restaurant had closed. With a warm flush of feeling she realized then and there that he was the only man she would ever love.

"Baby, you're exhausted. I'll finish." He kissed her lightly on the neck. "You go on upstairs."

"No. You're exhausted, too."

Loosening her apron, he wrapped his arms around her and hugged her tightly. "I'm okay. Now go on. I'll be up in about an hour."

Hesitantly, Spice walked away. Just before opening the door, she remembered, she stopped and turned back around. As softly as a shadow she said, "I love you, David."

"I know," he answered, meeting her gaze and smiling.

For twenty years, their marriage was perfect. Spice's love had grown for David every year. With the girls entering college, Spice and David began fantasizing about future grandchildren, and how they would fit into their potentially glorious business plans.

But it was not to be. On his way home from a weekend trip to Midnight, David had fallen asleep on the freeway and run into the back of a semi. His white Lincoln crunched up like an accordion, he was killed instantly. To protect her, David's brother, Otis, begged Spice to let him identify the body.

Now, widowed for five years, Spice still believed she would never again experience such an honest love as the one she'd shared with David.

"Who else made the list, Spice?" Carmen asked, her voice calling Spice back to the present. Dipping a wooden spoon inside a mixing bowl, the pixielike Carmen finished sprinkling English toffee over the top of the caramel pie cooling at the stove and placed it inside the refrigerator.

Spice called off five more names, listed alphabetically, and stopped at the last entry: Reverend Golden Westbrook. "I'm not familiar with that name. I wonder—"

"Mr. Westbrook is the pastor at Divinity Chapel in De-

4

troit," Carmen answered. "He's the Detroit Chapter's President of NAABR. He'll be running again this fall."

"Really? I wonder if he's looking for a wife?" Spice was impressed. The National Alliance for the Advancement of the Black Race was a major advocacy organization. Its leaders held power positions high up in all kinds of business and government committees. "Now that's the kind of man Sterling should be dating."

"Sterling?"

"She may be needing a husband sometime soon." There was a bitter note in Spice's voice when she continued. "She'll be twenty-six in February, and she's still costing me a fortune every month." Spice flexed the paper forward. "Sit down and take a break, will you? You're making me feel guilty sitting here like this."

Carmen took a pull from her flask, which Spice knew was filled with vodka. Any time of day or night, no matter what the circumstances, something would cause Carmen to "need" a drink. For the twenty-seven years Spice had loved her friend, Carmen had always leaned on alcohol. And while Spice understood why Carmen felt the need to throw her life away, she was powerless to help her.

Spice waited until Carmen was seated. "I'll pay her bills for one more year, until she gets her degree—if she gets a degree, which I doubt. Degree or not, one year, then she's on her own."

Carmen uttered a short laugh. "I can just see Sterling with a preacher." Carmen removed the flask from her apron and took yet another quick sip.

"I think it's time for Sterling to change, don't you?" Spice put the paper away and headed back to the task at hand.

"What about you, Spice?" Carmen smiled. "When are you getting married again?"

"I'm not ready." Carmen's smile faded. "April marks the fifth anniversary of David's death. And to be perfectly honest with you, I enjoy my freedom and making all the business decisions around here. I married David because I needed a man to take care of me and my kids. My kids are grown now. I've

5

since learned how to take care of myself. I don't need a husband anymore."

Carmen didn't believe Spice was so independent. She knew Spice missed David terribly, but she also knew her friend could not afford to reveal her vulnerability.

When the timer went off, Spice removed the roast from the oven. Immediately the kitchen filled with the fresh scents of apricots, pecans and thyme. She added a subtle splash of bourbon to the robust sauce simmering on the range. Everything was ready for the succulent Apricot-Pecan Stuffed Pork Loin.

Soft steam formed on the windows, clouding the outside view as the women worked. With the subject of husbands dropped, they moved on to a safer topic—food.

"Don't you think this is a lot for just four people?" Carmen asked while stirring three pounds of fresh jumbo shrimp and lobster into the bubbling red pot of gumbo on the stove's front burner.

"Of course not! It's time for a celebration." Spice paused. "How often does a mother see her black child promoted to captain with a major airline, and a female child at that."

Spice expertly sliced the piping-hot pork roll then began arranging the circles of meat around a platter of roasted new potatoes, leeks and baby carrots. "However," Spice added, "whatever food is left over, we can wrap up and deliver to the Mother Maybelle's Soup Kitchen downtown in the morning." As she poured a hefty amount of the hot glaze into a separate dish, Spice dipped a finger in and gingerly sampled the tangy bourbon sauce. "Mmmm," Spice said, "perfect."

Carmen gave the gumbo one final stir, then replaced the cover on the pot and lowered the flame. "Everything else should be ready in about fifteen minutes."

Spice moved to the refrigerator and looked inside at its contents once again. On the top shelf, a Spinach Salad with Apple-Onion Vinaigrette glistened in a glass bowl. She checked Carmen's work of art on the lower shelf: five lotus-shaped stemware goblets filled with Peach Melba. She breathed in the sweet scent of raspberries, kirsch, and mint through the plastic wrap.

"I haven't even worked my usual shift yet, and I'm exhausted," Carmen said, sitting down and putting her feet in the opposite chair, and once again removing her small flask from her apron pocket.

Spice and Carmen had been cooking since six that morning. It was now 11:10 A.M. The brunch was set to begin in just under two hours. Everything would be perfect except for the fact that Carmen refused to come. Spice thought she'd try one more time to convince her. "Carmen, I'm having a problem with you not joining us. You know how important you are to this family. It won't be the same without you."

"Not today, Spice." Carmen rose to bring a dish into the living room. Stepping back, she automatically smoothed the swirled gold moiré skirt draping the buffet table that she and Spice had accented with gold silk bows. Fabergé silverware was laid out next to the red china. Ivory linen napkins were rolled through glittering cylinders of jewel-studded rings. "However," Carmen said teasingly, "if you'd like to offer me a bottle of your private cognac, I could be persuaded into accepting one of those."

"Of course," Spice said, hesitantly moving toward the bar.

The south wall of the living room was dominated by an elegant black lacquer Yamaha. Beside it sat three of her most prized possessions: two papier-mâché gilt, mother of pearl and cane side chairs with a similarly painted papier-mâché mother-of-pearl cave à liqueurs. Though she rarely drank, Spice kept the bar well stocked. There were several bottles of Dom Perignon and Cristal, along with the usual stock beverages. But what Spice was particularly proud of was the case of Louis XIII cognac, valued at $1,355 a bottle, which David had given her for their twentieth anniversary.

Carmen rested her hands on her narrow hips. "I was just kidding about the cognac, girl." She chuckled. "I could have sworn you'd say no, knowing how much those bottles mean to you."

Spice exhaled and felt her body relax. Truly, she would have given Carmen one of the bottles, or anything else that she wanted, but she was thankful her friend didn't feel the need to test her like that. She hugged Carmen's tiny body, then said seriously, "If you change your mind . . ."

"Spice, I know I'm family, but today should be just kin, your brother-in-law and your daughters. Anyway, it's been a while—"

"—since I've seen Mink and Sterling. I know," she said softly. "You've mentioned that before. I've just been so busy with this new project."

Spice removed her apron and sat down at the kitchen table to fill Carmen in on the progress of her latest entrepreneurial adventure. Though few people knew it, Spice was opening a second Southern Spice in downtown Royal Oak. But the project was bigger than the restaurant. The new restaurant was launching Spice into the rough and tumble world of business development. To prevail, Spice had often expressed the idea that she had to appear as creative as a woman yet with a man's strength.

Foxphasia, the $38-million hotel, restaurant and office center, was located on the northeast corner of the triple intersection of I-696 and Woodward and Washington in Royal Oak on a 6.8-acre site. Spice and two other investors had formed Foxphasia Corporation, which encompassed three office buildings of three, five, and fifteen stories respectively, a five-story condominium and a three-story children's museum. A bridge for pedestrians would be built between the existing Detroit Zoo on the corner of I-696, and the 154-bed hotel that housed Southern Spice's sister restaurant on the first level. The five-phase complex, due to open in the spring of 1998, was thirty percent near completion. When Spice finished telling Carmen of the plans, she clapped her hands like a child and exclaimed, "It's getting exciting, I can tell you that, girl!"

"I'd like to see it one day."

"Why wouldn't you? Anytime, kiddo." Then Spice added, "Even though my daughter is talented, I made a mistake in commissioning her to design the children's museum—she screwed up again."

"Sterling?"

"Yes. It took all of Otis' and my pull to get her hired temporarily at Zuller Architectural Firm. She has to work in partnership with another architect because she's not licensed yet. She seemed so excited about it last summer. Now she's a month behind the bank's deadline for approval of the plans. And the cold shoulder I've received lately from Zuller might never thaw."

"Don't worry, she'll come through." Reaching across the table, Carmen touched Spice's hand. "You need someone to help you with all this."

"Otis has offered many times to help me. But I don't want him involved. He may be my brother-in-law, but I see him enough already. He eats dinner here every Thursday night. Daily contact would be too much." She leaned back in her chair and turned to gaze outside. "I'm hoping to talk to the girls today about the development. It would be nice if they saw the possible benefits of building a family empire. Otherwise, it just doesn't make any sense to work so hard for much longer."

"Marriage is still an option."

"One more time: I'm still not ready," Spice said, turning to face her friend. "So it's not. If I could only convince Sterling how important— If only Sterling would get fired up over something—anything. You know how much talent she showed while she was growing up—those sketches she'd just whip up from designing hotels to log cabins."

"Yeah, but once she reached womanhood— Maybe she caught it from us—huh, Spice?"

"No. I don't think so. Sterling had so much more than me—more brains, more talent, help, schooling— Oh let's face it, it's hopeless."

"Sterling knows how to get to you, Spice. But she'll come through."

"I'm not so sure anymore about anything. I'd like to know that one of my daughters is being groomed to take over."

"You can still have another child, Spice. You're still a very young woman. I don't think you're being fair to yourself or the girls by trying to figure out their future."

"I'll tell you what. I won't discuss anything serious today. We'll just eat and have fun." Spice forced a smile that faded quickly.

With her hand still extended on the kitchen counter, Carmen touched her friend's arm. "Is there something you're not telling me?" she asked.

Spice looked Carmen squarely in the eye and held it before saying, "No."

"You've been acting funny since your birthday two months ago." Carmen turned her head to the side. "Personally, I partied through most of that year. So I really can't remember how I felt. But I've heard that turning forty-one is worse than turning forty."

"I'm not an advocate of that myth," Spice said, turning away and hearing, but not seeing Carmen take another sip from the flask.

In eight months Carmen would be forty-five. Her small body, with tiny breasts and hips, and even her full head of naturally curly hair, cut in a 60s shag, resembled a child's. To most, Carmen appeared undernourished, and the bones of her gentle hands looked like trembling branches. It hurt Spice to see her friend's frailty.

"It's never the physical that concerns me most. It's my mental attitude; staying on top of things, being in control. Life has been good to me, but I don't want the girls to make the same mistakes that I made."

"Mistakes teach us about life, Spice."

"David and I worked hard to build this business, and we assumed they would want to keep it." Spice removed the bread pudding from the oven and placed it on the butcher block to cool. "Mink's got her own career—" Spice added quickly, "Of course I'm happy for her. But Sterling . . . Sterling." She shook her head. "What am I going to do with her?"

"She'll learn."

"When? Sterling doesn't care about anything but shopping." Spice sighed. "I keep making excuses for her not delivering the plans at the bank, but I'm running out of lies. I didn't raise her to be an underachiever. I know I made some mistakes early on, but—"

"You did what you had to do, Spice."

Their eyes locked. A shared understanding was enough right now.

*　　*　　*

10

Sterling arrived first. Using her key to Spice's private-access elevator and residence, she entered the duplex and hung her coat up in the front closet.

"Spice?" she called out to her mother. "Spice!" she said louder, "it's me, Sterling."

"Hi, baby. I'll be down in a few minutes," Spice yelled from upstairs. "Open a bottle of champagne while you wait."

First, Sterling checked out the spread of food and sampled a piece of toffee before removing one of three chilled bottles of champagne on ice and moving upstairs to the library. Just as she settled down with a glass of champagne, she heard the elevator stop, followed by the sound of a key unlocking the door. In an instant Mink came into the library.

"Hello, Sterling," she said, giving her a hug. Mink stood five foot nine, Sterling, five foot one. Sterling wore her hair long, in waves of autumn gold; Mink wore a perfectly shaped half-inch afro. Sterling's complexion was ivory, like a delicate lily; Mink's flawless skin was chocolate-brown. Sterling's eyes resembled the goddess Athena's, a striking gray that at first glance appeared blue; Mink's eyes were a deep sepia, that mirrored the stars in midnight waters. The stunning high arch of Mink's sculpted cheekbones, broad nose and full lips called attention to her exotic appeal; Sterling's high forehead, sleek brows, aristocratic nose and narrow lips gave her a classical 1930's kind of beauty.

After setting her purse down on a lower shelf of one of the bookcases, Mink asked her sister, "Where is everybody?"

"Spice is still dressing, and Otis hasn't arrived yet."

Sterling rose, smoothing and adjusting her cuffed sleeves just so. She felt euphoric because she knew she positively shimmered in her stunning ivory Christian Lacroix pantsuit. Three rows of lustrous gumball-sized pearls hung from her neck. Her nylons, pumps and softly painted mouth were all in muted opalescent tones. She didn't need anyone to tell her that she looked terrific. Also, the heroin high didn't hurt.

"Join me in a glass of champagne," she said, reaching inside the library liquor cabinet for another crystal flute. Sterling poured a drink for her sister, then toasted her. "Congratulations on your promotion."

                                *   *   *

Leaning over her dressing table, Spice reapplied her make-up for the third time. She'd underestimated how nervous she'd be and couldn't get her hands to stop shaking. Consequently, at 1:20 P.M. she wasn't dressed.

Finally, make-up as good as it was going to get, Spice left her room with an air of forced relaxation and headed toward the familiar sound of her daughters' voices. She hesitated for a moment and took a deep breath just outside the entrance to the library. Just as she was ready to go in, she heard the catty tone in Sterling's voice as she spoke to her elder sister.

"You might as well hear about it from me," Sterling said loftily. "The dean's wife caught us together."

"Did she catch you in his bed or yours?" Mink was clearly having trouble controlling her voice to a low roar. "Never mind, I don't want to hear the vulgar details."

"Neither. It was in the back seat of his car in the school's parking lot."

"Jesus!" Mink exploded, "how stupid can you get. How stupid could *he* get?"

Sterling began detailing how their affair had begun. There was no remorse in her tone. The innocent meeting about her appointed advisor turned into a re-assignment to the dean himself. In this small school there wasn't anyone left in the liberal arts college to mentor her besides Dean Harris. The rest of the seamy business was as natural for Sterling as a lizard eating spiders. Dean Timothy Harris was a name and a body to add to her list. And he was bait for hooking Bennie, the only man she cared about—or so she told herself.

Cutting off Sterling's melodramatic tale, Spice walked into the room. "Hello, girls," Spice said, kissing Mink then Sterling on the cheek. As she stood back to appraise them, she said, "You both look stunning."

"So do you, Spice." Mink poured her mother a glass of champagne.

"Thank you," she said, accepting the drink from Mink. Turning to Sterling, Spice said, "Finish your story," then took a seat on the velvet ottoman in the middle of the room.

Mink took a seat beside Spice and gently patted her on the knee.

Even though Sterling had consistently won top grades in undergraduate school, her flagrant disregard of discipline policies was the core of all her problems. And the problem was getting worse. She'd been expelled from one architectural program after another. And the sad part was—soon she'd be out of options.

"Anyway, somebody spotted us in the car and called security, they found us and a half-gram of cocaine. The assistant dean suspended me. Harris took a paid leave of absence."

Spice had learned long ago not to react to Sterling's outlandish, self-destructive behavior. The more she showed she cared, the more her younger child rubbed her nose in her failure as a mother. When the telephone rang, Spice automatically jumped up, spilling her champagne onto her lap, staining her silk dress.

"Hello," Spice said, secretly glad for the intrusion. While reaching for a handful of tissues to dry her soiled dress, she listened to her head chef explain why he'd called. "What kind of emergency, Travis?" Out of the corner of her eye, she could see Sterling lighting a cigarette and listening to her every word. "I'll be right down." Spice put the receiver down.

"I've got to go," was all she said, before quickly leaving the room and her two stunned daughters behind in confused silence.

She knew that I'd been planning this for months, Spice thought, twisting her gold wedding band, which she wore on her middle finger, nervously back and forth. She was positive that Sterling had staged this whole school affair to draw attention to herself. They had played this game many times before. Getting suspended from another school! And drugs? Again? Spice was fed up with Sterling's second-hand theatrics. She was so angry, she welcomed the excuse to escape—not an unfamiliar feeling, unfortunately.

Spice had tried to teach her daughters that they could be more: more intelligent, more talented, more attractive—one better than anyone, just by being themselves. But somehow the message hadn't gotten through to Sterling.

When the elevator stopped on the main level, Spice stepped onto the pink and white checkerboard floor of Southern Spice's kitchen.

She waved to the employees as she made her way toward the head chef's office.

Just as she entered Travis Foxx's office, Spice heard a rumbling, rolling noise, then the sound of a file cabinet drawer clicking shut, telling her that Travis was wearing his manager's hat at the moment. Travis had filled some of the tasks left by David's death. Lord knows he was no David.

From the moment she sat down, Spice felt his eyes visually undressing her. "What's the emergency?" she asked.

She caught the snide smile on Travis's face as he moved from behind the desk, and facing her, rested his buttocks against his desk and leaned forward. He was a carbon copy of Will Smith on *The Fresh Prince of Bel Air*, especially the ears. Spice once had slipped and called him "Will," which had pissed him off.

"If you'd come downstairs with me a moment, I'll show you."

They took the elevator to the basement. All the way down, Travis complained about the freezer, which was costing a fortune in repair bills. His immediate bugaboo was with the new compressor system that currently ran their freezer and refrigerator. He'd voiced his concern over the hassles caused by the system last year. The system took up too much room and used double the electricity that a more compact unit would cost. Now they had the bills to back him up.

At Travis' suggestion Spice peered at the overburdened circuits. She tried to make some sense of what she was looking at. She'd never been able to grasp the necessity for all the wire and tubing that extended off into a zillion directions.

With a sudden movement, Travis was behind her, gently cupping her buttocks.

"Don't." Spice checked each breaker inside the circuit box to see if any were in the OFF position. Travis, ignoring her, continued to massage her breasts from behind her.

"Look," she said, pulling from his embrace, "I made a mistake. It's over. It can't happen again."

She watched his sly smile as he released her.

"You've got the most exquisite body that I've ever seen. Naked or clothed."

"I hope this isn't why you called me away from Mink's celebration."

"You don't give a rat's ass about that and you know it."

Travis' words stung. Was this dump on Spice day?

"Travis, how I love my daughters is none of your damn business. Now if you have no legitimate reason to need me now, I'm out of here."

After four years of celibacy, Spice had longed for sexual satisfaction without the emotional entanglements. She assumed that a young man could enjoy occasionally bedding an older woman without strings. But after one week of intoxication, she found that it just wasn't possible; he was too demanding of her time. His lack of discretion as her employee hadn't helped. Just like today, acting amorous while on the premises was typical of his immature behavior throughout their brief fling. And so she had ended it.

At twenty-six, Travis was an asset to her business. He had the perfect ingredients of good chef management: culinary creativity, menu vision, manpower efficiency, discipline and grievance flair. Combine these attributes with reason and common sense, and Travis was the epitome of a professional chef.

Spice silently chastised herself. She'd allowed Travis to take one too many trips around her mulberry bush. It was time to show him how pussy and power prevailed, and a mere set of balls had to step back when it came to running her business.

Sterling was livid. She poured another glass of champagne and quickly gulped it down before asking Mink, "Can you believe that bitch left us here?"

"Spice is our mother, Sterling. She's not a bitch. I think you've got the two confused."

"Fuck that. What kind of mother would walk out on her daughters' party and go to work."

15

"I'm sure it was important, Sterling. She'll be back in a few minutes."

"Bullshit. She didn't have to leave. Travis knows the business inside and out."

Mink was silent.

"Tell me, Mink, is there anything more important to her than that fucking restaurant?"

Each minute passed like a chrysalis of eternity as the women silently sipped champagne and picked at the buffet.

"I've told Spice all along that I didn't think I could make it at Crown." Sterling paused to light a Salem, then blew out a thin veil of smoke between them. "She wouldn't lis—"

"Hold on, little sister," Mink said, coughing. "You *can't* make it. Period." She fanned the smoke away from her face, and taking a step back, crossed her arms beneath her breasts. "Quit making these pitiful excuses. You're just plain lazy. You've never worked a day in your life. All that's expected from you is to get a degree and you *can't* even do that."

Drugs and sex were Sterling's passion; like fire and water, they were good servants, but ungodly masters. Yet, both had been key to Sterling's escape from responsibility and reality since age sixteen.

Like all addicts, Sterling felt she could handle drugs and was always in control. Still and all, she would not admit to herself nor anyone else that she was now hooked on Red Rum heroin, murder spelled backwards. For this and many other reasons, she kept repeating the same mistakes she'd been making for years.

"I'm not an overachieving martyr like you. If someone would just let me explain—"

Mink turned away. "It's cold in here." She retrieved her purse and moved downstairs to the living room.

Sterling followed a few feet behind her.

"Go on, I'm listening," Mink said as she moved toward the fireplace and sat down on the hearth. Carefully, she hoisted two logs into the fire, reviving the smell of burning hickory. Warmth quickly filled the cozy room.

As Sterling talked, she took in the finely detailed interior of the room, remembering how Spice had carefully chosen the black suede wall panels that were framed by cream gilded floor and ceiling mouldings. In one fell swoop, her mother had purchased the two nineteenth-century Chinese chairs, a pair of chic ebonized gilded stools and several Chinese porcelain figures. A week later there were matching Chinese cinnabar lacquer baluster-form vases to be placed on top of a midnineteenth-century black lacquer Chinoiserie floral and gilt cabinet. As the girls matured, it became increasingly obvious to both Sterling and Mink that all of Spice's fussed over "junk" was worth a lot of money. Sterling sometimes wondered if it was such a good thing that Spice and David had made it big. Once she had received a spanking for toying with one of the Ming dynasty vases. Ever since then, she had hated this room.

Nothing's changed, Sterling thought. She'd been talking for the past five minutes with no response from her sister. As usual Mink hadn't been listening. No one ever listened to her. Suddenly bored, she moved to the piano bench and began toying with the keys. In a piece of music, there were separate notes broken up by air. Sterling felt there was a lifetime of stale air between herself and her sister. As she started in on "Mary Had a Little Lamb," Mink startled her with a question.

"You're forever talking about how painful your relationship is with Spice. What you don't realize is that the drugs are causing you the pain. Not Spice. Can't you see that they're destroying your life?" Mink asked her sister.

"I enjoy drugs the same way you enjoy professional status," she stated calmly. "Can't you see what that game is doing to *your* family?" The corner of her lips curled up in a knowing smile.

Mink scowled. "You ain't doing nothing but burning up brain cells that you'll never be able to recover." Mink shook her head. "Why do you put yourself through this? Why do you put Spice through this? Whatever problems you have, drugs aren't the answer. You're high right now, aren't you? You don't have to answer. I can see it in your eyes."

"Girl's gotta do what a girl's gotta do."

"Can't you be honest for once. I'm your sister, Sterling, for God's sake. I'm trying to help."

"Why don't *you* try being honest for a change. You hide behind that pilot's uniform, but underneath you're a whore just like the rest of us."

"Where in the hell did you come up with some stupid shit like that?"

Sterling stopped playing and swung around to face Mink, laughing. "And the funny part! What's really funny is that you're so jealous of me it's pathetic!"

"You must be outta your mind, girl," Mink said, rising.

"The fuck I am. You bring your ass over here and I'll show you who's crazy."

"You don't know who you're fucking with, girl."

"Come on big sista." Sterling started to laugh again. "Come and get some of this," she said, rotating her open hand into her chest and bobbing her head forward. Sterling started shadowboxing as she moved toward Mink. She stopped for a moment and said with a smirk on her face, "Oh, by the way, Mink. I have *worked* today. The only kind of work I plan on doing—on my back." She paused, sneered, then sniffed the air. "I still got dick juice on me from this morning."

"You lowdown slut—"

"Slut?" She walked towards her. "Who the fuck you callin' a slut? . . . ol' bitch-ass trick!"

Sterling screamed as she grabbed Mink's lapel and swiveled her torso and right arm back in preparation to slap her. Sterling's open palm was half-way to her sister's face, when Mink caught her wrist with her right hand, then clutched Sterling's chin in the crook of her left elbow. She felt Mink's arm slide down her neck and apply pressure on her throat and larynx, cutting off her air. Sterling struggled, trying to weave her petite body from Mink's tight grasp, then managed to loop her foot around Mink's calf and tugged. Surprised by Sterling's strength, Mink lost her balance and slipped on the thick pile, bringing Sterling down with her.

"Lemmego muthafucka!" Sterling yelled in Mink's ear as she tried to break free.

Neither would relinquish her tight grip. Struggling for leverage, they moved like serpents, their curved bodies sliding, rolling on top of each other along the black carpeting.

Thump! Crash! The girls were clawing and scratching each other, returning blow for blow and tearing the room apart while they fought. Sterling grunted and let out a loud moan just as one of the Ming vases fell from the mantel and cracked. The papier-mâché chairs were knocked on their backs as they tumbled over them without noticing. Mink pushed in Sterling's face with her one hand and snatched a clump of her gold tresses with the other. "Ouch!" Sterling hollered, trying to shake her hair free from Mink's grasp.

Scrambling to her knees by the buffet table, Mink tried to pull herself and Sterling to their feet, but before she could, Sterling managed to grab one of the Russian china plates and break it over Mink's head. Mink winced, but didn't shout as the plate connected with her skull. Far too much adrenaline was flowing through her system now to feel pain.

Mink's suede heel caught on the edge of the tablecloth as she tried to stand and an avalanche of gumbo, rice, eggs and meat in warmed chafing dishes came tumbling down.

Layers of rice stuck in Mink's hair like maggots. Clumps of lobster slid down between her breasts. "I hate you," shouted Mink as she grabbed a fistful of Sterling's angora sweater.

Together, they rolled over, and over, through the porcelain shards and food, struggling for position. Finally, Mink managed to get her foot at Sterling's crotch. She pushed hard, pumping her stockinged heel against Sterling's pubic bone, until she saw tears forming in her sister's eyes.

"Now that was some *ho* shit!" Sterling shouted between clenched teeth. She managed to break away from Mink and scrambled to the other side of the room. She snatched a bottle from the top shelf of the bar. Cracking the neck open on the side of the baby grand piano, she wagged the top half of the broken bottle toward Mink as she licked the drop of blood from the side of her mouth with her tongue. "Now you come and get some of this," she hissed.

"Spice is going to kill you," Mink said, pointing to the broken glass.

"Fuck her! Fuck you. Fuck all y'all mutherfuckas." Sterling dropped the broken bottle, turned and started throwing bottles of champagne and cognac at Mink.

Mink ducked and dodged the battery of bottles aimed at her. A bottle hit the toe of Otis' shoes just as he entered the room.

"Ouch! Dammit, Sterling," Otis shouted. "What the fuck is going on in here?"

Sterling froze.

"Good God," Mink said, surveying the destruction of the room.

"Go home, Mink. The party's over." He grabbed Sterling's arm and released the unbroken bottle from her grasp.

Quietly, without a glance in Sterling's direction, Mink gathered her things and left.

Otis released the inside button of his elegant black and white houndstooth Versace jacket and steered Sterling to the sofa. Turning over one of the chairs, he sat across from her as she busily brushed food fragments from her hair.

The sharp smell of cognac and champagne grew stronger as it seeped through the room. "Damn, it stinks like hell in here." Otis snatched a handkerchief from his pocket and wiped off his shoes.

"Maybe it's your cologne," Sterling offered with a snide smile.

"You breathe trouble," Otis said, straightening his lapel, "you know that?"

Sterling's gray eyes were slippery with tears. The evil look on her face didn't represent her true feelings. She wished that her Uncle Otis, or someone, would just wrap their arms around her and say "everything's going to be all right, baby."